The Double-Edged Sword
Inspired by true events in Palestine—a land under siege

by F. Michele Ramsey

This book is sold subject to the condition that it shall not, by way of trade or otherwise, be lent, re-sold, duplicated, hired out, or otherwise circulated without the publisher's prior written consent in any form of binding or cover other than that in which it is published and without similar condition including this condition being imposed on the subsequent purchaser.

The Double-Edged Sword Copyright © 2024 Fiona Russell, writing as F. Michele Ramsey.

This is a work of fiction. Names, characters, businesses, places, events, and incidents are either the products of the author's imagination or used in a fictitious manner.
All rights reserved.

Palestine map Licensed from istock.com
Levant map CreativeCommons courtesy of ian.macky.net

No part of this book may be reproduced or transmitted in any form or by any means without written permission of the author.

A Note From the Author

I started writing this novel back in 1994, when I was living in Washington with my former American husband and was desperately homesick for the Middle East.

A few weeks after my initial attempts at writing (which subsequently got shelved for more than 20 years), my then husband got a job in Gaza and, lo and behold, two months later we were on a flight heading to Tel Aviv.

Having spent three years in the States, my understanding of the situation in the Occupied Territories remained somewhat vague with regards to the Oslo Accords and the issue of the settlements. And while I had visited Jerusalem when we had been living in Jordan, Gaza remained shrouded in mystery. Yet, driven by my spirit of adventure, I ventured in the Strip one bright spring day, undeterred by the shootings at the Eretz checkpoint and the bombings at Israeli settlements.

As we settled into our new life, checkpoints and harassment by the Israeli army became a way of life, leaving an indelible mark on my soul. I witnessed firsthand the brutality, the injustice, and the daily humiliations Palestinians faced. I understood then that desperation leads to a lack of fear when there is nothing left to lose.

As I write these words, my heart bleeds for the ongoing war raging against Gaza, decimating the place, and killing over 35,000 (and counting) civilians, mostly women and children, while world leaders remain silent.

If anything, Palestinians have taught me about resilience, courage, and the essence of true friendship.

Free Palestine.

PALESTINIAN LOSS OF LAND

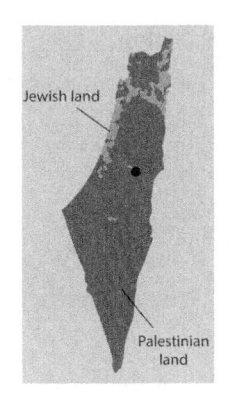

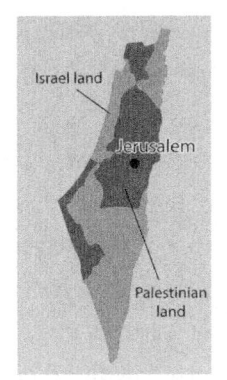

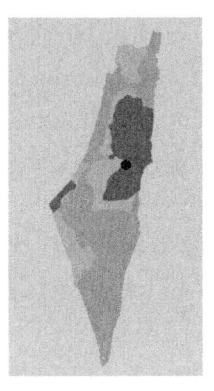

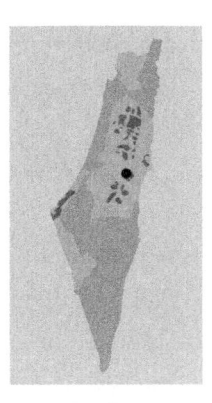

1946　　1947 UN plan　　1967　　Today

LEVANT MAP

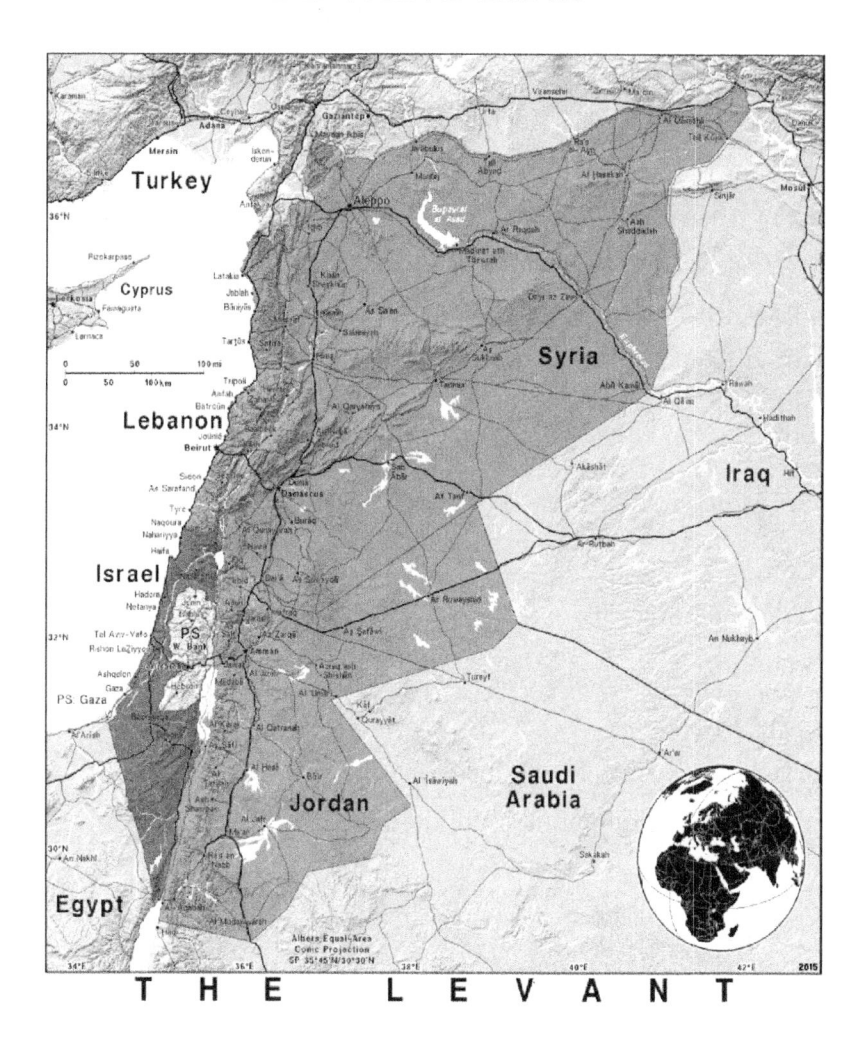

Cast of Characters

*

Gabriel Family

Farah Gabriel
Cyril Gabriel, her brother
Tammy Radwani, their half-sister on their mother's side. She is married to Jamal Radwani, a Palestinian Jordanian from a Jerusalemite family.

Marc Mercier, their French cousin

*

Avram Family

Moshe Avram
Carla Avram (Rosenburg), his wife
Yossi, Ruth, Jonathon, their children

Rebecca, Moshe's sister
Benjamin, her husband
Avi and Joshua their children

David Avram, Moshe's brother
Tamar and Deborah his daughters

Nathan Avram, Moshe's brother

*

Radwani Family

Ibrahim Radwani, Moshe's best friend from childhood and first cousin of Jamal, Tammy's husband
Hussein Radwani, his brother
Majid Radwani, his brother
Mariam Radwani, their sister
Alia Radwani, their mother

*

Khodeib Family

Ghassan Khodeib (Gus)
Layth Khodeib, his second cousin

*

Other Characters

Monique, Farah's best friend
Lucien, work colleague
Elise, work colleague
Gerald Naghton, an Irish archeologist
Hanna Lutfi, Farah's friend
Angela Lutfi, her mother and Mr. Lutfi, her father

To my parents and May
Not a day goes by without me thinking of you and missing you.

For the word of God is alive and active.
Sharper than any double-edged sword.
Hebrews 4:12

Prologue

Northern Tip of Jordan on the Border with the Golan Heights, July 1995

Screeching vehicles shattered the silence around the villa. A figure plunged through the open window on the second floor and swung down the pipes into the darkness, leaving Farah alone in the room.

The convoy of military jeeps rumbled to a halt. Members of the Jordanian Royal Desert Forces spilled out, their red and white checkered keffiyehs fluttering in the cool breeze that swirled off the Yarmouk River. They charged into the woods pursuing the shadow escaping through the olive grove.

A volley of gunfire lit up the dark sky while shouts echoed in the open space.

Farah flung herself on the floor, crawled behind a lengthy curtain, and curled up into a ball, cold sweat dripping down her back.

The front door burst open. Footsteps pounded through the empty hallway. The shouts grew louder.

"*Itala' lal tabeq eli fawq.*" Upstairs.

Farah pulled her legs tighter towards her chest. A cold chill enveloped her as she covered her ears with her hands.

"*Yalla! Yalla.*" Hurry.

A gun fired. At the next crack, someone shouted her name. She peeped through the gap in the curtain. A familiar profile appeared in the hallway before she fainted.

Part I

Chapter One

Paris, April 1986

Farah Gabriel stared at her wedding dress hanging on the back of her bedroom door and sighed in satisfaction. Her dream of a wedding Saturday in June was about to come true.

Her hesitant fingers touched the silk-satin fabric and the rosebuds on the corset encased with tiny pearls. A few sequins scattered the length of the full skirt and on the train.

A smile hovered around her lips. Everything was falling into place as if by magic.

She glanced at her watch. Justin should be calling any minute now. The phone rang, and Farah rushed out to the living room to answer it. The pips that preceded an international phone call sounded clear.

"My princess, I can hear the smile in your voice."

"Justin. How are you?" She plopped herself down onto the sofa with a contented sigh.

"Better now that I'm talking to you. And you? Getting ready for our big day?"

"Yes. *Maman* rang yesterday. They've ordered the flowers for the church and everything is set for the wedding reception. I'll organize the seating when I get to Cairo. Has your family bought their tickets?"

"Yup. We'll all be flying out of New York together five days before the wedding. We'll need a day to recuperate from the jet lag."

"Would your nieces like to be flower girls?" Her own niece was dying to be one.

"I'll ask Pennie and let you know in my next letter."

"I'm going shopping with Monique this week to buy her shoes, and I'll look out for children's dresses that would fit the color theme." She stretched her legs across the coffee table. The sun glinted through the window, flooding the room with brightness.

"What about that bag you've been saving up for months to buy? The one you want for the honeymoon?" he teased her.

Farah bit her lip. Should she tell him? They shouldn't have any secrets.

Except she did have *one*. And each time she had tried to tell him, the words froze in her mouth. She pushed the thought aside. "I -I've given the money to Monique."

"Oh? Why?"

Her face flushed. "She didn't have enough to pay for a fashion design class. And I have a million bags. She needed the help."

"You really *are* a princess." He chuckled. "Well, sometimes anyway."

They both laughed.

"How *is* Monique?" said Justin.

"Umm, not great. Did I tell you that Danny finished his military service a few weeks ago and wants Monique to move to Yugoslavia? She wants him to move to Paris. They just keep arguing whenever he calls her."

"I'm lucky you agreed to move to Washington."

She grinned. "I'd follow you to the ends of the earth. Fortunately, it's only to Washington. So, what's happening with you? How's work?"

"The same boring pushing paper stuff. Frustrating. That's *not* why I studied Arabic for three years. After the wedding, I'll start applying for new jobs."

A puff of air escaped her lips. He'd had such high hopes when he had started this job a few months ago. "Have you applied for Grad school?"

"Yes. Waiting to hear from them. Listen, I'm going to look at a one-bedroom apartment next week."

Her eyebrows shot up. "Oh?"

"We can't start our married life in a shared house, can we? We need our privacy, and you need to think of what you'd like to do when you move here."

She swallowed hard. With all the hype of the wedding, she hadn't stopped to think about what it would actually mean to move to the States. It suddenly hit her smack in the stomach.

"Would you prefer that I wait and we start looking at places when you come?"

"N-no." Her eyes wandered around the room. Her parents' flat in Paris had been home since she had moved over from Cairo ten months earlier. It would be weird to leave to a totally new place where she wasn't familiar with anything. No more chats with the baker around the corner when she popped in for bread. No more sitting at the cafe two streets down, exchanging jokes with the waiter.

"You went very quiet," said Justin.

She inhaled a deep breath. "I suppose the move *is* a bit scary."

"Yes, I can imagine. But I'll give you all the support I can, princess."

"I know. And I can't wait till we can be together, no matter where that is."

"Nor can I." He huffed a laugh. "How's your work going?"

She shrugged. "I shouldn't complain. At least I'm not waitressing like Monique. Even if the VIP Lounge gets its fair share of annoying passengers."

"I'm sure. What news of Elise?"

"She's organizing a hen night for me next month. Isn't that sweet of her?"

They exchanged a few more words then said goodbye, with promises to write and talk again the following week-end, when international calls were cheaper.

Farah placed the handset onto the receiver determined to relish every moment in Paris till she left.

Chapter Two

Caesarea, Israel – April 1986

Moshe Avram sat on the sofa and scanned the headlines of the local left-wing newspaper. An article opposing Israeli settlements in the Occupied Palestinian Territories caught his attention. He read a few lines then snorted. No matter how 'liberal' they claimed to be, the article was nevertheless pro-Israeli.

At the sound of his wife's footsteps, Moshe looked up and smiled as she entered the living room.

"Moshe." She sat down next to him, lines of worry creasing her attractive, delicate features. "I'm worried about Yossi. He's now started to mobilize people to demonstrate. I'm scared they'll kill him."

Moshe tapped his fingers on the arm of the sofa. It was three years since Emil Grunzweig from the Peace Now movement had been killed by a Zionist. They had been protesting against Israel's invasion of Lebanon and the Sabra and Shatila massacres. He was Yossi's idol.

"I understand you're worried, my dear. But you can't ask our son to be less than the man he is. He's simply following in the footsteps of our family, fighting against injustice."

"Moshe, please convince him to go to my father in the States. He —"

"No." Moshe flinched. He didn't mean to be sharp with his wife, but this was a sore subject. "Look Carla, I have plenty of respect for your father, but I'm not having my son become alienated from this land." He bounced his knee up and down. "If people like him start leaving, what hope do we have? Yossi's twenty-three. He's old enough to make his own decisions."

Carla sank back against the sofa. Her lips trembled. He wrapped his arm around her slender shoulders and drew her towards him, guilt eating at him that he had brought his American wife to live in this tormented part of the world.

"We just have to trust that things will turn out okay." He kissed her lowered head then stood up to open the window as the sun's pink glow faded into the Mediterranean.

The front door slammed shut. Yossi's smiling face appeared, his girlfriend, Judith, in his wake.

A surge of pride shot through Moshe as he looked at his firstborn.

"Mom, Dad." Yossi pecked his mother's cheek.

Carla looked up. "Hello, Judith. Nice to see you again."

"Hello, Mrs. Avram." The young woman then turned to Moshe. "Mr. Avram."

Moshe waved his hand towards the sofa. "Sit down, Judith. What would you like to drink?"

"I'll make some tea," said Carla.

Moshe couldn't help smiling. Tea was a sacred ritual Carla had picked up from her English mother.

"We only have a few minutes, Mrs. Avram. We're about to meet some friends."

Yossi lowered himself into an armchair. "Dad, we're organizing another march to the Prime Minister's office."

Moshe shot a glance at his wife. The anxious look in her eyes tugged at his heart.

Yossi carried on. "We still think Jerusalem should be the capital for both states."

Moshe nodded. The Palestinians had a right to an independent state, even if it *was* with the pre-1967 borders since Israel was now a *fait accompli*. And Jerusalem should have belonged to everyone, not just one group.

"You make me proud, son. I'm sure my father is up there somewhere smiling down at you."

Yossi's face turned bright red. "I'll just grab a jacket before we head out." He sprung up and made for the door.

"Is Ruth here?" asked Judith.

"We rarely see Ruth nowadays," said Moshe. He turned to his wife with raised eyebrows. "*Where* does that girl go?"

Carla's laughter tinkled out. "Your daughter has grown up, Moshe. She's not a little girl anymore."

"Meaning?" The amused glances Carla and Judith exchanged disconcerted him.

"Your daughter is in love."

"In love?" When did that happen?

The front door slammed shut again.

"Daaad. Mama." As if summoned, Ruth's singsong voice soared from the hallway. She floated into the living room with shining eyes, her mass of dark waves cascading down her back. Her smile reminded Moshe of Carla when they had fallen in love all those years ago back in the U.S.

Ruth threw her arms around her mother before turning to her father and doing the same. Humming *I could have Danced all Night*, she pirouetted across the floor, her happiness contagious.

"Are you going to tell us what this is about?" asked Moshe, in an amused voice.

Just then, Yossi walked into the room. "Hi, sis."

"Hi." Ruth spun around and noticed Judith. "Judith. How are you?" She didn't wait for an answer. "Where's Jonathon?" She looked around for her younger brother. "I have some news, and I want everyone to be here."

Moshe stroked his chin, joy and sadness coursing through him at the same time. It wasn't too hard to guess what his daughter was about to say.

Chapter Three

Washington D.C., April 1986

Justin turned the key and walked into the house. It had been a tiresome day at the office. From the kitchen, voices and sounds of pots and pans clanking drifted through. His housemates must be cooking dinner. A pile of letters lay next to the stairs. He rummaged through them. Two were for him. One was a bill, but what was the other?

He climbed up the stairs, two at a time while undoing his tie. Once in his room, he took off his suit and changed into something comfortable then sat down and opened the mystery letter.

As he read through it, a small frown played between his eyebrows. It was an invitation for an interview for a job he had applied for last July when he had just returned from Egypt.

They had invited him to take their exam, but he never heard back from them. Bitterly disappointed, he had assumed that they were not interested in recruiting him.

He reread the letter then looked at the calendar on his wall. They requested to meet him three days from now. He raked his hands through his hair as a thrill of excitement ran down his spine.

This was why he had invested time studying Arabic. Ever since he was a little boy and his grandfather had told him tales of his adventures, how he had travelled the world with such a job filled with intrigues and challenges, Justin had wanted to follow in his footsteps.

"Justin."

At the sound of his name, he jolted. He placed the letter on his bedside table and walked out to the landing. One of his housemates stood at the bottom of the stairs wearing an apron, a wooden spoon in his hand.

"Dinner's ready."

He dashed down the stairs and joined the other four in the kitchen.

Though he did his best to join in the conversation, Justin's mind was miles away. Once they had finished, he rushed back to his room.

Should he tell Farah now or wait till after the interview?

A grin played around his mouth. With his mastery of Arabic, there was a good chance he would be offered the job. Then, he and Farah would be able to return to the Middle East. Not only would he be working in the field of his choice, but he would also be able to offer his princess the ex-pat lifestyle with all its perks.

***

The following Thursday morning, Justin climbed into his car and drove towards Fort Meade. As he approached his destination his gut knotted. What kind of questions would they ask?

A few minutes later he caught his first glimpse of the "Puzzle Palace". He made for the high barricaded wall surrounding the forbidding looking building. It was enclosed with a barbed wire fence. Electrical no doubt. An armed guard stopped him in front of the gate. Another armed guard sat in an elevated booth that gave him a panoramic view of the scene below.

"Identification, please," said the guard briskly.

Justin handed him his driver's license. "I have an appointment with

Mr. Steven Salyard at eleven o'clock."

"Yes, Sir." The guard's face was expressionless. He scrutinized the document before returning it.

The car was waved through. A few meters later, Justin slowed down as he caught sight of a second barricade. Once again, he handed his driving license as proof of identification. He hadn't driven ten minutes when he came across a third barricade. What the hell was this? Did they expect him to switch places with an armed terrorist between one blockade and the other? This time, it appeared to be the last one and he was finally allowed admission into the compound itself.

As he drove through, his mouth fell open; this was a city within a city.

Totally self-contained, the National Security Agency had its own shops, hospital, and post office.

Justin parked and strode towards the entrance. A tall man with light brown hair stood waiting. He stretched his hand.

"Justin Naban? I'm Steven Salyard. Please follow me."

Salyard led him inside to a small room.

"This won't take a minute," said Salyard, as Justin was blinded by a flash.

Within seconds Salyard handed him an identity tag. "Make sure you wear this while you're on the compound."

Slightly dazed, Justin followed his escort down a huge hall.

They strode past rows of rooms on both sides filled with computers. No doubt this was a hub for unscrambling and analyzing data from around the globe. They eventually reached a door that was marked 'No Unauthorized Admittance'.

Salyard opened the door.

"Ah, Mr. Naban. Please do come in." The speaker swung around on his revolving chair to face them before standing up to shake hands.

He appeared to be in his fifties. Bald, slightly overweight, he had a commanding presence about him.

"Allow me to introduce myself. Peter Swift, Senior Officer for the NSA recruiting team. Have a seat please." He waved to an armchair opposite his desk.

Chapter Four

Paris, April 1986

Farah finished her breakfast and rang Monique.

"Farah, what happened to you? You vanished."

"Sorry. I was working non-stop. Elise's father died suddenly, so I was doing two shifts in a row to cover for her, poor girl. Such a shock. I finally have a day off today."

"How sad for Elise." There was a pause. "So, what about that postponed shopping spree?"

They agreed to meet two hours later in front of the C & A store.

Rue de Rivoli bustled with people. When Monique appeared, they sauntered to a nearby shoe shop but found nothing suitable.

Across the street was a small café. The pair headed there, settled for a table near the window, and ordered two cappuccinos.

"So how does it feel?" asked Monique with a twinkle, "only seven weeks till the wedding."

Farah pursed her lips for a moment.

"Justin's not happy at work. It's been playing on my mind. I haven't been able to talk to him for two weeks. I missed him each time I rang, and he didn't call back."

The waiter placed the steaming cups on the table.

"He's probably busy with his own arrangements. Have you decided on the honeymoon yet?"

"Well…" Farah hesitated. "We're going to a place called Cape Cod. His family has a house there."

Monique stared at her with raised eyebrows. "I thought you wanted to go to Italy?"

She winced. "He can't afford that right now. And as long as we're together, it doesn't really matter where we go." It had been a big disappointment, but she wasn't going to admit it to anyone. She brought the cup to her lips and took a sip.

"It's strange why his family doesn't offer to help him out. I mean, didn't he say he had a trust fund to go to Georgetown University?"

"I guess Americans do things differently to us."

"Your father didn't offer?"

"No. He's already paying for the wedding." In Egypt, the bride's family never paid for the wedding.

"Are you nervous about moving to the States?"

"A bit." Farah shrugged. "It's such a different culture. Plus, I'll have to find something to do. I can't work before I get my green card though."

"Why don't you take some acting classes? You enjoyed that so much at college, and you had such presence on stage."

"I gave up thinking about that as anything beyond a pastime after what happened with my dad."

Her father's reaction two years earlier when she was offered a part in a movie swam through her mind.

"Out of the question," he had said coldly when she broke the news that a famous director had approached her for a part in his new film. "No young lady from a good family goes into acting."

The next morning, as she and her brother cycled to the club, she had tried to enlist his help, but Cyril had been just as adamant as their father.

Monique leaned forward. "But that was in Cairo. You'll be in Washington now. I'm sure your dad won't have objections that you take it up there. Anyway, you'll be a married woman, free to do what you want."

Farah cast her a doubtful glance.

Monique touched her arm. "Farah, it's wonderful that you're marrying the man you love, but you need some other kind of fulfillment as well, you know? Married life can't be a goal in itself."

Farah didn't answer as she mulled over Monique's words. Then, twisting her lips to one side, she smacked her lap. "You know what? You're right. That's what I'll do. I loved being on stage, loved studying those characters and becoming them." She reached for her cup, a smile painted on her mouth. Wouldn't it be great if she enrolled in an acting school and got serious about it? Who knew where it could lead? She glanced at her watch. "Do you mind if we head back to my place? If we manage to get back by two-thirty, I'll be able to catch Justin before he leaves for work."

***

Farah pressed the receiver to her ear, her finger on the rotary dial. "The number you have dialed has been disconnected. There is no further information about this number," repeated the automatic voice.

A puzzled frown played between her brows as she peered at Justin's number in her address book. "How odd. Listen to the recording, Monique." She handed her friend the receiver, kicking herself that she only had Justin's personal number, not the main phone he and his housemates shared.

"That's strange. Are you sure you dialed the right number?"

"Yes, I'm sure."

"Did he not pay his bill? Can you call his office?"

"Yes, but in an hour. He won't be in yet."

Farah boiled some spaghetti and prepared a tomato sauce. Every few minutes, she glanced at the clock on the wall. The hands seemed to barely move.

They sat down for their meal, though Farah couldn't eat more than a fork full. Once they had cleared the table and washed the dishes, Farah dialed Justin's office.

After several rings, an operator picked up.

"Justin Naban, please."

"I'm sorry, but Mr. Naban no longer works here," said the female voice.

"W-what?" Farah blinked not sure she had heard correctly. "Since when?" A myriad of questions swarmed through her mind.

"Last Friday was his last day."

"Did he leave a contact number?" Confused, Farah found it hard to think straight.

"I'm afraid not. Will that be all ma'am?"

"Yes. Thank you." The receiver slipped through Farah's hand and hung mid-air. "I don't understand." The words spluttered out. "He didn't mention anything about resigning." She slumped backward in her chair and cradled her head in her hands.

Monique patted Farah on the back. "I'm sure he'll phone you today or tomorrow and explain. Did you check the answering machine?"

"Yes, there was only a message from my cousin Marc."

Monique stayed with her till late in the evening. "Try and get some sleep, Farah. There has to be a simple reason for all of this."

Farah tossed and turned before finally dozing off. She woke up in a foul mood. Fortunately, she was on the afternoon shift at work. As she left the building, the concierge came running to her with an envelope.

«Le facteur m'a donné cette lettre pour vous, Mademoiselle Farah.»

"Merci Yvette." Farah reached to take the letter. Her hand halted in mid-air. A sinking sensation filled her stomach. That was *her* handwriting on the envelope. It was the last letter she had mailed to Justin last week. 'Return to Sender' was stamped on the outside.

She grabbed the letter and ran back upstairs.

With trembling hands, Farah dialed his mother's number and waited. After ten rings, the line cut off. What if Justin had had a terrible accident?

Her heart sagging, Farah somehow managed to get to work on time.

Unable to reach Justin or his mother, the nightmare continued for the next few days.

On Saturday morning, after another sleepless night, she dialed his mother's number again. This time, Justin's stepfather picked up.

"Hello."

"Oh, Mr. King, this is Farah. I'm so glad I found you. I've been worried sick. I can't find Justin. His number's changed, and he's quit his job. Where is he? Is he all right? Is his mother there? Can I speak to her please?"

He clicked his tongue in annoyance. "Farah, it's 4:30 in the morning here. And no, my wife isn't available."

"I know. I'm very sorry, but I've been trying to reach you for the past week. Nobody picked up. How can I get a hold of Justin?" Her heart throbbed.

"Farah, I'm sure that if Justin wanted you to get hold of him, he would have contacted you by now. I'm afraid if he hasn't given you his new number, then neither can I."

"Wh—?" The words froze in her throat.

"I'm sorry, Farah."

Click. The line went dead.

Farah's stomach lurched. With each shallow breath, her chest heaved in and out.

She crumbled onto a chair like a piece of wood eaten away by termites.

Chapter Five

Seven Months Later
Paris – November 1986

Flight announcements boomed as passengers darted their way through the crowds to departure gates in Orly Airport.

Farah smiled at a middle-aged couple who had just entered the VIP lounge and accompanied them inside. The phone rang. She looked around for Elise, but she was at the other end of the lounge, and there was no one at the reception desk. Farah rushed over and picked it up.

"Bonjour. VIP Lounge."

"Farah? It's Eric." Her boss's voice rumbled down the line. "Aquilah Louhichi is off sick."

Why was Eric informing her about someone in senior management?

"She won't be able to attend the annual reception on Friday. You're the only other Arabic speaker we have."

Farah swallowed. Friday was the evening she planned to finish the application form for the London School of Drama, and write a letter to Dr. Osius, who had directed all the plays she had acted in as a student, asking him for a reference.

"The reception is being held at the Ritz. I want you there around 8.00. Evening dress code."

"Uuh yes, of cou–"

But her boss had already hung up. She glanced at the clock. Ten minutes till her shift ended. Farah shot into the back office and gathered her belongings. At five sharp, she was out the door.

It was rush hour and the streets heaved with people hurrying under a bleak sky. She caught the metro and in half an hour, was home.

Her parents' two-bedroom apartment was located not far from the Champs Elysees. She unlocked the door and headed to the kitchen. After heating some leftover lasagna, she sat down on the sofa, staring out of the window. November was always a miserable month in Paris, rainy and gloomy. Her throat constricted – this year in more ways than one. It was seven months since Justin had vanished like a fish in the Dead Sea. Questions stormed through her head, her soul palpitating with pain. *Oh Justin, how could you have done that to me?*

With a sigh, Farah pushed her plate of food aside and went into her bedroom. Might as well practice a scene in case any of her applications got accepted.

She stood in front of the bedroom mirror, her arm stretched in front of her as if entreating someone, while she recited Portia from Shakespeare's *Merchant of Venice*.

A ringing phone interrupted her rehearsal. It was her half-sister.

"Tammy. I'm so glad you rang. I just got my ticket for Christmas."

"Oh, wonderful. The kids are so happy you're all coming to Jordan this year." Her sister's voice echoed on the international connection. "How're you doing otherwise?"

"I – I'm okay, thanks." Farah's voice faltered but she continued. "Have you spoken to Cyril? When is he arriving?" It would be nice if her brother was already there when she arrived.

"Yes, he's arriving on the 21st. Listen, Mariam Radwani will be in Paris in a couple of weeks. I've given her your number and told her to get in touch."

"Great." She liked Mariam, her sister's cousin-in-law from Jerusalem. She hadn't seen her in four years. Not since Mariam had been working in a Palestinian refugee camp in Lebanon. Was it Sabra? Or Shatila?

All Farah could remember was that there had been a massacre there. At the time, she had been too busy with theatre productions and partying at university but recalled seeing banners by some group called 'Friends of Palestine' denouncing Israel. Politics didn't interest her.

"One last thing. I was talking to Mom. I should warn you that your father wants you to return to Cairo, and he's going to bring it up while you're here next month. He doesn't see any need for you to remain in Paris anymore."

Farah's stomach churned at the thought. She glanced through the window. Dark clouds circled the Paris skyline. The only thing she missed about Egypt at this moment was the sunshine during the short winter months.

Maybe she shouldn't go to Jordan. She waved the thought off as soon as it took root. Miss Christmas with the family? Not in a million years. Especially *this* Christmas. It would be so sad and lonely, like a bare tree without any decorations.

"Anyway, Farah, I've got to run Adam over to his soccer practice. Talk soon."

"OK. Give my love to Jamal and the kids."

The clock on the wall stated it was quarter to seven. Still an hour and fifteen minutes till Monique was due to visit. Farah chewed on the inside of her cheek, mulling over her sister's words about returning to Cairo.

She strode into the bedroom and changed into some running gear then stamped out of the apartment, shutting the door with a loud bang.

Once on the street, she inhaled a lungful of air and started fast walking before it turned into a jog. She dipped her hand into her pocket and dug out her Walkman, switched it on, and put the volume to full blast as George Michael's *Careless Whisper* streamed through.

She ran down a side street then turned left. A few meters later, she veered to the right, ran across another busy street, and continued up a pavement without noticing where she was heading. Car lights blared as they drove past. Drops of sweat trickled down her face, and she wiped them with the back of her hand.

Farah glanced at her watch. She'd been running for almost forty-five minutes now. Her heart thudded against her chest in rhythm with her breath. But then she lost her footing, tripped, and fell with a thud on the ground. Though her outstretched hands broke the fall, she grazed her knee.

She eyed the area, no idea where she was. As she sat on the sidewalk, tears stung her eyes but she blinked them back. This wasn't time to wallow. She had to be home before Monique arrived. Farah hauled herself up and limped forward. Still unable to get her bearings, she reluctantly asked a stranger for directions to the closest metro station.

It was only a short ride. As soon as she arrived home, she cleaned her wound, and stuck on a band aid.

The buzzer downstairs rang. A few minutes later, Monique, red-faced from the cold, stepped in and took off her coat, her auburn hair standing in tiny spikes.

Farah made coffee and they settled in the living room in front of the fireplace. The aromatic coffee tasted so much better in Paris than in Cairo. The whiff of the Colombian blend lingered in the room, but nothing dispelled the melancholic vibes that filled the place.

"You're so lucky, Farah, that your parents own this place."

"You could stay with me if you want, instead of paying rent in Ivry." Why Monique chose to rent in an area populated by desperate migrants scrambling for a better life was beyond Farah.

"Yes, but familiarity breeds contempt. Anyway, when have I not been here when you needed me?"

Farah couldn't argue with that. She was grateful for all the support Monique had given her over the past months. She stuffed some chocolate into her mouth, wanting to fill that big gaping hole inside her. "My father wants me to return to Cairo."

"And?"

"And what? I'm not going. I'm applying for another scholarship. This time at the London School of Drama." Farah shrugged. "If anything comes through, then –"

"What if nothing does, what will you do then?" Monique reached for her coffee.

Her head drooped. "Then…I don't know."

Farah gazed at a bookcase on the far wall. The sight of Naguib Mahfouz' *Midaq Alley* on the bottom shelf, the only book in Arabic, cut her breath like a serrated knife. Why hadn't she removed all of Justin's traces?

She turned to Monique. "*You're* the one who made me want to go back to acting. I realized that's the only thing I have a passion for, getting into the character's head to tell their story." It would also be the only thing to take her mind off the heartache. "Plus, There's also that rush of adrenaline when I'm in front of an audience."

Monique nodded.

"Why on earth did my parents send me to university if I can't make my own choices in life?" Farah shrugged and stared at her nails. "I'm also not willing to give up my freedom. Cairo stifles me. I can't bear all the cultural shackles over there. Besides, my father would control my life again if I go back."

"Maybe you could live alone –" said Monique doubtfully.

"Oh, come on. I have neither the money nor the courage to rent my own place. I can just see my aunts screeching into *papa's* ear if I even suggested living alone." Farah rolled her eyes. "Here, I'm anonymous. I can do whatever I want, whenever I want. No curfews, no interfering neighbors."

Outside, the wind whistled and gusted.

Farah jumped up and drew the curtains. "Plus, my Egyptian grandmother and aunts are intent on marrying me off to some *eligible* guy."

"But your mum would never allow that to happen."

"True. All those years of fighting with my dad. One Egyptian man in my life is quite enough."

Monique raised an eyebrow. "Yeah. It's weird being caught in the middle, one foot in each culture." She took another sip of coffee. "When my parents don't get each other's way of thinking it's kind of like…"

Farah puckered her lips. "Pfff. Sometimes I wonder why my dad married a European."

"I know. My mother said that when my father brought her to Egypt, he changed so much. It was like she was suddenly married to a different person. She said if they'd remained in Europe, their marriage would have been better," said Monique, with a shake of the head.

"Well, I'm *not* returning. I can't do that to myself."

Monique reached for a pack of caramelized biscuits lying on the table. "How's Lucien?"

Farah's lips crinkled upwards at the mention of the red-headed Breton. "He asked me out."

"He's a fast mover. But I suppose after crying on his shoulder for the last few months…anyway, a new nail pushes out another, you know what I mean?"

"We'll see how it goes." Farah wasn't even sure why she had agreed. Loneliness, probably. He was fun to be around, and a great listener, with a good sense of humor. She poked at the fire and waited till the sparks calmed down before sliding the fire screen over it. "I've been meaning to ask you, any news from Danny?"

"Yes." Monique's voice was flat. "He's getting married."

"*What?*" Farah swung around. "Oh, Monique, I'm so sorry. When did you find out?"

A muscle in Monique's jaw twitched. "I got a letter from him a week ago. Says he wants to settle down, start a family. He went to some school reunion a few months ago and met up with an old classmate who had a crush on him. Obviously still likes him and wants to settle down too."

"I can't believe -"

"It would never have worked. I wasn't going to move to Yugoslavia, and he wouldn't move to Paris."

Farah hugged Monique. "I'm sorry." She fumbled for some comforting words – but what was there to say?

"I didn't want to tell you – you've got enough to deal with already."

Farah stared at the crackling fire, the blue and orange flames spitting as they reached towards the chimney. "Did you ever think when we moved here last year that our lives would take such turns?" She sighed. "I really miss college. All our high hopes after we graduated…"

"Enough of that. Come on, let's dance." Monique slid a tape into the cassette player and pulled her off the sofa.

They danced to the Pointer Sisters' *I'm So Excited*.

Farah waved her arms in the air, and, for a brief moment, forgot everything and just enjoyed the music.

Chapter Six

Jaffa - South of Tel Aviv, November 1986

Moshe Avram parked his car and made his way to Ajami, one of the many historic cities founded by the Ottomans at the end of the 19th century.

Shading his eyes from the bright afternoon sun, he walked past the Lebanese Maronite monastery and church at the southern tip of Dolphin Street, close to the precipice overlooking the harbor.

Considering the enmity between Israel and Lebanon today, it was ironic how the Lebanese Christians had ever settled here. But in those days, this country had been called Palestine, not Israel.

Seagulls soared above, squawking.

Moshe was glad for the stroll. Too much pent-up energy from being cooped up in the office made his body crave the exercise. He chuckled as he glanced beyond the little path to his right, thinking of himself and Ibrahim Radwani as children running along, holding onto a brightly colored kite. Their squeals of delight had filled the air as they hurtled down that perilous slope, tripping, falling, but never letting go of their precious possession. But that was before the 1948 war that changed everything forever.

A couple of young IDF soldiers, automatic rifles hanging off their shoulders, stepped out of the house on the other side of the street where Ibrahim and his family used to stay during the long summers. They walked past speaking in Yiddish.

He crossed Dolphin Street. The salty sea air slapped him in the face. Waves frothed up before crashing against the shore, only to be subdued as they rolled onto the sand receding again leaving clumps of seaweed on the beach. A light breeze ruffled through and Moshe zipped up his windbreaker. The restaurant was situated on the northern tip of Ajami, still a bit of a walk.

Lunch with Ibrahim Radwani was always a treat, a time to unwind. The bond between them spanned almost half a century. Moshe's gaze fell on the scar on his right arm, the 'Pledge of Friendship' as they both called it.

Moshe chuckled at how two little boys of four, one Jewish and the other Moslem, had found each other one summer back in 1942 when he had run to the rescue of a stranger being bullied by a group of older boys. For all Moshe's scratching and kicking, had it not been for his older brother Nathan who had arrived on the scene with a few of his friends, Moshe and Ibrahim would have been turned into mincemeat.

Back then, both of them were blissfully unaware of the war raging on another continent, just across the Mediterranean, with consequences stretching into their own future.

The events that followed, Israel's declaration as an independent state in 1948, and Jerusalem becoming a divided city, left them all reeling. Suddenly, traveling overseas became easier than crossing from the Israeli side of Jerusalem to the Arab East Jerusalem.

Moshe remembered how he kept asking his father how come there was no country called Palestine any more, after East Jerusalem and the West Bank were annexed to Jordan.

Despite all that, the two friends managed to remain in contact. Whenever Ibrahim's family traveled to Europe, they sent telegrams with their news. As they neared school leaving certificates, Moshe and Ibrahim planned to study at the same university in the States. Young and full of hopes, nurturing dreams of a better world, Moshe immersed himself in his studies, Ibrahim hot on his heels.

Moshe reached the Old Man and the Sea restaurant before Ibrahim and sat down on the terrace. Plain wooden tables with wicker chairs dotted the place. A waiter swirled over and placed a giant pitcher of freshly squeezed lemonade in front of him. Moshe pushed it to the side; he wanted a beer, but would wait for his friend.

Anchored in the marina outside were a few run-down fishing boats, the kinds with oars, fragments of what had once been bright-colored paint peeling off here and there.

Within minutes Ibrahim Radwani appeared, greyer than last time—but then so was Moshe.

They exchanged loud greetings and pats on the back then settled on their food choice.

The waiter brought their drinks, beer for Moshe and *Araq* for Ibrahim who favored the anise drink over ale.

"How's the family?" Ibrahim rested his ankle on his knee.

"Yossi's as active as ever, and Carla's terrified something might happen to him." Moshe shifted his gaze towards the sea. "So am I, but that's part of living here. We never know when we go out if we will return home again or not. None of us do."

Ibrahim nodded. "True."

Moshe stroked his chin. "At times I blame myself for bringing her back here."

"How could you have known back then how things would change?"

No, how could Moshe have guessed when he and Carla eloped that the world would change irrevocably? It had been just after his graduation, when he was twenty-two and she twenty, with Ibrahim as his witness.

"I should have had the foresight, though foresight isn't one of our strong points, is it? But I'm working on it."

A comfortable silence hovered between them.

Ibrahim signaled to the waiter for a refill. "And Ruth? Jonathon?"

Moshe beamed. "You'll be getting an invite to Ruth's wedding soon, Ibrahim. In Galilee."

Ibrahim's face broke into a smile. "Who?"

Moshe gave a short laugh. "Jaleel. An Arab-Israeli from Nazareth."

"And your father-in-law?"

Moshe raised his shoulders, his palms spread outwards. "I doubt he'll care as long as Ruth is happy." He shook his head. "Do you know the number of times Gideon has visited us, and despite that, his understanding of the region is still shallow?"

"To be fair to your father-in-law, it's not easy to understand our screwed-up region. And the man has no interest anyway."

"He still tries to convince me to take the family back to the U.S."

"It's understandable that he wants his daughter and grandchildren closer," said Ibrahim.

"Well, it's not going to happen. But of course, I shouldn't criticize him."

Gideon Rosenberg had entrusted Moshe with opening a branch of Rosenberg Shipping in Tel Aviv. Moshe climbed the financial ladder, establishing his name among the scions of wealthy families.

"Forget that for now." Moshe reached out and took a big gulp of his beer. He offered Ibrahim a cigarette and pulled one out for himself before lighting them both. "Ibrahim, something's going to happen soon, and it's going to backfire on everyone."

Ibrahim leaned forward, a frown playing between his eyebrows. "Something like what? Isn't it enough what we're in already?"

Moshe snorted. "Is anything enough for this government? It's only a matter of time till this cauldron of simmering anger explodes. And when it does, the downward spiral will carry us all underground."

"I can't see what could be worse than their policy of apartheid," said Ibrahim, his voice riddled with sarcasm.

"The government plans to fund an Islamic movement." Moshe's nostrils flared. "Sheikh Ahmed Yassin."

"*What?!*"

Moshe nodded, his lips pressed together in a grim line.

"No, Moshe, that's impossible."

"Why? They learned from the Brits: Divide and conquer. Funding an Islamic movement is a masterstroke against the PLO and Yasser Arafat. Just like the United States funded the Taliban to fight the Soviets."

Ibrahim's face went white. "How do you know this?"

"*Ihud* may be small and insignificant, but we're still able to get information first-hand."

Joining the only political party in Israel boasting an assortment of Jews, along with Christian and Moslem Arab Israelis, had been one of Moshe's best moves. United in their anti-Zionist stance, they all yearned to live in a society where rights weren't determined by religious affiliations and ethnic backgrounds.

Moshe's thoughts darted back to the horrendous massacre of Deir Yassin back in 1948, when the head of the International Red Cross emergency delegation had bravely pushed through rows of armed militia, only to find that nearly the entire village had been slaughtered.

Shock and disgust had reverberated through the indigenous Jewish community. The Chief Rabbi of Jerusalem flew into a rage when the news reached him. But even he couldn't stop the mighty military machine of Israel.

A shudder ran up Moshe's back. "If this movement gets Israel's support, there'll be no end to the madness pitching Islamists against secular Palestinians. None of us know what the result will be. But we can be sure of one thing: the cycle of violence will never end."

"Even the current government can't be that stupid."

"*Fi Sehetak*, cheers my friend." Moshe raised his glass. "I hope I'm wrong, but my gut feeling is that very soon we will hear of the existence of this entity. We're dealing here with a government that has zero scruples – even less than the norm."

Ibrahim shook his head. "You're such a misfit, Moshe."

Moshe chuckled, a sense of determination surging through him.

F. MICHELE RAMSEY

"And *that's* why I'm going to make a difference."

Chapter Seven

Paris - November 1986

Farah scowled at the clothes in her closet. This damn reception Eric had roped her into attending. He probably expected her to be grateful – junior staff like her were never invited.

A sob froze in her throat. Here she was, alone and single as if the curtain had tumbled down in the middle of the play.

Lights from the street lamps flickered through the window while teardrops of rain pitter-pattered against it.

She reached for a black off-the-shoulder top and a long, velvet skirt.

The bottle of Nina Ricci *Eau de Toilette* stood on the dressing table raking up painful images.

Justin had called it her seduction technique. Compelled by the fragrance, he would draw her into his arms. The image, the sensations, were still vivid, how he sprinkled light kisses on her face leading to a passion that usually ended up making them late to wherever they were going.

Her chin trembled. God. The memories still hurt.

She sprayed a few drops behind her ears and her wrists then dabbed on her lipstick.

The nineteenth-century lithograph of the Sphinx by David Roberts hanging on the wall caught Farah's eye.

She and Justin had gone there during Ramadan, arriving at sunset, while everyone was breaking their fast and the touristic area was deserted.

Justin had climbed up on the wall that overlooked the Sphinx and stood there in silence staring at the grandiose monument. "Shall we?" A mischievous look spread across his boyish face.

With shouts of laughter, they both leaped down, ran to the Sphinx, and stood between its great paws, intoxicated with the thrill of treading where forbidden.

"Hail, mighty Sphinx." Justin's voice echoed off the massive creature into the endless desert. He had grabbed Farah around the waist and lifted her in the air. Her squeals pierced the silence. When he put her down, their arms interlocked.

And there, in the ancient desert that guarded secrets of countless generations, he bent down and kissed her, with all the tender sweetness of a first kiss.

Her sister's words echoed in her mind. "This too shall pass."

Would it? She slumped into a chair, her chest tight. Why did everything remind her of him?

The clock chimed pulling Farah back to the present. She stood up with a sigh, grabbed her bag and coat, and headed downstairs where she hailed a cab.

***

The classic façade of the Ritz stood unchanged since it had been founded in the 1800s, built to attract the rich and famous.

Farah handed in her coat at the vestiaire and crossed into a brightly lit reception hall clouded with smoke, and speckled with the orange glow of cigarettes. Conversation mingled with laughter and the clinking of crystal glasses to create an almost overwhelming din.

She scanned the room until she spotted Eric, waved at him, and waited till he acknowledged her with a nod, then sauntered off. As long as she made an appearance, Eric couldn't fault her. Anyway, he was too busy networking himself to notice who she spoke to.

A waiter edged his way through the throng of guests, carrying a tray of bubbling champagne flutes. Though she hadn't eaten, Farah grabbed a glass, smiled her thanks, and took a sip. At the sight of Lucien's head bobbing up and down like a goldfish in a tank, she ducked and hurried away. After their disastrous date, she didn't want to spend the evening with him – the chemistry just wasn't there. She headed to a far corner where she could observe without being observed, and avoid dreaded small talk with strangers.

Older, well-dressed men strolled around, puffed up like Arabian camels, with racy young escorts hanging on their arms. Their revealing outfits left little to the imagination.

A pianist, at a white grand piano at the far end of the reception hall, struck the opening bars of Charles Aznavour's *Hier Encore*. The lyrics touched a cord in Farah's soul and she inhaled a deep breath. The buzz of the champagne went to her head. She ventured off in search of more, a bit wobbly on her high heels. Amusing snippets of conversation drifted through, like an auditory mosaic. She paused to exchange a few words with a couple of patrons.

A waiter glided past.

Farah reached for another flute, almost toppling the rest of the glasses on the tray in her haste to return to her little hiding place. *Zut*. A group of businessmen had occupied her sanctuary.

A puff of annoyance escaped Farah's lips. Her eyes watered from the smoke. She wandered towards one of the open French windows, where a high table was tucked away, almost hidden by an enormous pale blue silk curtain.

A tall, broad-shouldered man with well-chiseled, Middle Eastern features and a thick black mustache leaned against the wall. A glass of whiskey in one hand, a cigarette dangled from his lips. He emitted an allure, magnetic and dangerous at the same time.

Farah stopped.

He must have seen her hesitation. Eyebrows raised and, with a hint of a smile, he gestured theatrically at the ample space around him.

She tried to read him.

His piercing eyes, the color of the desert sky at midnight, dared her to join him.

Farah's gut told her to walk away, but overcome with a sense of recklessness, she made for the table and acknowledged him with a small nod. She slid up onto a high chair, and half sat, one foot still firmly on the ground before turning to face the pianist, her head bobbing to the tunes. When she turned back to reach out for her flute of champagne, the stranger was perched opposite her, his drink on the table.

He held out his hand. "Ghassan Khodeib, but everybody calls me Gus." His voice was deep and sonorous.

With such a name he had to be Levantine. But which country?

Tongue-tied, Farah shook his hand then picked up her glass and pressed her lips against the rim, trying not to stare at his gold puzzle ring. They had always fascinated her, but she had never been able to put one back together.

His cologne, an intoxicating blend of citrus and cloves, drifted to her. It conjured up thoughts of exotic places, of beaches, palm trees, and languid summer afternoons.

Gus put out his cigarette in the ashtray. "Don't you have a name?" His penetrating eyes were still on her, an intimation of laughter in his voice.

Don't you have any manners?

"Farah." She stuck her nose up in the air. Why was his tone mocking?

He grinned. "Farah? Do you know what your name means in my language?"

"*Ma'loum*. Joy." She reverted to a Jordanian dialect.

"Ah…your pronunciation is excellent. One would think Arabic is your mother tongue."

"Well, it almost is."

"What's your *real* native language then?"

"French. My *real* mother tongue is French."

Again, that amused look which began to make her feel rather disconcerted. She glanced at his packet of cigarettes. He picked it up and offered her one, a gold lighter in his other hand. She coughed after a couple of puffs.

His lips twitched under his mustache, revealing a well-set row of teeth.

"It's not my first time. To smoke," she said, heat flaming her face as if a misbehaving child caught out. Her father's disappointment when he had caught her smoking had never faded from her mind.

"Oh, I never thought it was."

She fidgeted in her seat. "It's just that I haven't smoked for quite a while."

He nodded and flicked his cigarette, his eyes drinking her in. "I take it, with your features and complexion, you must be one of those …'Halfies', as they say?" His arched brows disappeared under a shock of coal-black hair.

He said 'halfies' as if it were some kind of alien species and Farah cracked a big smile.

"Ah, so you *do* have a sense of humor." He picked up his glass. "Suits you much more than that haughty look when you first sat down."

She stared at her drink, unwilling to meet his eyes.

He persisted. "I'm curious, Ms. Halfie. What are your halves?"

She failed to suppress a chortle. "French and Egyptian."

"Egyptian? Yet your accent – "

"I've spent time in Jordan and picked up the accent."

"And which half is French?"

Farah put her glass down, swishing her right arm upwards in an elegant flourish. "*Ce moitié.*"

They both laughed.

"My mum is French, and my dad Egyptian. And you?"

"Lebanese."

She toyed with her pearl necklace. "So, you're a fullie."

He chuckled and raised his glass to his mouth.

"And what is a fullie Lebanese doing in Paris? Do you live here?"

How old was he? Thirty-five? For someone more than a decade her senior, conversing with him was easy.

"*Oui*," he nodded and adjusted his gold cuff links. "And yourself?"

"I moved here last year after graduating from university in Cairo."

"The American University?"

She chortled. "How did you guess?"

"So many of my compatriots attended the AUC because of the civil war in Lebanon. It supplanted the American University in Beirut as the best educational institution in the region." He shrugged and picked up his glass. Finding it empty, he clicked his tongue in annoyance and gestured to a passing waiter for refills.

"And what do you do here, Ms. Halfie?"

"I work in the VIP Lounge."

There she went, giving him information.

"Why have I never seen you before? I'm sure I would have remembered those enigmatic eyes."

Her cheeks flushed.

Gus slipped a set of jade worry beads out of his pocket and began twirling them through his fingers.

The waiter arrived with the drinks, saving her from having to respond.

"*Santé*, Farah." The dark stranger raised his glass at her again. "So, tell me, Ms. Halfie, what do you like?"

Light-headed, Farah tilted her head to the side, while a slow smile spread across her face and blurted, "*J'aime la vie.*" I love life. She drew in a sharp breath. Why had she said that?

"An original answer." Gus nodded slightly and clicked away at the worry beads.

"Except it's full of heartache because of that damned liar." The words spilled out before she could stop them.

To her relief, Gus didn't react.

Her eyes smarted as tears threatened to roll down. She stood up and avoided looking at him. "Excuse me, I need to use the Ladies Room."

The possible embarrassment of exposing her shattered heart was enough. She didn't need to end up looking like Morticia from the Addams Family, with mascara smudging down her cheeks.

In the bathroom, Farah stood in front of the mirror and gripped onto the sink, breathing in deeply several times. Why wouldn't this damn heartache go away? After composing herself, she walked back out and slipped into her seat.

Gus inclined his head, acknowledging her return.

The soft music ended and the reception hall evolved into a disco club. A DJ played Madonna's *Papa Don't Preach*.

Couples moved on to the dance floor.

Farah reached out for the stem of her chilled glass with the tip of her fingers, her red nails resembling drops of blood on the crystal. She longed for another cigarette.

She raised her eyebrows at Gus and reached for his purple pack of Silk Cut.

He nodded.

What had come over her? It was ages since she had last smoked or enjoyed a distinctly warm encounter like this. While his presence was unsettling, it wasn't unpleasant. Her mouth turned dry so she took a sip of champagne. Should she switch to water?

She noticed him studying her through spirals of smoke. Did he know the effect he was having on her?

More champagne arrived. Shoving her reservations to the side, Farah downed another glass.

More bodies crammed the dance floor, gyrating as one mass. UB40's *Red Red Wine* rattled out of the sound system as people raised imaginary wine glasses in the air.

"I think I'm going to head home." With a pinched expression, Farah slipped off the highchair and clutched the table to steady herself.

Gus checked his watch then raised an eyebrow. "Why so early? Don't tell me you have a curfew?"

Farah threw him a haughty glance. "No, but my carriage might turn into a pomegranate if I don't leave now."

"Touché." He stood up. "I'll see you home." His voice was firm, the voice of someone accustomed to being obeyed.

"There is really no need." She pretended to protest, though secretly pleased by his offer.

In a protective gesture, he placed a hand on her back and steered her across the room. "You must know, *Chère* Farah, that no *honorable* Arab man would allow a lady to make her way home alone at night, *n'est-ce-pas?*"

In the lobby, Gus retrieved her coat from the attendant and held it out for her.

Still light-headed, Farah fumbled for the sleeves. She shot him a mortified glance.

The same amused smile from earlier played across his lips.

A chauffeur-driven black Mercedes stopped in front of them.

Gus opened the back door.

She stepped off the pavement to go around to the other side.

He caught her arm, and with a short laugh, indicated that the open door was for her.

Embarrassed at how gauche she was, Farah mumbled her thanks and stepped in.

Gus climbed in next to her. "I left my crystal ball at home, so would you be so kind to tell us your address?"

She laughed awkwardly. "16th Arrondissement, please. Avenue Victor Hugo."

Her hand brushed against his as she fastened her seat belt. Flutters swam down her stomach. She edged towards the door and peered out of the window to distract herself.

The driver sped along, weaving his way through traffic, overtaking other cars, and sliding in between them through impossibly small spaces. Like Cairenes, Parisians disdained traffic rules and had no compunction about creating road chaos.

A waxing moon hovered in the sky, its half-light casting shadows over the Seine.

The car halted in front of her building. Gus climbed out and opened her door.

When she extended her hand, he raised it to his lips. "I hope you will allow me the pleasure of your company again, Ms. Halfie." In the light of the streetlamp, his dark eyes glinted.

"T-thank you for the ride home." Annoyed at her stammering, she snatched her hand away.

At the entrance of her apartment block, Farah looked over her shoulder. Gus was leaning against the car, the amused smile had never left his face. With a farewell wave, she hurried inside as fast as her wobbling knees allowed her. Steadying herself against the cool paneled wall of the lift, Farah inhaled a deep breath, her palm against her chest.

Something about this man sent exciting tremors down her spine.

***

The next morning, the doorbell buzzing intruded through Farah's fuzzy brain. She dragged herself to the door, massaging her pounding temples with her thumbs.

A gorgeous basket of white roses rested on the doormat, their delicate scent filling the air.

The last time she had received roses had been from Justin for her birthday.

Farah opened the small envelope to find Gus's business card. On the reverse side, a handwritten quote from Rumi, the 13th Century Persian poet: *"You have to keep breaking your heart till it opens."*

Damn. Why hadn't she kept quiet?

She inhaled a deep breath. It was too early in the morning to think of such deep words, especially when her stomach was unsettled from all the champagne last night.

Farah took hold of the flowers, and instead of bringing them in, placed them firmly in the hallway outside her flat. It was as if by doing so, she was blocking Gus and his dark, penetrating eyes from invading her mind. She went into the kitchen and popped a slice of bread in the toaster.

Her thoughts drifted back to the three glorious weeks she had spent with Justin here in this flat two summers ago, right after her graduation.

Three weeks filled with the thrill of secrecy, and far from her parents' watchful eyes. She had cut the noose of the 'Mother of All Social Taboos' and lost her virginity.

Another relationship wasn't going to be the balm to her pain – or was it?

The roses perturbed her. As did Gus's panther-like allure. With his intensity and mystery, he had the appeal of forbidden fruit.

Yet wasn't it time to start engaging with life again?

After breakfast, she wandered back into her bedroom.

The packet of Justin's letters lay in the bottom drawer of her bedside table like some embalmed creature she shouldn't disturb. Tearing up, she retrieved them, recalling every detail of how their story had started in Cairo two years earlier, in 1984.

It had been Friday, 29th of November and the theatre was jam-packed. She was playing the leading role in the university production of George Bernard Shaw's *Caesar and Cleopatra.*

Farah shuffled through the letters – she didn't have the strength to burn them.

The empty frames that once held cherished photos of her and Justin stared at her like hollow eyes. Why hadn't she filled them with photos of her childhood?

She curled back into bed. What had she ever done to deserve getting her heart broken?

Waves of guilt and shame overcame her as the horrible secret she had squished for so long flared in her mind. If only she had shouted a warning to her mother all those years ago, the baby wouldn't have died. And this was life's punishment.

Chapter Eight

Farah sat at the reception desk at work checking the guest sign-in book.

"Farah, the boss wants you." Elise pointed to the door, her dark eyes conveying a look of sympathy.

Farah's mouth turned dry. Eric rarely called them in. When he did, it usually wasn't pleasant. She gripped the desk as she rose, her heart thumping. She reached his door and, after a few deep breaths, knocked.

"Come in," Eric called through in a brusque voice. As she entered, he looked up from the file in front of him and gave her a curt nod. His pale blue eyes were unsmiling. "Sit down, Farah."

Her spine pressed upright against the back of the rosewood chair, Farah waited, her stomach in a lurch.

"Do you know why I called you in?" Eric tapped the end of his pen against his desk and glared at her.

She averted her eyes. She had a pretty good idea. It was to do with the passenger in the white robe and headdress reeking of alcohol. He had snapped his fingers at her demanding she fetch him more vodka. When she brought him a glass, he had placed his hand on her hip and brought his leering face so close to hers she could have counted his uneven yellow teeth. Then, with overbearing arrogance, he informed her that her job was to look after his needs, whatever they might be.

Farah had sworn in Arabic, pushed him away, and stormed off, ignoring his drunken screech that she would pay a high price for her insolence.

"This is not the first time there's been a complaint about you from one of our passengers, Farah. Do I need to remind you that staff working in the VIP lounge *must* extend the utmost courtesy towards our passengers?" Eric narrowed his eyes. "Have you taken leave of your senses? Have we not drummed it into you enough that First Class passengers are irreproachable?"

Farah swallowed. "W-well, actually he touched –"

Eric put up his hand.

She fell silent and lowered her eyes. What was the point of trying to explain to a male chauvinist how uncomfortable she had felt?

"I don't need to hear shallow excuses. You should have learned by now that our motto is *the customer is always right*. This is your last warning. I don't care if you're the only Arabic speaker on the team. If there is one more complaint about you, it's back to the check-in counters."

Farah's lips trembled. Demotion. Lower salary. No more saving up for Drama school.

She *had* to keep her job. The prospect of returning to Cairo loomed over her like a flapping bat.

"That's all. You may go."

Once outside Eric's office, Lucien appeared with Elise right behind him. "What did Eric want?"

Farah sagged against the wall. "I got a warning. It's my second one."

Lucien leaned forward and laid a gentle hand on her arm. "What? Why?"

"A horrible passenger." She turned to Elise. "You remember?"

Elise nodded, her dark chignon bobbing up and down.

"Eric said that if there is one more complaint I'll be demoted to check-in." Farah covered her face with her hands. "It's not only the humiliation, but it's also less money."

"Look Farah, if you like, I'll tell Eric what happened." Elise turned to go.

Farah put out her arm to stop her. "No."

It was time for the shift change, and amid the hustle and bustle, Farah wanted to slip away and go home. She grabbed her stuff. "Bye – I'm off tomorrow and the day after." With a wave, she sailed through the exit into the corridor, groping in her pocket for some chocolate.

"Wait, Farah, I'll walk down with you," said Lucien as he caught up with her.

Elise stuck her head through the door. "Farah, phone call for you. They're waiting on the line." Her voice resounded through the corridor.

"Don't wait for me." Farah rushed off, not wanting to see the hurt look on Lucien's face. She picked up the phone at the reception desk. "Hello. Farah Gabriel speaking."

"*Mademoiselle* Halfie, I'm so glad I caught you before you left."

Farah's heart jumped. She had tried not to think of Gus during the past week but he had popped into her mind more often than not. At his silence, she wasn't sure whether to be relieved or annoyed. She savored the idea of seeing him again. She opened her mouth to say something then shut it.

"Farah? Are you still there?"

"Yes." She pressed the handset to her ear.

"I hope you haven't forgotten me already," Gus spoke in the same slightly teasing tone as the night they had met.

"Oh, no…"

"Since you've just finished your shift, would you join me for a drink?"

How did he know her working hours? She hesitated, her instinct warning her to keep away. Something about this man spelled danger. But a small voice in her head suggested that one drink wouldn't hurt, one drink and then not see him again. She glanced at her watch, ignoring her body's pleading cries for rest. "Sure, why not?"

"Great. I'm parked outside the Departure Hall."

"Ok. Five minutes." Farah peeked into the mirror, fluffed her hair, and applied some lipstick. It would lift her spirits to see him after Eric's nasty telling off. She hummed a cheerful tune. When she exited, she searched for a black Mercedes. "Oh." She raised her eyebrows when Gus drove up in a white Porsche.

He leaned over, opened the passenger door, and put out his cigarette in the ashtray.

"*Bonsoir Mademoiselle Halfie*. Nice to see you again."

She climbed in.

"Hello." Her cheeks burned. "Nice car."

"I'm glad you like it."

He shifted to first gear.

"You had a driver last time."

"Yup. I only use him for work-related matters, not personal. It would be slightly uncomfortable having him now in this car, *n'est-ce pas*? No privacy." Gus grinned and threaded his way out of Orly Airport.

She lowered her head, intimidated by his answer.

It was peak hour. Along with hordes of other cars, they crawled along the arteries of the French capital. Horns blew incessantly around them while exhaust fumes choked the air.

It took her a few minutes before she ventured a question. "Where are we heading?"

"Didn't I mention? How remiss of me." Gus shot her a fleeting look, a teasing note in his voice. "Montmartre. A charming way to unwind and work up an appetite for dinner, don't you think?" Without waiting for an answer, he picked up the car phone. "Since I'm driving, would you mind dialing a number, please? I'll need to inform Maxime so my table is ready."

Farah swallowed as her stomach clenched. Maxime? The most exclusive restaurant in Paris? This was only supposed to be a drink. How had it turned into dinner as well? She rubbed the back of her neck. The sheer force of the man's personality swept over her like a great rolling wave. If she didn't back out now, it would be too late.

"But…I can't go there." She fidgeted in her seat, her knees pressed tightly together. "I'm not dressed to go to such a place."

He waved his hand dismissively. "I wouldn't worry about that."

He seemed accustomed to breaking the rules with no repercussions.

She dialed the number he dictated to her with some reluctance.

"Bonsoir, Maxime."

"B-bonsoir. I'm calling on behalf of M. Khodeib. Is it possible…I mean, he's planning to go to your restaurant this evening and wants –"

"M. Khodeib's usual table is always ready for him. Thank you for calling."

She placed the phone back. Did he always get his way like this?

Gus parked the car not far from Montmartre.

They made their way through the narrow streets, their footsteps echoing on the cobblestone as they began their slow climb to the main square. The grey November sky faded to black and shops switched on their lights, transforming the place into a fairyland.

Starry-eyed tourists loafed around soaking in the Bohemian ambiance, as they jostled one another to have their portrait drawn by a Frenchman in a beret.

The last time Farah had been to Montmartre was right after Justin had abandoned her. She had wandered around, blinded by tears, with no particular direction. When she reached the hilltop where the famous Sacre-Coeur perched, she had filled her lungs with one gulp of air after the other, staring at the expansive view of Paris below.

Afraid her face might reveal feelings she wasn't willing to share, Farah blew into her hands, chasing away the morbid thoughts. Why hadn't she brought warm gloves with her?

"Shall we have a quick aperitif before we head to the restaurant?"

He didn't wait for her answer. The light touch of his fingertips as he guided her into a bistro sent a tingling sensation down her back.

A waiter led them to a table for two in a secluded corner.

"You're very silent today, Ms. Halfie." Gus took out a packet of cigarettes, offered her one, and then lit it for her before lighting his own.

Farah took a long drag then squinted at the menu.

The waiter arrived and took their order.

Drawing on her cigarette emboldened her. "Can I ask you something?" Farah looked him straight in the eye.

Gus nodded. His lips twitched. Digging into his pocket, he took a set of worry beads.

They were lapis this time, not jade, like the last.

She bounced her heel up and down under the table. "How did you know I'd just finished my shift?" Her spurt of courage ebbed away.

The corners of Gus's eyes crinkled as he angled his head to one side. "Is that what's upsetting you?"

What was so funny? How rude of him.

Gus clicked away at his worry beads, his intense gaze making her squirm.

"Don't you find it flattering that I went to the trouble of finding you? I rang a friend in management – I assumed you hadn't noticed my phone number on the card with the flowers."

Farah's conscience tweaked. She hadn't kept the roses, let alone thanked him. But she wasn't going to be sidetracked. "Who do you know in management and how?"

"In fact, I know several people, some who were posted in Beirut, others through work contacts here. Does it matter?"

She shook her head, hoping Eric wasn't one of them.

"Was I wrong to want to see you again?"

She lowered her eyes. Could he guess how much she had hoped their paths would cross again?

The waiter placed the whiskey, mulled wine, and a plate of olives on the table.

Farah wrapped her hands around the glass of mulled wine, enjoying its warmth shooting through her cold body after the chill outside. She inhaled the aromatic scent of orange peel and cloves before bringing the glass to her lips.

Gus raised his glass at her with a quick wink. "How long have you been with the VIP Lounge?"

"Oh, you mean you didn't find that out as well?"

Gus chuckled. "You're even more charming when you're on your high horse. But to answer your question, no. I thought it would be more interesting to find that out from you."

Farah squirmed. Gus's gaze lingered like a warm caress down her spine. She stared at the ground and struggled for composure, wishing some smart retort would come to mind.

He stubbed out his cigarette, leaned back into his chair, and rested his ankle on his knee. "Your tongue seems to go on holiday at the most inopportune moments, Ms. Halfie."

She huffed a laugh. It *was* flattering that he was interested in her. Why deny it? "I've been with them for a little more than a year."

"And what made you decide to work for an airline? What did you study at AUC?"

"Literature. Comparative Literature and Drama." Relaxing back, she began to unwind. "Well, I mean a B.A. in Literature broadens your view but doesn't get you anywhere – you need a master's degree for a job you can make a career out of." She raised a hand, palm outward. "But I realized acting is what I want to get into. I need to save up, though, as my father doesn't support my dream." She shrugged. "I took this job because it allowed me to travel, which I needed then." One of the perks of working with the VIP Lounge was discounted tickets on various airlines. Her first trip had been to New York, to visit Justin. Enveloped with feverish excitement, she had run into his arms, the months of separation dissolving into nothingness.

"You don't need to travel anymore?" Gus's voice no longer held a teasing note.

Though his question rubbed at the raw wound, Farah forced herself to be cheerful.

"Not anymore." She glanced at her left hand where a faint mark of the engagement ring was still visible on her finger. Life had turned out nothing like the fairy tales her mother used to read to her as a little girl.

"*Très bien.* As the Romans said, *Carpe Diem.* Live in the here and now." His strong voice shook her back to the present, and he raised his glass at her again.

Farah stared at the burgundy liquid in her hand. "*Carpe Diem* indeed." She muttered under her breath. She half-expected him to comment about her acting aspirations. He probably disapproved like her father. She stole a glance at him. He brought to mind a prince out of the Arabian Nights.

He interrupted her train of thoughts. "What kind of literature did you study?"

"A bit of everything. Greek, Roman, Medieval, Shakespeare – not that I studied much at all…" A regretful laugh escaped her lips. "I spent most of my time at AUC socializing or rehearsing when I was cast in leading roles in theatre productions. I wish I'd studied harder, appreciated the privilege more. But…I was young and foolish, I must admit."

Gus chuckled. "You're still very young, *ma chère* Farah."

"I'm almost twenty-three!"

Her response elicited another hearty guffaw. "Ah, to be so young again and beginning the big adventure called life, not knowing what's around the corner." His voice took on a dreamy tone. "Just like me when I showed up at the reception last week, simply out of courtesy. I didn't know that I would be charmed by a young woman with magnetic eyes the color of an angry sea."

She dipped her chin. "Well, it was a fluke that I got invited to the reception in the first place."

"One chance encounter - it's the old story – a simple twist of fate. Destiny had its say." He fingered his worry beads, caught the waiter's eye, and ordered another round. "You know, I understand your father's reluctance to pay for acting school."

Farah rolled her eyes. "Typical Arab male reaction."

Gus stroked his mustache, his eyes resting on her lips. "Perhaps. But as I see it, he's trying to protect you."

"But it's my life." Farah looked at the ceiling. "It's all I have left now," she muttered to herself.

They finished their drinks, rose, and moved towards the entrance.

Gus held the door for her. "How about we ask one of the artists out there to draw your portrait?"

"No." Her answer spilled out almost before he finished the question. A frisson ran through her. She'd had her portrait done when she had visited Montmartre with Justin.

Gus's eyes widened. "Ok. Are you hungry?"

They reached the car. He opened the door for her and she slid in. "Yes, but…"

"But what?" He backed out and headed off.

Her mind raced, searching for a response. "It's just…I don't feel comfortable…" she paused, thoughts of 'just one drink' out the window, "going to Maxime," she said, lamely. Would he scoff at her?

"*Bas Heyk*?" Only that? "I'll take you somewhere else. What about a small Lebanese restaurant on the Left Bank?"

"Much better." She grinned. Surprise mingled with relief that he changed plans without any objections.

***

The Lebanese Maître d' welcomed Gus like a long-lost friend and ushered them in with great fanfare. He and Gus exchanged news in Arabic while three young waiters trailed behind.

They settled into a bright red and green divan which contrasted sharply with the dimly lit atmosphere.

Gus nodded to the Maître d'. "The usual, please."

He must be a regular here too. What if I don't like 'the usual'?

Within minutes, one waiter placed the Lebanese *mezze* on the low-legged round brass table, while another brought a bottle of Lebanese *Araq* and poured it into the traditional small glasses filled with ice.

"Can I have a coke please?" asked Farah.

Gus unfolded a starched, white napkin, whipped out a pen from his jacket, and began to draw on it.

Her hand flew to her mouth. "You're ruining their tableware."

He chuckled then handed her the napkin, a perfectly proportioned rose drawn on it.

Speechless, she stared at it.

"Go on, take it," he laughed.

"But –"

"Don't worry about it."

So, he could draw as well.

Her face broke into a smile at his carefree attitude. A flutter ran through her stomach. She placed the napkin on her knees but didn't help herself to any food.

He raised his eyebrows. "I thought you were hungry?"

She lit a cigarette and puffed away. Her tummy rumbled as the waiter fetched her drink.

"Don't you like Lebanese food?" Gus dug his fork into a vine leaf smothered in yoghurt and offered it to her.

She shook her head. When he had mentioned dinner, she had expected a whole meal, not *mezze*, which might dribble down her chin.

The Maitre d' rushed to their table. "*Seedna.*" He bent down and whispered something to Gus.

The vein in Gus's forehead pulsed. "Excuse me for a minute, Farah." He rose in a swift panther-like movement and strode towards a door with a 'Staff Only' sign on it.

How bizarre.

Farah stuffed a meatball and a couple of vine leaves into her mouth.

Gus returned, a hard look in his eyes. He remained silent. The tension was palpable. He glanced at his watch then turned to her. "You seem tired – I'd better take you home." It wasn't even a question – just a statement.

Farah pasted a smile on her face.

Gus finished his drink in one gulp, his hand already in his pocket for the car keys. They hurried past bowing waiters. Gus nodded at the Maître d' as they swept out.

How come he didn't pay the bill?

During the hair-raising drive, she kept her eyes shut. The brakes screeched as he halted in front of her apartment block and with a quick goodbye, she bolted inside, bewildered.

The following morning the phone rang while she was having breakfast.

"Hello."

"Mademoiselle Hafie."

"Oh. Hello."

"Just phoning to make sure you're all right. Sorry that yesterday evening was cut short. How about if we meet up tomorrow?"

Farah swallowed and played with the buttons on her cardigan. "What…time?" *Zut*. She had just agreed. Why hadn't she said she was busy?

"Pick you up at one o'clock?"

She hung up not sure whether she was annoyed with herself or pleased about seeing him.

Later that evening, when Monique was visiting, the phone rang again. This time Monique picked up.

Eyebrows arched, she handed the phone to Farah.

It was Gus asking if it was okay to postpone their appointment the next day till two o'clock.

"Who was that?" Monique asked after Farah hung up.

"Someone I met at the reception the other night."

Monique leaned back in her chair and crossed her legs, swinging the top one back and forth. "Oh? Well, come on, spill the beans. Why all the secrecy? Who is he? What does he do?"

Farah swallowed. "He's Lebanese. Much older." Her stomach lurched, knowing what would come next.

"*Lebanese?* What if he's Moslem? Your father would be livid – and Cyril too."

"I don't know if he's Moslem or Christian. Look, it's nothing, just a bit of flirting. Why are you making such a big deal? I can stop seeing him anytime. But …I don't know. It's fun, I suppose. I enjoy the attention, that's all." Farah's voice faltered. *What if he were a Moslem?*

"You're not very convincing."

"Do you think I'm stupid? The minute I want to end it, I'll do it just like that." Farah snapped her fingers, annoyed at the insinuations.

"That's the way it always starts, do you know what I mean? But it can spiral out of control." Monique rose, put on her coat and hat, and headed for the door. "I've got to go. I need to do some shopping. Talk soon."

Farah stretched out on the sofa, buried her head in a cushion, and groaned.

Chapter Nine

Gus opened the file in front of him, took out his Montblanc pen from the top drawer of his mahogany desk, and signed the documents his secretary had placed in a neat pile.

He glanced at the calendar on the wall. His vision turned hazy as events of long ago rose to his mind.

Tomorrow it would be eight years since he had fled to France.

He and his older brother Yazan had been walking towards the car, heading home to their father's mansion, where three generations lived together. They wound their way through the streets of Tripoli, crawling with Syrian soldiers.

They seem to multiply every day.

A wave of recklessness rolled over Yazan. "Ghassan, let's head north. I want to see the cedars."

"Are you crazy? The curfew's in half an hour. We need to rush home." The streets were deserted of civilians though it wasn't even six p.m.

"No. I'm starved to see the cedars. Lebanon without cedars is like an opera without arias. What are they going to do? Kill us? It's OUR country."

Gus rushed over to his brother and grabbed him by the arm. "This isn't the time for poetry. Yazan, please—"

Yazan snatched his arm away and ran, singing the song that eternalized Beirut by Lebanon's national treasure, Fairuz.

They turned a corner, then another, leaving the soldiers behind. When they had almost reached the car, a lone Syrian officer materialized out of nowhere.

"Halt."

Yazan ignored him and continued running, his voice soaring.

Gus's heart pounded in his ears. He stopped, his gaze following his brother in desperation.

Without hesitation, the officer raised a revolver and pointed it at Yazan, his eyes narrowed.

As if paralyzed, Gus sucked in a gulp of air, unable to grasp what was happening.

The officer aimed for Yazan's heart.

Crack.

Yazan collapsed onto the ground as the officer looked on impassively.

For a split second, Gus stood immobile before charging forward. He bent over Yazan's lifeless corpse, rage rocking him like an avalanche. His hand flew to his pocket and he seized his pistol. He pulled the trigger. The bullet hit the Syrian in the forehead.

The officer crumbled onto the ground his eyes wide with surprise, blood flooding down his face.

His breathing shallow, Gus threw a furtive look around. He pressed Yazan's wound to staunch the bleeding, placed his brother's warm body over his back, and staggered to the car. Trickles of sweat dripped from his forehead, burning his eyes. He pulled the back door open and lay his brother gently on the back seat and tapped his cheek to wake him. Yazan's head rolled to the side, his face deathly pale. Gus squeezed his eyes shut as a sudden coldness expanded into his core. Yazan was gone. He hyperventilated, then, shaking, Gus covered the corpse with his jacket, and jumped in, the back of his throat throbbing. Though it was only a fifteen-minute drive back to the house, it was the longest drive of Gus's life as he replayed the events in slow motion. The car raced through the empty streets. For the first time in his life, Gus prayed. *No checkpoint. Please.*

The gods must have been listening.

He drove into the garage, parked the car, flew up the stairs, and bolted through the door before bursting into his father's office. "A Syrian officer killed Yazan. I shot the officer dead," he said, as he panted for breath.

His father paled. He gripped the desk and stood up then collapsed back onto the chair.

"My firstborn. Where's my son?" he cried.

"He's in the car, *baba*. I wasn't going to let them desecrate him." Gus's hands shook and his mind went blank.

Gus's two brothers rushed in at the commotion.

"We need to get you out of here NOW," said his father, "call the family."

One of Gus's brothers rang a relative. In no time, the house swarmed with cousins and uncles.

Gus stumbled onto a chair. Someone shoved a glass of whisky in his hand. He knocked it back.

Outside in the garden, his cousins dug a grave.

His father bellowed to one of his daughters to pack a bag for Gus.

"Ghassan, are you ready?" asked his father, "you need to get to the port now. You'll board a boat to Cyprus, and from there, take a plane to Paris." He opened the safe and flung wads of U.S. dollars into a briefcase. "Take this. As soon as you've opened a bank account there, I'll transfer enough to buy a flat. You won't be returning for a while."

The sound of a baby screaming floated through from the next room.

"But—"

His father pushed him out of the room. "Don't worry about anything. Just get yourself to safety."

In the hallway, Gus's mother almost collapsed, her unrestrained tears pouring like a waterfall.

"Mama—" His voice broke.

Someone knocked at the door, snapping him back into the present moment. He tapped the pen on his desk and sighed impatiently, expecting his new secretary to pop her head in with yet another question.

Instead, it was his cousin.

"Layth." Gus beamed and stood up. "I thought you were arriving tomorrow."

"Abu Omar."

Gus slapped his cousin on the back, motioned to the chair across the desk and they both sat. "You're the only one here who calls me by my *kunya*[1]. It brings back the warmth of home. Why did you change your travel dates?"

"I finished the pending matters in Amman and decided to catch today's flight. How are things here?"

Before Gus had time to answer, there was a timid knock at the door. His new secretary, Cecile, entered.

"Mr. Khodeib, Madam Chantal rang. I told her you were in a meeting. She wanted to know if you're going to attend the dinner tonight at the residence of the Cypriot Ambassador."

"Please call her back and let her know I won't be able to."

Gus went towards the little cabinet under the window and bent down. "A glass of *Araq*, Layth?"

"Sure. How come you're not going to the dinner? It's a good networking opportunity."

Gus shrugged, reached out for a couple of glasses, and poured the anise-flavored alcohol. He topped it up with water and dropped in a couple of ice cubes pulled from the small fridge beside the cabinet. He handed Layth his glass and lowered himself into the chair opposite his cousin facing the door.

---

[1] A kunya is a component of an Arabic name, a type of epithet, in theory referring to the bearer's first-born son or daughter.

Viewed through the side window, the Eiffel Tower soared into the blue sky. Sunbeams filtered down. The hands of the wall clock pointed to one fifteen. He'd have to make this quick; he was picking Farah up at two.

Gus took a large sip. He reached into his pocket for his packet of cigarettes, lit one up, and drew a long breath.

"So, the shipment–" But before Gus could finish his sentence, another knock sounded. He grunted.

Cecile poked her head through the door, her face flushed.

Not again! I'll have to train her better.

"I'm s-sorry, Mr. Khodeib, but the florist is on the phone. He wanted to know if he should send the flowers to the same address as last time or if you'll pick them up."

Gus glared at Cecile as she shuffled from one foot to another. With her black hair, round babyface, and big eyes, she reminded him of Betty Boop. What a pity his old secretary had left – she would have known how to respond in various situations without having to ask.

"I'll pick them up. Thank you."

A look of relief spread across her face as she hurried to close the door behind her.

"Flowers, Ghassan?"

Well aware of the anger that simmered underneath his cousin's mild voice, Gus ignored the laden question. He rose from the chair and walked up to the other end of the room.

He straightened the crooked frame on the wall. The oil painting of Berbers on horseback in the Moroccan desert had caught his eye in some tiny shop in Montmartre when he had first moved to Paris. Struck by the beauty of the endless golden desert, the sky's hue of blue, and the noble stance of both horses and men, Gus had purchased it. As an avid art collector, he had never bought anything by an unknown artist before.

Satisfied at the angle of the painting, he turned to face his cousin.

"I'm afraid I have an appointment now, Layth. Why don't we do lunch tomorrow and have a proper catch-up? You can brief me about the shipment issues."

Gus slipped into his jacket, patted his pocket to make sure he had a set of worry beads, then opened the door and they headed out.

***

Farah glowered at the crumpled half-finished letters as she sipped her coffee. Her half-hearted attempts at drafting Gus a goodbye note lay strewn across the table. She glanced at her watch. Her pulse quickened. Time to get ready. The jeans she slipped into were a snug fit. She rummaged through her wardrobe before choosing a green top to match her eyes.

When it was time, she hurried to the elevator, an exciting thrill enveloping her, purposely ignoring Monique's advice. It was ages since this bubbling sensation filled her chest. As soon as she saw the white Porsche and Gus standing next to the passenger door, her insides quivered.

He kissed her on the cheek then opened the door for her.

She climbed in, heat creeping up her face.

Gus sped off. "I thought we could take a drive to Malmaison this afternoon."

Farah shifted in her seat. What and where was Malmaison?

Gus reached out to the back seat, pulled out a bunch of pink roses, and dropped them on her lap. "*Pour toi.*"

She buried her nose in their sweet fragrance. "*Merci.*" She felt like a glamorous film star.

He overtook a silver Peugeot. "Have you been to Malmaison before?"

"No."

"It was the private home of Josephine and Napoleon Bonaparte. Magnificent gardens. She had exotic flora imported from all over the world. As for her collection of roses," he waved his hand in the air in a languid movement, "it was in its day unsurpassed."

She slid down in her seat conscious of how poorly informed she must appear in front of someone so cultured.

Gus parked, then walked around to open her door, but she jumped out before he had a chance to do so.

The wide gravel path leading to the chateau was flanked on both sides by trees trimmed into cone shapes, with rows of white and red camellias between, creating a perfectly symmetrical design. The sun peeped through the gathering clouds, filling the place with an air of nostalgia for the elegant times Malmaison must have seen.

They wandered through the opulent rooms, past bronze figurines and ornate dinner sets of fine bone porcelain reflecting a by-gone era where life and chatter once resonated through its hallways and reception rooms.

"Poor Josephine – she ended up here alone and broken-hearted after Napoleon divorced her. I bet these walls have some tales to tell." Gus's voice was low, tinged with a husky edge.

An involuntary shudder ran through Farah as the echo of Justin rose to her mind. She thrust it away and focused on the sumptuous surrounding, admiring in silence. Why had she never bothered to visit before? She should make an effort to learn more, know more, in case…

"No time to see the gardens today – they close in fifteen minutes." His voice cut through. "My fault for picking you up later than planned."

She lifted her hands in regret, still too awestruck to say much.

Gus winked at her. "But that means I'll have to bring you back another time."

She looked at the ground and bit her lip. What was this strange effect a man she barely knew had over her?

They ended up at Fouquet, the famous bistro on the Champs Elysees.

A young waitress welcomed Gus by name, led them to a corner table, and without being asked, returned with a bottle of chilled champagne.

Uncomfortable at all the attention the waitress showered on Gus, Farah stared at the menu before putting it down with a shake of the head.

"Nothing? OK." Gus called the waitress to open the bottle. The cork popped with a loud smack, letting out a spate of bubbly liquid that splashed over Farah's top.

The waitress reached for a napkin. "*Excusez-moi, Mademoiselle.*"

Farah laughed and dipped her serviette into her glass of water wiping her chiffon blouse. "No problem."

"What have you been up to since I last saw you?" asked Gus.

Farah shrugged. "Not much. Work. And Christmas shopping."

"Ah, of course. Christmas. Around the corner. Where will you spend the holidays?"

"We're all traveling to Jordan this year."

"I thought your family lived in Egypt?"

"My parents live in Egypt. But my sister lives in Amman. She's married to a Jordanian. Well, Jordanian Palestinian."

"What's his name?" he asked.

"Jamal Radwani –"

"Ah, so you're related to the big Jerusalemite family."

"Kind of. What about you? Do you usually do anything for Christmas?"

He glanced up, his gaze sharp, then shook his head. "No. We never did. It's not our feast. We joined in the celebrations with the community back in Lebanon when I was growing up, of course. But at home, we didn't do anything special."

Half of Lebanon was Christian. Why did she have to meet a Moslem?

"Do all your family drink, or just you?" she asked.

"The men do. My mother and sisters don't. They're quite religious." He raised his glass. "Then again, wasn't *Issa's* first miracle turning water into wine?"

Farah looked at him straight in the eye. "Why do Moslems call Jesus *Issa*?" It was a question she had never dared ask any of her Moslem friends – religion was such a sensitive subject in the Middle East. She had been thrown out of class numerous times for arguing with her Arabic teacher over Jesus' name.

"That's his name in the Quran. Does it matter?"

"I guess you're right. It doesn't matter." Farah sipped her champagne.

A group of five people arrived and the waitress led them to a nearby table. Their chatter and laughter drifted across.

Gus leaned forward. "What school did you go to?"

"*Sacré-Coeur* – a French convent. In an area called Heliopolis, where my parents live. Do you know Cairo?"

"Kind of –"

"The Baron Empain, a Belgian, built it at the beginning of this century. First, he built my school, then a bizarrely beautiful castle for himself, and a huge Basilica, where he's buried."

"So, you're nun-educated then?"

"Unfortunately. Because once *they* found out I was Protestant, they had it in for me. One of them was Spanish, from Granada – and she made my life miserable. I was the only Protestant in the whole school."

Gus shot her a look of pity.

"How come you're Protestant?"

"Huguenots from my mother's side - survived persecution here in France, and lived to tell the tale.

"I'd have thought that in Egypt, like the rest of the Middle East, you'd have had to take after your father, not your mother."

"My mother's one condition when she agreed to marry my dad– kids get baptized in her church – much to the fury of my dad's family, who are devout Orthodox. And my maternal grandmother drummed that into us when she was alive." Farah rolled her eyes. "All of us cousins know *ad nauseum* about St. Bartholomew's Eve and the persecution under Louis XIV."

Gus didn't say anything. He took out a set of onyx worry beads and started to click away. "When are you leaving?"

"Two weeks." She rubbed her hands together, a wide grin on her face. "It's the one time during the year when we're all together without fail. Christmas is sacrosanct."

He chuckled. "Do you only have one sister?"

"No. I mean yes." Farah shook her head in confusion. "Tammy is my half-sister, from my mum's side. She's ten years older than me. My mum married an American when she was very young, but he died and his family wouldn't allow my mum to take Tammy when she returned to France." She flinched, still embarrassed by her reaction when she found out she had had an older sister. She had been ten years old at the time, and the anger at having to share her mother with another sibling still ran vivid in her mind – so stupid. Tammy had turned out to be the ideal sister. After the first summer holiday together, Farah became strongly attached to her, elevating her to the role of confidante.

Farah flicked her hair. "But I also have a brother. A full brother. He'll be flying in from Rome. Cyril."

"Rome? Studying or working?"

Farah's face darkened. "Both. Kind of."

He tipped his head to the side, a puzzled look in his eyes. "Kind of?"

"Well," Farah stopped, pressed her lips together, and looked away. "He's studying at the Vatican."

Gus frowned. "Vatican? But I thought you said you're Protestant?"

"Well, yes. But for some reason, beyond anyone's comprehension I might add, my brother decided he wanted to become a monk, so he converted to Catholicism." She shrugged half-heartedly, and propped her cheek on her fist, images of the family drama caused by his decision playing in her mind.

Why am I telling him so much? Isn't it enough that I already blabbed about Justin? I should shut up – now that I've told him almost my whole life story.

"And your sister married a Moslem." Gus sounded amused. "Well, in the end, there's no black or white, more like a kaleidoscope of colors that are constantly changing, depending on our choices." He clenched the worry beads into his palm before releasing them again and returning to his usual clicking. "That's life, with all its complexities and uncertainties, with all the pain in people's souls. Nobody knows the internal battles each one of us faces. But, if despite all this, one manages to find a path that will give him some peace, then so be it."

Maybe it was time to start asking some questions of her own?

"What about you? Do you have brothers and sisters? Are your parents still alive?" She held her breath, waiting for Mystery Man to reveal some details.

Gus's eyes went blank. "I have three sisters, and one of my three brothers died." He paused, took out a cigarette, and lit it.

"Oh. I'm sorry. Was it recent?"

"A few years ago. He was killed by the occupying Syrian army." Gus exhaled a deep breath and fingered his mustache as he stared into space. His voice was miles away.

"Oh my God. How awful."

"I made sure my brother wasn't the only one to die that day." His eyes had a hardened look in them.

Farah inhaled a sharp breath and her hand flew to cover her mouth. He had *killed* someone? Pulled the trigger? Did that make him an *assassin*? True, it was someone from an occupying force, but still…he had killed a man. A thrill of danger raced through her like an electric shock. She should be horrified but somehow, she wasn't.

"You…carried a gun?"

He snorted. "Everyone in Lebanon has a gun. We're in a civil war. There's nothing easier than buying weapons there."

"Oh."

"They're literally on display in the streets."

She stiffened.

Gus leaned over and brushed her cheek with the back of his hand. "We're in Paris, not Lebanon."

They came from such different worlds.

She shook her head sideways, her hands clasped together. Under the chair, her legs folded beneath her, too weak to remain upright.

"You don't know what it was like, seeing the officer pull out his gun and shoot him. My older brother, my hero, my best friend. Only a year between us. We did everything together. And in a matter of seconds, Yazan was gone." He shut his eyes for a brief moment. "A non-entity for the Syrian who killed him." Gus's voice cracked.

There was something unnerving about seeing this strong, unshakable man bare his soul to her.

"In those few seconds, before I got out my gun and pulled the trigger, I envisioned my mother's agony when she heard the news. My father's grief at losing his firstborn. How Yazan's death would affect our entire family. I reacted without a thought for the consequences."

She swallowed. "That's such a sad story. I can't even imagine what it would be like to lose your brother." Farah leaned forward and touched his arm. "I mean, I know about the war in Lebanon, but one never thinks of the horrors that happen to individuals unless it's from someone who lived through such an experience. I'm so sorry you went through such a tragedy."

So different from her own experience of war.

It was 1967. She was three years old. The Israeli air force bombed the nearby Almaza military airport. At home, the windows, covered in dark blue paper to prevent enemy planes from detecting lights at night, shook and rattled.

Her parents grabbed her and Cyril and dove under the bed, cradling their children between them while they waited for the bombing spree to end.

"Can you hear the bombs?" Her father, who had held her tightly in his arms, spoke into her ears.

Farah nodded, not knowing the difference between sound and vibration at the time. "Oh yes, *papa*. Even my legs can hear them."

They had remained like that for an hour. The next day, her father bundled them all into the car and drove them to her uncle's house in the Nile Delta for safety.

That was what she could remember of war.

Poor Gus. Who would have thought?

Farah met his eyes, seeing him in a new light – a noble hero.

Lebanon was such a paradox to outsiders, an exciting enigma, a tension-filled civil war zone, affecting the geopolitical scene of the entire region. Maybe there was a dignity about fighting for what one believed in?

"There's nothing as awful as war." Gus's words shattered her illusions. "So many of those fighting consumed copious amounts of drugs all the time. Even fifteen-year-olds were sent on top of buildings with automatic rifles to act as snipers."

"Whew." She reached for her glass and pressed her lips to the rim, his grim words vivid.

Et si tu n'existais pas, the famous song of Joe Dassin, one of France's idols, drifted through the speakers.

Gus rose from his chair and stretched his hand out to her. No one was dancing – it wasn't a dancing place, but then, who cared? What was that phrase he liked to quote? *Carpe Diem*.

Farah stood up and he wrapped one arm around her waist, her hand firmly in his while they glided between the tables as the romantic words floated through the speakers. Her stomach fluttered, unpleasant thoughts receding in her mind. As an incurably romantic teenager, she had hummed this song so often, dreaming that one day someone would murmur these words into her ears.

Gus pressed his cheek against hers as he held her firmly, his muscular chest pushing into her, his breath on her neck.

Her heart raced. She closed her eyes, relishing the feel of his arms around her.

But then, he moved a step back and twirled her around, out of sync with the song, before laughing and leading her back to the table.

Some of the other clients clapped, faces creased into surprised smiles.

Gus winked, a wide smile on his face. "You're a pretty good dancer." He waved at a waiter to bring the bill. "I suppose I'd better get you home."

Farah finished her drink in silence, caught off guard by the sudden change in attitude. She had anticipated spending the rest of the evening with him.

It was a short drive back. He pulled up in front of her building. "I'll call you in a few days. I've got some guests arriving tomorrow, but once they leave, we can catch up."

She hid her disappointment with a smile, said goodbye, and went upstairs.

That night, Farah replayed the dancing scene over and over, reliving the feeling of his touch and how he had chosen that song. She fell asleep, her lips curled into a smile.

Chapter Ten

Farah sat with Lucien in an airport cafe, surrounded by passengers coming and going. Announcements of arriving and departing flights interspersed with the clatter of the crockery being piled up behind the counter.

"How was your weekend? You've been pretty silent – like you're in some kind of dream." Lucien raised his voice to be heard over the noise.

"Fine, thanks." She sipped at her coffee, her face expressionless.

"I tried to call you yesterday afternoon to see if you wanted to go out, but you never picked up."

"I mostly slept over the weekend," she drained her cup and stood up.

"Already?"

"I want Eric off my back. You stay if you like."

Lucien stood up. "I'll come with you. Not much fun sitting here by myself."

They stepped onto the escalators.

"What are you doing after work?" he asked, as they headed towards the VIP Lounge.

"I'm meeting a relative who's visiting from Jerusalem."

When they reached the Lounge Farah slipped behind the counter to relieve Elise.

Elise smiled. "How was Fouquet? I saw you there yesterday afternoon, dancing away with that Arab client."

Farah tilted her head in Lucien's direction. "Shhhh."

"What's that about Fouquet?" Lucien's eyes shifted from Farah to Elise and back again, a hurt look on his face.

A taut silence hovered among the three of them. Lucien gave them both a glassy stare and stormed off.

Farah exhaled slowly. Lucien had offered her so much support, had always been there for her; she didn't want to hurt him. But she couldn't help it if she didn't have romantic feelings towards him.

***

Farah shot through the entrance of Café de la Paix, biting the inside of her cheek. *I hope Mariam hasn't been waiting too long.*

The sumptuous Second Empire style of the café never failed to impress Farah. The soaring columns, ornate gold moldings, and breathtaking ceiling frescos always triggered sighs of admiration. The combination of classical and baroque artwork infused the place with an air of grandeur that blended in with the Opera house across the street. Were the rumors true? Had the fateful Marie Antoinette met her Swedish lover there while attending a performance?

Out of breath, Farah searched the crowded room for her cousin-by-marriage. Mariam Radwani's head was down as she studied the menu. Farah recognized her by her mass of dark curls tumbling down like corkscrews around her shoulders. Mariam looked up and her face broke into a wide smile.

She rose and hugged Farah. "*Habibty,* how are you?"

"It's so good to see you."

Farah dragged a chair and sat, eager to hear news of Mariam's family in Jerusalem.

After the waiter took their order, Farah turned to her cousin-in-law. "You haven't changed a bit since I last saw you – what, four years ago?"

Mariam's eyes clouded. "Five. Before I moved to Lebanon."

Farah wanted to bite her tongue. "I'm sorry. I heard you had a terrible time there, but I don't know the details."

Mariam's hand shook slightly. "Yes, it was awful. I was working in the hospital in Shatila Refugee Camp with British colleagues from the university," she said, working to steady her voice. "The Christian militia attacked the camps. They placed the camp under siege and trapped the Palestinians in there like animals. The Israeli army didn't allow anyone to leave for two days. What a bloodbath. We were running between the injured trying to control the bleeding amongst those who were still alive, terrified of getting killed ourselves."

"Oh my God." Farah clapped her hand to her mouth. "I'm so sorry. That must have been awful." She raised her brows. "How did you get out of there?"

"Somehow the Lebanese Phalangists knew there was a British medical team in the camp, so they let us through. If it hadn't been for my British colleagues, I would've ended up like the rest of the Palestinians there. Dead." Mariam raised her hands, palms outwards. "I'm lucky to be here."

Christians attacked the camps, not Israelis? Why did the Christian Lebanese slaughter all those innocent people? No wonder the students at AUC plastered the campus with posters denouncing the massacres and demonstrated so ardently.

Heat flushed through Farah's cheeks. Throughout her time at university, she had basked in her newfound freedom, paying little attention to the political upheaval across the border. Farah had partied her way through those four years, studying the bare minimum to pass.

The waiter placed their order on the table.

With the mention of Lebanon, Gus rose to Farah's mind. Why

hadn't he ever mentioned any of this?

"You're so courageous, Mariam. I would've been terrified to go into a refugee camp. I think I might've died on the spot seeing men in military uniforms barge in with guns." She sunk her teeth into the French pastry then sipped at her coffee. "Are you here on holiday? Tammy didn't mention why you were coming."

"I'm attending a medical conference. It's a miracle my exit permit was approved."

Farah put down her fork. "Permit?"

"Yes, we can't travel anywhere unless the Israelis issue a permit. Didn't you know?"

"No. I didn't. It sounds horrendous." She raised the cup and took another sip. "How's the family?"

Mariam chuckled. "Good. I think Hussein might be getting married."

Farah grinned; she liked Hussein. "Oh. So, your playboy brother is finally settling down? Congratulations. Who's he marrying?"

"A Jordanian girl. Her family fled from Palestine to Amman during the 1948 war and settled there. You should come and visit us in Jerusalem, Farah." She stood up. "I need to go to the ladies."

Farah brushed away a few crumbs from her blouse.

Jerusalem was like a myth to her, not a real place. All the stories she had heard since childhood jostled in her memory. Sunday school at Church and catechism classes with tales of mystics wandering in the desert. Then there were studies in Arab history and the quest for the Holy City. The saga of the Crusades, with legends of Saladin and Richard the Lionheart. Jerusalem the coveted, Jerusalem the mysterious, Jerusalem with tales of knights and princes, romances of kings, queens, and princesses. Jerusalem the anointed with a volley of prophets and holy stories.

Mariam returned and sat down. "Come to think of it, you have a French passport so it shouldn't be too much of a problem for you." Mariam's lips curled downward. "Apart from standard Israeli harassment."

Farah shrugged. "Well, who knows. Maybe one day."

There was a slight pause. Someone at a nearby table laughed out loud.

"What's been happening with you? Are you happy here in Paris? Don't you miss home?" asked Mariam.

Farah offered a weak smile. She would have loved to confide in Mariam. But after hearing Mariam's tale of the Lebanese slaughtering Palestinians in the camp, she wasn't going to mention Gus.

"Paris is also home. I have family here. And my best friend moved here too."

Mariam tilted her head. "Of course. I remember you enjoyed acting. Has that gone anywhere?"

"I've been auditioning for parts in small productions here, but it's hard because my work shifts are so unpredictable. Sometimes I can be on night duty, so I can't commit to being in a play unless I make arrangements to swap with colleagues. But I've applied to different acting schools – the latest is in London." She smiled as hope surged through her. "*Inshallah*, something will work out."

"It's good to follow your dream but acting is tough. Not just breaking into it but what people may be forced to do to be cast regularly. Just keep in mind having a dream and grasping it are two different things."

Farah crossed her arms and leaned back in the chair, Mariam's words filling her with an unpleasant sensation. She pushed away the unwelcome thoughts.

Mariam picked up her cup. "Why don't you give yourself a time limit? If it doesn't work out, find something else. You don't want to wake up one day and realize you've flitted your life away without doing something meaningful."

Farah admired Mariam, even if intimidated by her cousin's success. A medical degree from Cambridge and becoming an orthopedic surgeon was no small feat. By comparison, Farah had little to offer society. "I never thought of anything else."

"Maybe social work? There's plenty of need back home."

Farah shook her head. "That would mean I'd have to study again and I have zero interest." Her dream didn't involve traveling to Palestine to serve 'the cause'.

"Don't mind me." Mariam placed a hand on her arm. "Living under occupation and witnessing the daily misery of lives around me, I've become more philosophical about the human condition."

Farah nodded, though she had a hard time trying to visualize what military occupation looked like. It was almost as if she and Mariam came from two different planets.

A couple sat down at the table next to them, conversing loudly.

Farah cocked her ear. "What's that language?"

"Hebrew," Mariam muttered, with a scowl. She folded her arms. "They're Israeli."

"You sound as if you hate Israelis."

"They kicked us out of our homes, stole our land, and killed our people. They came to escape what was happening to them in Europe and have been doing much the same to us ever since." Mariam stabbed her fork into her éclair, her frown deepening. "How do you think I feel about them?"

Discomfort tugged at Farah's stomach. Would Mariam start a confrontation?

The couple's conversation continued.

Mariam stiffened. "They're Zionists." A sour expression spread across her face. "They're discussing one of the illegal Israeli settlements established last year." Mariam spoke in Arabic, loud enough for the Israeli couple to hear. "It's ten kilometers south of Jerusalem."

The chatter at the next table ceased, and the two Zionists threw Mariam a dirty look.

Farah raised her coffee cup to hide her face.

Mariam continued. "They confiscated land from two Palestinian villages and diverted the little water that had been allocated. They built an electricity plant then steal our electricity and make us pay for it." She waved her hands, "They also built a highway to Jerusalem which Palestinians are not allowed to use."

"Oh." Farah wasn't sure she understood.

"Not all Jews are Zionists, of course. My brother's best friend is Jewish. But then Moshe always refers to himself as a Palestinian Jew."

Farah shuddered. It sounded so complicated.

Mariam gestured to the waiter for the bill. "I've got to meet some colleagues from the conference."

Once the bill arrived, Mariam paid, gathered her stuff, and stood. "You need to come visit us. You'll be able to see for yourself how bad the situation in Occupied Arab East Jerusalem is, instead of listening to the pro-Israeli western media's rendition of it."

She pushed her chair and sailed out of the café, a bemused Farah following in her wake.

Chapter Eleven

Washington D.C. – December 1986

Justin buttoned up his wool coat against the icy wind assailing the Capital as he walked out of his office building. Christmas holiday lights flickered, offering a cheery warmth against the winter cold – or was it his heart that was cold and lonely ever since he had jilted Farah?

It was dark when he left home in the morning. Stuck upstairs in his tiny office, Justin hadn't seen the sun all day, and now it was dark again yet it was barely five in the afternoon. On his way to the metro, he stopped at the supermarket to buy a few things, though the thought of returning to an empty apartment and eating alone didn't do much for his morale. Thankfully, the Christmas break was in a couple of weeks and he'd head over to his mother's place in Arizona.

He was looking forward to seeing his sister Penny, her husband, and their two daughters. His six and eight-year-old nieces would cheer him.

At home, Justin put away the groceries, and shoved the pre-cooked dinner into the oven. Another thrilling evening in front of the television awaited him. While his food was heating up, he picked up the phone and dialed his mother. They chatted for a few minutes, and he gave her his flight details so she could pick him up.

"How's work? I bet Washington looks rather pretty now with the lights and the snow," she said.

He sighed as he ran his fingers through his hair. "Work's okay."

"*You* don't sound okay." His mom's voice rose with concern.

"Well..."

"You're dwelling on how this Christmas would have been different if you'd gone through with the wedding, aren't you?" His mother's words pricked his already-troubled conscience. "I wish you'd listened to me, Justin, instead of believing what *they* told you. And it's not like you to be stubborn. I just don't understand what got into your head."

"Mom. Please." He didn't want to hear all that. Wasn't it enough he lived with his regret day in day out?

"Listen, why don't you get on a flight and go to Cairo for Christmas? Explain to her what happened?"

Why won't she lay off? "No. Anyway, I have no idea where she'll be for Christmas this year. Imagine if I go all that way and she's not there."

"Call her."

"After all these months? No way. She'd slam the phone down on me."

"You don't know that. Why don't you get in touch with her best friend?"

"Monique? Mom, I can't just call out of the blue. She'd eat me alive."

There was a pause on the line. His neighbor's front door banged shut.

"I suppose the phone call never came." His mother's voice was deprecating. "Well, at least that means that you're no longer under any compunction to listen to them anymore. How many months has it been now?" she sighed, "I could have told you stories and stories about your grandfather going down that route, and how it affected our family life when your uncle and I were children. Such a disastrous choice. I don't get why you wanted to follow in his footsteps."

Justin bit his lip feeling like a fool.

"It's only till we finish the background check," they had said. "Once your security clearance comes through, it'll only be a matter of a few weeks."

And he had believed them.

Justin stared down at his shoes, a dullness filling his chest. "Mom, I'm living with the result of my bad choice all the time. Please don't rub it in."

"I wish you'd contact her and explain, Justin. She deserves that. I'm sure she must think that you got cold feet. She might understand if you tell her the real reason. Anyway, think about it. See you in a couple of weeks."

He hung up feeling worse than before.

Of course, he had thought of contacting Farah, but he couldn't bring himself to do it. He wouldn't know what to say and this wasn't something to discuss over the phone. This needed a face-to-face conversation. Ringing Tammy had also crossed his mind. She was older and American. She might have understood. But then again, that wasn't a given. After his behavior, he deserved the pain he was living through.

The smell of food burning wafted through from the kitchen. Shit! That must be his dinner. He rushed in, opened the oven, waved at the smoke, and groaned.

***

Paris – December 1986

Farah sat at the reception desk her mind miles away. She hadn't heard from Gus in more than a week.

What was she to him? An extra in a 'movie' he was directing?

The phone rang. "Bonjour. VIP Lounge."

"Ah, so you *are* alive, Ms. Halfie. I was starting to worry."

She closed her eyes for a second. Why couldn't she find a witty comeback?

"I was in your neighborhood yesterday evening, so I stopped by to say hello, but you weren't home," he said.

Did he expect her to sit around waiting at his beck and call? How dare he treat her like a naughty child?

"Oh?"

"I wonder if you might accompany me to a reception at the residence of the Lebanese Ambassador this evening?"

She scratched her neck. Damn. She had promised Monique to meet up after work. "I'm sorry. I'll have to decline. I've already made plans with a friend."

"No problem. Another time then. I've got to rush to a meeting. Talk soon." He hung up.

She pressed a fist to her mouth, her stomach in a knot.

An hour later she rang him back. "You were so kind to invite me. I've postponed my engagement, so I'm free to go with you tonight after all."

A lighter on the other end broke the silence. "What a pity you didn't offer to change your plans earlier, Ms. Halfie. In the meantime, I'm afraid I've made other arrangements and it would be *very* complicated to change them now. I do hope you understand."

Her cheeks burned. Mentally, she kicked herself for not having left things *status quo*.

"Yes, of course. Enjoy your evening." She slammed the phone down her eyes smarting.

***

Four days later, Farah fingered the large envelope on her desk. Her name was written out boldly across the front. It was an invitation to a Christmas dinner party to be held at the Ritz for the 12th of December, hosted by M. Ghassan Khodeib.

Why would Gus send her a formal invitation when all he had to do was pick up the phone and call her? His silence since the fiasco of the Lebanese Embassy reception unnerved her. Her brow furrowed, Farah dialed the RSVP number.

A female voice answered.

Farah turned the card over in her hand. "*Bonjour*. I'm calling about the invitation I just received."

"Yes, of course. May I have your name, please?"

"Farah Gabriel."

"Ah, Ms. Gabriel. Monsieur Khodeib requested I put your call through. Just a minute please."

Before Farah had time to protest, the extension rang.

"Yes?" His tone was sharp as if he had been interrupted from something important.

"Umm, hi. It's Farah. I'm sorry, I didn't mean to interrupt but someone put me through." She rubbed her cheek. "I was calling about the invitation to your dinner party."

"Ah, Mademoiselle Halfie. Good morning."

"I'm sorry. You sound very busy."

"*Never* too busy for you." Gus chuckled. "So, should I take it you won't be too *occupied* that evening to join us?"

She swallowed. "No. I'm free." She was too shy to ask who else was invited.

"Excellent. I look forward to seeing you."

"See you then." Disappointed, Farah hung up. Maybe Gus's interest in her had waned? He knew she was traveling to Amman soon. Why hadn't he mentioned meeting her before?

She busied herself with some paperwork.

Elise and Lucien clattered in. Lucien acknowledged her with a faint smile. At least he wasn't ignoring her today.

Farah glanced from one to the other. "Why don't the three of us grab a bite together today?"

Elise slipped in behind the counter and began filing a report.

"Lucien and I planned to eat after work."

Farah waited around for a few seconds before leaving to fill out the logbook, hoping Elise would ask her to join them.

She didn't.

Chapter Twelve

The night of Gus's dinner party, Farah walked into the Ritz right on time.

Her high heels clicked against the marble floor as she made her way to the l'Espadon restaurant; the sign on the door indicated it was a private event. When she spotted Gus in a black suit with a striking blue and turquoise silk tie, her heart fluttered.

As soon as he noticed her, his face lit up. He held a glass of whiskey in one hand and a cigarette in the other. "Welcome, Farah." Next to him stood a dark, slender man in a grey suit who couldn't have been more than twenty-eight.

A troop of smartly dressed waiters rushed around, their eyes darting from the white starched tables to the meandering guests.

Farah almost choked at how much it must have cost to reserve the entire restaurant for the evening. Obviously, a large crowd was expected.

Gus clapped the young man next to him on the shoulder. "Farah, this is Layth, my cousin. Second cousin actually. The Jordanian branch of the family."

Layth nodded perfunctorily, a sullen look on his face. He placed his hands in his pockets, his dark eyes wandering around the room.

Why was he so unfriendly?

Gus hurried to the door muttering that he had to greet the Lebanese Ambassador. The older, grey-haired gentleman was accompanied by an elegant brunette in a long black evening gown, her arm linked to his, sparkling stones dripping from her ears.

Farah ordered a whiskey-cola.

A waiter arrived with a tray of drinks.

Farah reached for the glass. When she turned around, Layth was gone.

She stifled a yawn then sipped her drink and looked around, self-conscious. Why hadn't she opted for a chignon? From the official invitation card, she should have guessed that this would be a formal evening attire event, with the ultra-chic descending onto the restaurant in droves, their outfits probably costing more than she earned in two months. Her simple knee-length black velvet dress clung uncomfortably to her stomach and hips – she'd have to cut down on the chocolate.

A seemingly never-ending flow of guests crowded into the sizable restaurant, with people maneuvering around not to bump into one another as they broke into groups.

Two heavily made-up women greeted one another with air kisses, their cheeks grazing, and their jewelry clinking. "*Keefik Hayati?*"

"*Mais vous avez entendu les dernières nouvelles? Les Israéliens…*"

Farah wandered around as a medley of nationalities mingled exchanging information and opinions on a variety of topics from food to international politics.

A hand slid over her back. "I'm so sorry to have left you alone, but duties of the host…" Though Gus stood beside her, his eyes continued to flick the doorway.

"Oh, no. That's ok." She smiled, concealing the tedium of being on her own.

He pulled out a packet of cigarettes.

She reached for one.

Suddenly, Gus gave her a quick pat on the arm and, before he even had time to light her cigarette, sailed off.

He headed straight for a curvy blonde, swathed in a full-length red satin dress with a décolleté dipping down almost to her mid-riff before expanding into a full sequined skirt. The outfit was jazzed up by a string of dazzling diamonds.

Who was this cross between Red Riding Hood and a Christmas tree?

The woman wrapped her arms around Gus, who, for once, appeared nonplussed.

Farah narrowed her eyes, spun around, and headed off in search of a light. Layth stood nearby, a scowl on his face. She ignored the unpleasant sensation in the pit of her stomach and lit her cigarette from the candle in a centerpiece, then blew smoke out through her nose, mimicking Marlene Dietrich as a *femme fatale*.

Why had Layth taken an instant dislike to her?

A voice whispered into her ear. "Ms. Halfie take care you don't do that too often or you might get used to it."

Farah swung around to find Gus behind her. Her cheeks seared that he caught her in her make-believe persona.

Gus took the cigarette from her, drew a few puffs, and handed it back to her. He tweaked her nose before ambling off and leaving her again to grapple with feelings of longing and confusion.

A small brass bell tinkled.

Guests searched for their names on the seating plan, found their places, and sat down.

Seated at Gus's table, Farah found herself placed between an older gentleman, with thinning brown hair and a bulging belly, and the Lebanese Ambassador. The curvaceous blonde sat next to Gus, right across from them.

Gus tapped a crystal glass with his fork, and the conversation hushed. He stood and cleared his throat.

"*Mesdames et Messieurs,* I would like to thank you for honoring me this evening by being here. This year we are graced with the presence of both the Greek and Cypriot Ambassadors." He raised his glass first to one, then the other. "They join us to emphasize the strong historic ties our countries have shared for many centuries and will continue to do so. *Inshallah.* I hope everyone enjoys themselves tonight." He raised his glass. "I take this opportunity to offer an early toast to 1987. May it be a prosperous year for all of us."

Everyone raised their glasses and echoed his wishes.

Farah's stomach grumbled. A waiter placed a zesty lobster salad mixed with avocado before her. She raised a forkful to her mouth.

The fat gentleman next to her turned his head, his eyes resting on her breasts. "I'm Tim Wilson."

She nodded. "Farah Gabriel." Her skin tightened as his lecherous looks roamed up and down her body.

"How do you know Mr. Khodeib?" he asked.

"Family friend."

How dare this man ogle her like that? Why had Gus placed her next to him? Farah shot Gus a frustrated glance, but he missed it as the lady in red demanded his full attention, her diaphanous sleeves almost hiding his face from view.

Why was he allowing her to monopolize him?

Despite the woman's ridiculous attire, her graceful mannerisms exuded elegance far beyond Farah's level of sophistication. She stared down at her hands; how plain and lanky she must appear by comparison. The thick tablecloth buffered the sound of her drumming fingers.

"Excellent food, isn't it?" said the Lebanese Ambassador.

Farah turned to him. How on earth should she address him? "Yes. Delicious."

"But then Ghassan has a reputation for his gourmet taste." The Ambassador peered at her from above his round-rimmed glasses, reminding her of Professor Calculus in the Tintin comics.

The lady in red leaned towards the ambassador, her ample breasts almost spilling out of her dress. "That was a lovely reception the other night, Your Excellency." Her voice held the satisfied note of someone who had licked clotted cream off bare skin.

"My pleasure, Chantal. I'm so glad Ghassan convinced you to come along."

Farah's stomach hardened as she stared at the voluptuous blonde. She gritted her teeth. So, the minute she had *stupidly* declined his invitation to the reception at the Lebanese Embassy, Gus must have immediately rung this odd specimen and invited her instead.

Rocking slightly on the chair, she spun the gold bracelet on her wrist to stop her hands from trembling, a taste of bile in her mouth.

Fine. If this is what Gus wants there's really no need for me to even be here. I'm nothing more than an amusing pastime…

Her throat dry and scratchy, Farah reached out for a glass of water but found it difficult to swallow.

The waiters cleared the first course and brought in the main dish, poached salmon with roasted vegetables.

Farah looked down at her plate, all desire to eat gone. She sucked in a deep breath and forced herself to take a bite. The conversation continued around her, but she barely heard a word. Unable to face another mouthful, she cut up her food into small pieces and spread it across the plate.

How could she slip away without drawing attention?

The opportunity arose when, in the midst of the dessert being placed on the tables, the brunette companion of the Lebanese ambassador knocked over her drink. The wine splashed over the white tablecloth.

Two waiters rushed over, and everyone at the table stood up so they could do their job.

Farah stretched her hand to the Lebanese ambassador. "I'm afraid I have to leave. Nice meeting you, Your Excellency." Grabbing her bag, she strutted off.

She was halfway down the hall when Gus caught up with her.

He caught her arm. "Farah, is something wrong? Where are you going?"

"I feel sick. I'm going home."

"Sick? Your stomach?"

"You could say that," she said in a dry tone. The sarcasm was lost on Gus. "I really need to leave. I don't want to disturb your evening. Enjoy your 'Christmas tree'." Darn. Why had she let that slip out?

He raised an eyebrow. "Christmas tree?"

"Thank you for the invite, Mr. Khodeib. It was a very *interesting* evening. I won't keep you any longer," she said in a sour tone.

Gus threw her a puzzled look. "I'll call you, so we can get together before you leave."

Farah swept out without looking back.

***

The bus didn't take long to arrive. Farah leaned her head against the window, staring out as they drove past well-lit streets, still busy with traffic. She got out at her stop. The evening wind picked up as she walked towards her building.

When the elevator reached the third floor, Farah exited and headed down the corridor. The door leading to the fire escape creaked. She glanced over her shoulder. It swung back and forth. After a moment's hesitation, she scurried across to the fire exit and crossed to the landing. At the sound of rushing footsteps, she leaned over the railing. In the half-light where shapes and shadows merged, she caught a fleeting glimpse of a man's profile. A bright lamp from outside shone over a freckled hand, which slid on the rail as he bounded down the fire escape.

Farah shrugged. *Odd.* She retraced her steps, entered her flat, and switched on the lights. Kicking off her high-heeled shoes, she hurled her bag on the sofa and made for the bathroom. The jar of cotton balls wasn't in its usual place on the shelf. She clicked her tongue. What was it doing on the opposite side?

Once done, she went into the kitchen. A herbal drink was just what she needed.

Mug in hand, Farah plonked down on the sofa. She glanced around the room and frowned. The family photo on the bookshelf had been moved. Only that morning, she had positioned it in the middle of the shelf. She raised the mug to her mouth but stopped mid-air. The key to the second bedroom wasn't in the door, yet it had been there earlier when she had rushed out to the Ritz.

Someone had been in her apartment.

What if they were *still* there?

Dread coiled in her belly as her breathing came out in bursts. She flew off the sofa, grabbed her bag and shoes, and ran out.

Once in the entrance foyer, Farah took a few deep breaths to calm herself. *There's a payphone around the corner.* She fumbled in her bag for a coin, then with trembling fingers, dialed the Ritz.

Gus would know how to handle this.

"I need to speak to M. Ghassan Khodeib. The Espadon restaurant, please."

The operator asked Farah to speak louder. She repeated her request and waited on hold, running her hand across her forehead to wipe away the beads of sweat.

"Hello." Gus's strong voice resounded through the line.

Farah could have sobbed with relief. "Someone's broken into my apartment. I'm scared he…they might still be there."

"Leave the flat immediately. I'll be right there."

Fifteen minutes later Gus strode into the building.

Farah collapsed into him, still shaking.

He wrapped his arms around her. "Shhhh. Calm down. How do you know someone broke in? Is anything missing?"

"I…I d-don't know. I didn't stick around long enough to find out." Her voice was strangely quiet to her ears. She pressed her hand to her stomach. "But my family p-photo and a couple of other items were not in their usual place and the key to the spare bedroom wasn't in the lock."

Behind them, the elevator door slammed shut.

Farah started.

Gus took a firm hold of her hand. "Come with me to the car."

Farah clung to him as they walked to the Mercedes.

Gus barked an order at the driver. He placed his arm firmly around her back and they headed towards the building. "Let's go upstairs. Nothing to be afraid of. I'm here."

She handed him the keys.

He opened the apartment door and entered.

Farah hesitated, then, with a deep breath, followed him in. She sat on the edge of a chair, her eyes darting around, while Gus went in the kitchen to fetch her a glass of water. She gulped it down then pointed towards the bedroom and whispered. "What if there's someone under my bed? Or in the other room?"

Gus marched towards her bedroom then stopped. A key lay inertly on the floor. He picked it up and placed it in Farah's hand. "Is this the key that was missing?"

She nodded.

"Look around and make sure nothing's been stolen."

Her string of pearls and three gold bracelets were still in the top drawer, as were the five hundred francs she had withdrawn the day before.

Farah rolled her shoulders back and forth.

He led her to the sofa and they both sat down. "Relax."

The doorbell rang, startling Farah.

"Shhh." Gus got up. "I asked Layth to come."

"Layth?"

The young Jordanian entered with the same dour look still etched on his face. He gave the impression that this was the last place he wanted to be.

Gus took him aside and spoke to his cousin in a low voice.

Layth headed to her bedroom. Fifteen minutes later, he entered the second bedroom. When he came out and ran a device underneath the dining room table, the bookshelf, and the pictures on the wall.

Farah started to rise from the sofa.

Gus held her back. "He knows what he's doing."

"What *is* he doing?"

Gus laid a hand on her arm, his eyes sharp and focused on his cousin.

Layth appeared and shook his head.

Farah tugged Gus's arm. "What's he looking for?"

Layth jerked his chin upwards his eyebrows raised. "Nothing. Clean."

She snapped her eyebrows together and turned to Gus. "Clean?"

"Just checking to make sure your place isn't bugged."

"Bugged?" Her mouth dropped. "Why would it be bugged? How can Layth tell?"

"Layth…owns a security company. He's well-versed in all of this."

"Why would anyone want to bug my flat?"

A knowing look passed between the two men.

"Gus?" A note of panic crept into Farah's voice.

"Our cousins."

Farah turned her head from one to the other, her eyebrows in a puzzled knot. "Your cousins?"

"Mossad," said Gus, in a flat tone. He didn't pronounce the guttural letter in the middle, denoting a man's name in Arabic.

Why is he mispro-? OH MY GOD! The Israeli Secret Service!

Her lips trembled. "B-but I don't know any Israelis."

"You know me." Gus shrugged and lit a cigarette. "Farah, pack a bag for tonight." He held up his palm silencing her objection. "Don't even think of arguing. I'm taking you to my place – you can stay in the guestroom. I'll feel better."

A wave of relief rolled through her.

They arrived at Gus's duplex in Neuilly. Despite her state of nerves, the array of priceless Persian silk carpets impressed Farah. On the bookshelves, Sartre's work rubbed shoulders with Amin Maalouf and Sagan's novels. Dostoevsky and Tolstoy's masterpieces stood beside the works of Flaubert and Baudelaire. An eclectic collection of books on the Crusades were stacked in an entire corner.

Intricate bronze chandeliers hung from the ceiling, flooding the place with a warm glow. Crystal vases filled with cream roses adorned every room, their sweet scent hanging in the air.

"Why don't you get settled in? I need to return to my guests, but the staff is here, in case you need anything."

She bit her lower lip and looked into his eyes. "Thank you."

Gus ushered her into a bedroom decorated in white and yellow, with matching curtains and bed linen. A pair of yellow towels lay folded on the bed.

He patted her on the shoulder. "I think you need to get some sleep. Tomorrow is another day."

Tucked up in Gus' guestroom, Farah tossed and turned as spying agents and Chantal blended into one.

Chapter Thirteen

Later that evening, after the reception finished, Gus returned home and sank into an armchair, a cigarette in one hand and a set of amethyst worry beads in the other. Pavarotti's voice rose from the stereo to the strain of *O Sole Mio*. He rested his head back and closed his eyes for a moment.

Had someone broken into Farah's flat? If so, there would be only one reason, since nothing was missing. A warning to *him*. He shook his head. No, that was an unlikely scenario. Not Mossad's style.

His thoughts drifted to her dramatic exit and he chuckled under his breath. Farah had made her point by storming out from the dinner party, trying hard, but failing, to mask her feelings. Her glittering green eyes expressed her anger louder than words. And underneath the anger, hurt.

He should have checked the seating arrangements, but it had slipped his mind. His new secretary had simply followed the same seating plan used for the last few years with Chantal next to him.

Even if he *had* checked the seating arrangement, he wouldn't have been able to change it. Chantal had been a lifeline for him when he had first arrived in Paris six years ago after he escaped Lebanon.

They had met at the opera through mutual friends, and not long into the conversation, discovered their similar tastes in art. Gus had immediately enlisted her help in furnishing the apartment he had bought.

As an art connoisseur, Chantal knew where to go to procure original paintings and collector's items.

They had spent many an afternoon browsing around together in antique shops, enjoying one another's company. With her invitations and introductions, she had opened doors for him that would have taken him years to cultivate.

At the time, naturally, Gus had sought comfort in her arms. Though more than twenty years his senior, Chantal, with her laidback attitude, provided the relief he craved in his mandatory exile, easing his longing for home if only momentarily.

It was an easy arrangement for both of them, but there had been a clear understanding between them from the beginning.

"We can play, Ghassan," she had said after they slept together the first time, "*mais pas plus que ça*. At my age, I'm no longer interested in a commitment with any man, not even one as young and handsome as you."

She had listened to his incessant ranting about the political turmoil in Lebanon, the ongoing civil war, and how the Syrians and Israelis carved up his beloved country between them.

Gus clenched his jaw, staring at the wall opposite, seeing nothing. His thumb rolled bead after bead, the familiar clicking filling the silence.

And then Farah appeared, a mirage in his emotional desert.

Hard to believe it was only three weeks ago.

From the minute he set eyes on her, Gus saw through her thin defensive veneer right into her vulnerable and suffering soul, stirring in him feelings long since buried. He identified with her pain, although hers was that of a first love, no doubt.

The emotions she arose in him went beyond a longing to stretch out his arms, gather her to him and provide her with safety. He was overpowered by something he had never experienced before with a woman.

Love shifted the balance of his life as he crossed unchartered territory. Except he was the last person who could offer her stability.

What a joke that he, Ghassan Khodeib, who had never allowed his sentiments for a woman to get in the way, would finally plummet for a slip of a girl in her early twenties. How had she managed to invade his soul in such a way?

He stood up, poured himself a glass of whiskey, and faced the window, looking out at the star-strewn black sky.

Footsteps sounded against the marble corridor. He turned around.

Layth entered. He perched on the arm of the sofa, swinging one leg back and forth. "Is she asleep?"

Gus nodded and sat down again.

"Do you think it was the Mossad?"

Gus shrugged. "Anything is possible. It could also have been that she is hypersensitive - she seemed a bit…emotional this evening. After all, the key was on the floor. Doesn't mean anything, I know. Still."

An awkward silence hovered between them.

"You know you can't, Ghassan."

"I don't need you to remind me."

Layth reached out and helped himself to some nuts in a bowl on the ebony coffee table. "I think I do. I've never seen you like this."

Gus lit another cigarette and turned to his cousin with a heavy sigh. "*Le Coeur a des raisons que la raison ne comprend pas.*" The heart has reasons which reason does not understand.

After a few more puffs, he crushed his cigarette, threw back the remains of the drink in his glass, and rose, his heart weighing him down like an anchor.

***

The next morning Farah showered and dressed, then stepped out into the hallway.

"*Bonjour,*" she smiled at the maid carrying a tray with empty glasses, "*ou est Monsieur Khodeib s'il vous plait?*"

The maid pointed her towards a closed door.

Farah knocked timidly.

"*Entrez.*"

She entered Gus's office.

He sat behind a desk, a file in his hand, and a cup of Turkish coffee next to him.

A map of Lebanon was spread out on the table, paperweights on each corner. An ashtray full of cigarette butts lay on the side, next to a single framed photo of a smiling young man with a goatee holding a curly-haired little boy.

Gus stood up and took her hands. "Did you sleep all right?"

"Yes, thank you."

An antique-looking sword hung on the wall behind his desk glittered in the sunlight.

Farah stared, eyebrows slightly raised.

"*Al Badee Azlam,*" she read aloud the framed Arabic calligraphy hanging below the sword. "He who initiates is the guilty one?"

"That sword was given to one of my ancestors by Saladin after the Battle of Hittin when he defeated the Crusaders. Legend has it that when my forefather returned to his township, he discovered the neighboring ruler had attacked his castle and taken the womenfolk to be sold as slaves. So, he wrote a hurried message to Saladin for help. The Sultan sent this sword to aid my ancestor's revenge."

"What happened to the women?"

As Farah uttered the question, she remembered she wanted to ask him about Sabra and Shatila.

"He rescued them. He used that sword to cut off the heads of the men involved and paraded them on spikes. With Saladin's blessing, he added his enemy's land to his. My family adopted that motto, and it's been part of our heritage ever since."

"Oh my. That's quite a story."

On a corner table, a big mother-of-pearl box rested half-open, worry beads of different stones spilled out.

Farah ambled over.

"Ah, you spotted my treasure trove," Gus said, a note of pride in his voice. "I collect them."

"Oh."

She lifted the cover, struck by the rainbow of colored stones that met her eyes. Aquamarine, lapis, opal, and many others. How did he decide which one to take each time? She reached out for a pink set, a color she hadn't seen before.

"That's my *pièce de résistance*." Gus huffed a laugh and walked up to her. "Pink sapphire. Only for *very* special occasions."

"Stunning."

He brushed a wisp of hair from her face. "Come, we'll get you some breakfast."

As she followed Gus to the kitchen, Farah gazed in appreciation at the paintings on the walls, recognizing a still life by Monet. Was it an original? Were they all originals?

He poured her a cup of coffee and offered a croissant on a plate. "I went out especially this morning to buy that for you."

"Thank you." Her unseemly scene of the previous night flashed through her mind. She looked down.

Gus cut an apple and placed the plate in the middle of the table.

Farah reached for a slice. "You know, I've been meaning to ask you about Sabra and Shatila." She paused to gather her thoughts. "I thought you might, perhaps, explain to me the complicated situation in Lebanon – it's very hard for an outsider, you know? I mean, Lebanon, Palestine – it's sort of intertwined, right?"

Would he think her stupid?

Contrary to what she expected, his face broke into a smile.

"I'll be more than happy to explain it to you. As you said, it's very complicated." He winked. "What about a lesson a week?"

Farah chuckled. "Sounds good." She looked at her watch. "I'm sorry but I have to leave after breakfast. I hope you don't mind."

"I'll take you home whenever you want. What time is your shift today?"

"I start at 3.00. I have a few things to do before I go to work."

As he shepherded her toward the front door, she cast a quick look into the office at the centuries-old sword hanging like a dark shadow.

Chapter Fourteen

"Mossad?" Monique choked and spattered the coffee all over her clothes.

Farah delivered a couple of back blows then ran from the living room to the kitchen to fetch a cloth.

Monique's coughing subsided and she sat back in her chair, wiping her stained clothes.

"What on earth have you gotten yourself into?" Monique raised her eyebrows. "This guy's dangerous. You know what I mean?"

Farah massaged her head with the tips of her fingers. "I'm not sure."

"What does he do for *Mossad* to be after him?"

Farah pursed her lips and frowned, recalling how Gus had vanished with the Lebanese Maitre d' on their first date, then had been in a hurry to leave.

She opened her mouth to reveal that Gus actually killed a Syrian soldier, but held back. She didn't need another lecture.

Monique took another sip of water. "Fishy."

Farah drew in a sharp breath. What if she was on the cusp of becoming part of something big? She shivered in excitement. This felt like a thriller movie with all the elements in place, and her playing the part of some tragic heroine.

"It's a good thing you're leaving to Amman soon – you need the distance. Hopefully, by the time you get back, you'll be over this infatuation." Monique checked the time. "Anyway, I have to go." She stood and picked up her bag. "I'm not sure I'll see you before you leave so I'll say goodbye now." She gave Farah a quick hug. "Have a lovely Christmas, Farah, and send my best to your family. See you in January."

***

The next morning, when Farah walked into the back office, she froze. Elise was huddled on a chair, sobbing.

Lucien crouched next to her, wiping her tears, her hands clasped in his.

Farah scurried over. "What happened?"

"Her mother's been rushed to the hospital for emergency open-heart surgery," he answered without looking up.

"Then what are we doing here? Come on, quick! Elise, I'm coming with you. I'm sure Eric won't object. This is an emergency."

Elise's chest heaved up and down with sobs, tears streaming down her cheeks.

Lucien helped Elise to her feet. "It's ok, Farah, I'll go with her."

"I'll come too."

Lucien put out his hand to stop her. "No, Farah. We can't all just leave. Someone needs to stay here."

Farah swallowed. "Yes, you're right." Lucien had never been so firm before.

He guided Elise out, his hand resting lightly on her back.

Poor Elise, she still wasn't over her father's sudden death a few months ago, and now this? No wonder she was so distraught.

Her thoughts consumed with her friend's predicament Farah went through the motions of greeting incoming passengers. Though Lucien had promised to phone as soon as they knew anything, she found it difficult to concentrate and kept glancing at her watch. After what seemed like an eternity, the phone rang.

She grabbed it. "Bonjour, VIP Lounge."

"Farah. I n-need -" Elise broke off sobbing.

"Elise, has your mother gone in for surgery yet?"

More sobs.

"Farah," Lucien came on the line. "Elise needs to go home and rest, but she forgot her keys in her desk drawer. Can you find some way to have them delivered to the hospital?"

"What's happening with her mom?"

"She's in the operating room. Please, can you send the keys?"

"Yes. I'll find someone to bring them to you. Don't worry."

Farah rushed into the back office where they all had their desks. Under the glare of the harsh lights, she opened Elise's drawer and rummaged beneath the papers till she found the keys. Then a document caught her eye. She jerked her hand back in disbelief and staring at it, she dropped onto a chair her hand flying to her chest, the blood draining from her face. Elise was her friend. How could this be possible? Yet the proof was right there in front of her, in black and white. A draft complaint letter about her, allegedly from a disgruntled passenger. The clock on the wall ticked in the silence. Frowning, Farah took a deep breath. Snippets of conversations came back to her. The shrill ring of the phone made her jump.

"Hello."

"Farah, what's taking you so long?" It was Lucien on the other end.

"S-sorry. I've found them. I'll call you back once I've organized delivery." Farah stammered through a mist of hurt and confusion.

***

That evening, as Farah lounged on the sofa ruminating over her discovery, the phone rang.

She picked it up. "Hello."

"Farah, it's Gus. Listen, I'll drive you to the airport on Sunday. Unfortunately, I won't be here when you get back."

Farah gripped the receiver and swallowed, attempting to keep the disappointment from her voice. "How come?"

"I have to go to Lebanon. There's …on family business." Gus paused. "You understand what family obligation is like."

Farah's stomach churned. Returning to Lebanon? Visions of military forces and explosions, which daily news depicted, came to life. "I thought you couldn't go back to Lebanon. I mean, after what you told me." She chewed the inside of her cheek. "What about Mossad? You never explained."

"I'll fly to Cyprus then go by boat to Tripoli." He ignored her last question.

She had created this entire scenario about how their reunion after New Year would unfold. "How long will you be gone?" she asked in a small voice.

"Three or four weeks."

She slumped into a chair. "I see. So, not before the end of January?"

Paris in the January doldrums would be horrible without him.

Chapter Fifteen

Amman – December 1986

Farah slipped out of bed quietly not to disturb her sleeping niece. She drew her dressing gown closer around her as she tiptoed out of the bedroom. Down in the kitchen, she put on the kettle, made herself a coffee, and sat down at the table.

"Why are you up so early?" Cyril's voice boomed into her ear.

Her hand flew to her chest. "God, you scared me, Cyril."

Her brother grinned, ruffled her hair, and joined her. "Another Christmas over. Next year in Cairo."

She nodded and sipped her drink, warmed that they had ten more days with all of them together as a family, despite the day's chill.

Cyril opened the fridge and poured himself a glass of juice. "I think we should plan a visit there soon. You know *Teta* is getting on – she'll be 87 next month."

Farah chewed on the thought. Her relationship with her Egyptian grandmother had never been easy. She disliked the way the Matriarch treated her foreign daughter-in-law. Plus, *Teta* always favored the firstborns among her grandchildren; in this case, Cyril.

And then that time she had been sitting in the back seat of the car, a little girl not more than eight or nine, with *Teta* in the front rambling on about some distant relative getting married to a foreigner, *but* a good one.

Her father had reacted by shouting repeatedly "What do you mean foreigner *but* decent? Are you trying to say that *most* foreigners are bad?"

Her grandmother's feeble attempts at self-justification had convinced no one.

Still, it was hard to imagine life without *Teta*.

Farah placed her empty cup in the sink, grabbed a packet of cigarettes, and went to sit on the big stone steps outside the kitchen door.

Cyril followed her.

The rising sun's incandescent rays endowed the world with a new day, a fresh start. Birds twittered, springing from one tree to another, and broke the stillness.

Cyril removed his scarf, wrapped it around Farah's neck, and cradled her head on his shoulder. "How are you doing, Majoie? How's work?"

She smiled at the fond memories of her childhood nickname Cyril had given her. Her mother had often recounted how, as a little boy of three, he had been unable to pronounce the guttural consonant at the end of his new sister's name in Arabic. He had invented the nickname and it had stuck.

"Work sucks, if you want the truth. There's too much backstabbing."

"You could always go back to Cairo."

She wrenched her head from his shoulder and glowered at him. "To suffocate there? I don't think so. Most of my classmates are already married and probably have kids by now. I'm a misfit in Egypt."

"But that's the way things work there," he said gently.

"I'll live my life the way I want, *do* what I want. Just like you did. You didn't give a damn about going against everyone." Her voice grew louder.

Her brother put a finger to his lips. "We're only trying to protect you. Because we love you."

"Speak for yourself. For Papa, acting isn't 'proper'. *That's* why he refuses to pay. All he cares about is what the family would think." She inhaled a deep breath. "Cyril, acting is the only thing I really enjoy. When I read a play, I feel a deep emotional connection to the characters, and fuse into them."

Would he understand?

For the last six months, she had been trying to climb out of the ashes, to forge out a new direction, a new identity, while her mind exploded with unanswered questions.

Farah sighed and closed her eyes. Fortunately, Cyril didn't know that she had lost her virginity to Justin, something which still haunted her.

The shocked look on Justin's face at the sight of blood on the sheet flashed through her mind. It gnawed at her, like the conversation that followed, still clearly etched in her mind.

"Farah, I have nothing to go back to, no job, no home since my mother's about to get re-married," Justin had said.

"But your family has money. Ask for help," she had blurted.

"Never! This isn't Egypt where parents pay for everything. I don't have the right to ask. If I can't afford to get married, I won't."

Cyril drew her close to him again. "Justin's still on your mind? You'll get over it. One day you'll meet someone else."

Farah flinched. She had no intention of mentioning Gus right now.

"You're hiding something. I can feel it."

She didn't answer.

"Fine. As long as you know the rules. Only a Christian – whichever denomination."

She stared at him. "Isn't that a bit hypocritical, Cyril? We *are* staying in the house of our *Moslem* brother-in-law, aren't we?"

"We grew up in the Middle East, Farah. No negotiating on religion."

"But Tammy's happy with Jamal. I mean, interfaith marriages *can* work."

Cyril shot a warning glass to their parents' bedroom right above them. "Don't go there. You'll only hurt yourself," he said in a hushed voice.

Farah's heart sank at how Cyril unknowingly echoed Monique's words. "I don't know why we're even talking about this," she whispered.

Best to change the subject just in case their father overheard anything. He would physically stop her from returning to Paris if he had any suspicions that she was involved with a Moslem man.

"I wish I could do something more to help you get over Justin. But I do what I can – pray."

Farah rolled her eyes. "Oh, please. Not that again."

"Prayer changes situations. It transforms people."

"Cyril, please shut up. I've already had enough with Tammy's preaching. I don't need yours as well."

He opened his mouth but she cut him off. "You chose that path when you converted to Catholicism, and I supported you against *Maman* and everyone. All I ask is that you support me now."

"I'll continue to pray."

She pointed a reproving finger at him, her eyebrows snapping together. "Papist."

They both burst out laughing.

"Farah, God is good. I know sometimes it just doesn't seem like it, but…"

Farah blocked her ears with her fingers and stuck out her tongue.

Cyril laughed and tried to pull her hands away, starting a game of tug of war, with both talking at the same time to drown out the other's voice.

Farah threw up her hands. "I give up."

Together, they headed back upstairs.

Her niece was still sleeping. Farah changed into a training suit and went down to the basement. The trampoline stood in the middle of the floor. She climbed onto it and started jumping, her eyes closed.

Gus's specter rose like a dark, looming shadow, jeopardizing the warm, tight-knit family nest.

She jumped faster, adrenaline shooting up her body.

What was he up to? Too bad she hadn't been able to give him Tammy's number. They both knew he couldn't ring her there in case someone else picked up and the questions that would follow. '*Who is that? What does he do? How do you know him? Why is he phoning you?*' Plus, there was zero privacy at Tammy's since the telephone was in the hallway and anyone could hear the conversation.

Exhausted, with sweat trickling down her chest, she slowed down to a stop and fell onto the trampoline out of breath. If only she could stop thinking of him so much.

Later that evening, the family gathered around the table for dinner, with the aroma of the spices and onions rising from the roast lamb lying in the center, garnished with potatoes and bits of parsley.

Farah's father finished and pushed his plate away. "Great meal, Tammy, as usual. *Yeslamoo edeiki.*" Bless your hands.

Tammy smiled. "Thank you." She herded her daughter out of the dining room. "C'mon Sarah. Time for bed."

Farah sprung up to join them – she loved reading her niece bedtime stories and spending quality time with Tammy. In a way, it made up for all the years she had grown up without even knowing she had a half-sister.

"Farah, I want to talk to you alone," said her father.

Farah's stomach muscles spasmed. It wasn't difficult to guess the reason. Now that Christmas Day was over, her father would get to business.

Her mother followed her into Jamal's study and the three of them sat down.

Her father lit his pipe. "Ok, Farah. So, your mother and I think it's about time for you to come back to Cairo. There's no reason for you to remain in Paris. It's not like you're going to make a career from your current job. Back home you can find a much better job, something you can grow in."

Farah clenched her teeth. "I want to go to Drama School."

"Drama School?" her father asked in an incredulous tone, "enough of that nonsense, Farah."

Fury flashed through her. She turned to her mother with pleading eyes.

But her mother remained quiet, her lips pressed shut.

"Papa, please. There's nothing else I want to do."

If she left Paris, she would never see Gus again...

"Farah, you either come home or I'll take measures you won't like." Her father's voice turned grim.

She rubbed the back of her neck not sure what he meant.

He banged his hand on the desk. "If you insist on staying in Paris then you can take full responsibility for yourself. You'll have to pay your own utility bills from now on. You can stay in the flat since nobody's using it at the moment, but that's about it."

She shifted in her seat her jaw jutted out. "I'm staying."

"Fine, Farah. To every choice in life, there are consequences. Remember, as of next month you pay all the utility bills if you don't want the services cut." He took a deep puff at his pipe. "And the maintenance fees as well."

Farah pursed her lips but didn't say anything, grateful for the Middle Eastern custom that parents never charged their children rent.

Chapter Sixteen

A dull grey Paris awaited Farah upon her return. The sense of loneliness in the empty apartment wrapped itself around her like a heavy mantle. What a relief that Monique was stopping by later. Farah couldn't wait to swap holiday news.

Much to her disappointment, there were no letters from any of the drama schools waiting for her.

The phone rang.

She picked up the receiver to the pips of an international call. "Hello."

"Ms. Halfie?"

"Gus? Where are you? Are you ok? Are you back?"

"Slow down, kiddo." He laughed. "In Lebanon, though I wish I were in Paris. I knew you were returning today and wanted to say hello."

A warm feeling slid down her body. He had remembered.

"Unfortunately, I have to postpone my return," he continued.

The sky turned a shade darker as if it were going to cry.

She swallowed. "When —"

The line went dead. She closed her eyes and sighed in frustration.

What if he didn't come back? What if something happened to him over there? A tremor ran through her body.

When Monique arrived, Farah shelved the conversation with Gus to the side.

Monique took out her manicure set and placed a bottle of red nail polish on the coffee table. "Can you believe we're back already?"

A fierce wind gathered strength outside. The bare branches of the trees convulsed in the cold while the windows rattled.

"There's been something I've been meaning to tell you," Farah paused, a nasty sensation spiraling down her chest. "I found out who was writing the complaint letters about me."

"Who?"

"Elise."

"*What?*" Monique's mouth fell open. "That's impossible Farah. You two are so close. She even organized that surprise party for you."

"That was before."

"Before?"

"Before she started seeing me as her rival – she's in love with Lucien."

"There must be some mistake."

"Nope. I found the draft in her desk."

"Oh no!" Monique knocked the bottle of nail polish. It spilled onto the floor. She rushed into the kitchen to get something to wipe it up.

"I felt so shocked. I still feel hurt and so let down," said Farah.

They were both on their knees wiping the carpet vigorously.

"Are you going to confront her? Or tell your boss?"

Farah shook her head. "No. She might lose her job. Her dad passed a few months ago, and her mother just had major heart surgery – she's in a wheelchair. Elise is her carer and the only breadwinner now. I couldn't do it. Better be the victim than the culprit."

"That's so nice of you. I'm not sure I'd react the same way."

Farah went into the kitchen to rinse the rags. "I wish I could say I forgive her but I can't."

"The atmosphere at work must be horrible."

"Pretty much."

The phone rang again. Farah rushed to grab it. Raindrops trickled down the windowpane.

"Sorry, Farah. The lines here are very bad." Gus's voice faded in and out.

"Never mind. You were saying something about when you're coming back –"

"I'll know better next week."

The line cut for the second time.

Farah clenched her teeth as she twiddled with the cord, the receiver pressed against her ear. Seconds passed. Giving up, she slammed the phone down, went into the kitchen, and rummaged in the fridge for some chocolate.

Monique crossed her legs, a scowl on her face. "I suppose that was that Gus guy?"

"Mmmm."

How could she explain to Monique how she felt if she herself was confused? It wasn't only his flamboyant aura or his casual disregard for money that impressed her. When she was with Gus, Farah forgot everything else, even Justin. Gus made life exciting again, and he drove away the melancholia she had been wrapped in since Justin had disappeared.

"Easy on the chocolate. I see a few new curves." Monique's harsh comment cut through her daydreaming.

Farah stared down at her stomach in dismay. Drastic action was needed.

Chapter Seventeen

Nazareth, North of Israel - March 1987

Moshe Avram was unable to take his eyes off his radiant daughter. Ruth glowed.

She and her new husband, Jaleel, went hand-in-hand around the tables, greeting their guests. Huge smiles wreathed their faces, and their eyes shone with the soft look of people in love. They made a striking couple. Ruth had inherited Carla's delicate features, but had taken his olive complexion, big, brown eyes and dark hair, giving her an exotic air.

Music reverberated through the speakers. Friends and family crowded the place, chatting and laughing with the newly-weds.

Moshe glanced at his wife. At 50, Carla was in great shape, her dark blonde hair cut to frame her face. She looked stunning in the forest green Mother-of-the-Bride dress.

Yossi, their oldest, stood not far off, his arm around Judith's waist. He bent over and whispered something in her ear. She laughed, stood on her tiptoes, and kissed him on the mouth.

A smile tugging at his lips, Moshe exchanged a meaningful look with Carla and winked. Perhaps another wedding was on the horizon?

Moshe's three siblings and their families sat at adjoining tables. The women clapped to the music's beat. He headed towards them, smiling and nodding at the guests.

Would Avi, his sister Rebecca's son, show up? Something weird was happening with Avi. The change in his attitude regarding Israel's politics was obvious whenever they met, becoming more marked each time. The caustic remarks about 'Arabs', the constant mention of Greater Israel, an offensive term for Moshe and his siblings – their father had denounced the creation of a Zionist state and was among the founders of the Jewish-Palestinian Peace Alliance.

Avi's allusions created a growing rift in the family. Moshe sighed. Pity he was so different to his brother; he had neither Joshua's positive, helpful attitude, nor his sense of responsibility.

His brother David cleared some space between himself and Ibrahim. "Here, Moshe, have a seat."

Ruth and Jaleel bounced over laughing, her long veil trailing behind her.

Ibrahim rose, embraced Ruth, then handed her an envelope. "The most beautiful bride." He turned to Jaleel and clapped him on the back. "This girl is the daughter I never had. Make sure you cherish her, or else."

Ruth laughed and landed two resounding kisses on his cheeks. "Thank you, Uncle Ibrahim. I'm so happy you're here."

"I wouldn't miss this for anything."

Jonathon, Moshe's youngest son appeared. "Dad." He jerked his head towards the door.

Avi stood in the doorway, his dour face casting a shadow on the festive ambiance.

Moshe forced his lips into a smile and stood up to welcome his nephew. "Avi, glad you could make it. Come and meet the groom's family."

Avi glowered and didn't move.

Moshe clutched Avi's arm. "Differences should be set aside on a day like this."

He led him over to Ruth's in-laws. Moshe waved his hand in introduction. "This is Avi, my nephew. Joshua's older brother."

"*Marhaba, ahlein.* Welcome," smiled several of them.

One of Jaleel's sisters leaned forward to kiss him, but Avi recoiled.

"He's very shy," said Moshe, curbing a desire to clip his nephew around the ear.

They all laughed except Avi.

Dinner done, the guests clamored around the bride and groom.

"The Hora, the Hora," they cried.

Guffawing, Yossi and Judith dragged two chairs into the growing circle of people. The bride, pulling along her husband, entered the circle, and screaming with laughter, they sat down. With shouts in the air, several of their friends and cousins lifted them up.

An Arabic song rang through the sound system. The surrounding guests clasped hands and shouted as they moved counter-clockwise to the Arabic beat.

Moshe and Carla stood behind the circle clapping, their feet tapping to the rhythm. They were soon joined by the rest of his siblings.

Scowling, Avi remained apart.

Moshe walked up to him. "Avi, come on, join in the fun."

Avi's bitter voice cut through the noise. "The *Hava Nagila* wasn't good enough for my cousin?"

Moshe glared at him. "Strange indeed that Palestinians wouldn't want to play a song that celebrates the Balfour Declaration. I'm sure they must have been delighted with the British Government supporting a Jewish homeland in Palestine."

The ululations of joy from Jaleel's female relatives drowned his voice.

With a sudden woosh, ten young women in traditional Palestinian embroidered dresses clasping hands appeared in a line. Their headscarves and jewelry clinked as they jumped up and down dancing the Palestinian *dabke*. Ten men holding hands thumped their feet and uttered guttural sounds as they encircled the women. The men at each end waved handkerchiefs.

Guests stood clapping in a semi-circle around the dancers.

A vein in Avi's temple throbbed and he narrowed his eyes, like someone demented. He clenched and unclenched his hands.

Moshe grabbed his oldest son. "Get your cousin out of here."

"Dad, Aunt Rebecca and Uncle Benjamin will be offended—" said Yossi.

"Too bad. Get him out of here."

Yossi shrugged and went off.

Moshe sat down next to his brother Nathan and grabbed a glass of wine. "Am I the only one, or do you also think that Avi's gone nuts?"

Nathan twisted a tumbler of beer in his hands. "I hope I'm wrong, but I heard from the kids that Avi is hanging out with some strange people these days."

"Father must be turning in his grave. So much for his dream of an inclusive society."

Nathan sighed. "It's better that entire generation is gone now. At least they can't witness what this place has turned into."

"I'm going to have a serious talk with Rebecca and Benjamin. They have to put a stop to this."

Chapter Eighteen

Paris - May 1987

Farah sauntered down Boulevard Haussmann past the pleasing eyeline of apartment blocks, appreciating the symmetry of design. She glanced at her watch and quickened her step as she threaded her way through the crowds to meet Gus.

He stood with his back to her in front of *Galeries Lafayette*, the upmarket French department store with its iconic 19th-Century dome of glass and steel.

She tapped him on the shoulder. "*Salut.*"

He spun. "Ah, Ms. Halfie. Ready for some shopping?"

"Uhh…shopping?" He hadn't mentioned it when he had asked her to meet him here.

With his arm around her waist, he led her into the *Coupole*, the department store's main building. The massive atrium buzzed with throngs of people.

Though it was morning, iridescent lights glimmered from the impressive dome.

Gus steered her quite purposely through the shoppers. With a firm step, he led her towards the Haute Couture shops.

Farah tensed and slowed her steps, surrounded by the displays of the latest fashions with prohibitive prices.

People with garments draped over their arms drifted in and out of the fitting rooms.

Gus stopped near a rack of cocktail dresses. "I'd like you to choose a special dress. And if we don't find anything that suits you, we'll pay a visit to Avenue Montaigne."

She blinked. "Why do I need an expensive dress?"

"Because I'm whisking you away on a surprise trip for a special event." He tweaked her nose. "I want you to look stunning. Choose whatever you want – don't even look at the price."

A lightness fluttered within her.

"Wait," she held up a hand. "What trip?"

Gus grinned. "Surprise."

She shifted her weight from one foot to another. A warm glow spread through her as his words sank in. But then she faltered. "I'm sure I'll find something in my wardrobe that's suitable." Or borrow something from Monique.

"No. I insist. Let's say it's a belated Christmas gift. Or an early one, whichever you like."

Gus stopped a young shop assistant. "*Mademoiselle*, we're looking for cocktail dresses. Elegant and chic." He laughed and put his arm around Farah. "Unique, like her."

The clerk nodded. "*Bien sur, Monsieur.*" She smiled and turned to Farah. "Perhaps this would appeal to *Mademoiselle*?" She whipped out a royal blue silk dress from the rack. "This arrived today."

"Let her choose several, please." Gus headed for a bank of chairs near a set of three-way mirrors. "I'm going to wait for your fashion show."

An excited laugh bubbled up inside her. After browsing through the racks, Farah selected her favorites.

The shop assistant followed alongside. "This way, *Mademoiselle*."

She hung the five dresses in a fitting room.

In the next cubicle, two women discussed buying the same style in all colors in the Gulf Arabic dialect.

Farah slipped into a royal blue dress that clung to her body like a second skin. She smoothed a hand down the silk fabric and exited the fitting room.

Gus leaned back in his seat. "How do you like it?"

Farah glanced in the mirror and shook her head. "It's not my style – too tight. And silk creases too easily."

He smiled indulgently. "It shows off your figure, but if you don't like it, try another."

Next, she tried on a sleeveless lilac chiffon dress. Farah twirled in front of the mirror. She glanced at the label. Dior.

She walked out to show Gus and stopped short. A buxom woman with fuchsia lipstick approached him with outstretched arms. Chantal.

Farah's throat went dry. What was it with that woman and her brazen colors? This time she was wearing a pink and yellow skirt and jacket with matching shoes and handbag. Who was she trying to be? The Easter bunny delivering an Easter basket?

Yet whatever Chantal wore, even the most outlandish clothes, she carried it off with incomparable elegance and style.

Easter Bunny reached Gus first, clutching him in a theatrical embrace that seemed to smother him. "Ghassan, what are you doing here?" Chantal's voice rang with a musical lilt.

Farah slid up to Gus and laid a hand on his arm. "Helping me choose a dress for our trip."

Chantal's face wore the stunned expression of a dead fish but quickly regained her composure.

"Well, how charming." She stopped and furrowed her eyebrows. "I'm sorry, I don't recall your name. I'm Chantal."

Farah inclined her head. "Farah."

The heavy perfume Chantal wore enveloped them, making Farah slightly nauseous.

Gus's lips twitched. "Uh, well if you ladies will excuse me, I need to pick up something. I'll be right back."

He sauntered off without a backward glance.

Farah stared at his back, inhaled a deep breath, and held it. *Damn him.* She turned to Chantal. "If you'll excuse me." Her heart thumping, Farah marched off, unable to suppress a gleeful smile.

Inside the safety of the fitting room, Farah exhaled a loud breath and changed back into her clothes. No point trying on any more dresses. This was the one she wanted. She draped the lilac Dior dress over her arm and walked out.

Chantal was nowhere in sight but Gus stood waiting near the entrance to the fitting rooms, a small parcel in his hand.

Farah flipped her hair and walked up to him, a slight flutter in her stomach. How would he react after the little outburst?

Gus cocked an eyebrow. "I thought you were going to try on a few other dresses?"

She tugged at her jacket. "No need. I like this the one."

"Good choice. The color flatters you."

Gus paid for the dress and asked for the item to be delivered to the house.

She wondered why he had left but was too shy to ask.

He placed an arm behind her back and steered her towards the exit. "Satisfied?"

A warmth crept up her cheeks. "Yes. I love the dress. Thank you."

"No, I meant with how you put Chantal in her place," he said. He threw back his head and laughed.

Chapter Nineteen

Verona, Italy. May – 1987

Farah waited in the reception of the hotel in the heart of Verona's historic center, a stone's throw away from the Arena where the opera she and Gus were to attend would be performed.

Gus approached with two room keys.

Her insides jostled. Was it disappointment or relief that shot through her? Or a bit of both?

"Maria Callas suite," he said to the bellman collecting their luggage.

Farah stepped into the suite and stopped. "Oh my God. So luxurious."

Gus leaned against the wall, his arms folded, wearing a wide smile. "This is my usual suite, but since it's your initiation to the classics, I want you to take it."

"And you?"

He twirled his mustache. "I managed to wrangle something for myself."

She walked into the bedroom and bounced up and down on the bed laughing.

"I specifically chose *Aida* because of its Egyptian connection." He winked. "It's one of the most beautiful operas of all time. I hope one day, opera speaks to you as it does to me – to your soul." Gus's voice took on a dreamy tone. "Another language. Transporting you into the metaphysical. It can move you to tears. You lose your sense of time and place as the music elevates you beyond your human attachments or desires. While it lasts."

Farah sat immobile, afraid of breaking the spell.

He blew her a kiss. "I'll let you settle in."

What was this invisible power that enveloped her senses whenever she was around him? As if he were her harbor in a storm.

An hour later Farah was ready for the evening. She glanced in the mirror. The sleeveless lilac chiffon dress pulled into a high neckline before it clinched tightly at the waist, flattering her slim figure. She was smoothing down the lower part of her dress when there was a knock. She opened the door.

Gus walked in and handed her a gift wrapped in exquisite gold paper, tied with a golden ribbon, and topped with a bow. "*Pour toi.*"

Her heart raced. She stripped off the wrapping. Wide-eyed, she held up the dark green box of Poison, Dior's latest perfume. "Oh."

"Time to change your *parfum, ma belle*. That floral L'air du Temps you wore at university has run its course. *Et les temps ont changé* – the times have changed."

She stared at the bottle then at him. "*Les temps ont changé*," she repeated, then drew in a deep breath.

Gus didn't take his eyes off her as he removed the crystal stopper, tilted the deep amethyst bottle, and dabbed a few drops onto her inner wrist. He blew delicately till the fragrance seeped into her skin, then raised her wrist to his lips to inhale the scent mixed with hers.

Farah's heart throbbed as she stared at the cloud of dark hair lowered over her hand. A soft smile played around her lips as he began feathering her wrist with kisses.

"Being in the presence of a beautiful woman who lives it naturally is a uniquely satisfying experience."

He raised his head and looked into her eyes.

"Beauty is an attitude. It's in her transcending existential passion. It glows through her fearsome soul, her strong mind and her amazing heart, ever-manifested in the delightful artistic act of being herself."

She tipped her head back. "Who said that?"

"Masoud Dawoudi, a Palestinian philosopher."

A raw shiver of desire ran through Farah. What would it be like to wake up in this man's arms?

They headed out of the hotel and wandered their way to the performance.

Verona enchanted Farah with its old cobblestone streets, gothic cathedral, and 2000-year-old Arena. Its hint of pink marble rendered it the same fairy tale quality Gus had lent to her life. Suddenly, a tremor of guilt shot through her. The sight of her mother falling came back to haunt her.

She shoved the unpleasant thoughts back into a dark deep hole and slammed the lid shut.

They walked down the red carpet, surrounded by a babble of different languages, and a crowd of international opera fans in evening gear. In step with Gus, Farah walked to the front row seats and waited while he fetched some champagne.

The gong sounded.

The spectacle unfolded, with hundreds of cast members and horses entering and leaving the stage.

The surreal experience proved riveting. Farah couldn't tear her eyes away from the show.

In the half-shadow of the moonlight, under a dazzling canopy of stars, divine voices soared to the heavens, while a zephyr stroked her cheeks.

Gus, eyes smoldering, leaned over and kissed her lips, his gentle hands cupped her face and caressed her hair.

Her pulse raced as heat radiated through her body.

THE DOUBLE-EDGED SWORD

When she tried to speak, he shushed her, wrapping his arm around her shoulders, and turning their attention back to the stage.

For the rest of the show, her face creased into a permanent grin.

After the last notes faded, deafening applause burst from the audience. The crowd began to disperse.

Gus took hold of her hand. They strolled across the first-century flagstones, past a life-size statue of Garibaldi mounted on his horse. Conversations and music drifted from the many restaurant tables spilling onto the square. Soft lights cast elongated shadows on the walkway as they headed back to the hotel.

Humming to herself, Farah bounced up the stairs. When they reached her suite, she handed him the key without hesitating, desire overtaking her.

He laughed, lifted her, and carried her inside.

She laced her arms around his neck and pressed her lips to his.

He stopped in front of the bed.

When she drew back, she glanced around. "Oh!"

Dozens of red roses covered nearly every space in the room, their delicate scent infusing the place.

Gus lowered her onto the bed and leaned over as their mouths met in an explosion of passion. "The night is still young," he whispered, and undid the zipper of her dress, his hands gliding down her back.

Enveloped in the afterglow of their lovemaking, Farah reached out for Gus's cigarette. She took a couple of puffs, laid her head contentedly on his chest, closed her eyes, and drifted into sleep.

The sound of the phone woke her with a jolt.

She rubbed her eyes and looked at her watch. "Hello?"

"Farah, thank goodness I found you."

"Monique? It's three-thirty in the morning."

"I'm really sorry. Cyril just rang me. Your parents are going berserk trying to reach you."

Farah's mouth went dry. She reached out and squeezed Gus's hand, her nails digging into his flesh. "Why?"

"I hate to be the one to break it to you, but your grandmother passed a few hours ago."

"*Teta* died?" said Farah in a small voice. She gulped back a sob. "No…"

"Farah?" said Monique on the other end.

She swallowed. "Thanks for letting me know," she said in a small voice, "I'll return to Cairo tomorrow." She hung up.

Gus wrapped his arms around her, his cheek pressed against her face. "I'm so sorry."

A wave of remorse shot through her. "I feel so bad. I didn't visit her last time I was in Cairo even though my dad suggested it. I snapped at him that I didn't have time." Farah's head hung, tears smarting her eyes. "How could I have been so selfish?"

Gus handed her a glass of water. "Drink." He stroked her cheek.

"I need to make travel arrangements." Farah blew her nose into a crumpled tissue.

"I'll get you back there by tomorrow. We can leave first thing in the morning."

"You can't come, Gus. They'll pick me up from the airport," she said in a matter-of-fact tone. Funny how she remained lucid in such a situation.

Gus pounded the side table cursing.

She darted into the bathroom, slammed the door, and scrubbed her teeth till her gums bled. There was no way she could ever bring Gus home at the best of times.

She returned to bed. "I didn't bring anything black with me."

"I'll buy you something once the shops open."

A few hours later, Gus flew her to Rome on his private jet.

As they made their way to the boarding gate, she broke down and clung to him. "I don't want to travel alone." Her voice cracked.

He hesitated for only a minute then shook his head, cupped her face, and trailed his fingers down her cheek, a brooding look in his dark eyes. "You know I can't."

She struggled to find the right words about what last night meant but they escaped her. She turned away, an ache in her throat.

They announced her flight.

She tore herself away from him and, heavy-footed, entered the jetway, waving over her shoulder to Gus.

***

The funeral took place the following day.
Her face tear-stained, Farah clutched at Cyril's arm as they climbed the steps leading into the church. Once they reached the top, they separated according to tradition. Cyril headed to the left, where the men sat, and Farah to the right to the women's section to join her mother, aunts, and cousins.

The coffin lay in front of the altar lengthwise, wreaths on either side. The loud sobs of her three aunts in the first pew filled the air. Farah's eyes drifted up to the icons hanging on the church walls as members of the Orthodox clergy chanted in Coptic in an atonal rhythm.

She glanced at the casket. Hard to believe *Teta* lay in there lifeless.

When Mass ended, a convoy of cars followed the hearse to the cemetery and stopped outside the family mausoleum, a plain edifice from the outside with an iron door which, once opened, revealed a structure divided into narrow cubicles.

Farah shuddered as her grandmother's coffin was slid into the space next to her husband.

The maids wailed, and Farah's youngest aunt screamed as she tried to reach for the box before the gate was closed. Tears rolled down Farah's cheeks. Her spine bowed, she covered her face with her hands. Her limbs felt so heavy she could hardly lift her legs. Cyril put his arm around her shoulders and squeezed her close.

She pulled out a tissue and wiped her eyes. "There's nothing comforting about the funerary rites here, is there? Not like in France.

Remember when *Mémé* died how beautiful the service was? And how peaceful the cemetery is? This is just awful."

Her brother nodded. "Different traditions, that's all."

Back in the family house, lunch was a somber affair. Farah wandered around the various rooms of the spacious villa remembering how her grandmother's keys used to jangle on her hip.

That evening, instead of joining the rest of the family in the sitting room as they received condolences, Farah sat in the orchard under the orange trees. A faint citrus scent lingered in the light spring breeze. *Teta* used to make bitter orange marmalade every year, a labor-intensive task that took up an entire day.

Arms hanging to her side, Farah struggled to process her pain. Thoughts of the sanctity of life and how fleeting it was crowded her mind.

Another scene rose before her; her own mother crying for her unborn child.

Farah covered her face with her hands and wept.

Chapter Twenty

Caesarea, Israel – June 1987

Moshe shut his bag, lifted it off the bed and placed it on the floor. He turned to his wife, his eyebrows raised, "Are you sure you don't want to come with me to Jordan? We could stay a couple of days longer, you know. Visit Jerash, maybe some of the castles?"

He hated traveling without Carla.

"If I'd known earlier, I could have planned it. But to decide last night that you're traveling today…" She opened a jar of hand cream, dabbed some on her hands, and rubbed them together.

"Well, The Israeli Civils Affairs Office only issued the travel permit for Ibrahim and the rest last night. It's only valid for a few days.

"I'll never get used to how this country is run. Anyway, I'll be able to spend time with Ruth."

Moshe's face broke into a smile. Two months after the wedding, their daughter had announced that she was expecting.

He reached for his wife. "Come, let's have a few minutes in the garden before I go."

Hand-in-hand they walked out and sat by the pool.

"What time are you meeting Ibrahim?"

"Eleven-thirty at the American Colony."

"How many people are going with him?"

"About fifteen with his brothers, uncles, and cousins. Some other cousins who live in Amman will be joining for the *Jaha*."

When Ibrahim had asked him to join them, Moshe agreed without second thoughts, honored to be included in such an important event.

Carla huffed a laugh. "Fancy so many people traveling to another country to make a marriage proposal."

"That's the tradition. And they consider Jordan almost like home. Half its parliamentarians are from the West Bank."

He glanced at his watch and rose from his chair. "I'd better leave in case there are any road blockades." He raised his eyes towards heaven. "The half-hour drive could turn into a few hours."

He kissed his wife and headed out.

The highway to Jerusalem, dotted with hills on either side, was a pleasant drive. Clusters of green trees scattered around the open landscape. Cars whizzed past, with no respect for the speed limit.

Moshe fiddled around with the radio channels for the latest news bulletin in case he needed to change routes due to some unforeseen incident. For once, everything was calm and he reached his destination on time. He parked and stepped inside the American Colony Hotel, one of the few oases of neutrality in Jerusalem, and made for the Courtyard Bistro.

It lay tucked in between leafy trees offering respite from the blazing eastern sun. The calming sound of water spouted from the central fountain with an air of Ottoman grandeur.

Conversations floated around, with French, Italian, and Spanish mingling with the usual English, Arabic, and Hebrew.

Expats, mainly from the United Nations, as well as upper-crust Palestinians and leftist Israelis, frequented the place.

Hussein's party sat in the far corner.

Moshe embraced the groom and his brothers with big hugs,

Palestinian style. After a hearty round of handshakes with all of Hussein's cousins and uncles, he was offered a coffee.

He turned to Hussein. "Ready, *ya 'Arees?*" he teased while the rest of the group joked at how finally someone had been able to wangle a commitment out of the family playboy.

Hussein grinned and smoothed his dark hair with one hand. "Eh, it had to happen at some point. So, it's a good thing I met Rola, otherwise…"

"As long as your mother approves of her, then you're all set."

Moshe's words produced a clap of laughter from the prospective bridegroom while everyone nodded in agreement. Arab mothers-in-law were a force to be reckoned with.

They spent a pleasant half-hour chatting then Hussein stood up. "We need to leave. If we get to Jericho in forty-five minutes, we can be at Allenby by two o'clock. After that, it's us and our luck with the crossing, depending on the mood of the Israeli officials."

Moshe wondered how the Israelis and Jordanians went about the coordination with Jordan still refusing to recognize the Israeli occupation since 1967. [2]

At the crossing, Moshe had to enter from the one side and the

---

[2] In June 1988, the Arab League gave the PLO financial control of support for the Palestinians, thereby virtually acknowledging 'Arafāt as their spokesman. In response, King Ḥussein renounced all Jordanian claims to the West Bank, allowing the PLO to assume full responsibility there. He dissolved the Jordanian parliament (half of whose members were West Bank representatives), ceased salary payments to 21,000 West Bank civil servants, and ordered that West Bank Palestinian passports be converted to two-year travel documents. When the Palestine National Council recognized the PLO as the sole legal representative of the Palestinian people and proclaimed the independence of a purely notional Palestine on Nov. 15, 1988, King Ḥussein immediately extended recognition to the Palestinian entity.

https://www.britannica.com/place/Jordan/Renouncing-claims-to-the-West-Bank

Palestinians from another.

Unsmiling, armed Israeli police and immigration officials at the border control filled the place with fingerprints of military occupation.

He handed his U.S. passport to the immigration official, grateful to his father-in-law who had insisted that he remain in the States till he got naturalized.

"Moshe Avram?" She smiled. "*N'siah tovah,*" she said and handed him back the passport.

Moshe pocketed the document. "*Toda.*"

I bet my last shekel no one's telling Ibrahim 'Have a good trip'.

It didn't take much of an imagination to guess the rough time the Radwanis must be having. Hadn't he seen for himself how Arab Israelis were treated at Ben Gurion airport, intimidated and harassed? Even though they carried Israeli passports, they were still considered second-class citizens.

He opened his bottle of water and took a sip.

On the other side, a young Palestinian man, his shoulders slumped forward, waved a European passport as if entreating the officer.

The stony-faced official looked through him as if the young man didn't exist.

Moshe, ignoring orders from security to stop, dashed across to find out what was happening.

A member of the Military Police grabbed his arm.

Moshe turned to him with narrowed eyes. "Let go right now." He spoke in Hebrew almost spitting out the words.

The official shuffled back a step.

Moshe looked at the young Palestinian. "What's the problem?"

"We're visiting from Norway. They let my wife and my son enter but they're refusing to let me through. I have my son's medication with me. He'll suffer severe complications if he doesn't get it and it isn't available in Ramallah." Lines of worry covered the young man's face.

Moshe turned to the official and spoke in Hebrew. "He has a Norwegian passport. Why aren't you letting him in?"

The official folded his arms across his chest, his legs apart. "Orders," he said, curtly.

"Orders to stop European citizens from entering the country? Who gave such orders?"

The official ignored him.

Moshe glared at the official before addressing the young Palestinian. "Give me the medicine." He put out his hand. "And your address in case your wife has gone ahead. I'll make sure it reaches them."

The young man, his hands shaking, took the medication from his bag. "Thank you."

Moshe headed to the Entry booth and handed in his passport at the counter. The Radwanis probably still had a couple of hours ahead of them until the Israelis let them through.

The official took one look and pushed the passport back. "You can't re-enter. You just exited."

Did they enjoy being difficult?

Moshe narrowed his eyes, and, with one swift movement, slammed his Israeli id card on the counter. "Oh yes, I can. Don't you dare treat me like you do the Palestinians. *I know my rights very well.*"

The young official stared at Moshe, opened his mouth to say something but closed it again. Scowling, he allowed Moshe back into the Arrivals terminal.

Moshe scanned the area. His eyes fell on a forlorn young woman matching the man's description of his wife. She clutched a two-year-old close to her chest, her eyebrows drawn together, craning her neck to peer at new arrivals.

"Excuse me, I think this is yours." He handed her the bag of medicine. "It seems the Israelis are being difficult and won't allow your husband into the country."

The young woman's shoulders drooped. Tears rolled down her cheeks. "We haven't seen our families for two years. My husband's father is dying. He came to say goodbye."

Moshe clenched his jaw, then muttered a few words of comfort before turning away, his cheeks burning.

The female official at the booth who had waved him through the exit the first time stared at him with raised eyebrows.

Moshe placed his palms on the counter. "Emergency."

She let him through.

There was no sign of Ibrahim and the rest.

"I came in with a group of Palestinians. How long will it take for them to come through?" he asked the young Israeli standing at the gate.

The guy glowered at him as he escorted Moshe to a small bus waiting to drive them across the Allenby Bridge, over the Jordan River.

"I'm waiting for the rest of my party, but they haven't come through yet," repeated Moshe.

"What party? There's no one else in the Departure terminal."

"Not this one, but the side the Palestinians go through."

The driver's face darkened. "You'll see them on the other side," he said abruptly, "we need to go now. Get on the bus. You can't wait around here."

Moshe clenched his jaw, grabbed his bag, and climbed into the minibus muttering to himself.

Before he knew it, they were already on the Jordanian side, without even time for a thought.

Within a few minutes, his passport was stamped by smiling Jordanians and he was waved through.

"When will the next busload of Palestinians arrive?" he asked one of the officials as he exited the terminal.

"My friend, go to your hotel because you could end up waiting for a few hours."

Moshe hesitated then decided to wait. Pity there was nowhere he could sit down and have a meal until the others came through.

Two hours later, the rest of his party appeared.

Ibrahim clapped him on the shoulder. "They try to break us – but it only helps build our resilience. Come on, my friend, let's shake off the dust of this place and do what we came to do."

Chapter Twenty-one

Amman, Jordan – June 1987

Gus opened the door of the navy Mercedes and Farah slipped into the back seat. He shut her door then slid in next to the driver, a cigarette dangling from his mouth. The driver pressed on the gas as they made for Jerash, one of the best-preserved Greco-Roman cities that existed, located half an hour north of Amman.

Gus turned to face her, a mischievous smile playing around his mouth. "So, what excuse did you give your sister this time?"

Farah rolled her eyes. "I told her that since she had a Bible Study, I'd go shopping. But it's hard finding reasons to go out without her insisting on accompanying me."

"Nothing we can do about it."

"No." It was too early to broach the subject with Tammy.

He shrugged. "I'm not complaining. I knew the deal when you agreed to come."

She rolled down her window. "It's so weird that you're going to meet my brother-in-law this evening. We don't have this tradition in Egypt. When a guy wants to propose, he goes with his parents and siblings, not the entire clan." Suddenly, a thought occurred to her. "Gus, does Layth know that Jamal is my brother-in-law?"

"I never mentioned it."

"Why does Layth dislike me so much?"

Gus whipped his head around. "Why do you say that?"

"It's just that he's always so unpleasant to me whenever he sees me."

Gus's face darkened. "It's nothing personal, Farah. Layth is very… family-oriented."

"What? And I'm the outsider so he has to always remind me of that?"

He reached out for her hand. "Don't let it worry you, *ma chérie*."

"As long as he doesn't let on that he knows me. My sister would grill me. I don't want to deal with that now."

It didn't take long to reach their destination. Traffic in Jordan was light, unlike Paris and Cairo.

They trapaised around the ruins then made their way to Hadrian's Triumphal Arch through the Colonnaded Street. Tourists of different nationalities strolled across the site voicing their admiration.

Gus pointed towards the left. "Do you know that not far from here there are two Palestinian refugee camps? People fled there after '48 and '67."

The mention of refugee camps reminded her of what Mariam Radwani had witnessed in Lebanon. Farah shivered. That was one place she *never* wanted to step foot in.

***

Gus returned to the hotel, reviewed some files then took a siesta. What a pity Farah wasn't here next to him.

The alarm went off two hours later. He hauled himself up.

It had been a good idea to come to Amman without prior warning and see how the office was operating. Though very different to Beirut before the war, Amman was pleasant in its own way.

He took out a clean shirt from the drawer and jumped into the shower.

The *Jaha* promised to be interesting, mainly because he would meet the Jerusalem branch of the Radwani family. And of course, Jamal Radwani, Farah's brother-in-law.

Shower done, Gus slipped into a black pair of trousers and was buttoning his shirt when someone rapped at the door. He opened.

Layth walked in dressed in a smart grey pinstripe suit.

"Ghassan, aren't you ready yet?" Layth crossed his arms. "I don't want to be late." He picked a banana from the fruit bowl, peeled it, then dug his teeth into the fruit. "It's important to Tarek that we be there before the bridegroom and his party."

"You said we had to be there by 8.00. It's only 6.30 for goodness' sake. It can't be more than a twenty-minute drive if that."

"It's just that Tarek needs the support – he only has one uncle. And it seems Hussein Radwani is accompanied by half his tribe for the *Jaha*. The groom's family have to know that Rola also has *rejala waraha* – support of male relatives– even if her father's dead." He glanced in the mirror and adjusted his tie. "I'll be in the coffee shop waiting."

In fifteen minutes, Gus, dressed in a black suit and a flashy silk tie of blues and greens, joined his cousin. Together they made for the car.

Fifteen minutes later, Layth rang the bell. A maid answered the door and led them to the sitting room where Tarek and his uncle waited.

"*Habibi. Alf Mabruk, inshallah,*" said Layth, offering his congratulation as he embraced his friend before shaking hands with the uncle.

He introduced Gus. "Ghassan Khodeib, My cousin."

They shook hands and Gus was offered a seat.

Gus sat down in an armchair and glanced in appreciation at the colorful display of expensive crystals in the glass cabinet.

The bride-to-be brought them coffee in delicate white cups with golden Arabic calligraphy decorating the outside.

According to tradition, since the young lady was already in

agreement, she should not appear when Hussein with his family came to formally ask for her hand. This was an affair between the men now.

The Radwani party soon arrived.

When everyone was settled in their seat, Gus threw a discreet look at a slim man in his late thirties with straight brown hair, thin lips, and a slightly hooked nose. So that was Jamal Radwani, Farah's brother-in-law.

The lady of the house offered coffee.

Ibrahim cleared his throat. As Hussein's older brother, his role was to formally ask for the bride's hand in the presence of her male relatives.

He addressed the bride's uncle as the oldest male family member present. "We would like to suggest that the wedding take place here in Amman in six months' time if you find that agreeable. I know the bride and groom would have it next week if they could."

Everyone laughed, and Hussein's eyes gleamed.

Ibrahim placed his coffee cup back on the table. "But we need some time for preparations to receive our esteemed new bride in Jerusalem."

The bride's brother and uncle glanced at each other then nodded.

"That sounds reasonable," said the uncle.

A date was set. Faces lit up with smiles as the men stood up and shook hands to seal the matter. The bride's mother placed her hand above her lips and let out a loud ululation.

Gus mingled with the guests repeating the congratulatory *'Alf Mabruk.'*

Jamal Radwani raised his voice. "In honor of the future bride and groom, everyone is invited to my house tomorrow evening for dinner."

Gus turned to the middle-aged man next to him. "The groom looks like he's in seventh heaven."

The man laughed. "He does indeed."

Gus stretched his hand to the stranger. "Ghassan Khodeib."

"Moussa," said the stranger, with a firm handshake. "Looks like the happy couple won't have to wait too long."

Gus nodded. How was he related to the groom? "Are you one of the cousins who live here?"

"No. We all crossed over today."

Gus took out a packet of cigarettes and offered the man one. "Do you come over to Amman often?"

The dark man shook his head. "First time, actually. And yourself?"

Gus swallowed his surprise. "I'm visiting from Paris. So, you're based in Jerusalem?"

"No, actually I –"

Just then, Ibrahim Radwani appeared, his face beaming. "Moshe."

Gus's back stiffened. Was this man *Israeli*? With an imperceptible flinch, he forced his lips into a smile. "Moshe? I thought you said Moussa?"

Ibrahim, oblivious of the tension, chuckled. "Moshe, Moussa – when it comes to Moshe, *kollo nefs el shi*." Ibrahim gave his friend a clap on the back. "Moshe is family."

Gus cracked his knuckles with his thumb.

Ibrahim sauntered off to talk to the bride's uncle, leaving Gus and the stranger together again.

"So, you're not related to the groom?" Gus's voice was smooth despite the palpitating pain shooting through the right side of his stomach.

"No. I'm a close friend."

Anger coursed through Gus's veins. He had *shaken hands* with an Israeli.

His fists clenched, Gus nodded politely, and, with a vague excuse, walked away, not trusting himself to remain calm. He grabbed Layth. Within minutes, they left.

Pale moonlight filtered through the window shield. The only sound from the back seat was the worry beads in Gus's hand, as he clicked away furiously. The string snapped, and the aquamarine stones rolled over the seat and onto the floor of the vehicle. Gus brushed away the ones clinging to his suit.

Layth opened the window. "I'm sorry, Ghassan. I had no idea."

Gus raised a hand to silence him. He narrowed his eyes and stared ahead, specters from the shambled past rising up to haunt him.

There was no escape. The die had been cast in Beirut that fatal morning five years ago after Israel invaded Lebanon.

Chapter Twenty-two

Next morning, Farah stepped into the midst of a heated argument between Tammy and Jamal in the kitchen. Her sister scowled as she clattered pots and pans on the counter.

Farah sat down and helped herself to some cereal. "What's happening?"

Tammy threw her hands up in the air and glared at her husband who leaned against the counter, his arms folded. "Jamal has invited everyone, *everyone*, over for dinner tonight."

Jamal raised his eyes to the ceiling. "It's a special family occasion." He shook his head and walked out.

"What are you talking about?" said Farah.

"I mean everyone from the *Jaha* last night. So, not only the family but Hussein's future in-laws as well. And apparently, some friends of theirs too, to celebrate the engagement."

Farah's hand stopped mid-air. She put her spoon back in the dish, her muscles rigid. Did that mean Gus was coming here tonight? Should she avoid the dinner?

Tammy opened the fridge, grabbed the milk, then slammed it shut. "I'll be busy for the rest of the day, Farah. You'll have to sort yourself out. Sorry."

"Do you need a hand?"

"Thanks, but you'll just be in the way. I'm afraid I wasn't expecting to have to feed the multitudes."

"Umm, don't worry about it."

Farah gobbled down her breakfast and slipped out of the house before her sister changed her mind.

She hailed a cab to Gus's hotel, breezed through the reception, and knocked at his room.

He opened the door. "Oh, you're early."

"I escaped Tammy's wrath."

"Wrath?"

"I hear my brother-in-law invited everyone for dinner tonight. I guess that includes you."

Gus strode over to the coffee machine. His hands jerked as he picked up a cup. It fell with a soft thud on the carpet. He muttered something under his breath.

Farah raised her eyebrows. "Excuse me?" He had never been so agitated.

"No, don't worry. I won't be going tonight."

"Why not?"

"I thought you wouldn't want me to go?"

She stared at him indignantly. "I didn't say that."

Gus shrugged. "Just teasing you. I need to finish some work. Layth will go, of course."

Farah drew in a sharp breath. She didn't trust Layth. *He'll probably let it slip that he knows me then pretend it was a mistake.* Gus would be annoyed if she brought it up again, but...

His voice cut through her thoughts. "I know what you're thinking. I promise you Layth won't open his mouth."

Though unconvinced, she dropped the matter and they headed for the pool.

The morning sun blazed down, and the pool area was quite crowded. The staff rushed forward to set up an umbrella and chaise lounges for them in a corner.

Farah plunged into the water to cool off. Why was Gus so distracted today?

When she climbed out, a Mojito was already waiting for her.

"You never even mentioned what happened at the *Jaha*," she said, as she sipped her drink.

His face darkened. "Nothing to tell. Just a normal *Jaha*."

"Okay." She checked her watch. "I'm going to need to leave soon. I'll have to help Tammy set the table."

This time he didn't try to persuade her to stay a bit longer.

***

At the sound of cars parking in front of the house, Farah peeked through the window. Jamal stood outside, shaking hands with his cousins and uncles.

The Radwani clan entered amidst chatter and laughter.

Ibrahim took Tammy in his arms. "Tammy, so wonderful to see you. And thank you for this invitation. So kind of you."

Tammy kissed him on the cheek. "We're so glad you could make it, Ibrahim."

Farah repressed a snort and walked up to him. His jaw dropped. "My goodness, Farah, I haven't seen you in ages. Quite the young lady, now."

She hugged him, then went on to greet the rest of the guests. The only ones she knew were Hussein and his younger brother Majid.

She looked around, curious to meet the woman whom Hussein had fallen for. "Where's the bride?"

Hussein winked. "On her way."

Farah went into the kitchen to fetch a bottle of *Araq*, ice, and glasses.

The doorbell rang.

Hussein sprung up and rushed to open.

A young woman with dark, shoulder-length hair, and wearing a teal knee-length dress stepped in, her long gold earrings jingling.

Farah gaped. She looked like Rita Hayworth.

"*Marhaba*," said Rola as she walked into the sitting room, followed by her mother, brother, and uncle. A minute later, Layth appeared behind them, a smile on his usually sullen face.

Hussein introduced his fiancée and her family to Tammy and Farah.

When it was Layth's turn, he raised Tammy's hand to his lips. "Thank you so much for inviting me."

Farah's mouth dropped open. Layth *did* have manners after all – when he wanted.

A small laugh tittered through Tammy's lips. "Our pleasure. This is my sister Farah."

Layth didn't even bother to extend a hand. He gave a curt nod then he moved to the other side of the room.

Farah clenched her teeth.

Tammy tapped her shoulder. "Farah, can you see to their drinks, please?"

When it was Layth's turn to be served, she extended the tray without any eye contact.

Not so with Hussein's fiancée who offered a smile that would brighten up a moonless night.

"Would you like a glass of *Araq* or something else?" asked Farah, warming to the attractive young woman.

Rola fluttered her eyelashes. "Better not shock the elders so soon," she laughed mischievously and tilted her head in the direction of Hussein's uncles. "A soft drink will do fine."

Farah grinned and went to fetch one.

Soon after, Jamal invited everyone to the table where a roast lamb lay in the middle, encircled by a medley of dishes.

He raised his glass with the traditional Arabic toast on such occasions. "To Rola and Hussein, *bil rifaq wel baneen, inshallah.*" Wishing you prosperity and good descendance.

To Farah's relief, Layth was at the other end, next to Jamal. She had no clue who the other gentleman sitting opposite Layth was, but from his facial expressions, it was obvious he was passionate about what he was saying.

She leaned towards Majid, Hussein's younger brother, who sat next to her, and gestured with her head. "Is that one of your cousins?"

"No, that's Moshe, Ibrahim's best friend."

"Moshe? That's a strange name."

"It's the Jewish version of Moses," said Majid as he cut up the slice of roast lamb on his plate.

"Jewish?" Farah spun her head around, a puzzled frown on her face. "I don't understand. Do you mean he's Israeli?"

"He has an Israeli passport, but he's on our side."

Confused, Farah didn't answer. There were Israelis who sided with the Palestinians?

With everyone talking at once, it was difficult to follow any conversation. She looked over to the man again. Layth sat immobile, his eyes fixed on the stranger as he listened.

At one point, Moshe's voice rose, drowning everyone else's. "It's going to happen but no one will listen."

Suddenly everyone went quiet. All attention turned to Moshe.

"What's going to happen?" Farah whispered to Majid.

"Ask him."

Layth's voice cut across. "You can only blame yourselves."

Ibrahim quickly intervened. "You mean the Israeli government. Moshe is fighting the system as much as he can."

Moshe picked up his glass. "The problem is that when it does happen, the consequences on the younger generation will be horrendous. Children are always the victims because they are the most vulnerable."

There was a moment of silence broken only by the sound of cutlery placed on plates.

"You're right," said Layth in a grim voice, "the children *are* the most vulnerable. And the world needs to do something to protect them."

Farah's mouth fell open. This was certainly an evening of surprises. An Israeli who sympathized with the Palestinian cause, and Layth who not only turned out to have manners, but also a heart.

Chapter Twenty-three

Washington D.C. - June 1987

Justin sat in his office and stared at the phone for a long time. *Mom was right all along.*

He pulled his address book from the drawer, picked up the receiver, and dialed a number he once knew by heart.

A female answered but the voice kept cutting in and out on the trans-Atlantic call.

He braced himself not knowing what to expect. "May I speak to Farah Gabriel, please?"

"Sorry, but she's not on duty now. Can I take a message?"

Relief flooded through him. *At least she's still in Paris and still in the same job.* "No thank you. I'll ring back later. Can you please tell me when she'll be in?"

"Hold on, let me check." She put him on hold with some elevator music in the background. "Farah's on morning duty this week and next."

Justin ran his fingers through his hair contemplating his next step. He glanced out of the window at the cloudless blue sky as he twirled a pen in his hand.

It had been more than a year since he had last spoken to Farah. What a fool he had been to think that his feelings would fade with time.

God only knew how she must have felt when he had vanished without a word of explanation. All the deliberations, the agonizing waiting he had gone through flooded his mind making him wince. He had been so sure everything would work out and he would be able to surprise her with good news. Even when time had run out, he kept giving himself another day till it was too late. His chest tightened at the thought of her green eyes filled with pain.

The dozens of letters he had written asking for her forgiveness, telling her he would explain everything when he saw her, still littered his drawer.

Justin shut his eyes and rolled his neck around. The office clock pointed to eleven. An idea formed in his mind. He rose, picked a leave request, filled it out, and strode towards his boss's office.

His boss peered at him through his glasses. "You want all of next week off?"

"Yes, something's come up unexpectedly."

His boss nodded and signed the form.

Back at his desk, Justin tried to concentrate on the report he was writing but his eyes kept darting to the clock – time crawled.

At one o'clock sharp he rushed out, the office door swinging shut behind him. With an adamant step, Justin headed towards the travel agency around the corner. To his good luck, the place was almost empty. He approached the first available agent.

"I want a roundtrip ticket to Paris, please."

"Sure, sir. May I know your dates?"

"I want to leave Friday night. Return the following Saturday."

That way there would be time to recover from jet lag before starting work on Monday.

The agent made some phone calls, then held the receiver far from his ear. "I'm sorry, sir. The flight on Friday night is full. Would Saturday night do?"

Justin let out an annoyed stream of air. Of course, flights were always full in summer. He nodded.

The travel agent wrote the flight details on the ticket.

Justin placed it in his pocket and went to grab a bite, his mind already on the City of Light.

***

Paris – June 1987

Farah stood in the office and stared at the letter in her hand, an ache at the back of her throat. Why hadn't she reported Elise?

She crumpled the letter unsure what to do.

Elise walked in with Lucien, little peals of laughter escaping her lips.

Farah whipped her head around, stomped over, and shoved the letter under Elise's nose. "So, you finally managed it, didn't you?"

"What do you mean?" Elise stared at her wide-eyed.

"Cut your innocent act. I know it was you."

"You know it was her what, Farah?" asked Lucien, placing himself between them.

"Ask Elise. She acts as if butter wouldn't melt in her mouth but in fact–"

A fleeting look of satisfaction crossed Elise's face but she quickly shook her head. "I've no idea what she's talking about, Lucien."

Farah stared at her in disgust. "I *saw* the letters, Elise. With my own eyes. In your drawer."

"What letters?" Lucien's eyes darted from one to the other.

Farah placed her hand on her hip. "Tell him."

"I've no idea what you're talking about."

An overwhelming desire to wring Elise's neck swept over Farah. She took a step closer, her eyes screwed up. "You wretched—"

Eric walked out of his office. "What's going on here?" He faced Farah with an accusing look. "I assume you got the letter?"

Farah nodded, averting her look. She opened her mouth to denounce Elise but Eric strode past.

Her shoulders slumped. She hesitated for a moment then strode over to the counter, filled out a sick leave form, and placed it in Eric's tray. The toxic environment suffocated her. Farah grabbed her bag and raced to the door, her eyes stinging.

Instead of going home, she headed to the Jardin du Luxembourg.

Her fingernails biting into her palms, Farah trudged past a bevy of statues of kings and queens of France, turbulent thoughts shooting through her mind.

The soothing sound of water bubbled through the monumental fountain.

If only it were easy to find another job here, but with an American degree, her chances were minimal. And not many companies needed Arabic speakers. It had taken her several months before she was offered the job with the VIP Lounge. There was no way she could afford to remain jobless now.

And none of the acting academies she had applied to had responded. With this demotion, she wouldn't even be able to save up.

Maybe Gus, with all his high-up contacts, could put in a word with someone more senior than Eric?

She straightened her back and rubbed her hands together.

Eventually, Farah headed towards the metro, stopping at a phone booth to call Gus. He offered to pick her up from her place in an hour.

***

Paris – June 1987

Justin sat upright in the café his knee bouncing. How would Farah react when he showed up at her door? He glanced at his watch, drained his cup, placed some francs on the table, and strode out.

The Quartier Latin swarmed with tourists. He threaded his way across to the Seine. The sun sparkled on the rippling currents and the Notre Dame Cathedral stood resplendent on the other side of the river. Yet Justin barely spared a glance.

He jumped into the metro and exited at Place de la Concorde. He preferred to walk the rest of the way. His stomach in a knot, Justin made for Farah's place.

According to his estimation, she should be arriving home within the next half hour.

In spite of himself, he chuckled as he walked past the obelisk. Farah had always argued that the French army under Napoleon had made off with it when they departed from Egypt. Funny how she could argue for either side, France or Egypt, with all the passion she possessed, depending on her mood.

The Champs Elysees crawled with tourists, with hardly a French word to be heard.

He found a bench not far from her building, stretched his legs and closed his eyes as he inhaled a calming breath.

He replayed his time with Farah in Paris two years earlier, how they had rushed upstairs with impatience after he had picked her up from the airport. She had been so alive, so full of *joie de vivre*.

Had she changed?

The first time he had seen her was at the student production of Caesar and Cleopatra at the American University in Cairo. She had been playing the part of the Egyptian queen. The long black and gold dress with a snake—headed crown over her dyed black hair, flowing to her shoulders, had rendered her an air of majestic magnificence in the final scene.

That same evening, mutual friends introduced them as they stood on a busy street, cars zooming past. A never-ending stream of people crowded the pavements with some *kamikazes* attempting to cross the busy road. Farah had been eating a *shawarma* sandwich with *tahini* dribbling down her chin. Justin had suppressed a laugh at how only a couple of hours earlier, she had been a queen on stage.

When they began dating, Justin had confessed that as he had watched her flit around on stage, he had thought to himself how nice it would be to go out with a girl like her - so dainty and fairy-like.

He glanced at his watch again. Surely, she must be arriving home soon?

A flurry of movement approaching the entrance made him squint. A group of schoolchildren and their mothers blocked his view.

Irritated, he clicked his tongue, stood up, and crossed over.

Too late. Several people had already entered the building, with only their silhouettes visible.

Had Farah been among them? Should he go up and ring the bell? Probably best to give her enough time to unwind before he appeared in front of her like a ghost.

Justin ran his hand through his hair, pacing up and down on the pavement.

An increasing number of cars whizzed past.

Then he caught sight of her.

She sailed out of the building and onto the street, her hair up, her eyes scanning the traffic.

His heart palpitated. He walked towards her.

A white Porsche drew up, and Farah jumped in. She offered her lips to the dark-haired man behind the wheel. They kissed a slow, long kiss, her hand traveling down the man's face before they drove off.

Justin stood in his spot, his arms slack at the side. He slumped forward slightly, his chest aching, and clenched his fists. He wanted to punch the wall. Punch this guy. Punch himself.

It took him a few minutes before he was able to move away, his steps jerky.

I guess all I can do is wish her happiness and hope this man doesn't hurt her.

Tomorrow he'd call the airline and change his ticket.

THE DOUBLE-EDGED SWORD

***

Gus reached for Farah's hand as they sauntered down the Jardins de Tuileries. "You haven't said much since you got into the car. What's wrong?"

A light summer breeze ruffled through the leaves of the trees lining both sides of the path.

He led her to an empty bench.

Farah chewed her lip. How should she start the conversation? In a halting voice, she recounted all what had happend.

"I can't handle work anymore. I thought Elise was my friend, but she was backstabbing me all the time." She rubbed her hand down her trousers. "And now I'm no longer in the VIP lounge. I'm back at the check-in counters downstairs, and I hate it."

Gus fingered a set of opal worry beads while he listened. "What do you want to do?"

She shrugged. "There's nothing I can do." *Unless you pull strings.*

"If you want your job back, you'll have it. But is this really a career? It's not like you have ambitions to climb the promotion ladder. Suppose you return to the VIP lounge, then what?"

She opened her mouth but he silenced her with his raised hand. "You talk about saving up to go to Acting School. No matter how much you save up, you still wouldn't be able to afford it. From what you've told me, none of your attempts for scholarships or grants has been successful."

"I'll keep applying —"

"That's *not* the point. Acting is a dirty *milieu*. If a director will only give you a part on condition that you sleep with him, what would you do?"

Her lips curled downwards. It had occurred to her, of course, though she had brushed it aside, preferring to ignore it.

"You wouldn't be able to handle it." His eyes scorching her, he took a deep breath before pulling out his wallet from his back pocket. He opened it, extracted a golden credit card, and placed it in her hand. "You needn't worry about money, Farah. At all."

She stared at the card uncomprehendingly then raised questioning eyes to him.

"You don't need to work, Farah. Move in with me."

Move in with you? You mean shack up?

Farah looked down at the card again and frowned. Her stomach churned. His implication made her feel cheap.

For an Arab, this was the gallant thing to do, as long as it was within the confines of marriage. Provide for the woman so she wouldn't have to work.

Neither her mother nor her aunts had worked after they got married.

Except Gus hadn't mentioned marriage.

"You don't need to answer me straight away. Think about it then decide."

She clenched her teeth onto her lower lip, then handed the card back to him, her face burning.

"Keep it. I insist." Gus pushed her hand away and stood up. "Come on, we'll go have lunch somewhere."

She shook her head. "I'm sorry. I don't feel like it. I want to go home."

Gus drove her back. When they arrived, he reached for her hand and pressed it to his lips, his dark eyes burrowing into hers. She gave him a vacant stare then struggled to take off the seat belt before bolting into her building, barely bidding him goodbye.

Disconcerted by the turn of events, Farah spent the rest of the evening mulling over Gus's offer, his implicit condition, and the deception it would involve.

As she paced up and down her flat, Farah weighed the pros and cons. *Acting in exchange for him. But would he propose? And what about her family?*

Her father would never accept her marrying a Moslem. It would be a choice she would have to make. Her own mother had married outside the Protestant faith, and even though she had married an Orthodox

Christian, Farah's grandfather had disowned his own daughter.

Shacking up, on the other hand, would mean lying to her family. If they ever found out…

A cold chill slithered down her spine at the thought of her father's reaction. The thought of his green eyes flashing with anger made her squirm. Would he too disown her?

The next morning, Farah arrived at work her mood glum, with a ton of make-up to cover the dark rings under her eyes. She slipped behind the check-in counter, conscious of the unfriendly stares around her.

The unspoken rivalry between staff in the VIP Lounge and those at the counter downstairs always bristled, with everyone striving to be promoted to the upper floor.

The mortification of having to go back down after reaching the coveted VIP lounge seeped through Farah's body.

The day dragged on. Muttering under her breath, Farah called Elise an assortment of insulting names. The only option was to find another job. There *had* to be something she could do to escape this drudgery.

She took the papers home that evening. Over the next few days, she sent out her CV to a dozen companies, her hopes high.

For the following two weeks, Farah did her best to be pleasant to her new colleagues, smiling constantly and showing interest in them but was met with cold stares. She even baked a cake and brought it in, only for no one to taste it.

It was so hurtful how they all ganged up against her, snubbing any attempt at friendliness from her side. There was no one to chit-chat or share a joke with during breaks. A deep sense of loneliness overcame her at the lack of connection as if she were a pariah.

Gus rang her several times suggesting they meet. Each time she put him off, pleading a physical ailment.

On Friday afternoon, following a particularly hectic morning, Farah was checking in a well-dressed middle-aged woman. The passenger checked in her suitcase. Farah overlooked the few kilos overweight. She was handing the woman her boarding pass when she caught sight of an extra piece of hand luggage.

"I'm sorry, Madam, but you're only allowed one piece of hand luggage. I'll have to check one in for you in the hold, and you'll have to pay excess baggage for that."

The woman glared at her and snatched the boarding pass out of Farah's hand. "You'd already seen it. Why are you making a fuss now?"

"Madam, please. These are the rules. If I allow you, then I have to allow everyone."

The woman picked up her two bags and walked away, ignoring Farah's protests.

"What's happening?" Isabelle, one of her new colleagues, approached.

"That woman who just left. She -" Farah eyed Isabelle warily. She was a close friend of Elise.

"Yes?"

"She's got an extra bag with her she wouldn't check-in."

"Don't you know the policy? Management is very strict when it comes to excess baggage. Why did you let her get away? You're not working in the VIP Lounge anymore, you know."

Farah cowed at her sneering tone. "I'll handle it at the boarding gate," she mumbled.

Isabelle and another colleague smirked.

Her cheeks burning, Farah turned to the next passenger. Judging by the length of the queue, she'd have to work super-fast so the flight could leave on time.

At the departure gate, Farah and Isabelle checked the boarding passes before allowing the passengers to board the flight.

"Whoa. What's this?" Isabelle glared first at the lady with the two carry-on bags then at Farah.

The woman pointed a well-manicured finger at Farah. "She said it was okay."

Isabel turned to Farah accusingly. "Don't you know it's against the rules?"

"I did—"

Another colleague scurried up to them. "Can you hurry up, please? The captain is complaining that at this rate, the take-off will be delayed."

"He can thank Farah for that. I have to clean up her mess," Isabelle snapped.

Farah swallowed hard. She looked at her watch. For the flight to depart on time all passengers should be on the plane in eight minutes. This was no joke. Any tardiness, especially due to check-in matters, had grave consequences that impacted the take-off of not just this flight but other flights as well.

Farah waved the woman through.

"I didn't say she could go," Isabel raised her voice.

Farah clenched her jaw. "Just let her go, for goodness' sake," she hissed between her teeth. "Better have a passenger with an extra bag than face an angry Captain."

"I'm going to report you." Isabelle turned away.

Farah's stomach sank. Would she be demoted to cleaning the toilets now?

Miraculously, the flight took off on time. Farah headed upstairs to the office, her stomach muscles tight. She grabbed a piece of paper and jotted down her resignation.

Elise pretended not to see her as she swept past the lounge reception desk, her chin high. She knocked on Eric's door and went in.

"Yes?"

Farah cleared her throat and handed Eric her letter of resignation.

He read it, put it aside, and continued with what he had been doing without giving her a second look.

Her chest hurt. She spun around and walked out, not pausing to say goodbye to Lucien. Though he tried to stop her, she brushed past, anger propelling her forward. There was no turning back now.

Chapter Twenty-four

Tel Aviv – July 1987

Moshe crouched down before his sister, patted her curly hair, and cooed gently into her ear.

Rebecca's chest heaved up and down, sobbing, the sound filling the living room. She hunched forward, her tear-stained face buried in her hands, her plump body shaking.

Avi had just announced his engagement.

Avi's behavior has been so erratic lately. We should have guessed…

Rebecca wrung her hands. "I just can't believe it. How can he marry a Zionist like her? Where did I go wrong?"

Moshe cast a fleeting glance at her husband, Benjamin. Would he voice an opinion this time or as usual remain silent? A small pang ran through Moshe's conscience at his frustration with his brother-in-law.

Benjamin was a holocaust survivor, interred in Dachau with his family as a child. His parents were killed there. He had arrived in Palestine alone as a traumatized adolescent right after the end of World War II. The British sent him to a camp, with thousands of other Jews escaping the horrors of Nazi Germany.

He was a quiet man, but on the rare occasion he talked about his time in the concentration camp, the atrocities he related made Moshe's skin crawl.

Benjamin looked on, his bald head shining. Hands clasped together over his beer belly, he rocked back and forth in the wooden rocking chair.

What his sister had seen in such a man was beyond Moshe, but somehow the marriage had worked. Did Benjamin's passivity have anything to do with Avi's current political inclinations? Or had Avi just fallen in with the wrong people?

Once upon a time, Jews, Moslems, and Christians lived together at peace in a land we all loved. Before the rise of Zionism.

Moshe raised a glass of water to his sister's lips. "Drink."

She thrust it away.

Moshe stroked Rebecca's face. "Please calm down. Crying won't solve anything," he said in a gentle voice. If only David or Nathan were here to give their sister the support she needed.

But David was traveling abroad, while Nathan and Rachel were attending the Bar Mitzvah of the only son of Nathan's business partner.

"I can understand she's upset but what can we do?" Benjamin's voice cut through his wife's loud weeping.

"A settler? A settler? Zionist, violent, belligerent, and intolerant. The entire family is like that. What does he see in her? I just don't get it." Rebecca sobbed even harder.

Moshe pursed his lips together, suppressing his desire to call his nephew an idiot in front of his parents. He turned to Benjamin. "Which settlement?"

"Qiryat Arba," said his brother-in-law.

Moshe exhaled a loud puff of air. He hadn't been to Hebron in years.

The hotbed for the Israeli-Palestinian conflict, of immense spiritual value to both, the place simmered like a pressure cooker constantly on the verge of exploding.

Yossi, his girlfriend Judith, and their friends gave him first-hand accounts since Peace Now activists regularly went to Hebron to monitor and report what the settlers were doing there.

Judith's face had crumpled as she recounted what she had witnessed when they had gone there the previous week. What she related had caused the blood to thump in Moshe's head.

"Some soldiers barged into a random Palestinian home, grabbed the men, and beat them in front of their wives. The soldiers then forced them to go down to the street and pick up the garbage. They fired gunshots and laughed at how the Palestinians reacted when bullets whizzed past them. I even witnessed them detaining children, Uncle Moshe. Their orders are to make the lives of the Palestinians not worth living." Judith's voice had shaken with anger.

The clock on the wall chimed, pulling Moshe back to the current situation.

His niece Tamar stuck her head through the door, her long black hair swinging in a plait across her shoulder. He was glad David's daughters were here to support their aunt.

"Shall we bring out the food, Uncle Moshe?"

He nodded.

They moved to the table. A dish of succulent lamb lay in the middle, along with Dauphinoise potatoes and a mixed salad.

Moshe smiled at his nieces. "Your father would have enjoyed this meal," he said as Tamar passed him the salad. "What are you up to these days?"

"I'm heading to Gaza on the weekend," she said, "the family I was staying with last time need medicines that aren't available there."

This was *not* the time to bring up Gaza.

Suppressing his annoyance, Moshe put down his fork. "I thought you were given a warning by one of the officers not to go back?"

"She was arrested, Uncle Moshe." Deborah pulled out a chair and sat down. "They caught her throwing stones at the army."

Tamar glowered at her sister.

The doorbell rang and Tamar jumped up to open it. Angry voices drifted through.

Moshe pushed his chair back and strode across to see what was happening.

Tamar stood at the door, hands on her hips, her face inches from Avi who stared at her with unflinching eyes.

"Let him through, Tamar. He needs to see the distress he caused his mother."

Moshe stomped inside without bothering to greet his nephew.

At the sight of her firstborn, Rebecca dissolved into more tears.

Avi hovered over her, a scowl on his face, as he fidgeted from one foot to another.

"Why, Avi? How could you marry a settler? My father taught us…" Her voice broke.

"If we followed his ideas, Israel would never exist."

Moshe reached for the potatoes. "Not such a bad idea instead of dispossessing people of what belonged to them."

Avi glared at his uncle. "God gave this land to *us*. The Arabs encroached it illegally. *No one* will ever kick us out again." He crossed his arms in front of his chest. "Isn't it enough what Hitler did to us?"

"Why should the Palestinians pay for what Hitler did?" Moshe's voice got louder. "Israel doesn't even have the decency to form a binational state. Instead of equal rights we have this damn apartheid policy."

"Equal rights? After all the blood they spilled on this holy land?" Avi paused and eyed them all, a sour expression on his face. "The only good Arab is a dead Arab."

Moshe jumped to his feet and slapped his nephew, the loud crack resounding through the room.

Avi clutched his reddened cheek just as Moshe grabbed his collar and shook him.

Benjamin and Tamar pulled at him while Deborah managed to slip in between her uncle and cousin.

Rebecca's wailing pierced through his anger.

Moshe let go of Avi. Shaking, he closed his eyes and wiped his brow. When he opened them again, Benjamin was steering Avi out of the room. "I'm sorry," Moshe said, in a low voice.

Rebecca nodded.

A few minutes later, Avi returned head down. "I apologize," he said in a low voice, without looking at his uncle.

Rebecca grasped her son's hand. "Don't tell me you're planning to live there. Please."

Her pleading voice cut Moshe like a blade. He would have done anything to spare his sister such pain.

Chapter Twenty-five

Paris – September 1987

The small café in the Latin Quarter brimmed with people taking advantage of the glowing sun.

Monique arrived panting, her cheeks a rosy red as if she had been sprinting. "Hello." She plopped herself down next to Farah.

They ordered coffee.

When the waiter brought their cappuccinos, Farah cleared her throat, steeling herself for her friend's reaction. "It's been ages since I last saw you. I'm sorry. I know it's my fault."

"Yes, you're always *so* busy these days." Monique shot her a sideways glance.

"Monique, there's something I have to tell you." She paused. "I've moved in with Gus."

Monique's eyebrows shot up. "What?"

Farah picked up her teaspoon, and scooped some of the cream into her mouth, avoiding Monique's eyes.

"I can't believe you did that, Farah. Are you out of your mind?"

"No. I know what I'm doing."

Why was Monique so bloody patronizing at times?

Monique scowled.

Farah forced a cheerful note into her voice to dispel the cool breeze between them. "How's work?"

"It pays the bills."

A group of young tourists, toting bulging backpacks, lumbered past.

Farah broke the stony silence. "Look Monique, I'm really sorry I didn't tell you. It's just…" She twisted a lock of hair.

"Don't your parents get suspicious when they phone you at home and you don't answer?"

"I phone them regularly. And I constantly check the answering machine in case they've left a message."

"I honestly think Gus is bad news. You told me *Mossad* might be after him. And what's he doing here in Paris anyway?"

Farah sucked in her cheeks, a wave of annoyance running through her, both at Monique for asking and at Gus for never divulging. He always answered her question tersely with a vague 'family business' response and changed the subject.

The question of whether she had made the right decision hovered in the back of her mind. She dismissed it immediately.

"Many Lebanese people consider France the Mother Country. It's normal that he resides here while Lebanon is embroiled in civil war."

"I don't trust him."

Farah threw her hands in the air. "Can't you be happy for me? You of all people should understand. You lived through the whole Justin saga with me."

"I'm worried about you. You're lying to your family. You've given up your dream to study acting. What do you plan to do with your life?"

Farah sighed out loud. It *was* a pertinent question, except right now, this new life was far too exciting to be thinking of such complicated matters.

"Maybe look for some part-time work. Gus has loads of contacts here, I'm sure he can find me something."

And once he proposes, everything will change. Why would he have asked me to move in with him if he isn't serious about our relationship?

"Building your life around a man is a big mistake, Farah; he won't fulfill you. You need to find yourself first, not look for your identity through someone else. I told you that before when you were about to marry Justin."

At the mention of Justin's name, Farah's eyes stung.

"Doesn't it bother you that Gus is supporting you financially?"

Farah hunched her shoulder, her face tingling. She picked up her cup and took another sip.

A woman in a beige jacket and yellow silk scarf approached, tugging behind her a perfectly groomed black poodle.

Monique opened her handbag and took out her lipstick. A photo fluttered to the floor.

Farah bent down to pick it up and stared at it before turning to Monique. "Why are you carrying a photo of Danny?"

Monique's face went red. "I...I was sorting out photos and found it –"

"Are you in contact with him?" Farah asked with a puzzled frown.

"Uh –"

Farah tutted, her eyes raised to heaven in mock horror. "You *are*."

And you're lecturing me?

Farah handed back the photo, a sly grin on her face. Monique had some cheek.

Chapter Twenty-six

Paris – November 1987

Farah meandered out of the metro, the chilly gusts of the November wind slapping her in the face. She buttoned up her jacket. The red and gold leaves which speckled the pavement crunched under her shoes as she headed toward Gus's flat. A sense of autumnal melancholy hung in the air.

The 1930s building stood at the end of a quiet street dotted with Chestnut trees, their bare branches reaching out like bony fingers towards the sky.

Hopefully 'Sullen Layth' wouldn't be joining them this evening.

Farah turned the key. The whiff of cigarettes mingled with the delicate scent of roses, a strange combination, but one she had grown accustomed to.

Gus' office door was ajar. Snippets of conversation drifted through. At the sound of Layth's rising voice, Farah suppressed a shudder.

"…no change. We need to act, Ghassan. For both their sakes."

Gus mumbled an inaudible response.

A chair scraped against the parquet floor.

Farah inched forward.

"You can't keep postponing." Layth's voice sounded shrill.

"I need more time."

"For God's sake, *ya* Abu Omar, why?"

Farah stiffened, her body turning into lead. Abu Omar? Someone slammed a fist but that didn't shake Farah's thoughts. She gulped in a huge silent breath. *Could it be?*

"I just do," Gus said, with a determined note.

"It's her, isn't it?" Layth's voice was sharp and accusing. "Ghassan, your responsibility to the family comes first – and *she* can't get in the way. I *won't* let her. You leave me no choice–"

"Leave Farah out of this. I'm the one who decides here!"

Ever since Farah had known Gus, he had never raised his voice. A thousand questions swarmed through her mind – then Gus strode out of his study, his angry footsteps taking her by surprise.

At the sight of her, he stopped short. The vein in his forehead pulsated, in his eyes an inexplicable look of fear.

"Eavesdropping, Farah? It doesn't become you."

Without waiting for a response, Gus stalked past her to the front door and slammed it behind him.

Stunned, Farah stood immobile for a moment before scooting upstairs to avoid Layth.

An hour later, convinced that Layth would be gone, Farah ventured downstairs. But when she entered the living room, there he was, settled on the sofa, a drink in his hand, his feet stretched out onto the coffee table.

She stopped short, her jaw clenched.

Layth's expression turned sour. "I hear you have a brother. I'm surprised he doesn't drag you back home. If you were my sister–"

"Thankfully, I'm not. I'd hate to think what you'd do to a sister of yours."

In one swift movement, Layth removed his feet off the table and sat upright, legs apart, the contempt in his eyes matched her loathing of him. "I tell you, any sister of mine would have more self-respect than —"

He began to shake and his drink slipped to the floor. His forehead beaded with sweat as he crumpled on the sofa. The trembling continued.

He raised pleading eyes at her, his hair matted to his forehead. "My medicine."

Farah rushed to him and leaned over, wrinkling her brow in concern. "Layth, Layth." She shook his arm. "Where's the medicine?"

"J-jacket."

She cast her eyes around the room. Nothing. She rushed into the office.

Bursting in, Farah ran towards Layth's jacket which hung on the back of a chair. She rummaged in the pockets and grabbed the tablets. Glucose. Hurrying back, she pushed one into his mouth, got him a glass of water, and pressed it against his lips. He took a few sips then wiped his forehead with the back of his sleeve.

Farah placed the glass on the table. "You're diabetic? Were you drinking on an empty stomach?"

A sheepish smile spread across Layth's face. He took hold of her wrist. "Thank you. You saved me from going into a coma."

She shook her head. "Anyone would have done that. Let me get your jacket." She scuttered back into the office, a loud puff of air escaping her lips.

The room stank of cigarettes. Farah opened the window to air it and stood with her back against it, the cool night breeze ruffling her hair. It was then that she noticed the rolled-up torn shirt, so faded its color was indistinguishable, lying on a corner of Gus's desk.

She stepped across, hesitated, then unrolled the cloth, half-afraid of what she might find. A small black revolver fell out and a pungent smell assaulted her nostrils. She stared at the ominous brown patch staining the center of the material. Her stomach churned and she was filled with an uneasy sense of guilt. It would be useless asking Layth – plus it would mean admitting she had been nosy.

By midnight, Gus had not returned. Farah waited up for him, her thoughts giving her no peace.

It was already two a.m. when his footsteps sounded in the hall.

As soon as he spotted her, his face creased into a frown. "Why did you stay up?"

She ran her tongue across her lips. "Why did Layth call you Abu Omar? Do you have a son?"

Gus paled and looked away. Several moments passed. "No."

Chapter Twenty-seven

Caesarea, Israel – March 1988

Moshe Avram arrived home at lunchtime and joined his family at the dining room table. The warm domestic scene filled him with a deep sense of satisfaction.

He kissed his wife then smiled at the baby was asleep in his daughter's arms. Moshe bent over and stared at her, lying there so peacefully, as she slumbered in the sleep of the innocent, unaware of the events happening in the country.

Moshe's prediction about the *Intifada* turned out to be correct.

The Palestinian uprising protesting Israeli indiscriminate butchery in the Occupied Territories had started a year earlier. Stone-throwing, graffiti, barricading, and laborers refusing to work in Israeli settlements became the new norm.

Israel's lethal response was disproportionate, with Palestinian deaths ten times more than the Israelis.

When a sixteen-year-old Palestinian schoolgirl was shot in the back by the Israeli army on her way home, that sparked a new wave of wrath.

Hamas staged its first attack by kidnapping two Israeli soldiers. The cycle of retaliation began its downward spiral.

Enraged, Moshe voiced his opposition in the Knesset. He threw blatant accusations at both Mossad and the Military Governor of Gaza for digging a pit so deep no one would escape from it, Palestinian or Israeli.

The grandfather clock chimed, interrupting Moshe's train of thought.

As he walked past his son, Moshe ruffled Yossi's hair. "Big day today, hein?"

The Israeli Prime Minister was heading to Washington to listen to George Schultz's peace proposals. Peace Now had organized a big demonstration as a send-off.

Yossi nodded. "Yes, we're expecting around 100,000 people to show up. If Shamir rejects the peace proposal we'll continue to garner support till we topple him like we did Ariel Sharon after the invasion of Lebanon."

"Most of them will be there primarily for Israel's safety, not because they want to fight the injustice," said Moshe.

"True. But at least they're willing to swap land for peace," said Yossi, "though I'm sure some do have a degree of solidarity with the Palestinians and what they're going through."

"Is it true two hundred reservists have refused to serve in the Occupied Territories?" asked Jaleel, Ruth's husband.

Yossi nodded. "Yes. Booklets are being circulated to soldiers about war crimes and international law. Five hundred people signed the 'declaration of refusal' to take part in suppressing the *Intifada*."

"That's a negligible number," said Jaleel, "when you think of the support the Zionist settlers have—"

Yossi's eyes turned into slits. "Those damn *'Gush Emunim'* – they're the main obstacle. And Hamas, of course, and how they rode on the wave of civil disobedience. If only Palestinian civil society had the same network of schools and hospitals Hamas does, they could have counterbalanced the effect."

Jaleel shrugged. "Yes, Hamas appeared like a savior, with their financial structure, aid to the poor, making people believe they would improve their quality of life."

"It's to the government's advantage to pit Hamas against the PLO – so they can claim they can't achieve peace," said Moshe, as he raised a glass of wine to his mouth. "But none of us know how we'd have reacted if we'd been born on the other side. As they say in Arabic, *el eedoh fil may, mish zay el eedoh fil nar.*" He whose hand is dipped in water is not like he whose hand is being torched in fire.

Carla's chin trembled. "I hope there won't be any shooting at protestors today." Her pale face highlighted the dark rings under her eyes.

Moshe stole a worried look at her.

"Mom, we have to keep putting pressure," said Yossi, "the PLO is on the verge of acknowledging Israel and committing to a two-state solution. We're so close." He passed the salad to his father. "And so many people support us, academics, intellectuals, professionals. We're all protesting the administrative detention of Palestinian leaders and the horrendous collective repression—"

Ruth's baby woke up and started crying. Jaleel sprung up and went to warm some milk.

"Did you hear that the army radio banned Si-Hi Man's 'Shooting and Laughing'?" said Judith.

Carla stared at her son's girlfriend. "Si Hi Man's?"

"He's a popular musician. The song is denouncing the repression of the *Intifada*," said Yossi.

Carla crumpled the napkin in her hand. "The title is horrible."

"It's a pun on the settlers, mom. Instead of shooting and crying, they shoot and laugh."

"Like our teachers at school. They punish us then laugh," piped in Jonathon, who had been quiet so far.

Ruth swatted her youngest brother's arm playfully before taking the bottle of milk from her husband.

"By the way, I heard from a reliable source that *Gush Emunim* plans to hold a rally tomorrow to counter ours this evening," said Judith.

Yossi's brow creased. "Hopefully, that means they won't send their people today to stir up trouble."

"They might," said Moshe then wanted to kick himself. He shot Carla a glance.

Her lips were pressed together and, in her eyes, a frantic look.

I should be trying to calm her down, not fan the flames.

Carla flapped her arms around, the veins of her neck standing out. "Yossi, you've become a target for Zionists. Why can't you see that?" Her voice had turned hysterical.

Moshe rose from his chair and went over to her, placing a comforting hand on her back. "Carla, they'll be fine. Please."

She turned to him lines of fear crisscrossing her face. "Don't let him go, Moshe, please."

Yossi came up and wrapped his arms around his mother's neck. "Mom, why are you so worried? I've been to so many demonstrations. You were never like this. Come on."

Carla buried her face in her hands, her chest heaving.

Ruth finished feeding the baby and stood up. "Mom, come let's go sit on the sofa. You can put your feet up."

Moshe helped Carla up and gestured to Judith to go make some tea before propping a cushion behind his wife's back.

She turned to him tearfully. "Please stop him."

He knelt down next to the sofa and took hold of her hand. "Carla, he won't listen to me. But I'll go along and make sure he comes to no harm."

She nodded weakly and closed her eyes, tears staining her face.

***

An electrifying atmosphere hovered over Malchei Yisrael Square in central Tel Aviv.

Thousands of people held hands as they chanted, "Yes for peace, yes for peace."

The chanting carried on and on for hours as the group swelled. Moshe scanned the crowd. It certainly looked like the hundred thousand Yossi had predicted.

An Arab-Israeli along with a Palestinian professor from Birzeit University stood on an improvised podium with a microphone.

"Israel is still expropriating land to enlarge illegal settlements, while Palestinians are evicted from their homes and not…"

Some of the demonstrators booed, competing with the pro-peace crowd.

Moshe surveyed the scene, his eyes turning back constantly to his son. Yossi, Judith, and their friends stood together, jumping up and down waving banners with Peace written in huge letters in Hebrew, Arabic, and English.

Torches flashed.

People jostled one another against the crisp night air.

A few voices floated through singing John Lennon's *Imagine*.

Then a thunderous howl sounded in the dark.

A growing assembly of young men racing towards them, in their hands bike chains, wooden beams, and truncheons. Moshe's bowels twisted in his gut. Around him, people started screaming and running in all directions, oblivious to whom they knocked as they ran.

He tried to edge his way over to Yossi but the aggressors were already attacking the first line of demonstrators. A collective inhuman wail rose as people fought their way to escape the attack. With each push and shove, Moshe found himself further away from his son.

"Yossi," he cried out, but his voice was drowned amongst the screaming.

Curling his arms to cover his face, Moshe thrust himself forward. A few more meters.

A woman shrieked. "Help. Ambulance. Please."

Why was Judith shouting for an ambulance?

A large group of Yossi's friends formed a protective circle, pushing off the aggressors with punches and kicks as the level of violence exploded between the pro and anti-peace demonstrators. Some of them used the rods that held the banners to rain down blows on the assailants.

Moshe finally reached her. Judith was kneeling her chest heaving, her face covered in tears.

Yossi lay twisting on the floor in a pool of blood that was still spurting forth onto the ground, his clothes soaked. He moaned, clutching his side. The nauseous metallic smell of the crimson liquid lingered over them.

Shivering, Moshe fell to his knees and grabbed his son's hand. He tore off his jacket and pressed it against the bleeding wound. The bastards must have stabbed him in the liver. He wanted to retch.

Yossi's breath haltered, his face contorted from pain and shock. He tried to speak, but all he emitted was a tortured sob.

Moshe looked around frantically before turning to his son. "Yossi, Yossi, don't give in," he yelled, "you'll make it. Hang in there till we get you to hospital."

He won't die. He can't die.

The sirens of an ambulance pierced the night. Within seconds, paramedics lifted up Yossi on a stretcher and loaded him into the vehicle.

Moshe jumped in, his forehead bathed in perspiration. He gripped his son's hand and stroked his cheek with the other.

Yossi looked at him, his eyes filled with fear. "M-mom." His labored breathing tore at Moshe's heart. "M-make sure sh—" His hand went limp and his face turned deathly pale.

Bile churned in Moshe's throat. *No, please, God. No.*

The paramedic took Yossi's pulse. He looked up at Moshe and shook his head. "I'm sorry, sir. There's nothing we can do anymore."

Tears washed down Moshe's face as he stared at his son's lifeless body. Images of Yossi as a little boy learning to ride his tricycle rose to haunt him. He closed his eyes. *How can I face Carla?*

Chapter Twenty-eight

Paris – October 1988

The pregnancy test resembled the chemistry sets at school. Farah took a deep breath and forced herself to pee into the tube and set it on the mirrored tray at the edge of the bath, her heart in her chest.

Now there was an agonizing wait of two hours.

She paced up and down the spacious bathroom, constantly glancing at her watch, as she circled the jacuzzi bathtub that stood in the middle.

Someone knocked at the door.

Farah froze.

But it was only the maid wanting to change the towels.

Farah dropped onto the floor and hugged her legs close to her chest. She glanced at her watch again. Five more minutes. She closed her eyes and rested her head against the wall. How foolish to do the pregnancy test today since she was supposed to meet Cyril shortly.

When it was time, Farah sprung up and peered at the mirror at the base of the test tube. At the sight of the red ring, her breathing hitched.

The nightmare had turned into a reality. She must be at least six weeks by now. She threw her head back in despair. What was she going to do?

She threw the pregnancy kit into a plastic bag to dump, grabbed her handbag, and headed out of the building, wind lashing her face. She fended her hat with one hand while buttoning up her coat with the other, and hailed a taxi as it started to drizzle.

The cab pulled up in front of *Le Procope* and Farah stepped out.

A maître d' led her past a display of gilded oval portraits. The subjects' lifeless eyes followed her to the table. Farah nodded her thanks and sat down. Would she be able to continue with all the lies she had said over the past year, pretending she was still working? Her stomach churned. As to her current condition, it didn't bear thinking of.

Cyril entered the restaurant, eyebrows furrowed, his deep blue eyes scanning the bistro. In his somber monk's habit, he appeared out of place amidst the fashion-conscious clientèle.

He acknowledged her with a wave, strode over, pecked her cheek, and sat down with a grunt. "Why on earth did you decide to meet here instead of at home?"

"I thought you'd enjoy a place Voltaire and Moliere frequented. Lovely to see you too, Father. Or what should we call you now?" she asked with a flippant tone.

"My God-given name will do just fine." He flicked a speck of dust off his sleeve. "Sorry. I'm just tired – long train ride. And instead of going straight to our flat, I traipsed here on one of your whims."

Farah rolled her eyes. "Well, I can't say that spending time at the Vatican improved your mood in any way."

Cyril huffed. "Farah, I *didn't* spend time in the Vatican. Only the Pope does – and maybe some of the nuns."

"The Pope and some nuns." She was about to make a sarcastic comment when she flinched, remembering her own predicament. "Whatever."

A waiter placed a jug of water on the table.

"You could at least make an effort. Anyway, how is work?"

"Good." She lit a cigarette. "How's life treating *you* at the monastery?"

"Monastery life never changes. I'm much more interested in hearing about your *exciting* life." Cyril leaned back and crossed his arms. "Nice Chanel bag, by the way."

Farah didn't respond.

"Do you have a new job, by any chance? Are you now working for the *Lebanese* airline?" His tone dripped with sarcasm.

Farah's cheeks burnt. She stared at him in horror, her hand flying to her throat.

"Yes, I know." Cyril let out a weary sigh and shook his head.

Was it resignation or disappointment?

She unfolded her napkin and placed it on her knees, not wanting to meet his eyes. "You spoke to Monique, I take it."

An overwhelming sense of relief shot through Farah. She no longer had to hide behind a web of deceit, lying about her living arrangements. But the respite was followed by a rush of anger at her best friend's disloyalty.

Cyril nodded. His eyes simmered with anger. "You're ruining your life."

The waiter appeared. They placed their orders.

A young couple entered the restaurant their arms linked. The woman placed her hand behind her back, her loose clothes unable to conceal her pregnant belly. Farah glanced at her with a pang of envy.

Her brother's raised voice plucked her out of her morose thoughts. "How could you let go of your job for this man? HOW?" Cyril banged his hand on the table, attracting attention. People at neighboring tables turned to stare. "And have you dropped the acting for him as well? Isn't that why you insisted on staying in Paris, so you could get a job and save up to attend drama school?"

Farah grabbed the edge of the table with both hands and glared at Cyril. "Spare me your hypocrisy, *Father*. Aren't you forgetting how you hit the roof when I was offered a part in Cairo?"

Cyril had the grace to blush.

Though his disapproval still smarted the last thing she wanted was an argument. She had enough on her plate already.

Yet his words summoned up all that was wrong with her life, the drifting, with Gus as her only clear direction, one unacceptable to her family.

Centuries of tradition and culture hung around her neck like a dead weight.

The waiter placed a plate of fresh oysters in front of Cyril and a bowl of soup before Farah. She broke a bread roll into the soup then dipped in her spoon.

Cyril's voice softened. He stretched his hand across the table. "Farah."

After a moment's hesitation, she took it.

"Farah, you believe somehow that you deserve what Justin did, and deep down you're terrified of commitment so you gravitate towards this Lebanese man because, subconsciously, you know he'll *never* commit to you."

Farah's hand trembled as Cyril cradled it. He had triggered her deepest fears.

"You're behaving irrationally," he said gently.

Farah snatched her hand away. "Gus loves me."

"Farah, you have to let your wound heal."

She lit another cigarette and took a few puffs, her insides quivering. "What are you talking about?"

If you knew the secret that's been haunting me for so long, you'd be shocked.

"The lie you believe about yourself. That you're not worthy of a commitment. But you are!"

"You think you can understand what we mere mortals go through as you sit in your ivory tower looking down at us? You escaped into a monastery." Farah glared at him and crushed her cigarette. "A relationship doesn't end just because one partner makes a decision – the aftermath hurts like hell." Her throat ached as she swallowed back her tears. She rummaged in her bag for a tissue. "Gus gave me back my life…"

"Farah." Cyril cupped her chin, a tender look in his eyes.

She pulled back, exhaling loudly.

"I just want to protect you. Don't let your bad experience with Justin change you."

"Oh, please. Spare me your lectures and twisted psychological analysis." She slammed her hand on the table. "I'll live my life the way I want."

"Fine. Have it your way. You do realize that if papa gets wind of this, you'll be on the first flight back to Cairo."

Farah gritted her teeth. "You're planning to snitch on me?"

"No. I didn't come here to fight with you. You'll learn the hard way." A resigned sigh puffed between Cyril's lips. "I suggest you come home for the few days that I'm here."

"Cyril," she paused, a rare feeling of hesitation running through her. "I'd really like you to meet him," she said in a beseeching voice.

"No."

It was the same tone he had used when announcing he had decided to enter the order. No amount of imploring or arguing could change his mind.

Cyril leaned forward, a hardened expression on his face. "And how do you know this man isn't married?" He rose from the table and walked off without another word.

Farah watched him leave, a bitter taste in her mouth, and a shadow of doubt cast over her thoughts.

The words 'Abu Omar' wormed their way into her mind but Farah thrust them aside. Gus couldn't be married. Why would he be alone in Paris if he had a wife? She took a deep breath and squeezed her eyes shut, Cyril's words haunting her. Was she using Gus as an escape?

No. Gus enveloped her with a sense of security.

What security?

She paid the bill and rambled through the streets to Montmartre. At least her pregnancy was still a secret. She shuddered and broke into a cold sweat before taking in a lungful of air.

The Basilica of the Sacré-Cœur towered above her, its Romano-Byzantine white façade glowing pink in the fading sunlight.

Live music drifted across from the main square. Farah stepped inside the church, seeking refuge.

Candle flames flickered, forming dancing shadows in the half-light. She tiptoed to a bench and sat down, overawed by the grandeur of Catholic churches, so different from Protestant austerity. Farah bowed her head and wracked her brains for something to say to the Almighty.

Tourists crept about whispering to one another while clicking cameras, their footsteps pattering against the stone floor. A priest walked past the altar carrying candles.

She pressed her hands to her stomach and closed her eyes. "Oh God, please help me," Farah whispered over and over again, her mind in turmoil about telling Gus.

He was so hard to read. It was a sore point that no matter how intimate they were, his innermost thoughts were cloaked in silence.

Yet wasn't it Gus' decision as much as hers?

Then there were her parents who would have to face the shame of an unmarried pregnant daughter in a society where honor was so important, not to mention the deep pain it would cause them.

Abortion? The Catholic values ingrained into her at school made Farah shrink from the thought.

Pre-marital sex was one thing, abortion on the other hand…

She shuddered. Wasn't it enough that she had been the reason why her mother had lost the baby?

Farah buried her face in her hands. Was there any escape from all these problems?

She sighed, rose, and walked toward the boulevard to catch a taxi. At the green light, Farah stepped off the pavement and crossed the street. Would Gus finally propose now that she was pregnant?

The sound of thunder rumbled, while raindrops splashed her face, but Farah hardly noticed. She ambled along, heedless of where she was going. Brakes screeched. A car swerved, knocking her to the ground.

Farah hit the asphalt hard landing on her right arm.

The driver sped off.

Someone shouted for help.

She clutched her stomach with one hand and struggled for breath.

People crowded around and two men carried her to the pavement where she lay moaning, tremors running through her body.

Shrieking sirens neared as an ambulance arrived. The paramedics placed her on a stretcher and loaded her into the van. One of them placed a mask of oxygen over her face and held her hand, measuring her pulse as the vehicle sped through the streets.

The ambulance drew up to the Emergency Entrance. The doors flew open to a crowd of hospital staff. As she was unloaded, a familiar face bent over her.

Marc.

Farah stared at her cousin, her heart pounding.

Marc patted her hand as he ran next to the stretcher toward the E.R. calling the necessary tests to the nursing staff.

Farah pulled off her mask. "Gus…"

The nurse shoved the mask back on and pricked her arm with a needle.

***

Farah woke up in a whitewashed hospital room. A young female nurse stood beside the bed changing the drip. Farah tried to sit up, winced in pain, and sank back into her pillows.

"*Attention s'il vous plait. Ne bougez pas.*" Don't move, please.

"I need to see Dr. Marc Mercier please."

"*Bien sur.* Of course. He treated you since your arrival. You suffered a bad hemorrhage."

Farah did not need to ask; she already knew. She swallowed her tears, the pain in the back of her throat throbbing.

The nurse smiled and headed to the door. "I'll summon Dr. Mercier for you."

"Nurse."

The young woman stopped, her hand on the door handle.

"There's someone I need you to call, please."

***

Farah awakened to voices. Her brother and cousin stood near the window engrossed in conversation.

Farah raised herself slightly. "Cyril."

Her brother and cousin fell silent and approached the bed.

Marc took her hand, a gentle look in his eyes. "You'll need to stay here for a few days, Farah."

Her lips trembled. She turned her face away.

A life for a life.

The door to her room swung open. Gus rushed in.

Gone was the calm, cool, and collected man, shrouded by an enigmatic silence. In its place was a pale, disheveled stranger who reached for her with trembling hands.

Cyril shot across the room blocking his way. Gus shoved past him but, to Farah's horror, her brother punched Gus, connecting brutally with his jaw.

Marc sprung forward, placing himself between them, and restraining Cyril.

"You bastard," spat Cyril, "you got her pregnant."

A hand clutching his jaw, Gus staggered back. "What -?"

Cyril escaped Marc's grasp and slammed his fist in Gus's chest.

Gus grabbed the monk and pressed him against the wall, his face twisted into a snarl.

Farah yanked the intravenous drip out of her hand and thrust the pole to the floor, panting from the effort.

At the sudden crash, both men froze.

Gus rushed to her, held her close, and stroked her hair. "I had no idea."

Cyril glowered, his eyes bulging, and his lips pressed shut.

Farah rested her head on Gus's shoulder, desperate for his touch. "Gus."

"*Ma Cherie.*" Gus's voice was hoarse as he wrapped her into his arms. "Why didn't you tell me?"

***

The next morning, she woke up to find Marc hovering at her bedside. "*Bonjour,*" he smiled as she opened her eyes.

"*Bonjour.*" She swallowed, the stabbing pain in her stomach making her nauseous. She drew in a deep breath. "Marc, I need to tell you something. I miscarried because of what I did—" She looked down at the blanket, her mind replayed the scene from all those years ago.

He squeezed her fingers. "Farah, you miscarried because of the accident."

"No, you don't understand. I killed the baby." The tightness in her chest affected her breathing.

Her cousin threw her a look of empathy. "You can't blame yourself."

Farah sighed. "You don't understand. When *Maman* slipped on one of Cyril's toy trucks and her baby died, that was my fault. I didn't shout out a warning because I didn't want another sibling. I let *Maman* fall." She pulled out a tissue and wiped her runny nose. "That's why I'm going through this now." She didn't dare mention the sense of glee that had run through her at the thought that the baby was gone. She'd been nine at the time, old enough to grasp that this was bad, old enough for her conscience to torment her ever since.

Loud sobs wracked her body.

Marc stared at her frowning until understanding clicked. His brow puckered and he shook her gently. "Oh my God. You think you caused your mother's miscarriage all those years ago?"

She gulped and nodded miserably. This was her penance.

"My dear girl, the baby was already dead. Died in the womb from an infection."

"What?"

"It had nothing to do with you."

Her head fell back and she gasped in relief as the guilt of all the years was washed away with those few words. She gripped his hand, gratitude blurring with pain.

If only Gus was here to envelop her in his arms.

Just then Monique walked in, a bunch of flowers in her hand. "Hello Farah, Marc."

Marc's face broke into a smile. He pulled a chair forward for her. "Have a seat."

Farah kept her mouth shut. Despite being absorbed by Marc's revelation, she was still angry with her best friend.

Marc sat down on the bed, his body tilted towards Monique showering her with attention until a nurse came looking for him.

As soon as he left, Farah faced her. "Thanks for betraying my confidence, by the way."

Monique's face crumpled. "I agonized over it, Farah. I'm really sorry, but I've been so worried about you –"

"You could have at least discussed it with me."

Monique walked over and laid a hand on Farah's arm. "Please don't be upset with me," she said in a pleading voice.

Farah inhaled a deep breath and scrunched her eyelids. When she opened her eyes again, she nodded at Monique begrudgingly. "Fine. Let's forget about it."

Chapter Twenty-nine

Paris – November 1988

Gus stood in the living room. The soft light flickered rows of little star-shaped openings from the round bronze lamp hanging from the ceiling, casting arabesque-like shadows onto the wall.

There was so much on his mind. The civil war in Lebanon showed no signs of stopping. Both *Shia* factions, Amal and Hezbollah, were now fighting among themselves, adding fuel to the fire.

He lit a cigarette and stared out of the window without noticing anything.

In a land where allegiances shifted like sand patterns in the wind, the hope of reaching an agreement among the multitude of different warring parties appeared as far-fetched as roses blooming in the desert.

He stubbed out his cigarette and picked up a set of Swarovski crystal worry beads Farah had given him as a birthday gift. Placido Domingo's rich baritone infused the room like stardust in the air, dispersing his gloomy thoughts.

His hands clasped behind his back, Gus paced up and down as he clicked at the beads. The incident that had propelled him onto this path followed him everywhere like a black shadow. Except, in all his calculations, he had never considered an unexpected factor called Farah.

He tugged at his collar and shut his eyes.

Love could only be measured by what one was willing to sacrifice for it, and the pain of loss was commensurate with the strength of that love.

The doorbell rang. Expecting Layth, he called out.

"*Ahlein.*" Welcome.

"*Marhaba.*" His cousin dropped onto the sofa. "Where's Farah?"

"At her parents' place. Her brother's leaving tomorrow." Gus waved Layth to the bar. "Help yourself to a drink."

"Looks like the Israelis won't be getting out of South Lebanon soon," said Layth, as he plopped onto the sofa, drink in hand.

"At some point, we'll get rid of the damn Israelis," said Gus, his fist clenched.

"You'll need to get the Syrians out of the north as well, if you want to regain control of the country."

There was a pause.

Gus switched off the music. "Layth."

His cousin looked up, his glass halfway to his lips.

"I need to ask you something. It'll put my mind to rest." Gus shifted his weight from one foot to the other. "Did you have anything to do with Farah's accident?"

Layth slammed his drink down on the table. "WHAT? Have you gone mad?"

Gus leaned his back against the window, his arms folded, and stared at his cousin in silence.

"NO." Layth's hand clamped into a ball and he pounded the arm of the sofa. "We both know why I don't approve of your relationship, but that's not Farah's fault. She's a good kid. Just not right for you."

"Fine. Subject closed."

"But the family–"

"I don't need you, or anyone, to tell me where my duty lies." Gus spoke in a firm, calm voice.

Layth narrowed his eyes, knocked back the rest of his drink, and rose. "If you'll excuse me, I have an appointment."

When the door slammed, Gus walked up to the window, his shoulders drooping. He tipped his head back, and looked skywards.

Whichever path he chose would result in suffering, and there had been so much of that already.

Farah's eyes screamed out the pain eating her soul since she had lost the baby.

Gus reasoned with himself as he weighed his options, desperate to give her what she wanted. Straightening his shoulders, he picked up the phone and dialed a number in Paris.

Chapter Thirty

Tel Aviv – November 1988

"Make sure you cross-check the expenditures of last month against the projected budget, Joshua. I don't want any discrepancies this time." Moshe handed his nephew the file and glanced at his watch. He stood up. "I'll see you later. The Party's having a meeting. I can't be late."

"Sure, Uncle Moshe."

Moshe reached out for the car keys, his heart heavy. It should have been Yossi learning to take over the business. A sense of guilt flowed through him that his son had died before him.

He headed for the door when Joshua's voice broke through his thoughts.

"You're coming to Avi's wedding, aren't you, Uncle Moshe?"

Moshe glared at his nephew. "Do you imagine any of us would go to Hebron to celebrate a settler's wedding after those Zionists killed Yossi?"

He stormed out.

Climbing into the car, Moshe switched on the engine and pulled onto the roadway. He had not gone far when the vehicle began to swerve. He steered to the side of the road and jumped out. The left-back tire was flat.

With a curse under his breath, Moshe opened the boot and pulled out the spare tire and tools. When he finished, he hopped back into the car and flipped open the glove compartment for the pack of tissues. A crumpled-up piece of paper lay stuffed in the corner. Moshe pulled it out and skimmed the pamphlet which incited violence against Palestinians.

Moshe uttered a guttural roar and revved the engine. The tires squealed as he did a half-turn and raced back to the office. He marched in waving the leaflet at Joshua. "What the hell is this Zionist diatribe?" His voice almost cracked.

Joshua took one look and his face turned pale.

"Your brother was banned from riding in the company car, or was I not clear enough?" Moshe pounded his fist into the wooden desk. "It had better not happen again, do you hear me?" He struggled to find his breath, his heart weighing a ton.

A hint of relief shot across his nephew's face and Joshua lowered his eyes to the ground. "I'm sorry, Uncle Moshe. It won't. I promise."

Chapter Thirty-one

Paris – January 1989

Farah unpacked her suitcase, relieved to be back in Paris. Christmas had been tense, what with Cyril's reproachful looks and all the lies she told her parents. Although she no longer felt guilty about her mother losing the baby, the burden of what she was hiding weighed heavily on her conscience and she couldn't wait to escape.

When she finished putting away her clothes, she joined Gus in the living room. He was settled into a leather chair. He pulled Farah down sideways on his knees, his eyes locking into hers before he brushed his lips against her hair and inhaled her scent.

Farah's fingers traced the hard edges of his jawline, a thrill running through her at how this handsome and mysterious man had chosen her. His mustache tickled her face as his sensuous mouth sought hers. Yet despite the display of affection, a sense of resentment crept out like an insect sneaking its way through the ground, wanting to consume her blood.

His gold puzzle ring glinted under the light.

The scent of roses wafted through the apartment.

Gus closed his eyes.

"How
Did the rose
Ever open its heart
And bestow to this world
All of its
Beauty?"

"Hafiz?" she asked. The fourteenth-century Persian poet was his favorite.

He opened his eyes and nodded, then twirled a strand of her hair around his index finger in a distracted manner.

Unable to resist the urge, Farah pulled off the puzzle ring from his finger.

"You won't be able to put it back together again," he said with an indulgent smile.

The twelve gold coronets hung loosely against one another. She squinted and attempted at reconstructing the ring, but in a few minutes got bored. She handed it back to him.

Gus shook his head and pushed her hand away. "No. Keep trying. I won't take it back till you've fixed it."

Farah rolled her eyes and slipped it into her pocket.

"Are you going to tell me what's wrong?" Concern seeped through Gus's voice.

"What do you mean?"

"You're bottling something up. Why won't you just say what's bothering you?"

Farah stared into space inhaling the familiar scent of cloves and citrus fruit clinging to Gus's clothes. Why couldn't she muster up the nerve to tell him how she felt?

Gus grazed the bottom of her chin with his fingers. "My precious girl, if you only knew what you mean to me."

If I mean so much to you then why...

"I want to protect you from anything that could hurt you. Even from yourself, sometimes." He stroked her upturned face. "You had tears running down your cheeks last night."

Farah slipped off his knees. "Oh?"

Gus's latest gadget, the new compact disc player, stood on a table next to the bar. She walked over and shuffled through the pile of small discs, a far cry from the cassette tapes that had to be manually rewound with a pen whenever the brown ribbon loosened.

"You spoke in your sleep." His voice followed her across the room.

She tensed. The only thing on her mind now was marriage. Had she let it slip?

"Justin." He dropped the word like an atomic bomb.

Justin?! She flinched. Her thoughts spiraled out of control. The compact disc in her hand shook so much that she put it back down again. Fortunately, she still had her back to him.

Gus came up to her and curled his arm around her waist, forcing her to face him.

The sadness engulfing his dark eyes pulled a chord in her heart.

He raised her hand to his lips. "You must have had a nightmare."

The nightmare of relationships not blossoming into the 'happily ever after'.

"Gus, I need to tell you something." Her voice sounded strange to her ears as the words stuck in her throat, choked by all the cultural taboos that weighed her down, like thorns on a rose bush.

I'm not strong enough to fight my family and the way I was brought up. I can't continue to live with you unless we get married.

He waited.

The ticking of the clock ate at her. She rubbed her forehead with the back of her hand, avoiding his eyes.

The moment passed.

He tucked her arm under his. "Come on."

Farah opened her mouth but Gus pressed his finger to her lips. "No questions."

They headed out of the building. The chauffeur was waiting for them. Gus opened the door for her and she climbed in, scooting over for him to slide in next to her. The car zoomed through the city, going down familiar roads she knew so well.

When the car stopped in front of Place Vendome, Farah turned to Gus wide-eyed, her curiosity bubbling. "Why -"

He clasped her hand and led her into Van Cleef & Arpels.

The manager hurried out to greet them, a beaming smile on his face. «*Monsieur Khodeib, quel plaisir.*»

He ushered them inside before vanishing.

The glittering array of sparkling jewelry dazzled Farah's eyes. Her pulse raced.

The manager reappeared and handed Gus a box, who, in turn, placed in into Farah's hand. "*Pour toi.*"

Thunderstruck, Farah ran her thumb back and forth against the velvet.

"Open it." Despite his smile, the sadness on Gus's face was unmistakable.

Farah flipped over the lid and clapped her hand onto her mouth. She stared at the diamond ring in silence. The stone winked back at her, reflecting the faint rays of a winter sun sliding in through the window. She slipped the ring on and held out her hand to see the effect, unable to curb her little cries of delight.

"It's a *bleu blanc, Mademoiselle*. The finest we have. Nearly two carats."

Lightheaded, Farah turned it from one side to another, admiring how it glittered then flung her arms around Gus's neck. "It's beautiful, just beautiful. "

His dark eyes ablaze with passion, Gus took hold of her hand and pressed it to his lips. "Farah," his husky voice was tight with emotion, "you are what your name means: Joy."

Farah's chin quivered with excitement. She clung to Gus's hand, her face beaming. The set of pink sapphire worry beads dangled down from his other hand. His fingers curled around hers, his unfocused eyes staring into space.

The wind picked up. Within minutes the sky turned grey before it burst into torrents of tears.

Chapter Thirty-two

Israel - March 1989

Moshe opened the car window and waved at Carla as she led their guests toward the archeological site of Arsuf.

Hilda, Carla's cousin, and Barney, her husband, a self-appointed expert on the Roman Empire, sauntered off in quest of anything remotely to do with that era.

"We'll be with you in a few minutes," he called.

Moshe turned to face his father-in-law. "Gideon, I know for a fact that the Israeli government has opened the channels of communication – with the PLO[3], no less. Israel *has* to negotiate; there's no other option."

He held his breath.

As a non-Zionist, Gideon Rosenberg, while one of the richest Jews in the U.S., had no political relationship with the State of Israel. He had been among those contesting the legitimacy of the establishment of a State for the Jews.

"I honestly don't see how I can help, Moshe."

---

3   Palestinian Liberation Organization led by Yasser Arafat.

"Of course, you can help. One phone call from you and I'll be in."

"If I ask a favor, that means I'll be drawn into a situation I don't want to have anything to do with."

"Gideon, ignoring the problem won't make it go away."

"I've told you more than once, leave this place once and for all. Bring the family back to the States. Get out of this messed-up region."

Moshe's jaw jutted out. "My oldest son is buried here. He died because of this bloody conflict. If there is *any* chance of some form of peace, I owe it to his memory to be involved."

At the mention of his deceased grandson, Gideon twirled the edges of his silvery mustache, his face expressionless, then sighed. "Let me think about it. If I agree to help you, I'll have to do it in a way so a financial favor isn't expected in return."

The American opened the door and stepped out.

Moshe and Gideon caught up with Carla and their guests already gaping in the midst of the excavation site.

Carla pointed at the remains. "...and this is where the Battle of Arsuf between Richard the Lionheart and Saladin is supposed to have taken place during the Third Crusade."

The ruins incorporated the medieval city wall and moat, as well as what remained of the Crusader castle.

Their guests shaded their eyes and swept a look across the ancient citadel.

Barney spotted something and scooted toward it, returning with a piece of earthenware, turning it over and over. "Looks like I've found a piece of Roman pottery here." His loud voice boomed through the open space.

Carla and Hilda peered at the piece of pottery. Gideon stood, legs apart, with his hands in his pockets, his face turned the other way.

Moshe nodded politely. Each time a member of Carla's family visited, they were obligated to do the rounds.

"Actually, that looks more Byzantine to me." An unfamiliar voice sounded behind them.

They all turned towards the stranger.

He approached and stretched out his freckled hand.

Barney reluctantly let go of his prize.

After scrutinizing it, the stranger handed it back. "As I thought. I would say early Byzantine." He nodded. "Sorry, I didn't mean to interrupt."

"Not at all." Moshe waved away the apology. "It's always interesting to learn something new."

"True," said the stranger. He held out his hand. "Gerald Naghton."

Moshe clasped it. "Moshe Avram. Are you working on this excavation?"

"No. Just sightseeing. If you're interested in artifacts, or Roman coins, I suggest a visit to Tel Anafa or Antipatris. They were Roman Provincial centers, unlike here, which was just a medium-sized coastal town."

"Wow," said Barney, "can we go there, Moshe?"

"Antipatris is in a settlement." Moshe's voice was dry. "I don't set foot in settlements."

Plus, with the ongoing *intifada*, they might be met with a hailstone of small rocks.

Barney looked nonplussed. Carla drew him to the side to explain.

With a small wave of the hand, Gerald Naghton headed off in the opposite direction. "Have a good day."

Later that evening, they sat down for a meal by the pool. Moshe itched to ask his father-in-law if he had given his request any more thought.

A light Mediterranean breeze ruffled through the garden as Tchaikovsky's Swan Lake played softly in the background. The candlelight dinner was accompanied by an excellent Cabernet Sauvignon. Despite the pleasant atmosphere, a layer of sadness always hung over the house, like fog blurring their life.

Hilda sprinkled some salt on the roast potatoes. "Last time I visited, Yossi was just a little boy. It must be so hard for you, Carla." Her voice was laden with sympathy.

At the mention of their dead son, Moshe cast a worried glance at his wife.

Carla stared into space, her chin trembling as she fought the tears.

He wanted to go up and wrap his arms around her, but it would only stoke her anguish. The stiff-upper-lip attitude she had inherited from her British mother was her way of coping.

Gideon leaned his head backward and stared at the twinkling stars filling the night sky.

Was he too remembering his vivacious first grandson?

"So, what's the plan for tomorrow then?" Barney asked, his loud voice snapping them out of their reminiscing.

Moshe threw Carla a pleading look. No more sites, please.

**

"So, where's this Crusader's Restaurant then?" Barney drawled as they headed to the car the following afternoon.

Gideon rubbed his hands together. "It's by the port. Lovely setting with outdoor seating. Great fish too."

By the time they arrived, the terrace teemed with people.

A waiter led them to a table overlooking the water, shaded by a big blue and white striped canopy. Waves lapped against the rocks and spumes of water spouted like sprinklers.

They ordered beer and starters before going through the menu. The babble of conversation from the clientele filtered through to their table, some close enough to join in.

Hilda tilted her head towards the table behind them. "Hey, there's the guy we met yesterday. The one who told us about the coins."

Moshe glanced over his shoulder.

Gerald Naghton sat right behind him, accompanied by two other men. One of them spoke in Hebrew, but Moshe couldn't catch what he said.

Naghton answered in English. "Yes, we have our eye on a Lebanese guy living in Paris—"

A fight broke out between two six- or seven-year-old boys. They bumped into a waiter, his tray full of drinks shattered when it hit the floor, splattering everywhere.

"I sure hope those weren't our drinks," said Barney.

Moshe didn't react. The mention of a Lebanese in Paris reminded him of the dark, charismatic man he had met the year before in Amman. Striking magnetism. What was his name again? Moshe screwed his eyes. Ah yes, Ghassan Khodeib. From the powerful Khodeib clan. Hadn't there been a Khodeib Prime Minister in Jordan?

Of course, he had noticed the momentary tick on Khodeib's face once he realized Moshe was Jewish before he quickly masked it with his charm.

Interesting, multi-layered personality, without a doubt.

The waiter delivered the drinks and salads.

They dug into the food as Carla, Hilda, and Barney discussed the merits of using organic ingredients in cooking.

"Darn." Carla yelped in dismay. "I forgot my medicine in the car."

"I'll get it," said Moshe.

As he approached the car park, two men leaned on the back of the car parked next to his own. He opened the passenger door, poked his head in, and grabbed Carla's antibiotic from the glove compartment.

The two men, deep in conversation, didn't notice him.

A familiar voice rang clear. "They're one of the top intelligence agencies in the world. And if they think—"

Moshe slammed the door.

The voices stopped and both men turned around. Gerald Naghton stared at him in surprise.

Moshe nodded in acknowledgment and walked back to the restaurant.

Intelligence agency? Mossad? So, he wasn't a historian or archeologist?

Moshe shook his head. Too many weirdos got washed onto the

shores here.

Carla, Hilda, and Barney were still talking about cooking.

Gideon gazed at the sea, an absentminded look on his face.

Moshe sat down and turned to his father-in-law. "Did you give it a thought, Gideon?"

Rosenburg picked up his beer and took a big gulp. "I'll make some phone calls to the States later today. *If* anything is happening, then the U.S. Government will be aware."

***

Later at sunset, Moshe joined his father-in-law in the garden.
Gideon sat on the double swing, moving gently back and forth, a glass of whiskey in his hand. "You were right. Apparently, negotiations between the two sides are in the pipeline."

Moshe held his breath. He had been advocating for negotiations for years. "Who did you talk to?"

"I rang Jimmy Baker's office. The Secretary of State will travel here in the next few months to meet with both sides and prepare for an international conference," said Gideon. He raised his glass in a toast.

Moshe laid a firm hand on his father-in-law's arm, "I *have* to be involved."

Chapter Thirty-three

Paris - March 1989

Dressed in a dark suit, Gus sat on the edge of the bed, placed the cup of hot coffee next to Farah then held out his arms.

She snuggled into his chest.

He stroked her hair then drew her away gently, and lifted the tip of her chin, forcing her to look into his eyes. "*Ma chérie.*"

With the tips of his fingers, he traced the contour of her delicate features, carving them onto his mind.

Farah stared down at the ring on her finger then turned to him with reproachful eyes. "Why do you have to fly to Jordan now?" She sounded like a plaintive child.

He adjusted the band on his watch. Despite the diamond ring, he had never proposed.

She opened her mouth.

Gus cut her off. "My darling girl, I'll be back before you know it." He placed both his hands on her trembling shoulders. "Please don't make it more difficult, Farah." He glanced at the clock. "I have to leave, *mon amour*. We have a permit to take off in a couple of hours, and we can't miss our turn on the runway." He burrowed his head into the hollow of her neck and breathed in her scent. "When I return, we can start making some plans."

Her eyes lit up.

"Never forget that I love you - you are my joy, my sweet Farah."

"At least let me come to the airport. Please."

"No, Farah. I'm heading straight to the aircraft."

Her lips curled downwards, she nodded and clasped her hands around his neck.

Gus tore himself away. At the door, he turned around one last time and gazed at her tear-streaked face. He raised a hand and walked out. Before he climbed into the car, he looked up as though he knew she would be standing at the window. One last wave. He stepped in and the car sped off.

***

Farah craned her neck for a last glimpse as the car drove off, a burning knot in her stomach. The tormented look in his eyes left her shivering with a sense of foreboding.

A couple of hours later a delivery of red roses arrived brightening her morose mood.

Smiling, Farah held them up to breathe in their delicate fragrance before reading the accompanying poem by Omar Khayyam.

> *"Ah Love! could thou and I with Fate conspire*
> *To grasp this sorry Scheme of Things entire,*
> *Would not we shatter it to bits — and then*
> *Re-mold it nearer to the Heart's Desire!"*

Farah closed her eyes holding the note to her heart. Would this calm the stormy sea within her?

At lunchtime, she headed to the kitchen to grab some food, mulling over Gus's words. When he mentioned plans, no doubt he meant *wedding* plans. A honeymoon in Monaco would be *so* romantic.

As evening crept up, Farah's sense of uneasiness simmered. Gus still hadn't rung – on previous trips, he called as soon as he landed.

There was a knock at the door. It was the maid to inform her that Layth had arrived.

Confused, Farah hurried down the stairs and found him pacing in the hallway. "Layth? I thought you left with Gus this morning?"

He cleared his throat. "Farah, come into the office. I have something to tell you."

She followed him in and hovered next to the door. The hairs on the back of her head pricked her neck.

Layth gazed out of the window into the moonless night, his hands clasped behind his back. He turned around slowly. "Farah, I'm afraid I have some bad news."

Hardly daring to breath, she stood very still pressing herself against the wall, her spine straight as a rod, and her eyes glued on him. A premonition that some catastrophe had taken place clawed at her heart.

"Gus…there was a plane crash." Layth's voice cracked, visible signs of distress on his face. "There are no survivors."

Farah continued to stare at him.

A car honked outside on the street. The seconds ticked on the antique wooden wall clock.

Layth shuffled his feet.

He went over and laid a comforting hand on her arm, his face inches from hers. "I'm sorry. I know what he meant to you."

She clasped her trembling hands, the taste of bile traveling up her throat.

It wasn't true. Gus had just sent her roses.

Then her knees gave way. She stumbled forward, crumpling onto the floor in a heap.

Layth dropped down next to her, cupping her tear-stained face in one hand, and helped her up with the other. Gently he guided her to the chair, then opened the door and yelled for the maid to bring some water.

He crouched down and put the glass to Farah's lips. "Drink."

She took a few sips before pushing the glass away. Was that hysterical laughter hers? "He's not dead, Layth. Not dead." Her stricken voice penetrated through her fogged-up brain as she wiped her tears with the back of her hand.

Layth sucked in a mouthful of air. "Who can I call to be with you now?"

It took a moment for her reeling mind to respond. "Marc. My cousin. Monique." Unable to focus, her gaze wandered around the room, her breathing uneven.

I can't handle my world caving in again – so soon.

He helped her into the living room. She lay down on the sofa and stared at the ceiling, Layth remained next to her till Marc and Monique arrived.

As soon as they rushed in, she broke down again, loud sobs racking her body. Between them, they got her upstairs.

When Farah woke up the next morning, for a split second, she had no recollection of anything. At the sight of Monique lying next to her, everything came crashing back, heartache and confusion, like a shard, cutting away at her guts.

She sat up with a start, hugged her knees, and squeezed her eyes tight. Gus was *gone*. Would her chest explode from so much pain?

Time came to a standstill.

There was a knock at the door, and Marc stepped in, a tray in his hands.

Monique stirred, rubbed her eyes, pulled the covers towards her, and sat up.

"I brought you both some coffee." Marc placed a cup in Monique's hands then went round to the other side and put Farah's cup on the bedside table. He sat down on the edge of the bed and took her hand. "I've rung Cyril. He'll arrive later today. Monique and I will help you pack and take you back to your parents' flat."

She nodded her shoulders curled over her chest.

"Breakfast is ready downstairs." He lingered for a few minutes then left.

"Why don't you have a shower then eat something?" said Monique.

"I can't bear the thought of food."

"At least have some fruit." Monique slipped into her clothes. "Please, Farah."

With a deep sigh, Farah swung her legs onto the floor and headed for the bathroom.

Once showered and dressed, she made her way to the kitchen.

Voices drifted from the living room.

Farah poured herself some juice and sank into a chair but after a sip, she pushed the glass away, unable to swallow anything. A lump clogged her throat.

Monique walked in and placed an open newspaper in her hands.

Farah glanced down at it.

"18 March 1989 Plane Crash with No Survivors. Lebanese Multi-Millionaire Ghassan Khodeib died yesterday as his private jet landed at Marqa Airport in Amman, Jordan. The pilot had been warned by the control tower not to land because of an anomalous weather situation..."

Farah pushed it away and stared at the floor. "Both you and Cyril warned me – but who thought this was how I'd end up getting hurt."

Funny, she had never noticed the pattern on the carpet before, a weird mixture of lines, waves, and trapezoid shapes, beige, blue, and salmon pink. A Persian design?

Farah closed her eyes and groaned. Why had she ever been born?

***

Paris – April 1989

Three weeks later, Farah, flanked by Cyril and Monique, climbed into a taxi headed to Orly airport.

Monique squeezed her arm. "Are you excited about moving to Jordan?"

"Let's say I'm grateful I got a job."

Farah pressed a palm into her chest and took a deep breath. This was going to be such a massive change.

She rummaged in her bag and pulled out two small gifts, and pressed one into Monique's hand, and the other into Cyril's.

"Thank you for looking after me. I-I don't know what I would have done without you."

Monique stared at the little parcel. "Oh, Farah. That's so sweet of you." She tore open the paper and took out a dainty silver bracelet with little charms. "Thank you."

Cyril pressed his cheek against her hair. "Remember Majoie, light comes after darkness."

He unwrapped his present and a smile spread across his face. He held up a rosary made of lilac beads, a wooden crucifix dangling at the end. Cyril bent over and kissed Farah's cheek. "Thank you. I love it."

When they reached the airport, a sinking feeling filled Farah's stomach.

Monique linked her arm with hers. "Don't look back, Farah. Take care and stay in touch."

Cyril picked up her suitcase and together they walked into the terminal.

Part II

Chapter Thirty-four

Eight Months Later
Amman, Jordan - November 1989

Farah closed her copy of Shakespeare's *The Merchant of Venice* and gathered her stuff. "Girls, don't forget to paraphrase Morocco's soliloquy for Wednesday. Group A, I want you to use costumes and props for your scene."

The excited babble of her students rose to a crescendo as she headed towards the classroom door.

"Miss Farah, will we act it out here in the classroom?" Lena, one of the brightest students, looked around, her eyebrows hidden underneath her auburn fringe.

"Yes. It'll be so much fun." She glanced at her watch and sailed out. It wouldn't do to be late for her meeting with Hanna, a friend from college.

What a great coincidence that Hanna was now back home in Jordan.

Books in hand, Farah struggled to put on her jacket. Something slipped out of the pocket and landed on the hallway tiles with a clink. She bent down and started. Twelve gold circlets hooked together glittered in the light. Gus's puzzle ring. It had been stuffed in her pocket since that day in Paris, just last January. Another life.

Tears sprang to Farah's eyes, her throat tight.

Uncanny that she should find it here in Jordan, where his plane had crashed – and not even a grave she could visit.

Why couldn't she block those haunting thoughts from her mind?

Farah shoved the ring back in her pocket and continued with a determined step.

***

As soon as she stepped into the coffee shop, Farah spotted her friend sitting at a corner table.
Still just as attractive, Hanna's luxuriant black hair fell down in soft waves below her shoulders. She was staring intently at the news bulletin on the TV.

Farah tapped her on the shoulder.

"Farah, oh my goodness." She sprung up and kissed Farah on both cheeks. "It's been so long." Hanna had picked up an American accent when her father had been stationed at the Jordanian Embassy in Washington. "Have a seat and tell me all your news. Why on earth did you leave Paris?"

Farah grinned and sat down.

A waiter placed a jug of water and glasses on the table, took their orders, and left.

Hanna raised her eyebrows. "So?"

Farah pursed her lips. "Paris didn't work out too well." She avoided Hanna's inquisitive eyes as she dug through her bag for her cigarettes. She lit one, and drew a long puff. "I wanted a complete change, and the school offered me the job…"

"That's so brave of you – to take on 14-year-olds. You're not even double their age."

"Probably why we get on so well."

Hanna nodded and poured herself some water, her eyes reverting quickly to the screen.

Their cappuccinos arrived.

Farah picked up her cup. "What about you?"

Hanna placed her hand on Farah's arm, her eyes locked on the TV. "Sorry. There's been a shooting in *Al Ghor* – the Dead Sea."

"Oh?"

Hanna shook her head, a small frown playing between her brows. "Yeah, it's a bit weird. Some group called The Avenging Sword is claiming responsibility."

"Like Hamas?" Since Farah had arrived in Jordan, she followed the political situation avidly. As more than half the population in Jordan was of Palestinian origin, anything involving the Occupied Palestinian Territories dominated the local news.

Hanna shook her head. "No religious undertone. They seem to be very organized – but mysterious. It's good to know that, finally, there's someone who can put the fear of God in the Israelis." She slammed her hand hard on the table, her eyes burning with the same fervor as when she was a student. "Anyway, what were we saying?"

Farah suppressed a chuckle. It was amusing how Hanna, who was half-Irish, could swing from one extreme mood to the other – temperamental like the Irish weather. She took another puff at her cigarette. "What are you up to these days?"

"Not much other than job hunting. Hey, if you're teaching, you'll be here till the summer, right?"

"It's a two-year contract, so till the summer 1991."

"Brilliant. You're living with your sister?"

Farah hesitated, enough to stifle her qualms at breaking unspoken societal rules. "I'm moving into my own place next weekend."

Her stomach churned. For the first time in ages she'd be living alone; but after three months with Tammy, she needed her own space.

"You know, it can get kind of boring here at times – nothing exciting like Cairo," said Hanna, with a regretful sigh.

Farah nodded. No doubt Cairo was vibrant, but it lacked the peaceful quiet Amman with its different *Jebels*, or hills, offered – a safe haven for troubled souls.

The conversation moved on to whom they were still in touch with from college, who had married whom, how tough it had been for Hanna to return back home, and how she would have loved to stay in Cairo but couldn't find a job.

Later, Hanna's parents came to pick her up and offered Farah a ride. She took an immediate liking to them. Hanna's mother was a small, buxom woman with short, brown hair and a jolly countenance, and the father had a contagious laugh.

"Farah, why don't you come over for lunch next week?" said Angela Lutfi, pushing her eyeglasses up her nose.

"Our home is your home, my dear. You're welcome at any time." Hanna's father met her eyes in the rearview mirror and reiterated his wife's invitation, his bald head shining in the pale moonlight as he stopped in front of Tammy's house.

Farah smiled, a warm, fuzzy feeling inside her at their unequivocal hospitality.

When Farah opened the door, the phone started to ring. She picked up. The line cackled then the sound of pips. It was Monique, phoning to check up on her.

"Monique, what a lovely surprise."

"You haven't sounded so good in a long time. Obviously, Amman suits you."

"It does."

"Are you applying to any more drama schools?"

Farah took a deep breath. "No."

"Oh?"

"I guess I buried that dream a while back. It's…it's a different phase of my life now." Mariam Radwani's words came back to her. *Keep in mind having a dream and grasping it are two different things.*

"Really? I was sure you'd start applying again. Well, whatever makes you happy."

They chatted for a couple more minutes before hanging up.

Farah placed the receiver back when the front door opened.

Tammy stepped in, took off her shoes, and slipped into a pair of soft leather slippers. "Back already?"

They headed to the kitchen. Tammy heated up some Moussaka for supper. "I wish you'd come with me to church this evening. The sermon the pastor gave was so inspiring. He talked about -"

"Good for you." Farah scowled and helped herself to a bar of chocolate, omitting to offer her sister any.

"Farah, you need to be reconciled with yourself, and only God can help you do that – "

Farah's blood pounded in her head. "I've *no* time for God. He's a killjoy."

It was all right for Tammy; she had a loving husband, two kids, and a beautiful home – all the things Farah yearned for but which slipped through her fingers each time.

"Because you didn't get what you wanted? Perhaps God was protecting you from something worse?" Tammy chopped some carrots. "I think you're being very hard on Him, Farah. You're closing the only door that can give you relief."

"Maybe I should have been the one to decide what's good for me and what isn't. I'm old enough to make my own choices."

"As a parent, I can tell you how painful it is to watch your children make wrong decisions when you know what the outcome will be, but you are helpless to stop it." Tammy threw the carrots into a salad. "And yes, God gave us free choice, although sometimes He does intervene to save us from getting into a real quagmire. Because He loves us."

"Yeah yeah yeah. Bla bla bla. Funny sort of love that is. Oh, look, she might be happy. Can't have that. I think I'll just swish him away with my wand. Never mind if she has to remake her life from zero."

"Well, what doesn't kill us makes us stronger."

"The Justin fiasco was quite enough, thank you." Farah rolled her shoulders and continued her rant. "And then, I met Gus. But *nooooo,* that was too good for me. God saw that I was happy, and He was not pleased. So, He took Gus away from me. But you know what? I'm sure God must be happy now that I'm full of pain inside. I can guarantee you He won't take that away from me."

Tammy wrung her hands. "Oh, Farah, can't you see, the bitterness inside you is eating you up. It's ruining your life."

"If your life collapsed into shambles, not once, but TWICE. do you think you'd still be such a giving, loving person?" Farah jabbed her hand in the air, tempted to sweep everything off the kitchen table onto the floor.

Tammy flinched. "I don't know. But I *do* know that because God is in my life, it would be easier for me to bear. Believe me, Farah, He's hurting for you right now. He's stretching out his hand to you. Take it."

"*Hurting* for me? What a joke. Listen, if I've told you once, I've told you a million times: I'm NOT interested! Thanks for ruining the rest of my afternoon, Tammy. I've got a massive headache now from all your harping!"

Farah stormed out of the kitchen muttering to herself. She stomped up the stairs to her room and slammed the door behind her.

Would Tammy ever stop bleating about church? She drew in a large breath then expelled it loudly. Only a week now and she'd be in her own place.

Farah opened the window and stepped out onto the veranda, the expansive view stretching out ahead.

A skyline of flamboyant villas and splashes of mauve and yellow bougainvillea cascaded down white stone walls, with scattered patchworks of green fields filling the spaces in between.

Such a stark contrast to the noise and chaos of Cairo where drivers had their hands permanently on the horn as if that would make the cars go faster.

What a relief she wasn't there now but instead enjoying calm Amman, even with Tammy's nattering.

The latest hit on the pop charts drifted over from her nephew's room. A light breeze whistled through. Her hands shaking, Farah lit a cigarette, unable to cast the angry thoughts from her mind.

Damn Tammy. And Cyril. How would they know what I'm going through?

Neither Tammy—who had met Jamal at university, got married and lived the happily ever after fairy tale, nor Cyril who had escaped into a monastery—had a clue.

And it still hurt so much, raw wounds the tide of time had not erased.

She raked both hands through her hair. If only she could get rid of the crushing feeling of suffocation.

The problem with pain, though, was that it never really went away.

After Gus's death, she had been so vulnerable and fragile, struggling to face a bleak future, her soul battered. Thoughts of loneliness had loomed in her mind filling her with a sense of dread and deep loss.

It had taken so much willpower to come to Jordan and take on a job she had never done before. At least Tammy could have given her some credit for that.

As evening crept up, Farah's conscience pricked her. After all, Tammy had been so supportive of her from the moment she had arrived in Amman, bending over backward to make sure she felt at home.

She stood up, grabbed her bag, and snuck out.

It was a fifteen-minute walk to the best sweet shop in Amman. She ran her tongue over her lips, imagining Tammy's reaction to the surprise.

When she returned home, Tammy was in the living room ironing some clothes. Farah went up to her, kissed her on the cheek, and placed the box of *Baclava* on the ironing board.

"I'm sorry about earlier on, Tammy."

Her sister pulled her close and smothered her in a bear hug.

Chapter Thirty-five

Caesarea, Israel - December 1989

Moshe stood in the kitchen preparing tiramisu, Ruth's favorite dessert. She and Jaleel were joining them later for dinner. Both he and Carla couldn't wait to see Jessica, their granddaughter. Hard to believe she was turning two in a few months.

Carla walked in. "I went shopping this morning and picked up some clothes for Jessica." She opened a bag and held up a little pink and white lace dress then pulled out another, maroon velvet with ruffles. "What do you think?"

Moshe smiled at her indulgently, drew her to him, and squeezed her shoulders. Their granddaughter helped stanch the oozing wound of losing Yossi.

Carla folded the dresses and placed them back in the bag. "What do you think if we organize a trip for the New Year? All of us."

A flash of pain darted through him. It would never be all of them again.

"Sure." Moshe shrugged. "Perhaps a warm place where we could go to the beach? Ein Gedi?"

The Dead Sea was always warm, no matter the time of year.

"No. Somewhere abroad. You and I could take Jessica to give Ruth and Jaleel some time alone together."

"I'm not sure Ruth would want that." Their daughter never let her child out of her sight.

"Well, you know how Ruth always wanted to do a Safari? We could offer them a trip to the Masai Mara – and you and I take Jessica and Jonathon to Mombasa. Once the safari is over, they could join us."

"You have it all sorted out, don't you?"

Carla laughed then looked at her watch. "They're late. It's not like them."

"Probably half of Jaleel's family was at the hospital, so they couldn't get out as early as they planned."

Jaleel's uncle had just had heart surgery and this was the first day visitors were allowed.

"I hope Ruth didn't insist on going over to Jaffa Street afterward." Carla's voice had a high pitch to it.

Two weeks earlier, a bomb had gone off in the pedestrian area there killing dozens.

Jonathon, their youngest, sauntered into the kitchen and tried to dig a spoon into the tiramisu. Moshe pretended to cuff his ears. He shooed his son out then switched on the radio.

News that the Avenging Sword had conducted an operation with military precision from the Jordanian southern border of Aqaba killing three Israeli soldiers in the port of Eilat filled the airwaves.

Such an out-of-character group.

Who were The Avenging Sword?

A special bulletin interrupted the news. A suicide bomber had detonated himself in West Jerusalem. Hamas claimed responsibility.

The clock in the hallway chimed followed by the shrill sound of the phone ringing.

Moshe clicked his tongue in annoyance – he hated getting phone calls in the evening, his family time.

"Dad, it's for you," called Jonathon from the hallway.

Moshe strode over to take the call. He made a mental note to explain to his youngest son for the hundredth time that a civilized person didn't shout from one end of the house to the other.

Moshe picked up the receiver.

A male voice spoke on the other end.

The receiver dropped from Moshe's hand. He froze, his breath like thunder in his ears.

Dear God, we can't handle another tragedy now.

***

Amman – December 1989

A feeling of satisfaction fluttered over Farah as she jumped into a taxi heading to Tammy's for lunch, the brisk December air brushing her face. In just a few months, thanks to her diligent lesson planning, Farah's students, who had moaned and groaned about having to study Shakespeare, now appreciated the Bard's writings.

Tammy hugged her and they went into the kitchen for lunch. The maid had already laid the table and served the food.

Farah poured bolognaise sauce over the spaghetti. "I'm glad we're having Christmas in Cairo this year. Did you get your tickets?"

"Yes. We're leaving on the 20th. You know Marc is coming over from Paris?"

"Marc?" Farah's mouth fell open. Her cousin never had anything decent to say about the Middle East. Still, it was lovely he was visiting. "I suppose I'll have to act as tour guide. I'll be so busy that my aunts won't be able to produce any prospective bridegrooms."

"You'd have thought they'd have given up by now. After all, you didn't have a traditional Egyptian upbringing. How can they thrust these kinds of social norms at you and not expect you to rebel?"

Farah grinned. "If they dare arrange for me to meet some 'eligible young man' *again*, I'll just refuse and embarrass them."

Tammy chuckled and drank some water. "How's work? Still enjoying it?"

Farah nodded her mouth too full to answer.

"To be honest, Farah, when you first arrived, you were in such a terrible state I didn't think you'd make it. But you're living proof that strength grows through struggles, courage develops in challenges, and wisdom matures from wounds."

Farah raised her eyebrows. "That's very philosophical."

"Just quoting from the Book of Job."

"I thought it couldn't be you."

Would Tammy never shut up? She served herself some more salad.

"Farah, would you be interested in doing some voluntary teaching at a refugee camp when we get back?"

"Voluntary teaching?"

"My church is starting this initiative to help some of the kids –"

"Forget it. I'm not getting involved with any church activities."

"But —"

"No."

"When you came to Jordan, you said you wanted to do something worthwhile with your life, redefine your goals. I'm offering you the chance to do just that." Tammy had never sounded so exasperated.

Farah flinched.

After Gus' death, it became clear that the purposeless life, drowning in a cocoon of luxury, no longer held any appeal.

The words of Sister Berenice, repeated during numerous Catechism classes at school, rose from the past. "Girls, never forget, giving is better than receiving."

It was time to contribute.

Farah made up her mind. "Ok. I will."

***

Nazareth, North of Israel - December 1989

The sound of wailing pierced through the canopied garden, the makeshift condolence hall. A life-size photo of Jaleel, Ruth's husband, stood on a table, a black ribbon across the top left corner.
Moshe cradled Ruth's trembling body, her rib cage wracked while an occasional sob pierced her throat, her breath stuttering in uneven heaves.

Jaleel's sisters, aunts, and cousins encircled his bereaved mother, their faces red and blotchy from unbroken streams of tears.

On the other side of the hall, Jaleel's three brothers, ashen-faced, stood along with their father and male relatives receiving condolences as extended family, neighbors, and friends arrived in droves.

Carla walked in, wrinkles sagging around her mouth. Her black dress hung on her loosely instead of the snug fit it used to be. It saddened Moshe to see how she had aged.

She sat down on the other side of Ruth, covered her with a blanket, and placed a hand on her daughter's lap.

Moshe stroked his daughter's hair, his heart bleeding. He closed his weary eyes for a second. No doubt Carla was reliving the death of their own son.

His niece Tamar appeared with one of Jaleel's cousins carrying a tray with unsweetened black coffee. She offered him a cup but he shook his head. He had already drunk about five.

At least Ruth had been spared the ordeal of the burial; Islamic tradition forbade the presence of women.

Ibrahim Radwani arrived with both his brothers and Mariam. Moshe disengaged himself from Ruth, and easing himself out of his seat, signaled to Carla to take his place.

Ibrahim clasped Moshe's hand in a firm grip. "No words, Moshe. No words."

Moshe swallowed and nodded as he squeezed Ibrahim's hand,

grateful his childhood friend could be here.

Hussein and Majid Radwani offered their condolences, their faces grim.

When it was Mariam's turn, she hugged him. "I'm so sorry for your loss, Moshe. There's nothing to say in such a hard time," she paused. "Has Ruth managed to cry?"

"No. She's gone numb. She's not even responding to her own child."

"She can't access her feelings right now. She's probably going through the 'survivor's guilt'. She'll need long-term therapy to deal with that." Mariam closed her eyes for a moment then shook her head in a gesture of despair. "Until when do we have to live with this? So much anguish, on both sides. I don't want to lose faith in humanity but we live in a world of monsters." She placed a hand on his arm. "Let me know if I can help in any way. I trust the food arrived?"

"It did. Thank you."

The Palestinian tradition of friends and relatives providing meals to the grieving family was such a blessing.

Tamar appeared carrying a sleeping Jessica in her arms. She gave Mariam a half hug. "Thank you for coming."

The child woke up and looked around fretfully.

Tamar turned to her uncle. "Uncle Moshe, she's got a slight fever."

"I'll take a look at her," Mariam offered.

The women left.

Moshe headed back to the canopied area. Ibrahim and his two brothers were sitting with David, Nathan, and Benjamin, Rebecca's husband.

Continuous loud crying and endless conversations almost drowned the voice of the sheikh reciting the Quran.

Moshe scanned the area and frowned. He strode towards the women's section.

Rebecca was coaxing Ruth to drink some water.

"Where's Joshua?"

His sister looked up, and, with an absentminded shake of the head, turned back to her weeping niece.

Carla came to him. "Moshe, I want to get Ruth out of here. She needs to sleep or she'll collapse."

"Carla, we *can't* leave; it's not done."

Carla glared at him. "I don't give a damn what's done and what isn't. My daughter is my main concern."

He didn't blame her. A spasm of pain shot through him, coupled with guilt. If they had never returned here…

Just then, he caught sight of Joshua at the other end of the garden. Moshe stalked over his lips in a thin line.

"I'm really sorry I wasn't here for the burial, Uncle Moshe," said Joshua, a sheepish look on his face.

Moshe glowered at him. "You should have been here."

"It's just that—"

"Uncle Moshe."

At the sound of Avi's voice, Moshe swung around.

His nephew stood behind the fence, a sneer on his face, his automatic rifle hanging over his back. "I'm here for Ruth's sake. Too bad your dear Hamas kill their own people, isn't it?"

Moshe's jaw trembled with rage. Before he could say anything, Joshua rushed forward, grabbed his brother by the arm, and pulled him away.

Hyperventilating, Moshe staggered to the wall to support himself. Avi's words pierced his soul like a dagger. Why would anyone think that he supported Hamas? He hated them as much as he hated Zionists.

Chapter Thirty-six

Cairo – December 1989

As soon as Farah walked through customs at Cairo Airport, she spotted her parents and Cyril. Beaming, she rushed towards them.

Her mother hugged her. "*Ma chérie.*"

Her father leaned over and kissed her. "Welcome home."

"Good flight?" asked Cyril as he slung his arm over her shoulder and squeezed her.

"Yes. Are Tammy and Jamal at home?"

Cyril pushed the trolley along. "Yup. So is Marc. By the way, Monique was with us on the flight yesterday."

"Brilliant. Can't wait to catch up."

They climbed into the car. Her father started up the engine and in fifteen minutes, they were home.

***

The next morning, Farah moseyed over to Baghdad Street in the historic center of Heliopolis.

Colored glass baubles hung from the tiny flower shop displaying Christmas trees on the pavement – not *real* Christmas trees like those in Europe but a variety of Cedar, which was just as good.

A fairy-like castle stood a bit further on, its one tower jutting out into the clear blue sky.

Farah recalled walking past as a little girl and her mother telling her to be quiet or she would wake up Sleeping Beauty with her chatter.

Later on, it emerged that this was the house Queen Farida had stepped out of as a bride on her wedding day, to marry Egypt's last reigning monarch, King Farouk.

A stray cat brushed against Farah's ankle, its unusual mink color standing out amongst its black and ginger mates roaming the streets.

Baghdad Street teemed with life. With its turn of the century tawny brown buildings, adorned with intricate latticework on the balconies and porticoes, pedestrians found relief from the blazing sun running the length of each block. Shops lined the streets and bare trees dotted both sides of the pavements.

The popular Swiss restaurant, Chantilly, stood out with its orange awning. It had replaced Home Made Cakes, a pastry shop.

Farah had a vague recollection of someone sniggering that the Italian Pulli Bey, the owner of Home-Made Cakes, and who had been King Farouk's pimp, had moved from tarts to cakes.

At the top of the road lay the ornate brick and white Greek Catholic church.

Farah had only been inside once for a wedding and was surprised at how small the church was on the inside, despite the relatively big exterior.

The Cairo she had grown up in had metamorphosed from a stagnant city, smudged with Russian experts—who had flooded in after the 1967 war with their buxom blonde wives specking the streets—to one swarming with multinationals, many from the United Nations. These changes allowed it to regain some of its cosmopolitan past when Greeks, Italians, Balkans roved the streets of a city they called home.

Chirping birds fluttered overhead, flitting from one tree to the next while a chilly wind swished through the trees.

She meandered around, enjoying window shopping. Then, she spotted a laughing Monique climb out of a cab, followed by Marc, a big smile painted on his face. She stared in surprise. Wasn't Marc supposed to be visiting the pyramids with Cyril this morning?

Just as she was about to cross over and join them, a delivery boy cycled past, a big metal tray covered in Pita bread loaves balanced on his head as he whistled a catchy tune.

Farah jumped back onto the pavement deftly avoiding him. She leaned against a wall, inhaling short, fast breaths as the accident in Paris invaded her thoughts. When her heart stopped pounding, Monique and Marc were nowhere to be seen.

***

Back home, the tiny colored lights on the Christmas tree blinked on gifts strewn over the wooden floor, wrapped in glossy red and gold paper decorated with reindeer and snowflakes.
Such a different Christmas this year. No Gus to rush back to after the holidays. Farah's throat constricted, tears threatening to spill down.

She escaped to the sanctuary of her room and lay down, uninvited thoughts crowding her mind causing her heart to ache. After a while, she pushed herself to join the family, not wanting to spoil the atmosphere because of her morose thoughts.

Her father poured everyone drinks before they headed off to Midnight Mass.

She had expected Marc to resist going but, contrary to her expectations, he seemed agreeable to go with the general flow.

When she voiced her reluctance about attending, Cyril glared at her, a note of aggravation in his voice. "You could at least make an effort and join the family on Christmas Eve. It's not too much to ask. Even Jamal is coming."

Her brother-in-law shrugged and raised his glass. Marc made a failed attempt at covering up a snort.

She had no alternative but to acquiesce.

As she entered the Basilica, the uplifting music and the accompanying choir's heavenly sounds celebrating the birth of Christ swept Farah away. She closed her eyes and allowed herself to be transported to an ethereal place where a sliver of light sneaked its way in, quieting her troubled heart, and filling her soul with a feeling she could not quite put her finger on.

Chapter Thirty-seven

Jordan - January 1990

The phone line crackled, and Farah moved the receiver from her ear.

"Are you coming to the picnic, Farah?" Hanna asked in a coaxing voice. "It'll be lovely down at the Dead Sea today, sunny and warm."

Farah stared out at the gloomy sky through her window. Not even a hint of sun for the past two weeks. The Dead Sea sounded tempting. "No. I can't."

"That's a shame. Lots of people from different embassies are going."

Farah shrugged. "I've got something planned, Hanna. Maybe another time."

She hung up without giving any explanations.

Her muscles quivering slightly at the thought of heading to the refugee camp alone, Farah drove off in Tammy's car, banishing thoughts of the beach and sunshine out of her mind.

The radio played a famous song by Fairuz. The Lebanese Diva's words rang out. *Al Quds Lana*'. Jerusalem is Ours. Farah hummed along. What would it be like to visit the 'Holy City'? Her thoughts drifted to Mariam Radwani. She should give her a call to ask about her.

The song ended abruptly and was followed by a news bulletin, announcing that the Avenging Sword had struck Nahariya, in northern Israel.

Farah shuddered. Hopefully, life in Amman wouldn't be disrupted.

The drive to Jerash camp took an hour.

When Farah arrived, the grey skies eased. The sun appeared, changing the glumness in the air as its rays beat down on the surroundings. She parked and climbed out, self-conscious of her long woolen coat as women in dowdy clothes stared at her.

Garbage littered the unpaved, muddy roads. Barefoot, snotty-nosed children in dirty clothes chased clucking chickens that were about to become someone's lunch, while others played in a filthy channel of water.

Farah stopped to ask them directions to the Chacour family's house. The narrow alleyway was lined on both sides with crumbling houses that had corrugated rooftops.

Palestinian refugees wouldn't build concrete rooftops because it would be an admission that they would never return to their homes.

Farah ducked so the freshly hung-out washing wouldn't smack her on the head as it flapped about like a scarecrow.

She crinkled her nose.

A pervasive stench of sewers ran through the shantytown, mingling with the aroma of garlic and cardamom. It appeared that sewage was dumped into a ditch running the length of the street under people's homes, spilling into a gully and forming a pond at the bottom of the hill.

By the time she reached her destination, Farah's boots were caked in mud.

An older man slumped back on a rickety wooden chair dozing. This must be Abu Elias.

Reluctant to disturb him, Farah loitered around till a dark young boy of about eleven came running out from inside. He stopped in front of Farah, his brown eyes shining with mischief. He put out his small, cold hand to grasp hers. "*Inti ma'lemty?*" he asked her.

"Yes, I'm your teacher. Are you Fadi?"

The boy grinned and nodded.

Farah studied him, her heart heavy. What kind of future could this boy look forward to?

The man opened his eyes and blinked. "Forgive me, my daughter," he said in a hoarse voice, "I sat out here to wait for you, but I must have fallen asleep."

She shook his hand.

A sad smile crossed his lined face.

Waves of guilt rolled through Farah. She had almost refused to come, just because it was organized by the church.

Fadi led her inside the sparkling clean two-room shack that smelt of disinfectant and introduced her to his mother, Um Elias.

Um Elias gestured towards a faded floral sofa propped up against the wall for their guest to take a seat. "*Ahlein, ya binty.*" Welcome.

A tattered rug partially covered the cold, concrete slab of floor. Old newspapers lay strewn across the floor. A television, perched on a low, three-legged table of peeling wood.

From the doorway, she caught a glimpse of a big brass bed filling the second room.

In her mind's eye, Farah could see the family seeking shelter there on cold, rainy nights when the unmerciful wind howled in the darkness like a famished wild animal on the prowl for prey.

Um Elias offered her a glass of tea.

Farah settled into the sofa, Fadi next to her. She stifled an exclamation of annoyance at the sight of his torn English book. This wouldn't do. Next week she would bring him some new books.

The two hours flew by, filled with grammar explanations, reading, and writing. At the end of the lesson, Farah stood up, said goodbye, and stepped towards the front door.

Fadi clung to her arm, pouting. "Don't leave yet. Please."

Um Elias left what she was doing and came up to her. "You can't leave now, *ya binty*."

Abu Elias walked in. He waved his hand to the low table with a modest meal of labneh, strained yoghurt with the consistency of cheese, and *za'ater* – thyme – floating in golden olive oil, along with pita bread and olives. "You must eat with us."

Refusing their hospitality would be a terrible affront.

Filled with guilt that she was an extra mouth to feed, Farah lowered herself onto the floor and waited for the family to join.

When they were all seated, Abu Elias opened his mouth, and everyone closed their eyes.

"Oh Lord, we thank Thee for this food that Thou hast so graciously provided for us in Thy mercy. We thank Thee for watching over us today. We thank Thee for sending this young woman, Farah, to help Fadi with his studies. And we thank Thee Lord for all the blessings Thou hast seen fit to bestow upon Thy humble servants. In the name of your only son, our Lord Jesus Christ, our savior. Amen."

The peaceful expression on Fadi's face reminded Farah of one of the cherubs from one of Raphael's famous Renaissance paintings common on artwork for tourists in Italy.

"Amen," they all echoed.

Farah's neck burnt.

"Were you born in Gaza, Abu Elias?" She helped herself to an olive. "I understand that most people here came from Gaza."

"No, I was born in Ramle, a city that connects Jaffa to Jerusalem. When the Zionists attacked in 1948, I was fifteen years old. My parents were killed, and my brother escaped with his family to his in-laws in Ramallah. He still lives there." He dipped a piece of pita in the olive oil. "I fled to Gaza, away from the aggression of the Zionist Militias. Then in 1967, when the Israeli army entered Gaza, I had to flee once again, with my own family. Like thousands of others." The old man's eyes had a vacant stare. "I've been a refugee most of my life."

Farah's scalp prickled, kicking herself for stoking his painful memories.

When the meal was over, Farah bade the family farewell and headed back to Amman, promising to return the following week.

She had never been so humbled in her life.

Her cheeks flared at the pleasure-seeking life she had lived so far.

Chapter Thirty-eight

Washington D.C. - February 1990

Justin put the soufflé in the oven and glanced at his watch. His sister should be arriving soon. What a stroke of luck that Penny had come to DC for a few days for work.

The doorbell tinkled. He rushed to open it. "Hey, come in," he said leaning forward to kiss her.

Penny plonked herself down on the sofa and looked around. "Nice. You can give me the two-dollar tour later. Right now, I need a glass of wine – it's been a long day."

He poured her some white wine and handed it to her with a grin. They had always been close, the kind of closeness siblings developed when their parent's marriage didn't work out. As teenagers they had clung to each other, witnessing their mother's tears of anguish while their father dwindled into the abyss of alcoholism that had ended his life.

After a few sips, Penny placed her glass on the table. "How's work?"

He busied himself, not wanting to answer.

"Justin?"

It was useless to delay. With a big sigh, he sat down next to her and clenched his hands. "Not good, Penny."

"Why?!" Lines of concern creased her face. "Everything was fine at Christmas. What happened?"

"New boss. Not a pleasant character. Constantly calling me into her office for trivialities. Basically, a pain."

"How old is she?"

"Mid-40s."

His sister winked. "Maybe she's a cougar."

"Pfff." Justin ran his fingers through his hair. "But it's not just that. I'm fed up with DC. Writing grant proposals isn't what I want."

"What do you want?"

He sighed, not sure he knew the answer himself.

"How's Emily?"

Justin shrugged. True he was drawn to the pretty, blue-eyed blonde he had met a few weeks before Christmas. Except she didn't fill this sense of emptiness, *ennui*, as the French called it, which invaded his life.

"She's fine. Sweet girl."

"But not Farah." His sister finished off for him. "It's coming up to four years, Justin, and you're still not over her, are you? You need a total change of scenery. Maybe it's time for a move?"

Justin clenched his jaw.

"Yeah, but –"

"Why not join the Foreign Service? You've got the languages."

"Me? A diplomat?" Justin scoffed. "A diplomat is someone who sends you to hell and makes you look forward to the journey."

"You don't have to be a *career* diplomat. You could join the Public Information Section. The brother of one of my colleagues joined last year. He's moving to Singapore now."

Justin frowned. With his Arabic, would he get posted to the Middle East?

"I don't know, Pen. I had given up on working overseas. Plus, I've just met Emily."

"You mean you'd rather stay and get harassed by an older woman?"

Her dry tone made him wince. "Come on, Justin. You need to be more proactive. Not taking a decision to change your situation is a decision in itself." Penny huffed a laugh. "Plus, it might force you to take a step with her instead of dragging your feet."

Justin rose to check on the food. He placed the sizzling soufflé on a mat. As they ate, they chatted about his nieces and summer plans.

When they finished, Penny raised the subject again. "Justin, think about it. And about Emily – if it's meant to be, it'll happen. She can always visit you wherever you are."

"Just by virtue of applying for a job overseas would send her the message that I'm not interested."

His sister stared at him in exasperation. "Oh, for goodness' sake, stop being such a nitwit. Changing careers is a good move, especially if it will involve something you want. And you *always* wanted to live overseas."

Justin combed his fingers through his hair. Maybe it *was* time for a change.

Chapter Thirty-nine

Jerash Refugee Camp, Jordan – February 1990

Farah approached the Chacour's house with mixed feelings. Though she enjoyed teaching Fadi, a wave of guilt rolled through her whenever she contrasted her life to theirs.

Yet the Chacours possessed something that Farah lacked: inner peace *despite* their circumstances. Nothing ruffled them. They lifted everything to God in prayer and trusted Him to provide.

Some young boys kicked an old, empty tin, a makeshift ball. The dusty lane muffled the sound of metal as it rolled around from one side to the other amidst screams of delight.

She reached the door and knocked.

Um Elias opened, a wide smile on her face. "*Ahlein.*"

Farah entered, greeted them, then set the bag of clothes she was carrying on the floor.

The wind whipped against the creaking windows that wouldn't stay shut.

"Fadi, your teacher is here," called Um Elias.

Fadi rushed out of the bedroom buttoning up an old, moth-eaten woolen cardigan.

Farah pulled out one of her nephew's old sweaters from the bag and handed it to him, trying to appear jolly. "Look, Fadi, I've brought you some clothes. Let's see if they fit you."

As she waited for Fadi to reappear, she glanced around the room. Though the place was spotless, the peeling walls made it look drab.

Farah turned to Um Elias. "What about if we give this room a lick of paint?"

The older woman's face lit up. "I've been wanting to for so long but we can't afford it."

"Don't worry about that," said Farah, "I'll organize everything. We'll wait till the weather is a bit warmer and the paint can dry."

Fadi stepped out, a huge smile on his lips as he ran his hands down the new trousers.

They settled on the sofa. When the lesson was over, Farah asked her student to draw a picture that meant something to him.

Within minutes, Fadi presented her with the drawing of a house set among the fields.

The child was talented. Farah showed it to his father. "See, Abu Elias? You must be proud of Fadi's skills."

He stared at the picture for a long time, then beckoned her to follow him as he scuffled over to a worn-out chest of drawers set in a corner, a sad smile hovering around his weathered face. He reached into one of the drawers and pulled out a piece of frayed cloth.

He unfolded it as if it were an ancient parchment that he was afraid to tear. Then, with a gentle motion, the old man took out a big, rusty key and cradled it in his hands with something akin to awe. He looked up, his eyes glistening. "This is the key to my home in Ramle. The home I still pine for."

"Oh," Heat surged through Farah's face. "Have you seen your brother since you both left?"

Abu Elias shook his head. "We talk on the phone once a month. Neither of us has money to make the journey across. But we give thanks to The Lord for everything." He placed the key back in the cloth and put it back in the drawer. "Every Palestinian has a key like that."

"I'm so sorry for all that you've been through."

"*Blessed are those who grieve for they shall be comforted.*" Abu Elias quoted scripture in a soft voice. "That's what Jesus taught us in the Sermon on the Mount."

"Comforted? The world is so full of pain."

"The Kingdom of Heaven doesn't work on the same principles as the world. You can't apply the same rules. When our Lord tells us that those who are mourning are blessed, it means that when people are mourning, their true selves come to the surface, not the façade they put on for the world."

Farah crossed her arms. "But some people get more than their fair share of suffering here on earth."

"Perhaps that's the only way God can get their attention. When we go through pain, we become vulnerable, humble. People relate to vulnerability. It's in moments like these that we become dependent on others to be around us, and most importantly, turn to God for help." He patted her back, his eyes filled with compassion. "Unless we suffer loss, we cannot experience authentic reactions. People who live in comfort, whether physical or emotional, do not grow, are not stretched, and certainly are not being molded to become more like Jesus."

***

By the time Farah reached Tammy's house, sun rays peeped through golden-edged puffy clouds as the sky turned into hues of mauve before darkness fell.

"How did it go today? Did the clothes fit Fadi?" asked Tammy.

"Yes." Farah pressed her lips together not wanting to mention the family's faith. Tammy would take it as another opportunity to preach. She rubbed her temples. "Do you have any painkillers?"

"Yes. On my bedside table."

Farah climbed upstairs. She grabbed the tablets and popped a couple in her mouth. A Bible lay open on the bed. A highlighted verse caught her eye.

"Come unto me, all you who are tired and weary, and I will give you rest."

Her nephew and niece squabbled in the next room, their voices raised.

A sense of stillness came over her as she stood frozen and stared at the verse.

Chapter Forty

Hebron – Occupied Palestinian Territories, March 1990

Moshe parked the car as blood-curdling shrieks pierced the air. The hair on the back of his neck stood up. He hurried towards the screaming.

This was the first time for him to step foot in Hebron since the *Intifada* had started. For his sister's sake, he had driven over to congratulate Avi and his wife on their first child.

Soldiers from the IDF, Israeli Defense Forces, stamped around, their military boots pounding the ground.

Yitzhak Rabin had just given the order of breaking the bones of Palestinian youths. With broken hands, they wouldn't be able to throw stones for almost two months.

Hebron embodied the entire conflict. The Israeli army, present since before the *Intifada* to protect a handful of Jewish settlers fueled by Messianic visions, terrorized the local inhabitants.

The screams became louder.

Moshe rushed past the shuttered houses.

A handful of soldiers looked on, while a crowd of male and female settlers pushed and shoved what appeared to be three generations of a Palestinian family.

Moshe shouldered his way through to the center of the crowd. A Palestinian woman lay on the street, a hand on her pregnant stomach, the scarf covering her hair halfway down her head.

Five male settlers, probably in their late teens, kicked her stomach and head as they yelled out insults.

She writhed and twisted, moaning in pain. Her distraught family shouted and struggled against the settlers restraining them.

Moshe dove at one of the youths, grabbing him by his side curls, and encircled the young man's neck with his arm like a padlock. Pity he never carried a gun.

The soldiers closed in on him, their weapons pointed at him.

"One step nearer and you'll regret it. I'm a member of the Knesset," Moshe shouted but his voice was drowned amidst all the screaming and uproar.

A loud screech rose from the crowd.

Moshe whipped his head around.

The young woman lay motionless.

Moshe shoved the guy so hard that he tumbled and fell, then Moshe bent over the young woman and felt for a pulse on her neck. He dropped her lifeless arm. A feeling of heaviness hit his core as he stared at her pale face, the tears still wet.

An older man pushed his way through and fell on his knees, his face lined with anguish. He cradled her head in his arms, crying out *"binty"*. Her father.

The raw pain the night of Yossi's death flooded back.

An older woman collapsed with sobs loud enough to wake someone in a coma.

The settlers dispersed jabbering to one another, and the soldiers walked away.

Moshe rushed and grabbed one of them by the arm. "Aren't you going to arrest them?"

The soldier pulled his arm away. "We're here to protect the settlers. They can go to the police if they want."

"You mean you'll do nothing?" Moshe's guttural roar left his ears pounding. "Why do you have to kill people and destroy their livelihoods when all they want is to get on with their lives and feed their children?"

The soldier muttered something and marched off.

"You'll wake up one day and realize you hate yourself," Moshe called after him, a tightening sensation in his chest. Everyone on this tormented land was trapped in a never-ending cycle of indiscriminate blood spilling.

His heart heavy, Moshe returned to the grieving family to offer his help. Friends and neighbors surrounded them. There was no point in him hanging around.

Moshe tightened his grip on the steering wheel as he sped home. He would telephone Gideon tonight to find out the latest developments on the peace talks. He would also make sure this was on the agenda at the next party meeting. This bloody cycle of violence *had* to stop.

Chapter Forty-one

Amman – May 1990

There was dead silence in the classroom while Farah read from The Merchant of Venice.

"The quality of mercy is not strained, it droppeth as the gentle rain from heaven upon the place beneath. It is twice blessed – it blesseth him that gives, and him that takes."

Farah studied her enraptured pupils. "What does Portia mean with these words?"

"I think Portia is trying to say that mercy is like the rain. It can't be stopped," said Lena.

"Indeed. Mercy flows without being held back. It's not only important for the person who receives it; the person who is being merciful is also blessed."

Lena sat back, a pleased smile on her face.

After all the huffing and puffing, it was gratifying how her students had come to appreciate Shakespeare, despite English being their second language.

"Will the group acting out the assigned scene get ready, please?

Everyone else, help me rearrange the desks to create an empty space in the middle," said Farah, taking the lead.

Before long, the 'actors' entered in their improvised costumes.

The 'audience' giggled and whispered. Farah cautioned them, a finger on her lips.

The actors swooshed around with extravagant gestures. Then, Nida, who was playing the part of Jessica, forgot her lines and stood mute, her lips trembling.

Snickers drifted from some of the students.

Nida scratched her arm, her face turning bright red.

Farah whispered a prompt, but Nida was too agitated. With a discreet signal from Farah, another actor came to the rescue.

A tight-lipped smile tugged at Farah's lips.

When the actors had finished the scene, they took their bows and left to change.

"I'm *so* disappointed at your reaction when poor Nida forgot her lines. How *dare* you make fun of her when she was so nervous?"

Silence.

A couple of students looked down while others fidgeted in their seats.

"I'm sorry, Ms. Farah. I didn't think of that," said Lena, in a contrite voice.

The rest of the students followed suit.

"It's not me you need to apologize to."

The classroom door opened, and the actors returned.

"That was excellent work, girls. Impressive." Farah patted Nida on the shoulder. "Well done."

The girl blushed.

The rest of the class gathered around the cast, showering them with compliments and apologizing. Soon the classroom was filled with laughter and excited chatter.

Chapter Forty-two

Amman – June 1990

On the last day of term, Farah stepped into the classroom, a knot in her stomach. Her students would be moving to another class next year. Time had passed like water through a sieve.

Where was everyone?

"Surprise," shouted her students.

Farah's hands flew to her open mouth as flowers were thrown at her. "I'm so touched," her voice quavered.

The girls crowded around her, sobbing and hugging her. The commotion died down, and they sat in a semi-circle, munching on pizza and cake they had brought from home.

Someone switched on a portable radio. Roxette's voice sang *It must have been love.*

An unexpected sense of foreboding enveloped Farah, like a dark cloud ruining a sunny day. In the midst of such an enjoyable moment, she had a presentiment that this experience wouldn't be repeated.

"Tell us a bit more about yourself. We don't know much about you," said Nida with a bashful smile.

Lena leaned forward. "We tell you our secrets, but we don't know any of yours."

Farah chuckled. "Maybe because, unlike you, I don't have any secrets."

"Do you have a boyfriend?"

Farah's eyebrows shot up. It was Zena, Lena's twin who was in another class. The girl grinned cheekily.

"Shh." Lena elbowed her sister with a glare.

"Close the circle," said Farah, ignoring the question as she motioned to them.

The students drew their chairs closer. A hubbub of voices rose up at the same time.

"So, what did you want to chat about?"

Zena loitered close to the blackboard, as if unsure if she should join.

Farah patted the chair next to her with a smile.

The teenager bounced across a fizzy drink in her hand. Just as she was about to sit down, she tripped. The brown liquid spurted out and stained Farah's beige trousers.

Zena yelped and Lena shot over, in her hand a bunch of tissues.

"Not to worry. I'll take care of it," said Farah.

She headed to the bathroom.

Suddenly, the fire alarm went off.

Her pulse drummed as Farah rushed into the corridor to get back to her class. Fire drills were non-existent. This could only mean one thing.

Within seconds, students from the entire upper floor flooded downstairs, pushing and screaming.

Teachers failed to organize an orderly exit, their voices drowned under all the shouting and yelling.

Everyone moved like one massive wave towards the entrance.

Farah fought her way through the chaos as sweat trickled down her back. None of her students were in the hallway. She reached her classroom and stormed in. It was almost empty. Most of the girls had climbed through the window into the garden.

A screech sprang from the corner.

Farah rushed over.

Lena and Nida crouched over Zena, who lay on the floor. Her legs kicking in the air, the twin's head rolled back with only the whites of her eyes showing.

Farah knelt and placed one hand on Lena's shoulder with an encouraging squeeze.

"Epilepsy?" she asked.

Lena nodded, a palm pressed against her chest as she hyperventilated.

When the seizure stopped, Farah and the girls moved Zena close to the window.

Farah grabbed the fire extinguisher from a corner with clammy hands and pointed it towards the door.

The clock on the classroom wall thrummed. Seconds passed like hours.

The sound of screaming and sobbing in the garden flitted through, as did the voices of teachers trying to calm the students down.

Sirens screeched.

Nida ran up to the window. "The firemen arrived. Oh, and an ambulance."

Farah and the girls remained in the classroom waiting. Zena's epileptic seizure had subsided, and she lay motionless, her eyes closed.

One of the teachers pushed her head through the door. "It's all under control now. You can come out."

"What triggered the fire?" asked Farah.

"A short circuit in one of the classrooms. Luckily all the students evacuated immediately, and someone had the sense to close the door so it wouldn't spread."

Farah helped Zena to her feet.

Once in the garden, Farah and the girls dropped onto the grass all of them shaken.

Around them, students babbled in excited voices as streaks of water dripped down the sidewall, spilling onto the shrubs.

A stylish, well-dressed woman rushed over and took the twins in her arms, her lips pressing against their long, curly hair. She murmured comforting words, her beautiful face pale and drawn.

Lena whispered something into her mother's ear. The lady turned to Farah and reached for one of her hands, covering it with both of hers, while tears welled in her eyes. "Thank you for not leaving my daughters alone." Her voice shook slightly.

***

That evening Farah went over to her sister's place. She was leaving for the holidays soon, heading to Paris to spend the summer with her parents and Cyril, so it was good to spend time with Tammy now.

She recounted what had happened at school that morning.

"Oh yes, the twins. The girls get their beauty from their mother." Tammy bit the thread with her teeth, knotted it, and inspected the darned sock. "Quite a society lady, you know. I hear she holds the best dinner parties in town."

The next morning, a crisp white envelope lay in Farah's letterbox, an invitation from the twins' parents for dinner at their house on Thursday evening, the night before her flight to Paris.

***

Jerash Refugee Camp, Amman – July 1990

Farah parked the car and climbed out. Fadi and three sisters were waiting for her, huge grins on their faces.

Farah greeted them then opened the trunk, and handed each of them a bucket, then followed them to the house, a big bag with brushes and other tools in her hand. Um Elias was waiting for them, her eyes shining.

"You don't know what a difference this will make." She hugged Farah.

Farah smiled her thanks and pulled an overall over her clothes.

They began by covering the skirtings with duct tape, then pushed the furniture into the middle of the room.

Farah rolled up her sleeves and handed out paint rollers before opening a tin. "Right everyone, let's get to work." She poured some paint into a tray, dipped her roller, and began to paint.

Fadi and his sisters imitated her, laughing and joking. It wasn't long before one side of the wall was completed, the lemony yellow reflecting a warm glow into the room.

Um Elias made them tea and plied them with biscuits.

It took them four hours to finish, with Fadi and his sisters jabbering excitedly as they watched the transformation take place before their eyes.

Farah stepped back and stared at their work, a sigh of satisfaction on her lips. She peeled off her overall and went to join Abu Elias who was sitting outside.

He smiled at her. "Thank you. That was a wonderful thing to do, but I hope it's not a goodbye gift."

"No. I'm only going on holiday. I'll be back after the summer to help Fadi again."

"If the Lord wills."

Without meaning to, Farah nodded in agreement.

Um Elias arrived with a tray carrying mint tea in glasses.

"You know what I miss most about Palestine?" Abu Elias took a sip. "The olive trees. We had one in the garden of our house in Ramle. They said it was over three hundred years old. As a child, I used to sit and look at it for hours, till my mother would tell me off for not helping." The old man's face softened, and his voice took on the dreamy aspect of a man in love. "Harvest time was the best. All the families used to get together to pick the olives. We'd start around mid-September, and it would go on for two months." He sighed. "The blood of Palestine is in its olive trees."

The indistinct babble of next-door neighbors chatting in the background drifted through, accompanied by the sounds of a crying baby.

Farah drank her tea in silence, mulling over Abu Elias' words.

"Did you visit Jerusalem often?" she asked.

"No, not often. But I remember one Easter we went there, and we visited the Garden of Gethsemane. One of the trees there is supposed to be over two thousand years old. Since the time of Jesus." Abu Elias shook his head. "I'll never forget that trip. We stayed up all night on Easter Saturday, in the courtyard of the Church of the Holy Sepulcher, because we weren't able to go inside for Midnight Mass. We call it the Church of the Resurrection in Arabic, you know. We wanted to make sure we could get in on Sunday morning for the Easter celebration. The place was alive with people who had the same idea as us."

"And did you get in?"

"Yes. Somehow, we managed. I suppose it's even more crowded now during Easter." He turned to her. "One day you must visit Palestine. And when you go to the Church of the Resurrection, light a candle for us."

"Maybe one day."

The old man nodded.

Farah glanced at her watch. "Oops, I've gotta go."

Mariam Radwani's plane from London should have landed by now. She had a twenty-four-hour layover before she crossed over to Jerusalem tomorrow.

***

Later that evening, she and Mariam strolled past the Roman Amphitheatre in downtown Amman.

A light breeze wafted through, cooling the summer heat of the day and turning it into a rather pleasant evening. Families walked around in groups, filling the street with their chitchat and laughter.

"Why the olive trees?" Farah asked as they climbed down the steep stairs.

"Because the olive tree is the symbol of Palestine, of *sumud* -

steadfastness - our ability to hold on and stand our ground against all odds," Mariam answered, without a moment's hesitation. "They have the potential to live for thousands of years. In fact, the oldest olive tree in the world is found in Palestine, a place called Al-Walaja. It's between four to five thousand years old." They reached the bottom row and sat down, their legs swinging back and forth, as they took in the impressive landmark. "Olive trees survive harsh winters and scorching summers. They are resistant, just like we are. That's why the Israeli army is constantly destroying them, and why we try to protect them with our lives. They've probably destroyed almost half a million since 1967."

Farah stared at her in silence. No wonder Abu Elias talked about them like a long-lost lover.

"What time will you cross over tomorrow?"

"I'll leave at nine." A puff of air escaped Mariam's lips, and she raised her eyes to heaven. "Who knows what time I'll arrive home, though."

"Why?"

"Things have become so much more difficult ever since the *Intifada*."

"Difficult how?"

"Because Israeli emigration officials will leave us sitting at the bridge for hours, just as a form of humiliation. And we can't open our mouths." Mariam shrugged. "It's part of what it means to be a Palestinian. Except I never accepted it."

Chapter Forty-three

A box of expensive chocolates in her hand, Farah walked into one of the ornate mansions adorning the main street in Abdoun. Her heels clicked on the white marble floor.

A waiter stood in the massive hall with a tray of welcoming drinks. A loud hubbub of voices drifted through. Farah stepped into the reception area where a Fragonard silk tapestry depicting a pastoral scene dominated the wall. Members of Amman's upper crust society filled the place, conversing, laughing, and clinking expensive crystal glasses.

As Farah weaved her way through the guests, she caught a few words here and there, mostly people talking about the Avenging Sword, the same group Hanna had mentioned, and whether Saddam Hussein would invade Kuwait.

"– and the Avenging Sword stated that—"

"Who are they? No one knows anything—"

"They only target military, never civilians—"

"Their leader is elusive like mercury—"

"—if war breaks out—"

"—Kuwait would deserve it—"

The twins' mother came over to her. She looked like she had just stepped off the catwalk. Her dark hair was piled up in an elaborate chignon, a few strands hanging down on the sleeveless side of her one-shouldered yellow silk dress.

The woman smiled, exposing two rows of pearly teeth. "I'm so glad you could make it, Miss Farah. Both my girls have spoken so highly of you and my husband is eager to meet you."

She led Farah towards a tall, dark, middle-aged gentleman with long sideburns, dressed in cream trousers, and a starched white shirt with gold cufflinks.

"Bassam, this is Lena's teacher, Ms. Farah Gabriel. You know, who took care of the girls during the fire."

The man gave a little bow. "We are extremely grateful to you for helping our daughters."

"I'm sure anyone would have done the same, sir. You have two lovely girls. *Allah yehmeehom.*" May God bless them both. Farah parroted the cliché sentence so overused in the Middle East that it had almost become stripped of meaning.

It was a good conversation ender. With a wide smile, Farah excused herself, leaving the hosts to entertain more important guests.

A few people mulled past, chatting away, while Arabic music played in the background.

In the far corner stood a low rectangular glass table cloaked by framed photos.

Farah strolled over. The photo of a stunningly beautiful young girl caught her eye. She peered into the frame. It was the younger version of the twins' mother.

"I see that like all of us, you're taken with her beauty." The male voice floated from behind. "My uncle's wife was Miss Lebanon before she got married."

Farah swung around. "Layth!" Muddled, she extended her hand. *His uncle's wife? Layth was the twins' cousin? What a small world.* "I've wondered if you'd returned to Amman or were still in Paris."

"But you never got in touch." Layth took her hand in both of his. "How've you been, Farah?"

She lifted her shoulders with a half-hearted shrug. "Good… I guess."

It was weird seeing him in such a different setting. Farah's mind tumbled back to another time in her life, not so long ago. Her throat constricted.

Layth looked at her intently. "We all heard how you took care of the twins during the fire. Like you did with me once."

"Anyone would have done that, Layth."

She didn't want to talk about that time in Paris. Tempted as she was to ask if Gus had a grave, she didn't say anything, even if it meant no closure. Best to shelve unwanted emotions. Gus was gone. Nothing would bring him back.

"Come, let's sit." Layth ushered her to a velvet sofa strewn with colorful silk cushions in a secluded corner, far from the noise.

He cleared his throat and averted his eyes. "Actually Farah, there's something I want to tell you."

Farah's stomach muscles spasmed. She had a premonition his words would strike her like lightning.

A waiter approached but Layth waved him away.

From afar tinkling laughter rose amidst the babble. A bottle of champagne popped. Guest cried out *fi sehetak*, cheers, as they clanked their glasses.

Layth started talking. She hunched over. "It's only fair I tell you, Farah. I know you've been through a lot, but still." He pressed his lips together and took a deep breath. "Gus is, I mean was, married."

She drew in a sharp breath, gripped the arm of the sofa, and stared at him, a numbness hitting her.

Layth lit a cigarette then twiddled with the lighter. "I'm not saying Gus didn't love you. On the contrary. In fact, he loved you to the point of…" He stopped abruptly. His face closed up as if he had changed his mind. "I never saw him like that with anyone. Not even…his wife."

As she tried to grasp his words, Farah's thoughts turned into locusts on a rampage. How could she have been so stupid? Any Arab man Gus's age would be married. Cyril had warned her of that. But she had ignored him.

Shaking, she reached for his packet of cigarettes, her vision blurry as she tried to fend off tears. "Who was she?"

"Her name is Lara. She's our cousin."

Was it relief that shot through her? The fact that Gus had followed the Middle Eastern tradition of the wealthy, marrying from within their cousins to keep the money in the family, made it less bitter.

Farah bit her lip. It was no more than an arranged marriage of convenience.

"Were they still married while we were together?" She held her breath, her heart pounding.

Layth's eyes turned glassy. He reclined his head against the wall and grimaced. "Lara had been in love with him since we were kids. Like all the girls of the family. She's my age – a few years older than you. Their fathers decided on the match when we were teenagers."

Despite his attempt at nonchalance, Layth's voice was strained, as if there was an internal conflict raging within him. His hands clenched into fists. A pained look crossed his face. "They got married when she was eighteen. Gus was already in his mid-twenties by then."

He looked away.

With a rare flash of insight, it dawned on Farah that Layth had been in love with his cousin. He had watched her get married to the man he looked up to, powerless to change the course of fate.

No wonder his loyalties were torn.

"That's why you were so angry when Gus and I were together?"

Layth tapped the lighter on the table. "I never had anything against you personally, Farah. I also understand Gus. I warned him at first that you'd end up getting hurt. But …*le coeur a des raisons que la raison ne comprend pas.*"

Farah exhaled slowly then nodded. Indeed – the heart went against all logic. She stared glumly at her shoes.

"I'm sorry to burden you, Farah." Layth pulled out his business card from his pocket and handed it to her. "If you need *anything*, please don't hesitate to call me."

After a cursory glance, Farah shoved the card into her bag. Her shoulders drooped. A wave of nostalgia, mingled with sadness, settled over her. "Thanks, Layth. I'm leaving for Paris tomorrow. I'll call you when I return."

He struggled out of his seat, held his hand out, and ushered her into the dining room. "Dinner's served."

She couldn't stomach the thought of food.

It was already ten thirty. Her heart heavy, Farah used her early morning flight as an excuse to leave. It was only when she was safely in the car that she let out a gut-wrenching scream.

Chapter Forty-four

Paris – July 1990

The *café trottoir* heaved with tourists. Farah stretched her legs in front of her while she studied the choice of pastries on the menu. It was unusual for temperatures in Paris to hit the high 20s in July. A light cool breeze from the north safeguarded the city from stifling heat.

Bits of conversations floated through from nearby tables as a medley of languages mingled.

A warm hand touched Farah's arm. She looked up. Monique stood, her face gaunt with dark circles and puffy eyes, her appearance totally different from when they had met at Christmas.

Farah swallowed her surprise. "Monique." She rose and gave her a hug.

"It's good to see you, Farah." her attempt at a bright smile failed.

"Sit down. How's life?"

Monique hung her head.

A snooty waiter approached them, a bored expression on his face. Farah, using the generic term popular in Jordan, asked for two *Nescafés*.

The waiter's snarky response was that *Nescafé* meant nothing. Her cheeks burnt. In her haughtiest tone, Farah ordered cappuccinos. She waited till he turned his back then made a face before turning her attention to Monique.

"How are you?"

Slumped into the chair, Monique bit her nails. Her usually shiny and well-groomed hair was pulled back into an unflattering ponytail.

Farah leaned forward. "What's wrong?"

The scowling waiter planted their order on the table and vanished.

Monique dipped her spoon in her cup, a faraway look in her eyes.

Farah reached and touched her arm. "Monique?"

Monique dropped the spoon with a clank and buried her face with her hands. "I'm pregnant."

Still haunted by her miscarriage, Farah's stomach lurched. Images jostled through her mind, the hospital, her fear. Gus rushing in with that demented look in his eyes.

She forced herself not to dwell, directing her thoughts to Monique's bizarre announcement. "You never mentioned at Christmas that you were seeing someone."

Why hadn't Monique confided in her? Who was the guy?

Monique's cheeks turned bright crimson. "Danny …was in Paris a couple of months ago for work."

Farah stared at her, stunned. "Danny?"

Monique nodded, "It just happened. I know I shouldn't have, but…" She shrugged helplessly. "I've been living a nightmare since I found out."

Farah lit a cigarette and followed the silvery stream of smoke with her eyes. A smudge of regret clouded her thoughts. If only she could turn back the clock.

"Have you told him?"

"Of course not. I don't want to break up his marriage. Anyway, they have a young child now." Monique started sobbing. "I'll have to have an abortion. No other way out."

Farah squeezed Monique's hand. "It'll be ok. I'll come with you.

Don't worry."

The scene of Cyril aggressing Gus rose before her. She pushed it away.

"It's…it's just that I have nowhere to go after the hospital. I'll need to rest."

"What about your place?"

Monique swallowed. "I'm sharing now. I don't want my flat mates to find out."

"We'll figure something out. Worst-case scenario you could always come back to my parents' place."

Monique shook her head vehemently. "No."

Farah snapped her eyebrows together. "Why not?"

"I don't want them to suspect."

"Fine. We'll rent a hotel room." She certainly wasn't going to let Monique face this by herself.

The reversal of roles smacked Farah in the face like a *Khamassin*, the hot desert wind. Monique had always been the stronger one.

Taking charge made Farah uncomfortable. But then, wasn't that what friendship was about?

The next morning, they presented themselves at the private clinic. After it was over, they grabbed a cab to the hotel.

"How do you feel?" asked Farah, as she tucked Monique in.

"Incredibly relieved."

Farah pursed her lips. Hopefully, Monique wouldn't regret her action.

***

Paris - August 2, 1990

Cyril rushed into the living room like a thunderbolt, Marc at his heels. "Quick, switch on the news. Saddam Hussein has invaded Kuwait."

Farah gasped, her hands flying to her mouth. She stood up in one abrupt movement, her heart thumping. "Oh my God, what about Tammy and the kids?"

And Abu Elias and his family? Would they be safe? What would the implications be for Jordan? Would she be able to return to her job?

"I don't see what that has to do with Jordan," said Marc sounding puzzled.

"Saddam talks about liberating Palestine from the Jews, and more than half of the population in Jordan are of Palestinian origin," said Farah in a shrill voice, "King Hussein will be compelled to side with him if he doesn't want problems in his own kingdom."

"More than 100,000 Iraqi troops invade Kuwait as Saddam Hussein wants control of Kuwaiti oil," the TV blared, as the news splashed over the screen, the same scene replayed dozens of times — Iraqi tanks bulldozing their way into Kuwait City.

"Jordan's geographical location means it will be implicitly involved, regardless," said Cyril shaking his head, "If Saddam decides to send rockets into Israel, the king will need some guarantee that they wouldn't land in his country."

A map of the region flashed across the television, with Jordan sandwiched between Iraq and Israel.

They spent the remainder of the day stuck in the house following the updates.

Farah dialed Tammy's number, but much to her frustration, the lines continued to be busy all evening.

***

The next morning, Cyril voiced her fears. "I'm sure none of the foreign teachers will return to Jordan. The Americans will definitely get involved. They certainly won't allow their citizens to place themselves in danger."
"I'm planning to go back, Cyril. Screw the Americans."

"The French will also send troops. So will the Brits."

Farah glared at him. "Screw the whole bloody lot of them."

"I don't think that's a good idea, Farah. You may want to use your head instead of your heart." He buttered a slice of toast. "Anyway, it's early yet to see which way this will go. Let's hope Jordan will keep out of it. For everyone's sake, not just you and Tammy. The last thing the region needs is another war."

Within two days, the Jordanian monarch openly supported Iraq.
All over Jordan, people spilled onto the streets celebrating the king's decision.
The U.S. immediately deployed troops to the Gulf.

Farah flicked through different news channels desperate to glean as much information as possible.

"We will kill all Americans," chanted a group of Jordanian men on the screen in an interview with a French reporter on TV5.

Farah's dad entered the room, switched off the television, and drew on his pipe, the whiff of tobacco filling the room. "Lunatics, the whole lot of them."

A tremor of resentment rumbled through Farah. "Well, at least he talks about the right of Palestinian refugees to return to Palestine, not like the rest of the Arab world."

Her father snorted. "It's just a ploy he's using to rally the common man. Do you really think he'd be able to take on Israel?"

"The Iraqi army is the fifth most powerful in the world." *Why am I parroting Hanna? Just to annoy Papa?*

"Typical Arab rhetoric. Like Nasser claiming we were winning the 1967 war, whereas we'd lost from day one." A note of bitterness crept into her father's voice.

"But what about the Palestinians who were kicked out of their homes? Don't you think they have any rights?" asked Farah, the image of Abu Elias and his family vivid in her mind.

"Unfortunately, my dear girl, you'll learn that life is unfair and full of disappointments."

***

A week later, Farah's mother stood in the kitchen and flipped a crêpe in the pan. "Aren't you sleeping well these days, Farah? You've got dark circles under your eyes *again*."
She opened the fridge, took out a carton of milk, and placed it in front of her daughter.

Farah mumbled her thanks and poured some over her cereal before spreading out the newspaper to scan the news. Her obsession with the developments back in the Middle East had become addictive as she struggled to reach a decision on what to do.

"Farah, you're not thinking of going back to Jordan, I hope," asked her mother in an anxious voice.

"Of course, she mustn't go back." Her father's voice thundered across from the living room. He turned to his daughter, his eyebrows drawn close. "Saddam Hussein is calling for *Jihad*. And you know what *that* means."

"But that's against Israel. I'll be fine in Jordan. After all, I'm Arab." Farah stopped short. What a weird statement to make. Living in Jordan had taught her to identify with the Arab ancestry she had consciously smothered for so long.

"You'd have a hard time convincing Iraqi soldiers with your coloring." Her brother's caustic tone cut through as he walked into the kitchen. She glowered at him. He continued matter-of-factly, "plus, you'll have Hamas, Hezbollah, and now the Avenging Sword – they'll all start dabbling in murky waters, organizing attacks, which will accelerate Israeli intervention."

"Tammy's still there." She stifled the tremor in her voice.

And I have to go back and see Abu Elias. I promised I would. Would they still be basking in peace in spite of their circumstances and possible war at their doorstep?

"She won't be there for long." Her mother took off her apron and sat down at the kitchen table with a cup of coffee. "She rang early this morning. Jamal plans to send her and the children back to the States. He doesn't consider it safe enough for them to stay."

Farah's mouth fell open. That was a big blow.

Still, Tammy's absence shouldn't affect her own plans. Teaching had given her life a new sense of fulfillment, a purpose.

She thrust her chin forward. "I don't care if Tammy is staying or not. I have a job to do."

Chapter Forty-five

Farah's stomach fluttered as she boarded the Royal Jordanian flight headed for Amman. Many of the male passengers wore the traditional Iraqi *Thawb*, as if making a statement. There were no westerners on the plane this time, adding to the sense of foreboding.

The passenger sitting next to her, wearing a smart beige trouser suit and in her 30's, dropped her boarding pass. Farah bent down and picked it up.

"Thank you."

"Don't worry about it," Farah responded in Arabic.

The woman raised her eyebrows. "I was wondering what a westerner was doing, flying to Jordan." Her dialect was different and she turned out to be Iraqi, returning to Baghdad via Amman.

"Why are you returning to Iraq? Aren't you scared?" asked Farah in a surprised tone.

"It's my country. Where else shall I go? I cannot stay in France forever."

"What if the Americans start bombing?"

"Then I will die in my country with the people I love. We have nowhere else to go."

"You could always cross the border into Jordan."

The Iraqi shrugged a shoulder. "Jordan also is not so safe."

The short exchange with her neighbor unsettled Farah further. As the plane circled down in its final approach, she asked herself if returning had been the right decision.

The plane landed and they boarded the coach to take them to the airport building. Farah waved goodbye to the Iraqi lady and gave her the thumbs up before heading for passport control.

Pushing her trolley into the Arrivals Hall, Farah almost tumbled onto Jamal who didn't waste time with greetings but picked up her luggage and hurried out to the car.

Amman lay silent, cloaked with an atmosphere of tension, the deserted streets deluged with posters of the Iraqi dictator, hailed as "Hero of Victory and Peace".

Farah snorted to herself. Orchestrator of war was more appropriate.

Wherever she turned, there were posters of Saddam in military uniform adorned with medals, in a smart European business suit, in Iraqi *thawb*, wearing the Palestinian *keffiyeh*, the black and white chequered scarf. Other posters showed him posing with Yasser Arafat, and shaking hands with King Hussein.

"Jordan is pretty vocal in its support of Saddam," she said.

"He's the first Arab leader courageous enough to stand up to the West and speak out for Palestinian rights," answered Jamal, his eyes on the road. "Except now we're flooded with refugees. Filipinos, Sri Lankans, Indians, and of course all the Palestinians escaping Kuwait. We're on the verge of a major crisis. We can't continue to provide support without help."

"I read in the news that Crown Prince Hassan sent out appeals to the West. I guess they can't close the borders to all those people who are escaping."

Jamal nodded. "For all practical purposes, life goes on as normal here. But there's so much rage simmering under the surface." He shot her a quick glance. "Be careful where you go. You might be American."

"I suppose people are finally able to vent all the pent-up frustration. The double standards of the west *vis-à-vis* the Palestinians," she said as Jamal drove into the garage and parked the car.

Politics was the main topic, whether at the supermarket, cafés, or even on the street, as people speculated in aggressive tones about what could happen next.

The dawn prayer from the Mosques became longer and louder, with the preacher bellowing through the loudspeakers about a holy *jihad* against the infidel.

The backlash whirlpooled out of control as the Americans gave Iraq an ultimatum: Either Saddam withdraws his troops by the 15th of January, or they would strike.

Just like Cyril had foreseen, the Avenging Sword struck with a series of explosions at strategic points along the Jordanian-Israeli border, from Southern Syria, and South Lebanon, causing further hype with tensions peaking.

The Israeli army moved troops to three fronts, escalating the situation.

The local man on the street in Amman hailed the Avenging Sword as heroes. Governments seethed with frustration that they were unable to get hold of even a shadow of a hint as to how this group operated.

"The Avenging Sword is all we need now," muttered Farah to herself as she adjusted a veil over her head before going out, an added measure of protection from the anti-western sentiment prevailing on the street.

Chapter Forty-six

Jerash Refugee Camp – Jordan, September 1990

When Farah reached the Chacour's house, Abu Elias's face cracked into a smile. "We weren't sure if you would come back."

Farah shook his outstretched hand before sitting down. "Why wouldn't I come back?"

Fadi appeared and gave her a big hug.

"I have some gifts for all of you." She pulled out a couple of T-shirts and a pair of trousers for her student, a blue floral shawl for Um Elias, and a grey woolen scarf for the old man.

Eyes shining, Fadi picked up his presents, then gave Farah a hug.

"Thank you, my daughter. The Lord knows our needs, and He used you to provide."

This was definitely a new way of looking at things.

"How have you all been? It must have been difficult with what's happening now. Saddam, possible war."

Abu Elias shrugged. "I've lived through worse days."

His wife went to the kitchen to prepare some tea.

Farah nodded. "It looks like the whole region is going to explode, doesn't it?"

Um Elias arrived back with the tea. Abu Elias reached for a glass. "Perhaps. Perhaps not. The Psalms tell us that the angel of the Lord encamps around those who fear Him and protects them."

"But what if Saddam starts aiming rockets at Israel?" Farah raised her hands, palms upwards, "we're in the middle here."

"My child, each day has enough worries of its own. We trust in the Lord. What will we gain if we worry about tomorrow?"

Farah didn't know what to answer. This uncanny kind of faith that wasn't affected by surrounding circumstances unnerved her. She turned to Fadi. "We can start classes next week. What do you think?"

Fadi nodded with an enthusiastic grin.

Farah stayed for a bit then left, Abu Elias's words ringing in her mind.

She returned home to the sight of Tammy on the floor in the living room, scissors and packing paper strewn around.

"What's happening?" asked Farah eying the scene with a frown.

"The kids and I are leaving in three days."

"Why are you boxing all your stuff? You make it seem like you're never coming back."

"I don't know when we'll be returning."

Farah bit her lips. No more safety net, just loneliness. The security Cairo offered flitted through her mind but she shooed it away, adamant to stick with her choice. She picked up the scissors and cut some tape to seal the boxes.

"By the way, Mom called. Marc got engaged."

Farah spun her head around. "Engaged? To whom?"

A knot appeared between Tammy's brows. "What do you mean who? Monique, of course. That's why he came to Cairo last Christmas."

The scissors dropped from Farah's hand. "Monique?"

Farah's eyes widened. Monique had been seeing Marc for all that time? Then she steadied herself with her hands. Monique had seen Danny *after* Christmas – she had *cheated* on Marc.

A stab of jealousy raced through her. How come Monique found what constantly slipped through her, Farah's, fingers? A stable, loving relationship with a dependable, decent man. Did Monique even appreciate what she had?

***

Farah walked into the Lutfi's living room with a bunch of flowers.

Angela Lutfi, Hanna's mother, greeted her with a kiss. "*Ahlan wa Sahlan*, welcome back." She took the bouquet, thanked Farah, and called for the maid to put them in water.

Farah sat down.

"How's the teaching going?" asked Angela.

Before Farah had time to answer, Hanna piped in. "Mom thinks I should start looking for a teaching job too."

"My school is desperate for teachers, Hanna. Many of them didn't return to Jordan because of the situation, you know."

Mrs. Lutfi raised her eyes to the ceiling. "You could get out of the house and do something useful instead of moping around."

"That sounds like a great idea." The strident male voice belonged to Hanna's father.

The sixty-something-year-old walked into the room sporting a cheerful expression. His bald head shook, and he cackled a lively laugh.

"See?" Hanna turned to Farah, her deep blue eyes, rimmed heavily with black *kohl*, sparkled with fun. "They can't wait to get rid of me. I've been away for so many years, you'd think they'd be glad to have me back. But no. If I were Ida, it would've been a different matter. They put her on a pedestal because she's doing her Ph.D. in London. But I'm the stupid one in this family."

Mr. Lutfi shook his head, on his face a look of comic exasperation. "Oh, Hanna, don't exaggerate. Your mother and I love both you and your sister equally. You're oversensitive."

Hanna flashed her father an indulgent smile. He lowered himself into the seat beside her, and his wife brought him a glass of whiskey filled with ice.

"No more before lunch," she laughed.

He chuckled, sniffed the alcohol, eyes closed, murmured in pleasure, then raised it to his lips and took a long sip. "Is your sister still here?"

Farah shook her head. "She's flying back to the States after tomorrow."

"Then you must come and stay with us, right, Angela?" said Mr. Lutfi, without a moment's hesitation.

His wife nodded in confirmation. "I'm sure you'll be great company for Hanna."

"That's so kind of you," said Farah with a rush of emotion at the unexpected offer of a safe haven.

They moved from the living room into the dining room. Sizzling hot food was already on the table.

Hanna poured water into the glasses. "The western coalition is moving more troops to Kuwait. God damn them."

"If the Emir of Kuwait hadn't refused Saddam's suggestion to raise the price of oil, none of this would have happened. But he wouldn't even discuss the idea, the arrogant man," said her father.

His wife shook her head in disgust. "The American Ambassador is also to blame. She assured Saddam that the U.S. wouldn't get involved in regional skirmishes when he hinted at the invasion of Kuwait."

It was strange how Hanna's mother had become so immersed in her husband's culture. Though probably as the wife of a Jordanian Ambassador, she had absorbed his political views like a sponge.

Hanna's fist banged the table with unnecessary force. "Well, we fully support Saddam in this house."

Farah recoiled, uncomfortable at how the conversation had turned as if she were to blame for Egypt joining the U.S. coalition against Iraq.

She ground her teeth. It was too late now for regrets.

Chapter Forty-seven

With only a week till the Christmas holidays, Farah headed to her usual travel agency to buy a ticket to Cairo.

Her teeth rattled as she took a seat. "Did you manage to get me the dates I want?"

The travel agent shook her head. "EgyptAir no longer flies to Amman because of the flight insurance. And Royal Jordanian has cut back to only one flight a day. The first available seat is the 10th of January."

Farah's hand flew to her mouth. "Oh no."

That would mean only Cyril would be there with their parents.

Why hadn't she bought her ticket earlier?

Her shoulders drooping, she headed back to the Lutfis.

"What's wrong?" asked Hanna, as soon as she entered.

Farah swallowed. "No tickets to Cairo."

Hanna clapped her hands. "You'll spend Christmas with us." Her eyes gleamed. "Amman is fun during the festive season – it might even snow. We could have a White Christmas."

"Yeah." Farah tried to sound enthusiastic but breaking the

Christmas tradition weighed on her heart like an oversized rock.

***

Farah dabbed on some lipstick on then ran out to catch up with Hanna who was walking out the front door.

"Another party?" smiled Hanna's mother as she pulled out some red candles from a drawer.

"Come on, Farah," called Hanna, rattling the car keys.

Farah rushed out and climbed into the passenger seat. "I love all this party hopping, it's like college days," she said as she adjusted her seat belt, gloomy thoughts about impending wars forgotten for the moment.

They woke up on Christmas morning to find that it had snowed during the night.

Farah stared at the snow, a lump in her throat. Images of her parents and Cyril celebrating alone instead of the usual full house flashed through her mind, making her homesick.

She imagined her father smoking his pipe in contentment, the rich scent of tobacco wafting through the air while her mother stuffed the turkey in the kitchen. Cyril organizing a meet-up with his school friends. The decorations and candles that filled the house with a cozy, festive feeling.

Bloody Saddam.

The day passed quietly, with just herself and the Lutfis for lunch. To Farah's relief, no one mentioned the worsening political situation at the table. Instead, Angela reminisced about how her family celebrated the festivity in Ireland when she was a child.

New Year's Eve turned out different, a better kind of different.

A French diplomat hosted a big party at his villa. Guests spilled out onto the garden as almost every foreigner in Amman attended.

Hanna and Farah elbowed their way in through the masses.

Cigarettes flared.

Alcohol flowed.

Loud music blasted through the speakers.

"Come, Farah." Hanna pulled her onto the dance floor. It heaved with people enjoying themselves in a kind of frenzy.

"Five, four, three, two, one," screamed everyone as they ushered in 1991.

"Happy New Year, Hanna," said Farah and hugged her.

Kisses smacked all around.

Bottles of champagne popped one after the other, corks soaring towards the ceiling before bouncing back down. Guests hollered with laughter as they ducked.

Farah went out for a stroll to escape from the smoke inside. The street was deserted. She sighed wistfully.

If only there were someone special in her life right now, someone to share this moment. This was a night made for romance, and wishing on stars for the New Year.

The traces of love lost still seared her soul.

A spasm of fear shot through her. What if she remained single for the rest of her life?

She closed her eyes. "1991 will be a good year," she repeated, willing herself to believe it, as if somehow, it would drive out her demons and that crushing sense of loneliness.

Chapter Forty-eight

Farah sat on the sofa scanning the newspaper for details. Only a week till the January 15th deadline the Americans had given Saddam to withdraw from Kuwait. Would there or would there not be a war?

Hanna walked in. "Anything interesting in the news?"

"The Iraqi Prime Minister is meeting James Baker in Geneva next week. Maybe they'll reach an agreement so we can avoid this damn war."

Hanna shook her head. "No. They won't. Why should the Iraqis bow to U.S. pressure? The Iraqi economy is strong, and their army is well-trained and well-equipped enough to stand up to those bullies."

"But war would only cause massive devastation."

"We won't have the west bullying us and telling us what to do. Fuck them. And fuck their armies, the Brits, the French – all of them at the beck and call of the Americans." Hanna raised her voice, waving her hands for emphasis. "Isn't it enough how they support Israel? Let them attack. They'll find out soon enough how strong the Iraqi army is. Saddam *mustn't* compromise." Her eyes glittered with anger.

"D'you really think they'll attack Iraq?" Farah asked, fear creeping up her throat.

Up till this moment, she had convinced herself that somehow everything would be resolved, and war could be avoided.

Instead, the threat inched closer. The tension in Jordan became unbearable and Farah longed to be back with her parents in Cairo.

The meeting between the Iraqi Prime Minister and the US Secretary of State took place.

No agreement was reached.

War was now imminent.

***

When her mother rang, Farah dreaded explaining the flight situation from Amman.
"No flights at all? That's impossible, Farah. Loads of people will want to leave before the deadline. The Americans *will* attack. You *have* to get out, do you hear me?" Her mother's voice grew hysterical.

Farah's stomach churned. She didn't want to be in Amman with missiles flying overhead, bombs exploding, and curfews in place.

"I'm doing my best. But everything is fully booked." She twiddled with the phone cord, promised her mother she would ask Jamal for help, hung up, and rang Jamal immediately.

"I'll see what I can do, Farah," he said before hanging up.

For the next couple of days, whenever the phone rang, Farah held her breath, only to end up shaking her head in frustration.

Two days before the deadline, the phone rang late at night. Farah clenched her stomach, a sense of nausea filling her. She waited with bated breath as Hanna picked it up.

It was Jamal. She grabbed the phone.

"I managed to get you a seat on the flight tomorrow morning. I'll pick you up at 9.30."

"Oh, Jamal, thank you." She hung up and collapsed onto the sofa, burying her face in her hands. "Thank you, God," she murmured.

She started to pack at once.

Hanna sat crossed-legged on the bed, a pensive look on her face. "Don't take much, Farah. You'll be back again, right?"

***

Farah's eyes prickled as she bid the Lutfis goodbye the next morning, a hollow feeling in her heart.

"Bon voyage." Angela Lutfi kissed her. "You know you have a home here, whenever you decide to come back."

She hugged them all and headed towards the car, where Jamal waited.

A bad accident on the airport road delayed them. When they finally reached the airport, droves of Military Police patrolled the area as people jostled to get through.

Though the sun shone, a bitter January wind blew across from the desert.

Jamal parked the car and pulled out Farah's luggage from the back seat.

Farah wrapped her scarf in a tight knot around her neck before stepping out. She clutched her suitcase and hugged Jamal goodbye.

Flinging her baggage on a trolley, she rushed into the terminal her heart thumping with fear at how late she was. The fluorescent lighting glared in her eyes, and it took a few seconds for them to adjust.

She elbowed her way through a heaving mass of irate people till she reached the Passengers Only area, manned by Military Police. He stood legs apart, his eyes darting back and forth as he stopped anyone from entering.

Continuous announcements for departing flights blared through the PA system.

Nervous passengers shoved one another in front of the check-in counter.

Children screamed as they ran amok, adding to the racket.

Farah, hands shaking, waved her ticket at the uniformed official, the blood thudding in her ears. "I'll miss my flight. Please, please, let me through."

The desperation in her tone must have had an effect.

He stepped aside.

She hurried to the Royal Jordanian counter and joined the queue.

"What do you mean I'm not seated next to my family?" demanded a male passenger in a loud voice.

"I'll try to shift some passengers to another row, Sir," said the frazzled staff member as he peered into a screen.

Drops of sweat trickled down Farah's back. She shifted her weight onto her other foot.

At last, it was her turn.

Boarding pass in hand, she headed for the escalators. Once she passed Passport Control, she relaxed. As she strolled through the airport, she caught sight of the VIP Lounge. Her thoughts drifted to another life. Did Lucien and Elise still work there back in Paris? With a wistful sigh, she made her way to the departure gate and embarked on the flight.

Chapter Forty-nine

Cairo – January 1991

Farah hollered down the hallway. "*Maman*, where are your car keys? I need to go. I booked a squash lesson with the trainer."

"In my bag, *chérie*. Make sure to be home for lunch. I'm making stuffed vine leaves."

Farah grinned. Keys in hand, she blew her mother a kiss, and ran down the stairs.

She had been back a week now. Part of her was relieved that she had reached her safe haven and was spending some quality time with her parents, but she worried about everyone back in Jordan.

How were Abu Elias and his family doing? And the Lutfis? It was so odd waking up and not finding Hanna. Even Layth crossed her mind, along with the twins and their elegant mother. Then, of course, there were her students. She missed them and the fun they used to have in the classroom.

Jamal rang to update them after Saddam launched missiles into Israel. "Everyone here is thrilled. They're convinced he's going to win the war."

Later that evening the phone rang again. Farah picked it up. "Hello."

"Farah, when are you coming back?" Hanna yelled so loudly that Farah had to move the phone away from her ear. "I went out dancing at the Intercontinental last night. We're having some wild parties over here. I wish you'd come back."

"Oh Hanna, it's so great to hear from you. I don't know. The fares are still so high. I miss you all so much. How are your parents?"

"Everyone is fine. We're all waiting for this to be over, but meanwhile, life goes on."

"Oh my. Listen, do you know anything about my school? Did they recruit anyone else?" Farah's voice wobbled.

"I don't know. School hours are much shorter while this is going on. But I haven't heard anything."

Farah glanced at her watch. They had been talking for over five minutes – international calls cost so much. "Listen, give my love to everyone and take care. I'll call you soon." She hung up.

What was it like in Jordan now, with all the action taking place?

The geographical distance between Cairo and Baghdad seemed as if the war was on another planet. While security was amped up and hotels were empty, the daily lives of Cairenes didn't change much.

She should be grateful she was safe, but somehow, Farah's heart was in Jordan.

***

Farah switched off the TV and joined her mother in the kitchen. "I can't believe this bloody Operation Desert Storm is still ongoing. It's been a month and no signs of it ending any time soon."

Her mother sighed and stirred some onions into the sauce simmering on the stove. "Yes. Think of all those poor people whose lives have been altered by this war. Livelihoods cut - families separated."

"Awful." An involuntary shudder ran through Farah.

Abu Elias and his family would definitely be feeling the brunt of this war. The last glimpse she'd had of them when she had gone to say goodbye was the family sitting together for their evening meal, basking in an aura of serenity. How she had longed for an ounce of their faith.

"The ground battle will be the deciding factor." Her father walked in, a newspaper under his arm. Up until now, Kuwait and its allies had launched air attacks. "According to the news reports, that should be pretty soon."

Her mother looked up. "Any plans for the next few days?"

"Might try to get in touch with some school friends."

All of them were married now with kids. Her ribs squeezed tight. When would it be her turn?

The next morning, Farah woke up to the radio blaring from her parents' room. She yawned and rubbed her eyes. It was still dark outside. Why were her parents awake so early? She plodded into their bedroom.

Her father held a small transistor in his hand, the aerial sticking out like some outer-galactical antenna. He patted the space next to him for her to sit down. "The ground battle started."

All thoughts of sleep vanished. Farah rushed to the living room and switched on the TV.

Almost all channels broadcasted American and British tanks rolling through Kuwait, assaulting head-on, as the coalition forces flattened their way through the Gulf desert studded with minefields.

Farah spent the entire day stuck to the television as the coalition forces destroyed Iraqi divisions and rendered them ineffective.

By the second evening, she was about to suffocate from all the tension. Her stomach ached from all the clenching. Farah grabbed her coat and went for a walk.

The chilly evening air lashed around. Farah folded her arms across her chest and wandered around the empty streets aimlessly, her head clogged with worries and plans to return to Jordan.

Over the next few days, The Mother of All Battles unfolded.

"All those oil wells burning because of Saddam's stubbornness," said her father as apocalyptic images of dense, dark smoke shooting into the atmosphere crossed the screen.

Farah raised the volume a bit. "It's shocking how many Iraqi soldiers have surrendered."

Her father reached for his pipe. "Saddam was out of his mind when he ordered the army to attack U.S. Divisions. Now the Americans are shelling non-stop."

"Poor kids," said her mother, referring to the Iraqi soldiers, "they can't even escape now that the Americans have sealed off the exit routes." She sighed. "They're trapped."

In a few days, The Mother of All Battles was over.

Saddam Hussein lost face. The Jordanians turned against him.

Two days later, Farah traveled back to Jordan. Though she was eager to see everyone again, her heart tugged with sorrow for all the people who had been affected by the war.

***

Amman – March 1991

The school had replaced her. For the next two weeks, Farah scoured the newspaper daily for vacancies but without much luck. Each time a door shut, an ounce of hope ebbed away.

She met Hanna for coffee one morning.

"What if I can't find a job?" she asked, her throat throbbing.

"You will. Don't worry." Hanna reached and squeezed her arm with a comforting smile.

Farah wiped her clammy hands against her trousers, not so sure.

A few days later the phone rang. Farah picked it up. "Hello."

"Farah, it's Angela. Hanna told me you're looking for a job. I was wondering if you would be interested in working at my Montessori kindergarten. The main teacher resigned suddenly."

Farah's pulse quickened. It took her a couple of seconds to respond. "But I don't have any formal training." She bit her lips.

"I need someone with some teaching experience," said Angela, "I'll train you on the job, no need to worry."

Thrilled, Farah hung up. Was God looking out for her after all?

***

Amman – June 1991

Farah and Hanna sat in Hanna's bedroom chatting when Angela walked in.

"Farah, I need to talk to you for a moment." She peered through her thick glasses. "In the last three months, it's been clear that you have a way with children. I have to admit, you've managed very well, and this without formal training." Mrs. Lutfi smoothed a crease on the bedspread. "Why don't you think of doing a Master's degree in Education? It would guarantee you a job at any international school worldwide."

Farah's mouth dropped. "I…never thought of it. I only thought of studying drama. But when that fell through…"

"Teaching is a lot like acting except the audience is different. It's about connecting with them, grabbing their attention, and interacting with them. You have a natural knack and your students respond to you without making an effort." She rose. "Think about it. They have some great programs in the U.S. and I still have contacts there. You might even have a chance for some financial assistance."

Mrs. Lutfi patted Farah on the shoulder and left, closing the door quietly behind her.

That night, Farah lay in bed pondering Angela's suggestion.

There *were* similarities between teaching and acting. Except there was fulfillment in teaching she had never experienced on stage – probably the face-to-face interaction with her students as opposed to an audience.

Stevie Wonder's *'I Just Called to Say I love You'* drifted through from the neighbor's house.

Farah tried to ignore it. Each time she heard this song, it brought to mind the evening Justin had asked her to dance. It was so long ago now. They had been at one of those crazy college parties. The slight tremor in his hand. The warm, fuzzy feeling in her stomach.

The lyrics rang through her mind, the singer bemoaning that there wouldn't be a wedding Saturday in June.

"I want a wedding Saturday in June," she had murmured to herself as he twirled her across the floor, "with *him* waiting for me at the altar."

And it had almost happened.

A small shiver ran up Farah's spine. She pulled up the covers. Was Justin still in Washington?

Chapter Fifty

Madrid, November 1991

P*alacio de Oriente*, the Royal Palace in Madrid, heaved with thousands of journalists who had come to report on the historic event. It wasn't so much the issues they were there to cover, which were already well-known, but rather that Israel and the Palestinians, staunch enemies divided by decades of bitterness, had agreed to discuss them face-to-face.

Shamir, the incumbent Israeli Prime Minister, glowered.

Delegates from Syria, Lebanon, and the joint Jordanian-Palestinian delegation sat across the table on the other side.

Representatives from Egypt, the Gulf States, and Saudi Arabia were also in attendance.

It was, for all purposes, an unprecedented gathering.

Moshe finished photocopying a document and glanced out of the window. The autumnal scene spread out ahead, falling leaves carpeted the ground. A sense of feverish excitement raced through the palace.

Below, Dr. Haidar Abdel Shafi, the head of the Palestinian envoys, was in deep conversation with Faisal Husseini from the non-official "advisory delegation" dispatched by the PLO, despite Israeli objections.

Moshe sauntered to the garden. Faisal was a cousin of the Radwanis, and Moshe had met him before at Ibrahim's, so it was a good opportunity to be introduced to the esteemed doctor.

By the time he arrived, the pair had been joined by a younger man with light brown hair and a neatly-trimmed goatee.

Faisal looked up and smiled. "Moshe."

They shook hands and Faisal turned to Dr. Abdel Shafi. "Let me introduce Moshe Avram, a close friend of my cousin Ibrahim. Despite identifying himself as a Palestinian Jew, Moshe managed to get included in the Israeli Delegation."

"Thanks to my father-in-law's contacts." Moshe held out his hand. "Dr. Abdel Shafi, what an honor to meet you. I've heard and read so much about you. Your opening speech was incredibly moving. Your words captured the essence of the Palestinian tragedy that has unfolded since 1948."

A beatific smile lit the older man's face. "Thank you. We are a people's delegation. None of us are politicians. As academics and intellectuals, we can only present the plight of the Palestinians as we see it, real and raw."

Moshe nodded. "The fact that you are here is a huge step. The world can see that you're serious about peace. Israel is now compromised. They don't want to appear to be the ones refusing to negotiate."

"The Israelis put all the obstacles they could to stop this from happening. They refused to allow an independent Palestinian Delegation to participate, or anyone from the PLO or East Jerusalem. James Baker shuttled back and forth *eight times* until he convinced all the negotiating parties to sit together," said the young man with the goatee with a strong American accent. "Finally, we agreed to the joint Jordanian Palestinian Delegation so no one could accuse us of being difficult."

Moshe winked. "And good for you for accepting those terms. And even better that you acted independently once you got here. Now Israel will have to realize that you're an integral part of the political landscape and you're not going anywhere."

The young man chuckled. He put out his hand. "Jo Khoury."

Moshe grasped it.

Faisal Husseini clapped Jo on the back before turning to Moshe. "Jo grew up in the U.S., but his heart remained with us. He's here to assist with the bilateral and multilateral tracks after the conference for the Permanent Status negotiations and he's Hanan Ashrawi's right-hand man –"

"It was a brilliant move to have her as your spokesperson. I've watched all the TV commentaries she's featured in. She's the star of the show," cut in Moshe. He huffed a laugh. "Bibi Netanyahu and the huge professional public relations team Israel fielded are no match for her eloquence and the battle for the hearts and minds."

"Yes, we're making sure that she gives press briefings, interviews, and answers questions at every interval between the plenary sessions," said Jo.

"How do you feel about the term 'territorial compromise' Gorbachev used?" Moshe posed the question to no one in particular.

"That was his way of telling us to forget about land Israel expropriated in 1948 and concentrate instead only on what we lost after the Six-day war in 1967," said Jo in a tight voice.

A Spanish official from the coordination team appeared. "Dr. Abdel Shafi, kindly follow me to prepare for the closing ceremony."

"If you will all excuse me," said the doctor. He turned to Moshe and squeezed his hand. "When will we have peace?"

He walked off without waiting for an answer, flanked by Faisal and Jo.

Moshe stared after him. As long as there were people like Dr. Abdel Shafi, there was hope for peace.

He stepped inside the Palace and strolled past some of the Israeli Public Relations team, catching a few words on the run – something about corridor diplomacy and pulling procedurals to dampen the momentum. Basically stalling.

Moshe clenched his fists and went up to the small group, on his mouth a smile that didn't reach his eyes. As he approached, one of them nudged the other two. With a round of fake smiles, they changed the conversation, obviously wary of the new face.

After a few inane comments on how the conference was going and what the possible outcomes could be, Moshe wandered off.

He went back upstairs to find a large gathering of journalists. Their focus of attention was a member of the Israeli delegation who challenged a Palestinian university professor to be photographed shaking his hand.

Moshe stood nailed to the ground watching, along with a growing conglomeration from the media. He wanted to slap the smirk off the Israeli's face.

The clock ticked.

Moshe took a deep breath and shifted his weight on his other foot. Along with the mass standing there, he waited to see what would happen.

Would the Palestinian professor shake the hand offered to him or not?

Photographers stood poised, cameras in hand, fingers on the button ready to click.

Microphones pushed forward like some weird offering to an altar.

People jostled one another to get into a better position.

Cameramen swung their equipment back and forth, elbowing anyone who came too near.

Moshe's eyes drifted to the woman in a black trouser suit standing right in front of him. The young peroxide blonde faced the duo, her dark roots begging to be dyed. Being selected to come here was probably the most exciting event that would ever happen to her in her career as a journalist.

A guy with a state-of-the-art camera dropped down on one knee to tie up his shoelace, his eyes darting between his shoe and the two at the center of the attention in case he missed *the* moment.

Moshe glanced at his watch. The closing session would be starting in fifteen minutes. But like everyone present, he too wanted to find out how this moment would unfold as if the entire peace process was hinged on that one handshake.

The Palestinian academic gave a big smile and calmly took the Israeli's hand, posing for the cameras. The hall resounded with a cacophony of clicks and blinding flashlights, a buzz of approval reaching a crescendo.

From the surprised look on the Israeli's face, it was apparent that he hadn't expected the Palestinian professor to be so worldly and courteous.

After the audible collective sigh of relief, everyone dispersed heading in different directions. Moshe, along with a few others, scrambled towards the auditorium, where the closing ceremony would take place.

During Dr. Haider Abdel Shafi's closing words, an idea started to form in Moshe's mind to stop Zionists from sabotaging the peace process. A new entity was needed.

The conference ended on a note of hope, giving the participating countries a roadmap for future reconciliation, and Moshe a new purpose.

Chapter Fifty-one

Washington D.C.,
30th October 1993

My dear Monique,
I can't tell you how delighted I was to receive your last letter with your wonderful news. Congratulations. Amazing that you and Marc are going to be parents. I hope you're not suffering from morning sickness?
I wish I could be there when the baby arrives, but I'll be preparing for my finals then.
Last weekend, I went to a place called Adam's Morgan. Full of ethnic restaurants. The weird thing was that when we were driving there, we passed Kalorama Rd., where Justin used to live – may still be living there, for all I know.
It was quite tempting to go knock on his door. Can you imagine after all these years, and all that happened in between, it still bugs me that I don't know why he jilted me?
My graduation ceremony is in July. Maman, Papa, Tammy, and the kids are all coming. Cyril said he would try. I wish you and Marc could make it, but of course with a newborn

that would be impossible.

Mariam Radwani suggested I look for work in Jerusalem. I'm thinking about it, but first I'll come to France to meet the new addition to the family.

How is Marc? I hope my aunt is being a decent mother-in-law ha-ha.

Please write soon. You have no idea how cut off I feel from home here.

Lots of love,
Farah
P.S. Have you thought of names yet?

***

Washington D.C – April 1994

Justin steered Emily out of the National Art Gallery. He fumbled around in his pockets for his sunglasses as they headed down to The National Mall admiring the Cherry Blossom trees.
Delicate pink decorated the nation's capital as the small buds bloomed into exotic flowers before falling off the branches to carpet the ground.

"Did you enjoy your guided tour?" he asked her.

"Oh, I loved it. Thank you. It makes such a difference to do these visits with someone who studied art history." Emily turned shiny blue eyes to him. "You'll have to bring me again. There's so much we didn't see."

He chuckled. Her enthusiasm was contagious.

Justin led Emily into the park, and they collapsed onto the grass.

Jefferson Memorial, with its Roman Pantheon style and iconic columns, stood on the other side of the Potomac past the Washington Monument.

A gentle breeze wafted through the trees.

Emily slid a rubber band from her wrist and tied her hair into a ponytail. "For all your explanations inside the museum, you're very quiet now," she teased him.

Justin scratched his cheek, an uncomfortable feeling seeping through his stomach. Why couldn't he take this a step further? Emily was such a lovely girl with so many laudable characteristics.

They had been seeing each other for almost three years. It was only normal that she would have expectations. But he *still* wasn't ready to make a commitment.

Except now, the circumstances had changed.

"There's something I need to tell you," he said.

She focused her attention on him.

He plucked a blade of grass and tied both ends into a knot. "I just heard that I'm getting transferred in September."

Emily's eyes widened. "Transferred?"

"Well, the whole point in taking this job was to end up working in the Middle East. That's why I studied Arabic in the first place."

She stiffened. "I see. Any idea where?"

"No, not yet."

"Do you think it'll be Cairo?" There was a tremor in her voice. "Isn't that where Farah is from?"

He kicked himself that he had told her.

"I'm not sure, Emily. It might be Cairo. I'll know in July."

"If you go to Cairo, will you try to –" Emily paused and glanced away before continuing, "see her again?"

Justin stared at the trees in front of him. "No." An involuntary shiver ran through him. "I wouldn't worry about that, Emily." He shrugged, though a knife stabbed at his insides. "I don't think she wants to see me."

"That doesn't answer my question. Do you *want* to see her again?"

He combed his fingers through his hair. "The last time I tried to make contact she was still living in Paris."

It wasn't that he didn't care for Emily because he definitely did. It wasn't Emily's fault that his heart was somewhere else.

A few birds chirped overhead as they flew from branch to branch.

She shrugged. "So, if you leave, what does that mean for us?"

The dreaded question.

Justin weighed the pros and cons. He certainly didn't want to hurt her, but neither did he want to be cornered into making a promise. There would be time to think about it once he was settled in his new posting.

It would be Ramadan in September, the month of fasting in the Moslem world.

A scene from his time in Egypt flitted through his mind.

Farah had tugged at his arm. "But you can't be in Cairo in Ramadan and not experience the Bazaar. Khan el Khalili comes alive at night, and it's so much fun," she had giggled.

Cairo traffic came alive too, he had found out when they had got stuck in a jam at one-thirty in the morning.

Emily cleared her throat, pulling him back to the present.

Justin stood and stretched his hand to her. "Let's go over to the fountain. It's warm enough to dip our feet in."

She placed her hand in his and he pulled her up. "Don't avoid my question, Justin. I think after all this time, I have a right to know if you want to continue this relationship, especially since you'll be leaving."

"You're right, Emily. But I'm not going for a few months. Once I know where I'm posted, we can plan your visit. It'll be a new experience for both of us. We can see how it fits. What do you think?"

Her face brightened up, and his guilt lifted.

Justin tucked her arm under his, and they made for the fountain.

Why did Farah's shadow have to hover between them, reminding him that relationships suffered not from what was said, but from what was left unsaid.

Part III

Chapter Fifty-two

MARCH 1995
Allenby Bridge Crossing between Jordan and Israel

"You. Wait in there." An Israeli female soldier shoved Farah into a small, windowless room, lit by a single strip of neon lighting. More than two dozen people were crammed inside on the tiled floor, and on the sparse plastic chairs.

Her chest tingling with apprehension, Farah stumbled and stretched out her hands to catch her balance. All the seats were taken. She dropped down on the floor and hugged her knees to her chest. Next to her, a young Palestinian woman rocked a crying baby.

Thin, and with a haggard face, the young woman sat with her frail shoulders slumped as if they bore a massive weight.

"Why are we here?" asked Farah in Arabic, her voice trembling. She recalled Mariam Radwani's warnings to anticipate a difficult crossing. "The Israelis consider it an international border."

But this treatment went beyond her definition of 'difficult'.

"The usual harassment." The woman said as she adjusted her headscarf. "Your first time?"

Farah nodded, then frowned. "Why were some people allowed into Israel without any problem?"

"Anyone who has any connection to the Arab world gets a different kind of treatment. Many people in here have western passports but were either born in the 'wrong' country or their last name is Arab."

The woman flapped her hand, a sour expression on her face. "That's enough for the Israelis to treat them like they treat us Palestinians. They might even perform a body cavity search."

"Body cavity search?" Farah shuddered. Her shoulders curled over her chest. What indignity to have to go through.

"Are you here for tourism?" asked the young mother.

Farah shook her head. "I'm hoping to work with Palestinian children. I just finished my Masters in Education in the U.S."

Mariam's idea to work in Jerusalem has appealed to her, excited by the challenge, and the opportunity to help.

"Better not tell the Israelis that, or they might send you back."

Farah stretched out her legs. "How long have you been waiting?"

The harried mother cradled her baby as if to shield it from the harsh glares of the Israeli soldiers. "Three hours so far."

Farah nodded as her eyes met those of the young mother who sighed, then softly hummed an Arabic lullaby in her child's ear.

Farah bobbed her head in tune while her eyes scanned the room.

A gaunt old man, greying at the temples, lay curled up on the floor next to his bag. His olive complexion hinted at his Palestinian heritage. He used his jacket as a pillow, and after sneezing into a handkerchief, shoved it back into his trouser pocket.

A young boy with a bewildered look on his face sat with his family. "Mom, I'm so tired."

Not more than five or six, he pulled at his mother's dress, his accent betraying a North American connection while his features screamed his Arab roots.

His mother brushed a wisp of hair from his eye. "*Ana kaman taabanah ya elbi*," she echoed in Arabic.

A man with a pencil-line mustache, sitting beside her, reached for the little boy and sat him on his knee, rocking him up and down.

An Israeli soldier appeared and yelled. "Nadine Tarazi."

A young woman sprung up and rushed over to a cubicle where another soldier waited to conduct a search.

People pushed together to make space for newcomers.

Farah tried not to crinkle her nose. There was hardly any ventilation in the room. No wonder there was a prevalent smell of body odor even though it was only March.

The young mother next to Farah clucked her tongue and turned to a young man in a wheelchair next to her. "Are you all right?"

He grunted.

Farah mopped her sodden forehead with a handkerchief, exhaled in exasperation, and took off her leather jacket. Perspiration trickled down her chest and sweat stains spread under her armpits. She pinned up her hair and fanned herself with her passport. A fly buzzed and landed on her arm. She tried to swat it but missed. The hard-stone floor pinched into her skin. Farah fidgeted to find a more comfortable position, shifting her weight from one side to the other.

"Mohamed Khalafawi," shouted a soldier, his eyes scanning the room.

A thin, young man sitting in the row of plastic chairs cast a furtive look around before standing up. The bottle of water on his lap rolled onto the floor. He bent down to pick it up and walked into the cubicle where a glowering soldier stood waiting.

Farah turned to the Palestinian woman next to her. "Why don't you take that seat?"

The woman smiled but shook her head. "You take it," she said and gestured with her head to her sleeping child. "I don't want to wake him up."

Farah jumped up and collapsed into the empty chair. The upright back was almost as uncomfortable as the floor. Reaching into her bag, she took out a book, but unable to concentrate, snapped it shut and thrust it back inside. She crossed her legs, kicked her foot in the air, and glanced at her watch. How long would this debacle last?

Two hours later, above the ebb and flow of conversation, someone called out "Farah Gabriel."

Hands clammy, Farah grabbed her bag and headed over.

A surly female soldier jostled her into a small cubicle. "Passport." She held out her hand. "Take off your clothes."

Stone-faced, Farah held out the document in silence. Her hand shook as she unbuttoned her green shirt.

The young Israeli paged through the passport, not bothering to hide the sneer in her voice. "French?"

No, Japanese, Farah wanted to say but bit her tongue, recalling the forlorn group of Haitians lingering at immigration and refused entry.

With slow, jerky movements, she stepped out of her jeans and stood barefoot in her underwear. A pain shot up through her throat. It was so humiliating to be almost naked and on display.

The churlish young soldier picked up first the jeans, squeezed each leg and checked the pockets, then tossed them back on the stool. The silk shirt was next. The last item was Farah's white leather jacket. The soldier rummaged in the pockets, ran her hand down the lining, and patted the entire item before being satisfied that there was nothing hidden inside.

Farah pressed her lips. If only she could douse her with spittle.

"Your shoes."

Farah narrowed her eyes before jerking her head in their direction. "There."

She turned away avoiding the soldier's eyes on purpose, her jaw clenched tight.

The soldier glared at Farah, looked at the shoes, then glowered at Farah again before bending down. She picked up the shoes and stormed out muttering in Hebrew.

THE DOUBLE-EDGED SWORD

Farah threw on her clothes and remained standing inside the tiny booth, her nostrils quivering. She rubbed her temples. Did she have any painkillers in her bag? What a way to start her 'new page'.

The soldier returned, flung Farah's shoes on the floor, and handed her the passport. "You can leave."

She slammed the door behind her.

Farah shot out of the cubicle, past those still waiting their turn, collected her luggage, and burst out of the terminal, blinking at the intensity of the bright morning sun. Hands trembling, she adjusted the collar of her shirt. This must be the only country where authorities hurled a bucketful of humiliation at tourists before allowing them to enter.

Still shaking, she forced herself to continue walking, the wheels of her suitcase scraping against the pavement.

The sound of soldiers yelling at people to move away from the exit gate wafted through.

Farah fished out a packet of Marlboro Lights from her handbag, lit a cigarette, and inhaled a long puff. Following the spiral of smoke with her eyes, she enjoyed the bite of the nicotine for a few moments before stubbing it out and heading to the taxi rank.

All the taxis parked there were *'service'* taxis, taking off only when they had enough passengers to fill their eight-seater cars.

The taxi driver didn't raise his head, instead, wet his finger with his tongue and turned the pages of *Al Quds*, a Palestinian newspaper propped up against the steering wheel. "You can join the family waiting over there but we need to find one more person."

Farah squeezed her eyes shut and took a deep breath. Of course.

"The Israelis color code the car plates from the Occupied Palestinian Territories. It makes it easier for them to restrict movement. Only taxis with Israeli permits are allowed to wait at the crossing have green plates. And they're only allowed to go to Jericho," Mariam had explained over the phone yesterday, "you'll have to change cars there. Remember, green for Allenby Bridge, yellow for the Jerusalem area, blue plates for the West Bank, and white for Gaza."

But with all the tension, it slipped her mind. No wonder Mariam wouldn't set a time for them to meet but kept repeating 'see how it goes' and told Farah to call her once she reached Jerusalem.

How on earth could anyone know when they would get anywhere?

The Palestinian family of six waited on the pavement. The mother petted her four agitated children, two of whom howled at the top of their lungs.

Farah waved at the youngest child, crossed her eyes, and made a funny face. He stopped crying for a moment and stared at her. As soon as Farah walked away, he started to cry again.

His anxiety tugged at her heart.

She leaned against a lamppost, another cigarette in her hand, and waited for more people to exit the terminal.

It was twenty minutes before a young blonde with a backpack and a perplexed look in her blue eyes walked out of the terminal. The large cross around her neck swung to and fro in time with her steps.

Farah raised her hand to shade her eyes and called out. "Hey. Where are you heading?"

"Jerusalem."

A wave of sympathy ran through Farah at the girl's wobbly voice. "We're heading there too, and we need one more passenger for the taxi to move. Would you like to join us?"

The stranger nodded and followed her.

"Where are you from?" Farah spoke over her shoulder.

"Australia."

"That's a long way to come. Why are you here?" She stopped short. Would this stranger consider her nosey like her neighbor back in D.C. when Farah had tried to be friendly, falling back on the characteristic Middle Eastern chit-chat?

To her relief, the Australian smiled.

"There's a group of Christians from different countries meeting here to pray for Jerusalem – just like it says in the Bible."

Farah turned her head away and was about to roll her eyes, but then she stopped herself. Wasn't that precisely what Abu Elias had? Faith.

They reached the cab. Farah threw her suitcase into the boot and jumped in the car. Best to get as much distance between her and the Allenby Crossing as possible. She leaned her head back and closed her eyes. The first thing she would do when she arrived at the hospice was to call '*Atfaluna*', and get an appointment for an interview. Wouldn't it be fantastic if they offered her the job on the spot? She would call Mariam after that.

The car slowed down and came to a stop.

The young Australian arched her eyebrows. "Why are we stopping here?"

The driver got out and slammed the door. "Zis car only go between Allenby Bridge and Jericho. Now you take regular taxi to Jerusalem."

Farah rolled her eyes. She turned to the young blonde. "I'm Farah, by the way."

Her face broke into a big smile exposing her white teeth. "Chrissie."

Farah, Chrissie, and the Palestinian family each paid the driver, gathered their belongings, and trudged towards a white Mercedes that was dented in the back, with some paint peeled off, revealing the ugly puce brown underneath. They all climbed into the car and headed off.

The arid Judean desert stretched endlessly into the horizon, stark and menacing in its own way. As old as creation. And barren. No wonder foreign armies had found conquering this land a daunting task. But then again, the austerity of the place was cleansing and fed spiritual hunger, whether prophets, mystics, or ordinary people. Judging by the Old Testament, a horde of them had experienced some form of spiritual ecstasy.

Farah bit her lower lip trying to remember Sunday School lessons but shook her head in defeat.

The desert air blowing through the window slapped Farah's face, causing her tangled hair to fly wild.

Why does it touch a chord in my soul? You can take an Arab out of the desert, but you can never take the desert out of an Arab.

Her lips twisted into a wry smile. She no longer rebelled against *that* part of her heritage.

"So, this is…" Concern oozed from Chrissie's voice.

The car zoomed past barefoot, snotty-nosed children waving on the pavement.

"Refugee camb for Balastinians who losing their homes in 1948." The new driver acted like a tour guide for beginners. Like so many Arabs, he pronounced the P as B.

"Oh, dear God." The Australian girl covered her face with her hands. "That's just terrible. Those poor children!"

He slammed his hand on the dashboard, his bushy eyebrows almost touching. "Yeah, our life like zis from forty-eight."

The little girl sitting in her father's arms in the front seat wailed.

"No bossible get out. No money, no food. Many children. Very boor." The driver lifted both his hands from the steering wheel and cursed in Arabic then spat out of the window. "Israeel."

Farah's eyes followed the trajectory of his spittle through the window and inched away. "But won't there be peace now that the Oslo Accords have been signed? Isn't this the first step for setting up a Palestinian state?"

The driver switched to Arabic.

"Oslo Accords?" he asked in a deprecating tone. "What did we gain from the Oslo Accords? The Israelis have not stopped building their damn settlements on occupied territory. It's peace on their terms or no peace at all. Have you ever seen a State that is divided into Bantustans? People needing permits from an occupying army to move from one Bantustan to another. Do you consider that a state?" He swerved along the winding route his furious voice echoing in the empty expanse. "You foreigners have no idea what we have to go through here…"

The driver's reaction confused Farah. "I guess I didn't get the full picture. I thought that Palestinians were pleased with the Peace Agreement."

She rummaged in her bag then checked her pockets with rising frustration for her elusive cigarettes.

"Dr. Haidar Abdel Shafi and Hannan Ashrawi were right to withdraw. Israel has no respect for anyone, not even the United Nations. They flout every resolution. Why does the world allow them to get away with so much and does nothing?" asked the driver, his voice seeped in frustration.

The Palestinian father next to the driver pursed his lips in silence, his eyes darting towards Farah and Chrissie.

Farah took out a handkerchief and pressed it to her mouth, inhaling deep breaths. The bending roads made her stomach queasy. Unless the car slowed down, she would start vomiting.

"Please. *Shway shway,*" she said.

He lifted his foot a fraction from the accelerator. "They strip us of our dignity - made an art out of humiliating us. Do you know what it means when a man can't provide food for his family? That is what happens when they deny us access to movement. You wouldn't even treat animals this way."

"Then they wonder about the suicide bombings," murmured the Palestinian woman.

Her husband glared at her.

"My cousin's son had a scholarship to study at Oxford," said the driver, "the Israelis wouldn't give him a permit to get to the airport. Why are they surprised that Hamas resorts to violence?"

Farah forgot her nausea and moved forward, propping her hands on the edge of the front seat. "Oh no. So, what happened to your cousin's son?"

"What happened? He couldn't go. The British Embassy didn't help." The man let out a harrumph. "Imagine. Oxford! How many other opportunities like that will he get?"

An awkward silence followed.

Farah exchanged a sideways glance with the Australian.

"He sounds very angry," whispered Chrissy, "did he say something about Oxford?"

Farah nodded and summarized the conversation.

The Australian's eyes widened in horror.

The Palestinian woman buried her face in her youngest child's head, her husband muttering something under his breath.

The mother of four turned to Farah, breaking the silence. "How long are you staying here?"

Farah raised her shoulders. "I don't know."

The taxi wove its way across the barren desert road past Wadi Qelt, a natural rift in the hills between Jerusalem and Jericho where the Byzantine Greek Orthodox Monastery of St. George perched on the rocky hills.

Chrissie leaned forward to look out of Farah's window. "Oh, what's that?"

"The Mount of Temptation." Farah knew that from the guidebook.

The Australian stared, her mouth half-open. "Oh, my word. Imagine. Jesus stood there. In the flesh."

They had been driving for almost an hour, approaching the peripheries of Jerusalem from the north.

The cabbie pointed as the outskirts of the city appeared on the horizon, sprawling over the hills. "Look."

Farah sat upright to get a glimpse, her eyes never leaving the front window.

Holy for some, filled with mystery for others, and claimed by all. Moslems, Christians, and Jews gathered in Jerusalem for centuries from all over the world, religious nomads converging onto this bitterly divided city to pray to the same God.

No wonder it evoked such strong feelings.

What would Jerusalem deliver for her? Prophets and mystics were for other people. Especially after Paris, the dividing line between her past and future, the before and after, with a graveyard of 'what ifs' in between. Too much water had passed under the *Pont Neuf*.

The cab stopped not far from the Damascus Gate, the main entrance to the Old City.

All eight passengers tripped out, grabbed their luggage, paid, and nodded goodbye to one another.

In her rush to get out, Farah's shoulder bag fell, and her passport, wallet, lipstick, and mascara spilled onto the street. Aaakkhhh!

Chrissie rushed over to her help. She handed the stuff to Farah with a smile.

Farah muttered her thanks and turned to leave.

"Farah," Chrissie called out.

Farah turned around. "Yes?"

The young Australian put her hand on Farah's shoulder and looked her straight in the eyes. "Keep well, Farah." She hesitated before continuing in her broad Australian accent. "God is a healer – only He can heal the pain in your soul."

Chrissie fingered the cross around her neck, a small smile playing around her mouth.

Farah stood still, a hint of a frown between her eyebrows. She mumbled her thanks.

Chrissie waved goodbye and walked off.

Farah stared at the retreating figure. How had this stranger seen right into her soul, just like Abu Elias had?

It took Farah a couple of minutes to maneuver her way across the busy street dragging her suitcase along. She asked a passerby the way to the Notre Dame Hospice. He gestured to continue straight. She followed the wall of the Old City, nestled in the Arab side, with its trove of holy sites, in a fast-paced strut.

The Notre Dame stood on the invisible Green Line dividing Arab East from Jewish West. She reached into the outer pocket of her bag for a tissue. Buried among crumpled paper, lay her packet of cigarettes. Farah whooped in delight.

Cars flew past on the busy road.

Out of breath from the uphill climb, Farah finally reached the Hospice.

A life-size, white sculpture of the Virgin Mary perched on top of the pale, limestone building welcomed guests and pilgrims with open arms.

At the sight of the statue, Farah stopped and gazed at it, her pulse quickening.

Chapter Fifty-three

Farah flung her handbag on the bed before hanging her jacket in the closet. She pulled open brown curtains to allow the sun to brighten the room, unpacked her bag then peeled off her clothes.

As she stepped into the shower, she wrinkled her nose at the strong smell of disinfectant. The warm water splashed off her body and soothed away the unpleasant experience of crossing over the Allenby Bridge.

Once she toweled off and slipped on a long dress, she rang the organization.

The Director, Nora Khoury, gave her an appointment for Saturday morning at 10.00.

She then dialed Mariam Radwani's number.

"Farah, you made it, finally. Welcome to Jerusalem. How was Allenby Bridge?"

"The whole experience was awful. I'll tell you about that when I see you. When do you think you can be here?"

"Give me fifteen minutes. You have the address where you want to go in Ramallah? I don't know how long it'll take us to get there, of course."

"After this morning, nothing would surprise me."

"Don't forget to bring your passport," said Mariam, before hanging up.

With her jacket folded over her arm, Farah ambled downstairs to the reception. Not long after, Mariam arrived.

They embraced and headed towards Mariam's car.

"My mother wants to have you over for lunch."

Farah climbed into the passenger seat and grinned. "Of course. I'd love to see everyone."

Mariam backed out of her parking spot, took a left out of Notre Dame Hospice, and headed towards Ramallah in the West Bank.

At Qalandia checkpoint, Mariam checked the piece of paper where Abu Elias had written out the address.

Farah's throat turned dry as they waited for twenty minutes. Just as she was about to ask Mariam if there was a problem, an Israeli soldier waved them through.

"That was a breeze," said Mariam. "I take the same route to the hospital every day. Sometimes they make us get out of our vehicles and point their guns at us to see our reactions." She twisted her lips to the side. "So, the gentleman you're visiting lives a bit outside the city center. What's his name again?"

"Abu George." Father of George.

Come to think of it, Farah had no idea what Abu Elias's given name was. Only that Elias was his oldest son. It was weird how people in the Levant lost their identity once they had children. As if they stopped being individuals and turned into father or mother of so and so.

They stopped again at El Ram Checkpoint. The soldiers peered through the car window and waved them through.

"We're very close to his neighborhood now." Mariam turned into the street and slammed on the brakes, jolting Farah into her seat belt. A chill ran down her spine.

"*Imshoo min hown, yalla.*" A policeman bellowed through a megaphone that nobody should approach the building which had been razed to the ground.

Two bulldozers stood not far off. Empty crates of explosives that the Israeli army had used littered the area.

Hundreds of Israeli police marshaled the cordoned-off area, pushing the shouting Arabs back away from the rubble as sirens sounded, their orange lights flashing.

Soot and ashes filled the air.

Droves of people scurried down the road, their faces in shock. Some carried small bags or rolled-up blankets under their arms.

Women cried.

Children wailed.

An old woman lay moaning on a stretcher on the pavement.

Dogs sniffed around the trail of debris.

Farah gasped. She stared at the scene of devastation in horror, her skin tingling.

The remnants of the blasted building looked like Armageddon.

Mariam switched off the engine and tore out of the car towards the fleeing mass.

Drops of sweat gathered on Farah's forehead as she followed Mariam. When she caught up with her, Mariam was talking to a man in his mid-thirties with a huge mole on one side of his face. He carried a bulging suitcase in one hand and a little girl, not more than two, in his other, her green dress covered in dust.

Mariam turned to Farah with a grim face. "The Israelis demolished the building he lived in, claiming the owner didn't have a permit to build."

"Permit? I thought Ramallah was Palestinian territory?"

"Indeed. According to the Oslo Accords," said Mariam grimly. She fished out her cell phone and dialed a number.

Her chest hurting, Farah scanned the area. The screaming and wailing continued. Three little girls stumbled past. The oldest one, her face as white as a sheet, held the hands of the other two who kept asking about their parents in plaintive voices. One of them had lost one of her shoes and her foot was bleeding.

At the sight of their stricken little faces, Farah wanted to throw up. The shoeless little girl tripped and fell.

Farah rummaged in her bag, pulled out a band-aid, and rushed over to them. She knelt down, wiped the little girl's foot with a tissue, and fixed the strip on her bleeding foot.

"*Shukran*," said the oldest, her eyes darting around as if she couldn't wait to drag her sisters away.

Before Farah had time to ask them if they needed a ride somewhere, they scooted off.

Up on the hill, jubilant Israeli soldiers gave one another high fives.

She made her way back to Mariam who was on the phone, speaking in a business-like tone, organizing shelter and food.

Farah's mouth turned dry and her heart pounded against her chest. "What's happening? How…"

"I'm sorry to say this is what we live with all the time." Mariam wiped the back of her hand across her forehead. "It happens so often that we formed an organization to help the victims."

"I don't get why their building was blown up?"

Mariam waved an arm. "That's the Israeli justice system for you."

Farah rubbed her jaw. "B-but -"

Mariam snorted. "Farah, the longer you stay here, the more you'll see brutal injustice. And no one can stand up to them. Most of the time, none of this is reported in the foreign press." She walked towards the car. "Come on. I'll take you back to the Hospice. I need to organize logistics for these people for tonight."

Farah followed Mariam, her skin in goosebumps, unable to get her head around what she had just witnessed. "What about Abu George?" She shuffled back a couple of steps, her voice a pitch higher than normal. "Won't I be able to see him now?"

"I asked that man about him. It seems Abu George and his wife are in Nablus to see their daughter. He lives a bit further out, but everyone in this area knows each other."

Though she didn't know him personally, Farah wanted to cry from relief.

Did Abu George's faith sustain him through these kinds of situations like it did Abu Elias?

Twilight had fallen by the time Mariam dropped her off at the Notre Dame. They agreed to meet the day at noon in front of Damascus Gate.

As soon as she entered her room Farah dropped onto her bed. Still shaken by what she had just witnessed, she had no appetite for dinner.

***

The next morning after breakfast, Farah sat on the terrace sipping coffee and stared at the walls of the Old City beyond the precincts of the Notre Dame. Her thoughts drifted to the events of the previous day, and the scores of homeless people who had watched their homes destroyed before their eyes.

According to Mariam, they even had to pay for the machinery to demolish the building.

She would have to adapt fast to the eruptive environment here. The enchantment of being in Jerusalem waned.

Farah glanced at her watch. Time to head for her appointment with Mariam. She wandered down the wide steps that led onto the street.

Damascus Gate was a fifteen-minute walk. Farah set off at a leisurely pace, passing a row of small shops on the other side of the street. The whiff of the famous Palestinian *knafeh Nabulsiyeh* proved too tempting to ignore. She crossed over her mouth watering.

The shop attendant doused the heated slice of baked shredded filo dough stuffed with cheese in rose syrup. When he handed it to her, Farah grasped a paper plate from the shop assistant. She dug the plastic fork into the succulent sweet, savoring every bite with a sigh of delight.

"*Yalla, yalla, itharakoo.*" An Israeli soldier shouted through a loudspeaker from a nearby tank, ordering people to keep moving.

Farah jolted, her euphoria suspended. She scanned the street. Army tanks stood at every corner surrounded by scowling Israeli soldiers. A pang of guilt at the pleasure she just experienced darted through her. The military-infested scene was enough to kill any appetite. She looked at the remaining morsel on her plate, then placed the paper plate on the counter and walked off.

Taxis honked their way through the crowded streets.

Pedestrians spilled out from roadside buildings, brakes screeching to avoid hitting them.

Vendors crammed in front of Damascus Gate selling everything from seasonal fruits and vegetables to cheap, plastic toys.

The powerful voice of Om Kalthoum, the Egyptian diva celebrated across the Middle East, soared from a tape recorder. No fan of classical Arabic music, Farah quickened her step. She walked past a group of women with kohl-rimmed eyes wearing traditional Palestinian caftans. Farah stared at the vivid hand-embroidered red and green stitches in admiration.

Not far off, someone put on a song by Fairuz, the legendary Lebanese singer. Several people stood around singing along while a couple of little girls leaped around, hands on their waists as they attempted a Debke, the traditional dance in the Levant.

Farah stopped, her lips parted, and clapped along to the music.

The pungent aromas of cumin and coriander floated overhead. The same spices her sister Tammy used to make a delicious chicken dish Farah loved.

After two years in Washington, Farah relished the flurry of activity that made up daily life in the Middle East. She had missed the noise and the chaos when she was living in the U.S. capital.

As she continued her walk, the muezzin in the mosque chanted out the call for afternoon prayer, a reminder to the faithful to worship.

She skimmed the crowd and found Mariam waiting in front of Damascus Gate.

Farah hurried forward and hugged her. "Have you been waiting long?"

"No. Just got here. How are you doing?"

Farah shrugged and waved her hand around. "Pfff…"

Mariam nodded with pursed lips.

Arms linked, they entered through the ancient gate and took a sharp turn at the first corner.

Mariam pointed to a narrow passageway, with buildings on both sides. "This is the Moslem Quarter. It leads on to the Via Dolorosa."

Farah looked around with interest. According to her catechism classes, the Way of Sorrows was where Christ had painfully walked almost two thousand years before, doubled over by the weight of the cross. The nuns had taught her that He carried the sins of humanity on His shoulders and by dying on the cross, He sacrificed himself on behalf of all. A slight shiver ran up her back. Such a terrible death.

They edged their way through the crowds down the narrow street, bumping into people from all walks of life as they pressed against one another.

"What's that doing here?" Farah pointed to an Israeli flag that fluttered atop one of the houses, its blue and white contrasting sharply with the greyish buildings. "I thought this was the Moslem Quarter?"

Mariam curled her lip downwards. "That house belonged to my family for centuries until Ariel Sharon confiscated it."

Farah nodded. "I remember my dad and my uncles saying something about how Sharon ordered the killing of civilians living close to the borders in both Egypt and Jordan during the War of Attrition. Of course, I was very young then, but I could still feel this tension in the air."

Mariam nodded. "Yes, the War of Attrition and many other crimes."

They threaded their way through the Old City, that centuries-old melting pot of cultures.

Hassidic Jews, recognizable from their large-brimmed hats, long black coats, thick beards, and their dangling side curls, hurried through in twos and threes engaged in avid conversation, faces unsmiling.

Veiled Palestinian women dragged unruly children behind them, moving steadily through the crowds.

Tourists of different nationalities took their time as they strolled through, snapping photographs of old buildings at every turn. Each time they stopped they blocked the narrow street.

Armed Israeli soldiers on alert stood every few yards, their hands resting on their pistols, their M16 rifles slung around their shoulders.

The colorful diversity couldn't dispel the sense of sadness pervading the place, as if the anguish of the local inhabitants, century after century, had seeped into the stones. More often than not, each invading army had ended up massacring everyone inside these walls.

Mariam gestured toward the building on her left. "This is the Church of Flagellation, the first station of the cross. Do you want to go in?"

Farah's heart raced. This was where Christ had stood on trial in front of Pilate. Was meeting Chrissie a coincidence? What if it were a message from above? Was that what Abu Elias would make of it?

She shook her head. It was the Church of the Holy Sepulcher that she wanted to visit, to light a candle for Abu Elias, as he had asked her.

Mariam's cell phone rang. Farah still couldn't get used to these gadgets that had swept over the Middle East so fast. When she had left Washington a few months ago, they were not yet a fad amongst Americans.

"Farah, I'm sorry, but there's an emergency at the hospital and I have to go. You'll be all right?"

A small wave of panic rippled through Farah. What if some unpleasant incident happened? Would she be able to cope with it alone? She flicked away the thought in an instant. "No problem, I have my guidebook."

Chapter Fifty-four

Justin meandered along narrow, cobblestoned streets of the Old City of Jerusalem. Someone tugged at his arm.

A scrawny boy of about ten in a faded, tattered T-shirt, with a scar under his left eye, tried to sell him a piece of the "real" cross of Christ.

Justin dug into his pocket for some coins. Not finding any, he took out a note of twenty shekels. "*Khod ya baba.*" Here you go, lad. He handed the money to the young vendor with a wink.

The little urchin's eyebrows shot up at the foreigner speaking Arabic. He stared at the note with huge eyes, grinned, and pocketed the money. He gave Justin the thumbs up and handed him the piece of wood.

Justin shook his head.

The child limped away, a sad little figure - possibly his family's sole breadwinner.

Since Justin's transfer from Washington D.C. back to the Middle East seven months earlier, Jerusalem was the only Arabic-speaking area he was allowed to visit.

It still annoyed him that he hadn't been posted to an Arabic-speaking country instead of Tel Aviv. Especially since he was one of the few fluent Arabic speakers in the department.

Still, one of the upsides was being able to visit Jerusalem with its mosaic of different cultures blending together, still steeped in history, and practice his Arabic, recapturing some of his most enjoyable moments in Cairo.

Justin sauntered past the Austrian Hospice, built for pilgrims in the latter part of the nineteenth century. Next to it stood the *Ecco Homo* Basilica, another nineteenth-century construction, with its arches inside and out. Who had decided to name it after Pilate's famous words, 'Behold the man'?

Justin's mind drifted to work and the upcoming presidential visit.

What a nightmare if something happened to the U.S. President while in the Holy Land.

The official tour was an attempt to salvage the stalled peace process and exert diplomatic efforts for a solution to the Middle East quagmire.

The ongoing complexities of the region reminded Justin of a big, messy wound, oozing blood that no one would be able to stanch. It was almost impossible to unravel the mysteries of Levantine politics that changed without warning from one day to the next.

The only predictable thing about this region was its unpredictability.

Following the twisted path past the first seven Stations of the Cross, Justin reached a junction. To one side stood the lively souvenir bazaar of *Souq Khan el Zeit*, and to the other, the Franciscan chapel, with its bright red door, where the Catholic custodians of Jerusalem's holy places resided since the thirteenth century.

Hands in his pockets, Justin fixed his eyes on the uneven stones. He weaved his way through the narrow alleys catching bits of conversations here and there, a mixture of English, Arabic, and Hebrew. Shopkeepers bartered with tourists, and locals discussed amongst themselves. He stopped in front of a shop. T-shirts hung on a rail outside.

In no time, the owner appeared. He was of medium height, slightly on the plump side, with long, dark sideburns. "Can I help you, sir?"

Justin pointed to a white T-Shirt with *I got Stoned in Gaza*. "*Bedee hada. Qad eish?*" This one. How much?

Now that the Israeli army was out of Gaza, and only a few settlements remained, the resourceful Palestinians had come up with a pun on the *Intifada,* when they used to throw stones at the Israeli army.

"Very good, your Arabic. For you, twenty shekels."

"*Khamastaash.*" Bartering was part of the buying procedure here, like in the bazaar in Cairo.

"No, my friend. Bad tourism now. Five shekels won't make a difference to you."

Justin hesitated. Part of him would have liked to continue the conversation, a great opportunity to practice the language. But the other part knew that the man was saying the truth.

"*Mashi. Mishan khatrak bas.*" All right. Only for your sake, though.

The man laughed, took the money, and threw in a small olive wood camel. "Gift for you, my friend."

A warm sensation ran through Justin. "*Shukran, habibi.*" He thanked the man and walked away.

"You welcome here any time, my friend," the man called after him, like many Arabs, omitting the verb.

Justin turned around and raised his hand in acknowledgment.

East Jerusalem, with its hustle and bustle, always brought Cairo to mind. Magical, chaotic, and exquisitely alive. When he had lived there, he couldn't get enough of that happy-go-lucky existence that permeated through the different layers of life. It made routine a rare characteristic, with the unexpected always lurking around the corner.

What a pity he couldn't share with Emily how his year in Cairo had been a turning point that helped him define the kind of life he wanted to lead.

He crinkled his forehead. What was the name of the movie they had once watched together and which had been filmed in Cairo? Ah yes, 'Sphinx'.

Emily had visibly stiffened at the sight of the disorganized traffic and noise on Cairo streets, cars going in all directions, through red traffic lights, and even against the flow. She had turned to him, an expression of horror on her face. "It's really like that? It looks terrifying. What on earth did you enjoy about it?"

Ah well. She would probably enjoy Tel Aviv – it would remind her of back home in Washington.

His cell phone rang.

"Hello."

"Justin?" It was Paula, one of his colleagues at the embassy. "Just calling to invite you to our place next Saturday evening. We're having a reception."

"Sounds great. Count me in." *The lives diplomats lead – one reception after another.*

Justin looked at his watch. Still another couple of hours to kill before his meeting at the American Colony.

Shouts nearby drew his attention.

Not far off, a young man in a kippah, the skullcap Orthodox Jews wore, yelled in Arabic at a Palestinian shopkeeper old enough to be his grandfather, pointing to an old map of Palestine.

"*Hay Israeel, mou Filesteen.*" This is Israel, not Palestine.

Justin flinched.

More young men in kippahs appeared screaming and bellowing. One of them pushed the old man around. A dozen or so Palestinians materialized from nowhere, with Israeli police in their wake, using their batons to separate the group. Their truncheons slammed down on the Palestinians but not on the Israelis.

Justin slipped away, determined to keep a distance from the interminable, raw hostilities in this volatile environment.

***

Farah strolled along the crooked lanes gazing at the little stores before stopping in front of a pottery shop in the Armenian quarter.

A commotion erupted nearby. Farah turned her head, then drew in a sharp breath. The sight of a tall, blond man rushing around the corner reminded her of Justin.

If only she had bumped into him when she was in Washington.

The uproar grew louder, yanking her out of her nostalgic reminiscing. Not far from where Farah stood, some young Israelis pushed an old Palestinian man who stumbled and fell, unable to save himself.

I'd love to grab them by the neck and clonk their heads together.

A dozen or so Palestinians appeared, shouting and pushing through the aggressors to reach the old man, with Israeli police in their wake, thrashing the Arabs.

Just then, a well-built man with dark hair streaked with white, probably in his late fifties, arrived on the scene.

Farah frowned. He looked familiar. Moshe Avram! She was about to call out his name but the thunderous look on his face stopped her in her tracks.

Pushing his way through, Moshe shouted in Hebrew at the police, his eyebrows almost meeting. He gesticulated with his hands aggressively, stunning them into inaction. He reached the old Palestinian and helped him into a chair, barking orders in Arabic for someone to bring the man some water. At the sight of the man's snarling expression and ID card, the approaching officer backed off and called his men to withdraw.

Farah rubbed the back of her neck. Should she go and say hello? No. It was neither the time nor place. Moshe looked furious and there was no sign of his anger abating.

She darted into the Armenian pottery shop. Breathing rapidly, she watched from behind the glass as the commotion outside continued. The older gentleman inside the shop appeared used to it and gave her a sympathetic smile as he hung up hand-painted ceramic tiles.

It took her several minutes to calm down. How fortunate that Moshe had intervened.

A blue and yellow bowl with floral patterns caught Farah's eye. She picked it up, but when she saw the price, placed it back. With a nod of thanks to the owner, she exited the shop. Was Moshe still around? She peered right and left, but he was gone. What a pity. Perhaps she would have the opportunity to meet him again now that she would be living in Jerusalem.

She threaded her way in the direction of the Church of the Holy Sepulcher. From afar, an earsplitting sound, the clanking of metal, approached. It was followed by men's voices chanting what sounded like Byzantine hymns.

"What's that?" she asked a passerby.

"Friday Procession of the Franciscan monks."

Farah skimmed through her guidebook.

The procession was headed to the Church of the Holy Sepulcher. Someone grabbed Farah's arm. She struggled, her hands flapping around as she tried to push herself back but failed. In no time, she was swept into the hysterical crowd.

Brass censers, filled with incense, twirled back and forth with wisps of silver-grey smoke coiling upwards.

She coughed. Hemmed in by an impenetrable moving mass, Farah's eyes darted back and forth, her heart racing as she searched for an escape.

***

Justin paid for the children's books, a gift for his nieces, and headed out of the bookshop.

With the parcel tucked under his arm, he strolled over to the Christian quarter to exit from New Gate. A loud noise attracted his attention. Justin cocked his ears then remembered that it was Friday. That was the day the monks marched through all the thirteen stages of the cross that ended at the Church of the Holy Sepulcher, close to where he was standing. He leaned against the wall and waited.

People around him lowered their heads and crossed themselves, while others shot out of the way, shoving one another to make room as the procession moved along in a majestic manner.

Justin followed the swelling group with his eyes as it swept anyone in its path into its midst.

The procession drew nearer. Justin moved sideways but something caught his attention. His heart skipped a beat. It *couldn't* be. Unless his memory was playing tricks on him.

He strained his head forward to get a better look, but the crowds closed in on him and the face vanished in the sea of other faces. Justin barely managed to step into a small juice shop to avoid being knocked. He ordered a glass of orange juice and sat down, his brows furrowed. But it was hard to distinguish between his imagination and recollections shrouded by the shifting shadows of time.

A twinge of remorse, coupled with guilt darted through him. He closed his eyes for a second. If he hadn't been such a jerk, *she* could have been here with him now.

A woman's shrill scream interrupted his musings.

He quaffed down the remainder of the freshly squeezed juice, paid for his drink, and turned to leave, dismissing his thoughts with a rueful shake of the head.

Chapter Fifty-five

Terrified of being trampled on, Farah elbowed her way through, mindless of who she knocked in the process. The crowds pressed in, causing her to hyperventilate. A group of nuns crossed themselves. Next to her boomed the prayers of a perspiring fat gentleman who reached over her head to touch the holy relics. Farah almost fainted from the smell of garlic emanating from him.

Suddenly, an unexpected arm steadied her from behind.

"Easy now," said a male voice, close to her ear.

She half-turned to see who it was.

The man, with pale skin and light brown hair, shielded her with one arm, the other circling around her back. He shouldered his way and propelled them both forward through the swarms till they reached the inside of the church.

Farah sucked in gulps of air, and took the bottle of water he handed her without hesitation.

"Thank you so much."

"You're welcome," said the stranger.

Farah took off her jacket and wiped her forehead with a tissue. "I don't know what would have happened if you hadn't saved me. I had that horrible sensation that I was going to suffocate right there."

"Well, that's what happens when you join religious processions."

A sheepish smile spread across her face. "I wasn't planning to. I got dragged into it. Jerusalem ignites so much hysteria and religious frenzy…"

The man shrugged and looked around. "I guess people need an anchor, and religion fits the bill."

Tourists armed with cameras and guidebooks shuffled along, the hum of the conversations echoing against the elevated walls and arched ceilings.

"Yeah, I guess." She held out her hand with a smile. "Farah Gabriel."

He stretched a freckled hand. "Gerald Naghton."

She gave him the once-over. He was quite nice looking. A few grey streaks peppered his hair. In his early forties, perhaps?

"Nice to meet you, Gerald, albeit in bizarre circumstances." She rolled her eyes with a small laugh. "Well, thanks again for saving me. If you'll excuse me…"

Farah nodded to him and roamed down some steps, thankful for the shade and coolness.

With its Byzantine splendor, the Church of the Holy Sepulcher yielded a mystical hold over pilgrims for almost two millennia.

A few minutes later she caught sight of the group of nuns. They were now joined by a tour guide. Farah tagged along.

"The Church of the Holy Sepulcher is divided into four sections, controlled by the four major Christian denominations." The tour guide raised his right hand and wiggled four fingers. "The Roman Catholics, representing the Vatican." The nuns beamed. "The Syrian Catholics; the Armenians; and the Orthodox Copts, the Christians of Egypt and Ethiopia." The guide began walking again, waving at them to follow. "And now we will head to the tomb of Christ, built by Constantine, the first Christian Emperor."

More people milled in, some to pray, others to look, their loud voices resounding off the vaulted ceilings.

Farah sauntered over to the Latin part of the Church where Mass was in progress.

Small cymbals tinkled.

Chanting reverberated against the towering walls.

A young priest hurried past, his black robes flapping behind him, reminding her of Cyril. Farah chuckled. Her brother would be so surprised if he could see her now. A bit further on, she found a bench, sat down, leaned her back against the wall, and stared at the stone floor.

What if there *were* something in what both her siblings and Abu Elias believed? Could Christ give her the peace she was searching for?

***

When Farah returned to the Notre Dame Hospice, a silver moon emblazoned the dark sky. She went up to her room and placed her parcels on the bed. Wrapping a light cashmere shawl across her shoulders, Farah headed downstairs to the restaurant. Her eyes combed the place for a table as her stomach rumbled.

"Farah."

She looked to her left, her eyebrows flurried in confusion. "Oh."

It was the man from the church.

Farah stepped back in surprise, then headed to the table.

Gerald Naghton stood up and pulled out a chair for her. The wooden legs scraped across the marble floor. "Please, join me."

Farah smiled. "What a coincidence. Are you also staying here?" Her voice was louder than usual to be heard over the din filling the restaurant.

Gerald adjusted the rimless glasses that had slipped down his nose. "Yes."

"You seem to be spending your day getting me out of uncomfortable situations."

His brown eyes flecked with gold creased.

They both laughed.

A waiter jotted down their orders.

"First time here?" Farah asked.

"Yes. You?"

Farah nodded and leaned back on her chair, her hands clasped on the table. "How long are you here for?"

"Not sure. I'm here for work so it depends how long it'll take me to finish."

"What kind of work?"

"I'm an archeologist."

The waiter arrived with their first course.

"Are you here on a dig?"

She quaffed down the tomato soup and raised her eyes waiting for an answer.

"No." There was a slight pause. "Discovery of some scrolls down at the Dead Sea. Did you hear about it?"

"Like the Dead Sea scrolls that were discovered in Qumran in forty-seven?" She pushed her empty soup bowl to the side.

Gerald looked her straight in the eye before pouring them both some water. "Correct. What about yourself?"

"I'm here to teach."

He nodded. "Interesting."

The clatter of the waiters clearing plates away resonated in the big hall.

Elbows on the table, Gerald rested his chin on his hands. "Any advice on what to see for a first-timer? Which sites are you planning to visit?"

"Loads of stuff. Depends what you're interested in. I have a guidebook upstairs I can lend you if you like." Farah glanced out of the window. "As long as you give it back," she added as an afterthought, her tone playful.

His brogue induced her to ask where he was from.

"Ireland. Galway, if you've heard of it. Although I spent most of my life in London, I never got rid of my Irish accent. And yourself?"

"Half French, half Egyptian."

A Halfie.

Her lips curled into a small, wistful smile.

"What a fascinating combination. Do you join religious processions often then?"

Farah threw back her head and laughed. "No. My first time. I'm Protestant. We don't go for that kind of stuff."

The waiter placed a searing lasagna in front of Farah and a filet mignon in front of Gerald.

Gerald reached for the salt. "Do you think it's safe to go out or should I limit my forays to the bare necessity?"

"It depends. If you happen to be in the wrong place at the wrong time…" Scenes from yesterday's devastating incident jostled through her mind. "You just have to take care. New York is also dangerous, isn't it?"

"I guess it's just – well, you know…the media…"

"The media only cover what they want. There's a lot that goes on here that isn't relayed. I think one just has to be prudent, like any other new place you go to."

If he was so scared of the Middle East why work in a field that demanded traveling here?

Gerald wiped his mouth before folding his serviette and placing it on the table. "I suppose you're right."

"I don't think you should worry. I mean you can't be here and not do the sights."

A slight sense of guilt ran through her. Why had she made him out to be a bit of an idiot?

When they finished their meal, he ushered her out of the restaurant. "Maybe you would lend me your guidebook?"

"Sure." Farah nodded, her eyes creased as she smiled.

Chapter Fifty-six

Moshe swore out loud. Cars lined up along the length of Hayarkon St. meant only one thing: a roadblock.

He didn't have time for that.

Pulling into the nearest pavement, Moshe parked his car and slammed the door. The street was full of furious drivers complaining loudly to one another about being stuck.

He arrived at the U.S. Embassy two minutes before his scheduled meeting. Electrical barbed wire surrounded the area from the outside. A security official escorted him through rows of armed marines to the meeting room, enclosed with self-reflective, bulletproof glass. After the leaks of classified information fiasco at the U.S. Embassy in Moscow a few years back, the Americans had become hyper-aware of security.

The head of the security department, Matt Johnson, began at eight-thirty on the dot.

"Ladies and gentlemen, be advised that Operation White Minaret has now begun."

He emphasized the need to coordinate with Israeli Security before enumerating possible threats in view of the meeting in Tel Aviv between the U.S. President, the King of Jordan, and the Israeli Prime Minister in four months' time.

He then switched on the projector.

The words *Avenging Sword* appeared on the white screen.

In existence for six years now, the group vowed to continue attacks against Israel. Information about them was scant. No one had been able to penetrate nor find out who was the mastermind.

Moshe stared into space. Four years ago, after the Oslo Accords were signed, and there was a glimmer of hope that peace might be attained, he had enlisted the help of his father-in-law.

With the contacts his wealth afforded Gideon Rosenburg, he pulled the right strings and Moshe's idea had come to life.

Within months, the Israeli government agreed to the creation of Sechem, a security branch to keep hard-core Zionists on the radar.

He smiled bitterly. The vague terms of reference had meant that they were unable to stop Baruch Goldstein from massacring Moslems worshiping at the Ibrahimi Mosque last year, proving that Zionists posed as much of a threat as Hamas and the Avenging Sword.

Four years after the Madrid Conference, when there had been much optimism, the roadmap to peace now looked bleak.

With each day that passed, the 'Land for Peace' deal turned more and more into a lifeless dummy, thanks to Hamas and fundamentalist Zionists.

Moshe's thoughts drifted to his nephew. As a settler, Avi vehemently opposed any peace treaty between Israel and the Palestinians, even one as badly crafted as the Oslo Accords.

It wouldn't surprise him if one day a Zionist assassinated some high-ranking politician here for daring to negotiate with the Palestinians. Just like they killed Yossi…

But instead of allowing Sechem to concentrate on people like Avi, he had been called into his superior's office a year earlier to be informed of his change of role.

"We didn't start Sechem to investigate Arabs. Our task is to watch the Zionist threat." Moshe had answered, doing his best to control his anger.

"If you want Sechem to survive, you'll have to cooperate on other matters too. The Avenging Sword is targeting the Israeli Defense Forces with precise attacks. We're mobilizing all units now, including yours."

And that was how he had ended up here, at the U.S. Embassy.

Whatever it took, this high-profile visit *had* to take place without any mishaps. Moshe gritted his teeth. If anything occurred, Palestinians in the territories would be buried under a barrage of attacks and sanctions.

The man giving the presentation pointed to a map of Israel and the surrounding countries. "The Avenging Sword could be in any of these locations." He indicated the south of Lebanon, south of Syria, both to the north of Israel, its borders with Jordan along the Jordan River, and the Aqaba Eilat border in the south. "They could even be in the Sinai Peninsula to the west. We also know that the Avenging Sword was responsible for the attack on the Israeli Embassy in Switzerland last month. They're capable of infiltrating even the most stringent security measures." Johnson paused to take a sip of water. "Our aim is to catch their leader, alive if possible. We want to know who they collaborate with, Yasser Arafat and the PLO, Hamas, George Habash from the Popular Front for the Liberation of Palestine, or who."

He removed the transparency on the overhead projector and replaced it with another. ***Kahane Chai.***

"This is a group of ultra-orthodox Jews. The U.S., the Europeans, Canada, and even the Israeli government consider them terrorists. They pose another major threat. Their goal is to bring down the current Israeli government, using any means possible." Johnson turned to Moshe. "I'd like to introduce everyone to our counterpart from Israeli security, Moshe Avram. We'll be working closely with Moshe and his department to make sure this visit goes smoothly."

Moshe's lips pressed into a perfunctory smile that didn't reach his eyes.

The meeting broke for lunch. The participants trooped into the cafeteria.

"What do you do here?" Moshe asked the blond man sitting next to him at lunch, more out of politeness than interest.

Matt Johnson joined them amidst a shuffling of chairs.

"Moshe, I see you've met Justin Naban, one of our top Arabists. He's with our Public Information Department."

Moshe turned to Justin, his eyebrows raised. *"A'an jad? Wein daraset?"*

"I studied at The American University in Cairo. I was in the CASA program, it's –"

"I know what it is. How come you're not working with U.S. intelligence? A graduate of the Center of Arabic Studies has the ideal profile for that."

Justin winced. "That was the plan but…"

Moshe studied his face. "But?"

The young American shrugged. 'It didn't work out that way." His mouth twisted into a bitter smile. "Your accent in Arabic is flawless. Like a native speaker."

Moshe's lips curled. "I *am* a native. I'm a Palestinian Jew."

Justin's eyebrows shot up. "Oh. Can't be too many of you around."

"There's a few of us. My family for one." He purposely shooed away thoughts of Avi. "I was born here in 1935 when this place was still Palestine. My family lived here for centuries at peace with our Arab neighbors. Of course, we never expected anything to change. But then the holocaust happened, and Eastern European Jews started coming here. And after 1948," Moshe shrugged, "all Jews were given Israeli citizenship, and we, Palestinian Jews, Christians, and Moslems, were militarily separated, segregated by religion. Us on one side, and them on the other."

Justin shook his head. "That must have been a horrendous time for everyone. Hard to imagine."

Moshe winced, *the scene* playing out in his mind again. Though he had been only a child then, it seared his memory like a lump of burning coal. He remembered the day like it was just last week.

The frantic banging at the door wouldn't stop. Abu Youssef was panting, with a bleeding cut on his left cheek. He had stumbled in and fallen on his knees, wringing his hands in desperation.

"Help us. Please. They've told us to leave because we're in danger if we stay. But I don't believe them." Beads of sweat appeared on his forehead. "They threatened us. My family has already left with the rest of our village for the mountainside" His chin trembled and his breath came in bursts before he continued in a shrill voice. "They left everything behind. We're afraid we'll never see our homes again. They'll listen to you. You are Jewish, like them."

The Palestinian had slumped to the ground, wailing about his youngest son who had one leg shorter than the other and wouldn't survive the hardship of a long journey on foot.

The sight of Abu Youssef, a heartbroken, defeated man stripped not only of his home but of his dignity as well, and the fear in his voice still haunted Moshe's dreams.

They finished their meal and went back into the conference room.

Moshe listened with half an ear. This coming week was Yossi's birthday. His oldest son would have been thirty-two if he hadn't been killed six years ago.

***

It was almost six p.m. when Justin reached his apartment. He sank into the black leather sofa, leaned his head back, and closed his eyes. Would it be warm enough to go for a walk on the beach now that the days were getting longer? The ringing phone echoed in the empty apartment. He started.

"Hello."

"Hey, it's me."

Justin shut his eyes then opened them again and rolled his shoulders. "Emily, how're you doing?"

"Fine. But I miss you terribly."

He huffed a nervous laugh. "Did your request for leave come through?"

"Yeah, that's why I'm calling you."

There was an awkward pause. A pack of dogs barked on the street.

They had planned this trip together last time he was home. Why was he hesitant now?

"Great." He pressed his lips tight.

"You don't sound too thrilled," she said, in a hurt tone.

His throat felt dry. He kicked himself for not being more sensitive to her feelings. "No, I am. It's just that it's been hectic the past few days preparing for the Presidential visit. Bomb alert. I'm exhausted and stressed, that's all."

"Bomb alert?"

He ran his fingers through his hair. "Yes, part of the joy of living here."

"But when I spoke to you last time, you said you were so glad to be back in that part of the world."

"It's hard to explain." He didn't have the energy for that.

"You sound weird."

"I'm fine, Emily."

"Ok." She paused. "I'll let you know my flight details when I make my reservations."

"Sounds great. I look forward."

Justin breathed in long and then slowly exhaled. He went into the kitchen, heated up some soup, and began to plan what they would do when she arrived, dismissing that niggling doubt that started to sow its seed.

Chapter Fifty-seven

The lines on Farah's forehead deepened as she perched on the desk in her room, the phone pressed to her ear.

"What do you mean Nora Khoury can't meet me? I scheduled an appointment with her two days ago! I've traveled from Jordan to meet her."

"Well…" The person on the other end of the line hesitated. "I'll check when we can reschedule."

Farah drummed her fingers on the desk trying to control her mounting annoyance. "Thank you. I'll wait."

"Ms. Gabriel, would you be able to come in on Monday morning instead? Mr. Marco can meet you at 9.30."

A huff escaped Farah's lips. "Fine. Thank you."

She hung up annoyed at having to re-plan her entire day now. A slight doubt crossed her mind.

She frowned. Did they not think she was qualified enough?

With an exasperated sigh, Farah headed down for breakfast, slamming the door behind her.

Gerald sat at a table in a corner, but not in the mood for chatting, she didn't join him.

He stopped on his way out. "Morning. How are you today?"

Farah grunted. Then, remembering her manners, offered him a seat. He pulled a chair and sat down. "What's wrong?"

"My interview today has been postponed till Monday. Arrrgh."

"Well, a couple of days off doesn't sound too bad."

She shrugged.

"Would you be interested in seeing some of the sights?" he asked.

Farah hesitated. "Yes, I suppose that's a possibility." This unexpected free time might turn out to be quite pleasant. "We could wander around Jerusalem today. I might meet a friend for lunch. You're welcome to join us." Mariam was on an evening shift today. "I was planning to go to a ceremony I read about at the Church of the Holy Sepulcher this evening."

Gerald's eyes widened in surprise. "Mass?"

"Heaven forbid. I told you, I'm Protestant."

They shared a laugh.

"It's a ritual that was started sometime back in the 13th century." She tilted her head, her brow creased. "The key of the church is held by two Moslem families who have to open and close the door every day. Something about ensuring that all the different Christian denominations are equal that way, so none of them feel they own the church. Some Sultan decreed that and ever since, the keys have been handed down from father to son."

"Sounds most intriguing. And tomorrow?"

"Bethlehem?"

He quirked an eyebrow and smiled. "Great. Meet you in the lobby in about fifteen."

***

After a morning packed with sightseeing, they met up with Mariam in the courtyard of the American Colony Hotel in East Jerusalem and sat at a table shaded by a mulberry tree.

The conversation turned to recent excavations and the scrolls.

"Well, there's been enough archeological evidence examined to provide solid proof that—" Gerald's cumbersome Motorola phone rang. Its antenna reminded Farah of some spatial gadget from the future.

He glanced at it in annoyance, picked it up, and walked off to answer.

Farah turned to Mariam. "Interesting guy, don't you think?"

"Yes..." The Palestinian woman frowned. "Except, there's something that doesn't square here. I mean, he's very nice. It's just that..." She paused as if trying to choose her words. "It's strange that this is his first time here. He's an academic. He doesn't have field experience. This place is an open archeological site, a paradise for archeologists, especially those specialized in Roman and Biblical times. He should have been here a dozen times already."

Farah shrugged. "Well, he's here now, isn't he? How do we know why he didn't come before?"

"And why is he sitting around with you and not digging?" she asked in a puzzled voice.

Farah dismissed the question. Her thoughts drifted to the Garden of Gethsemane they had visited that morning. The two-thousand-year-old olive trees stirred something in her. She pictured Jesus praying there, sweating drops of blood.

How sad Abu Elias would never return to see his beloved olive trees again. *I'll frame the best photo and give it to him next time I'm in Jordan.*

She turned to Mariam. "Would it be possible to go back to Ramallah? I'd really like to try and see Abu George. I promised his brother I would."

"Why don't we make that next week? I'm busy at work for the next few days." Mariam looked at her watch and jumped up. "I've got to go. I've no idea how long it'll take me to cross the checkpoint, and I need to get to the hospital on time."

***

The closing ceremony of the Church of the Holy Sepulcher was over in less than half an hour.

Farah and Gerald wandered through the little streets towards New Gate.

"What about a slice of cheesecake at the best cheesecake parlor in town, according to your guidebook?"

Gerald's eyes gleamed, holding hers for a moment longer than necessary.

She hesitated. West Jerusalem wasn't that appealing, but it would be a pity for the day to end just now. "Why not?"

He grinned. "Let's go then."

They exited the Old City from New Gate and walked past the Notre Dame, continuing towards the west side of the city. Its wide clean roads, chic shops with the latest European fashions, and upscale restaurants provided a sharp contrast to the mixture of modern and archaic of the east side.

"It wasn't so bad having a free day, after all, was it?" Gerald winked at her, putting out his arm before her as a car passed in front of them.

"What's your impression of Jerusalem now?" she asked.

"I'd say it's twisted in its own way. Full of raging contradictions."

"I'm not sure I'd use the term twisted."

"I mean, there's so much emphasis put on religion, then boom, next day there's an explosion, and loads of people get killed. Incongruous."

"Well, it's not that simple, really."

They turned into the pedestrian area, the active part of west Jerusalem.

"What do you expect when the Israelis treat the Palestinians like members of a sub-human species? They have nothing to live for, so nothing to lose," said Farah.

"But human life can't be that cheap."

Farah raised eyebrows. "Well, that's rich coming from…"

"From what?"

Her cheeks flushed. "An Irishman."

"I'm against all bigotry if you must know, including sweeping generalizations about nationality."

She wanted to kick herself. After all, she had only just met him. "Sorry, I didn't mean…"

"Didn't you? You think you know how it is in my country?" said Gerald in a cold voice.

"No, but it's different here." The lame response spilled out of Farah's mouth before she had time to think. She grimaced, glad that it was dark.

"Is it really? I see people here fighting because they think they're right. You think you're right – are you willing to shed blood over it?"

Indignation flooded through her. "No. I'm against bloodshed."

"OK then –"

Farah's temper flared. "But if you strip an entire people of their humanity, what do you expect?"

"You seem to have made up your mind that bloodshed is acceptable –" He threw her a frosty glance and folded his arms.

She clenched her jaw. "What about all the UN Resolutions that Israel flouts without any compunctions?"

They fell silent, a cool breeze forcing them to keep up a fast pace. Farah zipped up her jacket and drew the collar closer to her neck till they reached the shop.

Groups of people stood on the street chatting and laughing, as bright lights glowed into the dark night.

Farah was ready for cheesecake, a hot drink, and to mend fences. She stole a furtive glance at him. Was he still angry?

Not much fun sitting with someone you're not talking to.

They got a table at the far end of the parlor.

"What should we have? The classic cheesecake? Blueberry cheesecake? Layered Turtle cheesecake? Layered Mocha cheesecake? Pumpkin Walnut cheesecake?" She peeped above the menu. "Caramel Pecan cheesecake? Chocolate Raspberry cheesecake?"

Gerald laughed and raised his hand. "OK."

She ordered a layered mocha and he asked for the classic.

"So, Gerald, why aren't you on a dig?"

Was it her imagination or was there a moment of hesitation?

"I'm here to determine the... authenticity of these scrolls I mentioned."

The waiter delivered their orders and rushed off.

"Is it complicated?" Farah shoveled a slice into her mouth and chewed in enjoyment.

"Kind of. Because the parchments are tightly compressed, the brittle leather they're written on tends to crumble easily. Of course, many of them are already fragmented. We use infra-red photography to decipher them."

Farah leaned forward, her elbows resting on the table.

Who were these Essene monks, living in caves out by the Dead Sea thousands of years ago? How strange that the only witness to their existence were these scrolls they had written.

"How can you determine what period they were written in?" she asked.

"By paleography, the comparative study of script." Gerald took off his glasses, cleaned them, and put them back on again. "We also conduct a scientific analysis of the leather, the ink, the linens they're wrapped in."

"I see."

Gerald rested his elbows on the table and crossed his arms. "I find it rather bewildering that you want to stay here - you could get a job anywhere else."

Farah shrugged. "Isn't it better, when you believe in a cause, to do something about it?"

"Maybe."

"Well, as we say in French, *les gouts et les couleurs ne se discutent pas*. To each his own."

"Don't get me wrong. It's very noble that you want to help children here. But why would you intentionally put yourself at risk, living in such a place?"

She raised her hands. "Let's agree to disagree."

Gerald nodded, took another bite of the cheesecake then, with a challenging smile, looked straight into her eyes. "Let me change the subject completely then. How come you're traveling here alone?"

Startled, Farah dropped her fork onto her plate with a clatter. "What do you mean? Why wouldn't I travel alone?"

The Irishman raised his eyebrows. "You're a very attractive woman, so it would be only normal to assume you're in a relationship."

Farah's cheeks burnt. She studied the pictures on the wall, his question drumming in her ears. "It's…complicated." Her voice wavered.

She reached into her bag, fishing around for her cigarettes. As she pulled them out, she fumbled, dropping the packet on the floor. Picking it up, she extracted a cigarette.

Gerald bent forward, matches in hand.

Farah drew a couple of puffs and crossed her legs, foot bobbing. There was no reason to get flustered and worked up. She didn't owe this man any explanation.

He cocked his head. "It's just hard to imagine that someone like you would be single."

"Well, I am."

Gerald grinned and stretched his legs out in front of him into a relaxed position, arms crossed. "I sense a story there."

"You're very inquisitive, aren't you?"

The conversation was taking a turn she didn't like.

He laughed, his eyes boring into her. "You're only making me more curious."

Farah puckered her lips and avoided his gaze.

Gerald continued to observe her with the same intensity.

Minutes passed, their silence amplifying the surrounding sounds.

Farah stubbed out her cigarette and racked her brain for a clever retort but found none. "So, are you married, Gerald?"

"I'm divorced. And to answer your next question, I have two teenage kids who live with their mum. Jason and Anna."

She nodded.

His brown eyes twinkled. "Your turn now."

She folded her arms across her chest and remained silent.

"OK, Farah" Gerald raised his hands. "I'm sorry. I'm being nosey – none of my business."

A small queue of people waited to be seated. The level of conversation competed with the background music.

They paid the bill and left, the crisp night air slapping them in the face.

"Are we still on for Bethlehem tomorrow?" he asked, as they reached the Notre Dame.

Farah nodded. "Of course."

"Perfect. See you in the lobby at eleven."

Back in her room and ready for bed, Farah glanced out the window before drawing the curtains. The sight of Gerald hurrying out of the Hospice caught her attention. She stared at him with narrowed eyes. Where was he going at this hour of the night?

Chapter Fifty-eight

The drive to Bethlehem took twenty minutes. The taxi dropped them in front of the Church of the Nativity.

Contrary to what Farah had expected, the church looked unimpressive from the outside, like the front wall of a fortress.

Surly Israeli soldiers, mostly young boys in their late teens doing their military service, patrolled the square, brandishing armed weapons in a menacing way as they glowered at the locals.

The small city of Bethlehem stood almost empty apart from a handful of tourists. A couple, with Canon cameras hanging around their necks, conversed in Spanish as they wandered around. Shopkeepers loitered in front of their souvenir stores offering 'best prices' for their carvings in olive wood.

Palestinians hurried along their way, eyes to the ground, avoiding the armed Israelis.

Farah hastened into the church without waiting for Gerald, ducking her head at the last moment at the low and narrow entrance. Was it this low on purpose to deter invading armies, or to ensure that visitors bowed as they approached Christ's birthplace?

The inside of the church was dark and pewless. Old mosaics depicting saints and angels lay scattered across the walls. A carved screen, adorned with icons, stood in front of the main altar while dimly-lit lamps provided light inside.

Gerald arrived and together they climbed down the stairs leading to the Grotto of the Nativity.

Farah grabbed Gerald's 35mm compact Kodak camera and pushed him towards the Manger.

Gerald sucked his cheeks in, opened his eyes as wide as he could, and made a rabbit mouth with his lips.

Farah suppressed her laughter and clicked a photo.

When they finished touring the church, they strolled back to Manger Square and walked into a jewelry shop, empty, apart from themselves.

Farah chose a gold Jerusalem Cross for Tammy's upcoming birthday and an olive wood rosary for Cyril.

She dug her hand in her pocket for the money when something hard at the bottom brushed against her fingers. She frowned and pulled it out. "Oh."

Gus's gold puzzle ring lay in the palm of her hand. Farah stared at it with a tinge of sadness before dropping it back into her pocket.

***

A small, down-market restaurant at the corner of the street on the other side of the square was the only one serving warm food. It was crowded inside, obviously popular with the locals.

They sat down and Farah ordered *Makloubeh*, a typical Palestinian dish made of chicken, carrots, cauliflower, and rice, cooked together with spices and herbs.

"The translation of its name from Arabic is 'Upside Down' because of how it's cooked," she explained, with a gesture as if turning a bowl over to dump its ingredients.

Gerald emitted a hearty laugh. "Brilliant. I love it."

The waiter brought their food.

They dug in, and as soon as they had finished, they paid and left.

Outside, ominous clouds gathered. With typical March treachery, drops of rain trickled down from a grey sky, replacing the perfect morning weather.

"Do I see more soldiers than when we arrived?" said Gerald.

Farah's eyes flicked back and forth, taking in the scene. IDF troops swarmed the square. She jammed her hands under her armpits, picked up her step, and followed Gerald, her limbs tingling.

They jumped into the first taxi that pulled up.

The radio blared with news of an attempt on the life of the Israeli ambassador in London. Farah slunk into her seat, her mind conjuring up a variety of repercussions, one worse than the other.

Soon enough they were stopped by a bunch of grim Israeli soldiers patrolling a newly erected checkpoint at the outskirts of the Holy City.

Farah's breathing quickened.

"It's okay," said Gerald, "we're foreigners. They have to let us go."

The thud of combat boots reverberated in the open space. The soldiers rounded up all Palestinians and shoved them to the side of the road. There was no shelter from the rain. Men and women crouched, exposed to the elements till they were allowed into a dilapidated booth for a full body search.

"*Inta, henik,*" yelled one of the soldiers at their taxi driver, motioning with his gun indicating they should all get out of the car.

Gerald leaned forward. "What on earth –"

Farah laid a warning hand on Gerald's arm, her eyes cautioning restraint. They climbed out, walked over to the soldier, and handed him their passports.

The young Israeli soldier snatched them and glowered.

"Welcome to the Occupied Territories," whispered Farah, her tone laden with sarcasm.

They hovered around, not sure what to do next. The wind picked up. Farah clutched her handbag close to her chest, her insides quivering.

"I'll get my jacket," said Gerald and headed towards the taxi.

On the other side, some young soldiers pushed around an old Palestinian woman, bent down by her years. In a shrill voice, she invoked the Almighty for help. A terrified child, not more than seven or eight years old, probably her grandson, clung to her letting out piteous shrieks each time the soldiers poked the old woman with their guns. One of the soldiers grabbed him and yelled. The little boy dissolved into loud sobs. The old woman collapsed onto the ground amidst a torrent of tears.

The child, still crying, managed to wiggle away from his captor and ran over to her with a piercing scream.

A soldier thrust him roughly onto the ground and manacled him.

The child kicked his little legs into the air as he was hauled into the open army truck.

Her heart thumping, Farah leaped forward and ran to the soldiers who stood around talking while they smoked.

"*Slikhah.*" At least she knew how to say 'excuse me' in Hebrew. She dug her nails into her clenched palms so hard that they hurt. With a huge effort, Farah kept her voice on a level tone. "Your colleague just manacled a child and threw him into that van." She pointed to the little boy behind her. "He can't manacle a child – the boy can't be more than seven or eight years old."

"Move away," one of them snapped, "it's not your business."

He must have been nineteen or twenty, but already had a callous look in his dark eyes.

"It *is* my business." Farah's anger overcame her fear. She glared at him and placed her hands on her hips, the muscles in her face tightening. "Your country signed the UN Convention on the Rights of the Child? You've just broken international law."

"Keep away," the soldier roared, jerking his index finger and almost touching her face. The veins in his forehead throbbed as if they were about to pop. "Or I'll have you locked up for obstructing our work."

"I'm a French citizen. If you want to cause an international incident, then go ahead and arrest me." If only she felt as brave as she sounded.

The soldier glared at her. He muttered something in Hebrew and went off to join the other soldiers standing with their guns pointed over the waiting Palestinians.

Gerald appeared his brows furrowed. "What happened?"

Scowling, Farah jerked her head towards the sobbing child cowering on the lorry bench.

He placed his jacket over her shoulders, "why don't you get into the car? I'll talk to them."

"The old woman and the child -" her voice trembled.

"I'll handle it."

He walked her to the cab then strode off towards the Israeli soldiers to inquire why their driver was detained.

Her stomach muscles quivering, Farah slipped out of the taxi. She crept over keeping enough distance but still within earshot.

"Excuse me." Gerald addressed one of the soldiers who leaned against the booth smoking a cigarette and staring ahead of him. "Our driver is detained for no apparent reason, and we're on our way back to Jerusalem. Is there a problem?"

"*Slikhah?*"

Farah chewed her inner cheek. *Slikhah up your butt.*

Gerald repeated himself but in a louder tone as if talking to a delinquent child.

The soldier shrugged, eyed Gerald from top to bottom, and turned away.

Farah started her way back to the taxi when something made her pause. Had Gerald just spoken Hebrew? She spun her head around.

Gerald was glaring at the soldier menacingly.

Unsure what to do, she stood there for a moment before scuttling away, her breath condensing on the air as if she had just opened the deep freeze.

A few minutes later Gerald appeared, a grim look on his face. He pushed his mobile phone back into his bag. "I'm sure they understand English, but only when it suits them."

"Mariam might be able to help us get out of here. May I use your phone?"

He grunted and handed it to her.

But there was no answer, neither on the mobile phone nor the landline.

Farah's heart pounded. Her interview was tomorrow morning.

***

It was a couple of hours before Mariam picked up the phone. "Sorry, Farah, we were all at a wedding."

In a few words, Farah summarized their predicament, unable to keep the panic from her voice. "I can't miss this interview, Mariam. I just can't."

"OK, I'll tell Ibrahim. I'm sure Moshe can do something about it. Don't worry."

At the mention of Moshe's name, Farah relaxed a bit. Her head leaned against the back of the seat as she fingered the puzzle ring in her pocket, shutting her eyes tight for a moment. This surreal experience could now be added to the movie script her life resembled.

The irony hit her as she stared into the black velvet night. A handful of glittering sequins swung in the backdrop stretched above them, a perfect setting for a romantic film.

Outside, soldiers shouted and transmitted messages over walkie-talkies in Hebrew without ceasing.

Exhaustion took over and her eyes closed.

She woke up to Gerald's nudging. For a split second, she had no idea where she was. Then she remembered. She sat bolt upright and glanced at her watch. It was two in the morning.

He waved their passports at her. "Let's go."

"Whew. Finally." So, Ibrahim *had* been able to pull strings. "What about the old woman and her grandson?"

Interview or not, she wasn't leaving without them.

"Apparently, they're free to go too," said Gerald.

A wave of relief shot through Farah. She hurried over to them, Gerald a couple of steps behind.

The old woman sat huddled in a corner her arms around the child who was rubbing his red wrists. He shivered so hard that his teeth rattled.

Farah scooped the little boy into her arms, handed him to Gerald, then bent down to help the old woman.

"*Haja*," Farah used the term of respect due to an older woman, "I'll take you both home. *Inshallah kheir*." All will be well.

The grandmother's groans echoed around them, and she covered her head with her hands in a gesture of resigned despair, tears trickling down her old, shriveled face. "One son already in an Israeli jail. Four months now and no news from him. We don't even know why he is being held."

Farah held on to the old woman's arm as she shuffled forward, Farah murmured soothing words. "Please tell me where you live."

They heaped into the taxi and headed to Bethany, the driver speeding through the quiet streets, away from the scene of humiliation. Everyone remained silent, engrossed in their own thoughts.

The car pulled up in front of a small group of terracotta white brick houses, the street lamps disgorging disproportionate shadows over the area.

Farah helped the old lady out and offered her an arm to lean on as they took small steps towards the second house.

Gerald followed, carrying the sleeping child across his shoulder.

A skinny woman in her mid-forties, face drawn, ran towards them, her arms outstretched as she emitted frantic screams. Swooping the little boy into her arms, she clasped him firmly to her chest. He woke up and started wriggling. When she put him down, she turned to the old woman and repeatedly kissed her head and her hands. Loud, wailing sobs wracked her body.

Farah and Gerald slipped away as sleepy neighbors spilled over to hear what had happened.

"If we don't leave now, they'll insist on inviting us in," said Farah, "I have to get some sleep. My interview is in less than six hours."

She fidgeted in her seat, her brain foggy from exhaustion, unanswered questions shoved to the side.

Chapter Fifty-nine

The interview ended.

Farah stood up and shook hands with Marco.

"I'm very sorry about the confusion, Ms. Gabriel. I apologize once again that Ms. Khoury was unable to be here, but we'll organize it for next week as she has the final say. I will strongly recommend we hire you. Your qualifications are exactly what we need."

Disappointed, Farah nodded.

Now the question was should she stay in Jerusalem, or return to Jordan then cross back again?

"Thank you very much," she said, "I'll contact you in a week then."

"Before you go, would you like to see the children?"

"I'd love to." She swept aside her morose thoughts; there was time enough later on to make decisions. "Would it be possible to go to the Ladies' room first?"

"Sure. It's on the other side of the corridor. I'll show you where to join us."

They passed down a corridor and up some stairs. To the left lay a row of offices, and to the right a large room encased with glass. A circle of wide-eyed children sat cross-legged on a colorful blue and yellow carpet, frayed around the edges, while a young willowy blonde stood in the middle telling a story.

Farah clasped her hands together and stared at them for a moment, a sad smile on her face.

Marco pointed down the corridor and Farah rushed off.

On her way back, raised voices emanated from one of the offices.

Farah peered at the metal sign on the office door. Nora Khoury – Director. How strange. Wasn't Ms. Khoury out of the country due to a family emergency?

Doubts flowed through her mind like lava. Farah strode towards the door. She wanted to get to the bottom of this.

Someone touched her elbow.

Marco stood behind her, a polite smile on his face. "Please, Ms. Gabriel. This way," he said in a firm voice.

Reluctantly, Farah allowed him to steer her back.

They entered the room just as the teacher reached the end of the story, the spellbound children still in a circle. As Farah shut the door behind her, several of them turned their heads, and, seeing Marco, ran over to hug him.

Laughing, Marco lifted first one, then another, asking them how they were and making a fuss of each one in turn. He waved his hand towards Farah. "Say hello to Ms. Farah. She'll be working with us *inshallah*."

A little boy with a black patch on one eye came over and hugged her.

Farah crouched down and placed an arm around him and asked his name.

Marco put his hand on the little boy's head. "An Israeli bullet took out his eye." He spoke in English so the children wouldn't understand.

Farah drew the boy close to her chest, her cheek against his curly brown hair, and kissed his head.

He pulled back, a bright smile on his little face, and placed a trusting hand in hers.

She squeezed it. If only she had a magic wand. Tears clogged her throat making it difficult for her to swallow.

The little boy pulled her towards a corner where a pile of soft toys lay in a messy heap. He picked up a long-eared dog and waved it under her nose, a big grin on his face.

"Who's this? What's his name?"

"Pluto," he said in a shy voice.

"Well, hello there, Pluto," she said in a deep voice. "How do you enjoy school?"

The child gurgled in delight.

Marco walked up to them. "I see young Basel has taken to you – first time he's come out of his shell despite all the coaxing."

"Really?" Farah was gratified, hearing that she had made such an impact on the boy. "I'm looking forward to working here."

At the door, Farah turned around and blew a kiss. "They need to live their childhood so badly."

Marco followed her through the door to the main entrance and bid her goodbye.

Outside the run-down building, a cloudless bright sky greeted her. Farah basked in the embrace of a blazing eastern sun. Chirping birds flitted from one tree to another. She drew in a deep breath.

In the taxi to the hotel, she brimmed with excitement at the challenging prospect. Her mind raced with different activities she could introduce to help these children deal with their fears and insecurities.

Farah was bursting to give Gerald an account of her morning. The curious incident of Nora Khoury bugged her, but it could wait for now.

Forgetting her exhaustion, she bounced into the lobby and spotted Gerald tucked away in a far corner, a piece of paper in his hand. He was engrossed in reading. She rushed over to him.

"Hello."

Gerald jumped and stashed the piece of paper in his pocket. "Hello,

Farah." He smiled. "You seem to be in a good mood."

She plopped herself down on the comfortable sofa opposite him and beamed. "I am. I think I've been offered the job."

"You *think*?"

"I have to go back next week to finalize everything. I'm almost sure I'll get it."

"I guess congratulations are in order. Tell me more."

"The interview went well. But the best part was when I went to see the children. It was… *amazing*." She flapped both arms in the air.

The sense of accomplishment when she got her Master's degree paled in comparison to the thought of a job where she could make a difference.

Suddenly, Farah yawned as the nervous energy that fueled her dissipated. She stood up with a regretful smile. "I'm afraid I'm done for the day. See you tomorrow morning."

Gerald nodded. "Have a good rest."

Chapter Sixty

Farah woke up early the next morning. She jumped out of bed, washed her face then plonked herself onto a chair.

What was she going to do for a whole week? Returning to Jordan was a bad idea. Remaining in Jerusalem wasn't so appealing either.

Farah hugged her knees to her chest. What about heading north to Galilee then meander down the coast? She could visit Michele whose husband was posted as Military Attaché at the U.S. Embassy in Tel Aviv.

"You're always welcome to come stay," Michele had said when they both graduated back in Washington.

Then Gerald popped into her mind. Farah placed her head in her hands. Why and how did he become part of the equation?

Because she enjoyed his company, that's how. And her biggest fear was never meeting anyone and ending up alone.

She took a deep breath. Was she ready to venture into mangled-up romantic territory again? With someone who probably carried a load of emotional baggage?

Her lips drooped. Why would Gerald be interested in her? Then she frowned. A thought niggled in the bottom of her brain; there was something vaguely familiar about him. She tried to focus but shook her head in defeat and gave up.

After a warm shower, Farah got dressed and went for a walk. The morning air would clear her head.

She ambled aimlessly in the empty streets and found herself in front of the Garden Tomb. The guidebook mentioned that this was where Protestants believed Jesus had been buried.

She ventured into the small, green haven, and sat under the shade her back against a tree for the better part of an hour. Birds tweeted overhead. The perfumed scents of flowers that sprinkled the garden, the bursts of vivid mauves, pinks, and yellows, was carried by the breeze. The paradox of such beauty existing side by side with so much injustice struck an uneven balance that would be hard to get used to.

Then, a sense of determination surged through her. For the first time, she was purpose-driven for a *worthy* cause – to make a difference in the lives of those kids.

But would the tiny drops she could contribute to a sea of change really count for anything?

***

When Farah returned to her room, she rang Michele and made arrangements to be there in a few days' time. Then she called Mariam to tell her about her travel plans.

"Well, in that case, my mother insists you come for lunch today. Unfortunately, I'll be working then. But I guess I'll see you when you're back next week," said Mariam.

"Great. I can thank Ibrahim for his help the other night."

The call ended. Farah sauntered down the corridor and knocked at Gerald's door.

"Hello there." He held a towel in his hand, the remains of shaving cream on his face. "I knocked at your door earlier to go for breakfast but you weren't there. The receptionist said you'd already gone out."

"I went for a walk. Coming down?"

"Give me a second."

Gerald waved her in.

She sat on the chair and glanced at some papers on his desk. He rushed over and snatched them. "Classified info. If you find out I'd have to kill you."

Farah jerked her head back.

Laughing at his own joke, Gerald opened his briefcase and shoved the document inside. "Just joking. I don't want to bore you with my academic stuff." He winked.

He put on his jacket and opened the door.

They headed downstairs to the terrace.

"What are we doing today?" He spoke as if he had taken her company for granted.

"I need to make some travel plans."

He raised an eyebrow. "Travel? Where are you going? I thought you were hanging around till next week to sign your contract?"

Farah toyed with a lock of hair. "No. I decided to visit some friends in Tel Aviv."

"Well, isn't that a coincidence? I too have to go to Tel Aviv for some meetings in a few days and was thinking of taking advantage to do some sightseeing too. I'm going to rent a car anyway. I was planning to leave tomorrow, but leaving today is fine. I can give you a ride."

The waiter placed a pot of steaming coffee on their table.

Gerald poured a cup for Farah, then for himself.

Astonished by his suggestion, Farah stared at him unblinking, not quite sure what to say. Did that mean they would do the entire trip together till they got to Tel Aviv?

"No, there's no need for you to change your plans, really. I mean why would you want to leave a day early?"

He raised the cup of coffee to his mouth. "Honestly, it's no problem. I'll be glad of the company."

She squeezed her lips tight and masked her vague annoyance at this last-minute intrusion from a somehow secretive stranger who had splashed orange paint on her palette of pastel plans.

"Really, Gerald, there's no need," she repeated.

"Well, obviously if you think I'm intruding..." He sounded upset.

Maybe he *was* interested in her after all?

"No, no, I didn't mean that. It's just—"

"So, we're settled then. Up north we go," beamed Gerald.

Forcing a polite smile, she nodded.

"What time should we set off? I'll look into car rentals this morning."

"I have a lunch appointment. We could leave right after."

They stood up and he put his hand in his pocket to pay when an identification card with his photo tumbled out.

Farah bent down to pick it up. In that fraction of a second, she glimpsed a three-lettered first name before Gerald's head bumped against hers as he almost toppled her pouncing on the card.

"Ouch." Her hand flew to her head.

"Oops. Sorry. Are you OK?"

Feeling a bit dazed, she rubbed her head as a flash of pain shot through it.

She nodded and walked off to hail a taxi, her head spinning.

As the cab headed towards her destination, Farah wracked her brain. Why would he lie about his name? It didn't make sense. She shrugged. Probably Gerald was his middle name and he preferred to go by it. She chuckled. Her cousin Marc's first name was Blaise, but since childhood, he refused to answer to it, till everyone ended up using his middle name.

***

Farah finished eating and leaned back in her chair, taking in the lavish dining room of the Radwani mansion in East Jerusalem, its period furniture and treasures hanging from the walls, many of them heirlooms.

With its arches, columns, and high ceilings, the manor steeped in the nostalgia of the past, evoking better times. That was when the Radwanis were the leaders of Jerusalem, with hordes of family members in notable positions, including that of the Great Mufti.

"Thank you, Auntie Alia. Delicious meal."

"*Ahlein habibity*, you're always welcome here." Alia Radwani, the matriarch of the family, poured Farah a glass of mint tea. "I'm so sorry you had to go through that awful incident at the checkpoint."

Ibrahim Radwani walked back into the room, his teenage son trailing behind. "It's a good thing you contacted us, Farah."

"I can never thank you enough, Ibrahim. I'm indebted to you big time."

A gentle smile lit up Ibrahim's face.

Hussein offered Farah some cake. "Why didn't you stay with us, Farah? Don't you consider us family?"

"Next time, *inshallah*."

"We don't want Tammy saying we didn't look after you."

Her face broke into a huge grin. "Of course not. Anyway, I'm leaving this afternoon to Galilee."

"Don't forget to tell Tammy we're expecting her soon," Alia reminded Farah as she kissed her goodbye.

"Of course not, Auntie. Thank you again so much, it was great seeing you all."

Farah slipped on her jacket and made for the front door.

"Wait, Farah." Keys jingling in his hands, Hussein rushed to catch up with her. "I'll give you a lift back."

It was a short drive to the Notre Dame. Hussein pointed out some landmarks. Within a few minutes, he turned into the parking lot and stopped.

Farah opened the door. "Thanks for the ride. See you when I return."

Hussein laid a hand on her arm. "Farah, take care, and please don't get into any more altercations with the Israelis–"

"Hey, Farah."

She swung her head around.

Gerald walked towards the car.

"Who's that?" asked Hussein.

Farah already had one leg out. "Somebody I met here. An archeologist who's dealing with the new scrolls that have just shown up."

Hussein put a hand on her arm and gently held her back. "Don't be so trusting."

The note of unease in his voice made her turn around and face him. She cocked her head, one eyebrow raised. "Don't worry, Hussein. I'm a big girl and I can take care of myself. But thanks for the warning."

She stepped out of the car, climbed the steps, then waved goodbye.

"Ready to set off?" Gerald pointed to the parking lot. "I loaded our bags; we can leave now if you like."

Farah nodded and followed him to the rental car, refusing to dwell on Hussein's cautionary words. Enough paranoia; they were going on a trip and she was determined to enjoy it.

Gerald opened the door for her then got behind the wheel. "Who was that?"

Farah hid a smile. "A relative." Would he pursue the matter or just let it lie?

The engine purred into action and Gerald swung the car onto the main road, heading north. "You're full of surprises, aren't you? I had no idea you have relatives here."

"There's a lot of stuff about me you don't know," she chuckled, "like thirty years' worth."

"Why are you acting as if this is some state secret?"

A peel of laughter escaped Farah's lips. She cut it short, afraid he might think she was flirting. "No state secret. He's Mariam's brother. I met him in Amman." She rolled down the window to let in some air.

Gerald took a swig out of his bottle of water. "Were you living there?"

"Yes."

"When?"

She fiddled with the radio trying to find some music. "A few years ago."

"How come?"

"You know what, you sound like the bloody Israelis at the checkpoint with all their annoying questions."

She mimicked their accents in English. "Vat is ze purpose of your trip to Israel?"

They both laughed.

"Have you ever been to Jordan?" she asked.

"Huh?"

"What? You think you have exclusive rights for questioning? Wouldn't Jordan be a fascinating place for an archeologist? All that history, Biblical, Crusades…"

"As a matter of fact, I have been." Gerald's voice sounded measured.

"When? Why? How long did you stay?"

"Oh, I was only there for a few days." There was a slight pause. He shifted in his seat. "On holiday."

"Holiday? Where did you go?"

"The usual touristic sights. Petra, the Dead Sea, Jerash."

"When?"

"About four years ago. Now *you're* starting to sound like the Israelis."

Farah ignored his attempt at joking. "During the Gulf war?"

Gerald gripped the steering wheel with both his hands. "Right after it."

He stepped on the brakes just in time to avoid a herd of goats moseying out from the field to the side of the road. They were followed by a goatherd in tattered clothes holding a stick.

Gerald gave them a stunned stare.

The goatherd raised his hand in acknowledgement, his goats taking their time crossing the narrow road, pushing and jostling one another.

Farah stuck her head out of the window and let out a loud 'Baa', scaring the closest animal into hurrying away.

"Oh my God – such a Biblical scene coming to life," said Gerald.

"Very unusual considering you are in Biblical land." Farah's voice was slightly mocking as she settled into a more comfortable position to sleep.

Chapter Sixty-one

The piercing sound of the phone disrupted Moshe's concentration. He clicked his tongue in annoyance and picked it up.

"Yes."

"Mr. Avram, Mr. Ibrahim Radwani is on the line," said his secretary.

"Put him through," he ordered, tapping his pen on the desk.

"Moshe, thank you for your help the other day with Farah."

There was a slight pause. "Actually Ibrahim, by the time I got through to someone responsible, she'd already left the checkpoint."

"Really? She said a phone call came through and they were able to leave."

"Well, whoever helped her, it wasn't me. Hopefully, Ms. Gabriel won't get herself in such a messy situation again. Though if she insists on playing Robin Hood, let me know."

They chatted a bit longer exchanging news and comparing calendars so they could meet up soon before hanging up.

Moshe heaved a sigh. Pity he couldn't see Ibrahim more often. He shook his head and picked up the file about an attack in Ashkelon a few weeks earlier.

He frowned. How were the Palestinians getting their weapons?

Several cups of coffee later, Moshe packed up for the day not wanting to be late for the monthly family lunch at his sister's.

Half an hour later, he reached his sister's street in Herzilya, just north of Tel Aviv.

With the manicured lawns, rows of neat villas, bougainvillea cascading down the white walls, its marina, and sandy beaches, today's Herzilya was a far cry from the semi-cooperative farming community Theodor Herzel had created at the start of the century.

Little wonder that affluent Israelis chose to live there, as well as foreign diplomats.

He slowed down, parked, then climbed out of the car.

Joshua opened the front door with a wide smile. "Uncle Moshe. Just in time."

"Hello, Joshua." He gave his favorite nephew a friendly slap on the shoulder before entering inside.

His brother David gestured to the empty chair at the end of a table laden with food, resembling a medieval banquet. "Moshe, sit down."

Moshe suppressed a wan smile at the number of dishes laid out and sat down. Rachel, his brother Nathan's wife, piled food on a plate for him.

His body turned cold. How different coming here used to be. Yossi was now gone and Ruth had become more dead than alive, not talking, not reacting. The doctors were unable to predict how long her state would last.

"Where's Carla?" asked his sister.

Moshe stared down at his hands, an ache darting through his chest. "At home. She didn't want to leave Ruth alone."

He forced himself out of melancholic reminiscing and turned to his brother-in-law, his body tensing. "So, Benjamin, do you think the Knesset is going to pass a law stating it's illegal to shoot Palestinian children?"

His brother-in-law shrugged a weary look on his face and continued eating.

Joshua looked down at his plate while Rebecca and Rachel exchanged news of children to the clinking of cutlery against plates.

The doorbell rang.

Joshua leaped up to open it.

Avi's voice drifted through.

Moshe clenched his jaw.

Avi bent down to kiss Rebecca before doing the rounds. "Hi, Mom."

At the sight of the AK 47 slung across Avi's shoulder, Moshe gripped his wrist with his hand. He glared at his nephew. "Why are you still carrying that thing in here? Isn't there enough violence outside?"

Avi grinned and slipped the rifle off. "Sorry, Uncle Moshe."

He was about to place it in the corner when his mother glowered at him.

"Not here, Avi, please. Why do I have to keep repeating myself? If you're going to bring that repulsive thing with you, it stays out in the hallway." Rebecca's voice rang out loud and clear.

She turned to her brother, a hint of concern in her voice. "You look exhausted, Moshe. Those dark rings around your eyes tell it all."

Moshe grunted and raised his hands in a non-committed manner. "Preparing for the visit of the American President."

He let out a long, loud breath of air. If only the visit would be canceled.

They continued chatting at the table for a couple of hours. By the time they finished, darkness had already fallen.

Avi left at the same time as Moshe, his gun back on his shoulder.

Moshe turned to his nephew, a hardened expression on his face. "I won't offer you a ride."

Avi grimaced. He raised a hand and continued walking up the street without looking back.

Moshe turned the key, but the car wouldn't start. He tried again. Still no luck.

"Aaaagh." He banged his hand on the steering wheel. He should have taken the car to the mechanic once the engine had started giving trouble – but like so much since tragedy had hit their family for the second time, he had just let it go.

A couple of young lads walking past obligingly gave him a push, and the car rolled.

Moshe popped the clutch and the dead car revved back to life. He switched to second gear and was off, waving his hand out of the window in thanks.

At the top of the street just as he was about to make a U-turn to get onto the highway, he watched as Avi jumped into a black Four-Wheeler with tinted glass and no lights. The vehicle sped off into the star-studded night.

Moshe frowned, his sixth sense on alert at the sinister scene. He swerved to follow the Jeep down the same route, having trouble keeping up.

The Four-Wheeler drove at an atrocious speed, spraying dust as it veered onto the road to Hebron, the ancient site of Abraham's burial place, with Moslems and Jews disputing ownership.

A cold, bitter wind whipped its way through the open expanse, shrieking like a starving animal.

Half an hour later, the city of Hebron lay before them, dark and quiet, as if someone had cast an evil spell, causing the inhabitants to sleep for a hundred years.

A sour taste filled his mouth. There was only one word to describe settlements. Warts. Big, ugly home-grown warts, watered and nourished by the Israeli government to suit their needs.

The black jeep halted in front of what must have been a house once upon a time, but now only a couple of walls still stood, the rest of it looking like a derelict building site. No doubt destroyed by a bomb. Or demolished.

Moshe slowed down and parked to the side, a good distance away. He opened the glove compartment and grabbed his binoculars.

It wasn't long before the passenger door opened. His nephew, a Palestinian *kuffeyeih* covering his face, stole towards the side of the house.

Moshe curbed the impulse to rush out and throttle Avi.

A sickly trickle of moonlight penetrated the darkness.

Moshe drummed his fingers on the steering wheel. The binoculars, no longer in use, hung limply from his other hand.

Another *kuffeiyeh*-covered head emerged on the side of the road and stalked over to the side of the remaining ruins.

Moshe shot the binoculars up to his eyes again. He crept out of the car, careful not to make noise, and inched his way closer.

The corner at the back of what remained of the house still stood, a partial roof supported by some pillars.

Avi was engrossed in a hushed conversation, though if the slight raise in tone was anything to go by, it seemed like an argument was taking place.

Moshe jotted down the number plate. He strode back to his car and turned the key. Fortunately, the engine switched on and he drove home, his mind bulging with questions.

Chapter Sixty-two

Gerald parked the car and leaned over Farah's seat. She pored over the map on her knee, tracing the route with her finger, the light breeze playing with her hair. "We can stop at the site where Jesus fed the five thousand."

"The Church of Multiplication." Gerald read out loud from the guidebook. "In Tab…" He turned to Farah with a confounded look. "How do you pronounce it?"

"Show me." She snatched the book from him and hooted with laughter. "*Tabgha.*"

He grinned and bit his lower lip. "What do I know? I'm just a stupid foreigner who can't pronounce your language properly."

Farah laughed all the harder and made a stream of guttural sounds from the Arabic alphabet. Traveling with Gerald had turned out be a lot of fun.

Her head hanging out of the window, Farah inhaled the earthy scent of grass with deep, contented breaths. The array of orange and yellow wildflowers swayed in the wind like a patchwork carpet hemming the road from both sides dazzled her eyes. Tufts of wild grass sprouted through the rocks.

The Golan Heights lay ahead, dwarfing the surrounding scene, a range of rugged mountains, idyllic to look at, a perfect adventure for mountain climbers. But thick barbed wire sticking out from big, rusty iron rods that pierced the air clamped the atmosphere with an ominous feeling, reminding her that the 1967 war had been fought on this ground.

Flocks of wild birds filled the air with an occasional squawk along with the swishing noise of cars passing them on the highway, their random colors dashing through the lush green setting.

They reached the ancient church that overlooked the water. Lake Tiberius shimmered like a mirror, reflecting the golden rays of the morning sun. Picturesque sailing boats of vibrant greens and blues glided gracefully along, like royal damsels in a Medieval court, their floating veils trailing behind them.

Much to their annoyance, the church building itself was locked.

School children in grubby clothes, chaperoned by several nuns and a priest, strolled around the area chattering away in Arabic, an occasional Hebrew word thrown in here and there.

Nudging Gerald, Farah nodded her head toward the group. "Arab Israelis."

He stared at her, his brow wrinkling.

"The Palestinians who didn't flee the country but remained here after 1948. Israel was compelled to give them citizenship." She smirked. How galling that must have been for the Israeli government.

Her ankle boots scraped against the rocky ground as she bounded off to explore the open space, a corner of her mouth lifted, mischief brewing in her mind.

How on earth had she ended up in Galilee with a man she barely knew?

Farah kicked a flat pebble and continued walking, hands shoved in her pockets. Her mind shuttled back and forth between a past she wanted to escape, and a present that was turning out to be as unpredictable as a snowstorm in the desert.

She removed her boots and ambled around, enjoying the feeling of grass against her bare feet, grounding her in nature. As she followed Gerald with her eyes, the sight of his light brown hair tousled by the wind stirred emotions within her that she hadn't felt in a long time. He was deep in conversation with the priest and some of the nuns.

By the time she decided to join him again, the Irishman acquired quite a following; a bunch of giggling teenage schoolchildren trying out their English on him and jostling one another to get close.

Farah sauntered up to him.

Some of the kids squabbled as they all took guesses about his nationality.

"*Min Irelanda.*" Ireland. Farah's voice cut through to settle the matter.

The students stared at her with big round eyes.

She chuckled to herself. Her response in Arabic shocked them into silence.

"*Men wein inti?*" Where are you from, asked the tallest boy amongst them, who couldn't have been more than thirteen.

"*Misr.*" Egypt.

Some of the children giggled nervously. Others grinned and shook their heads.

"No. Really, where are you from?" he insisted.

"And France." She grinned as she gave the same boy a thumbs up for speaking in English, then turned to Gerald. "Come on, let's go." She pointed to her watch and crooked her finger at him to follow her to the car. "Or else we won't have time to visit Capernaum today."

A dwindling number of the enthusiastic audience accompanied them, reminding her of a farewell committee. She and Gerald climbed into the car and waved as they drove away.

"That was an unexpected lesson in social history from the priest – fascinating to hear the viewpoint of an Israeli Arab. I suppose they must have become quite..." Gerald paused for a moment as if trying to find the right term, "'Isrealized', for lack of a better word."

"Israelized?" She grimaced. "I doubt they identify with the Israeli National Anthem, which glorifies the hope of returning to 'Israel'." She turned to face him. "Do you know that most employers in Israel stipulate proof of military service? That way the majority of Arab Israelis are shelved without even an interview because they won't join the Israeli 'Defense' Forces."

She squeezed her eyes tight remembering Gus's explanations. How did this stranger manage to dig up the demons of her past?

"I'm sorry if I offended you. Totally unintentional. I obviously need to educate myself more. Will you help me?"

The contrite look on Gerald's face made her smile. She nodded.

**

With a slight flutter in her stomach, Farah glanced at the mirror before heading to the lobby.
Gerald stood facing the elevator, hands crossed behind his back. A low whistle passed through his lips when she appeared.

She blushed and touched her hair, swept up in a French twist.

"You just look…stunning." He handed her a gift. "I got you something to say sorry."

She peeked through the bag to find a pretty blue and yellow ceramic bowl. "Oh my. Thank you. It's beautiful."

The same colors she had admired at the Armenian shop in Jerusalem.

On an impulse, she gave him a quick hug. A warm feeling spread through her heart.

They reached the waterfront. Small restaurants crowded together on the pier. They chose the first one with an empty table facing Lake Tiberias.

Strings of colored lights bounced off the water, and rows of set tables stood close to one another, flowing white tablecloths swaying gently in the breeze. Well-dressed people of mixed ages wandered about while Israeli music played in the background.

Following the waiter's recommendation, they ordered the famous St. Peter fish dinner.

Farah drank in the lively scene, so different from the tenseness of Jerusalem.

Gerald raised his gin and tonic towards her before putting it to his lips. "*Slainte*, as we say in Ireland."

She lifted a glass of white wine. "*A la votre.*"

"You're a real mystery lady, aren't you? Eyes like a forest in the mist."

A searing heat flushed through her cheeks. She took a few sips.

Gerald leaned forward, his elbows resting on the table, and continued to study her. "I bet you miss Paris."

She shrugged.

The waiter arrived with the food.

"*Bon appétit.*" Without waiting, Farah dug into her meal.

"You must've enjoyed living there, no? I mean, the City of Light. So beautiful. So romantic."

Farah's eyes wandered off towards the water, as scenes from another life played through her mind. She put down the cutlery onto her plate and crossed her arms against her chest.

Gerald reached out for his jacket. "Cold?"

She put out a hand to stop him. "No. Someone just walked on my grave."

His lips in a taunt line, he moved to the edge of his seat, like a cat about to pounce on a mouse. "For me, Paris is the *most* beautiful city in the world."

She looked away.

He swigged his drink. "Don't you agree?"

Farah shifted in her chair. Why couldn't he get the message?

"My goodness, Farah, trying to have a conversation with you is like trying to extract a tooth with a nutcracker!"

"I don't want to talk about Paris."

From now on she was taking control of the rudder.

To dispel any awkward silence, Farah rattled on about how she hoped to help the kids through her new job, ignoring Gerald's distracted look. By the time they reached the hotel, she had run out of steam and couldn't wait to get to her room.

Gerald pushed the button of the elevator. "By the way, I meant to ask you, how long are you staying in Tel Aviv?"

"Three days. Why?"

"I just thought we could drive back together since I also need to return to Jerusalem."

Her thoughts momentarily froze. "Umm, well, yes, I suppose we could."

***

The next morning, they drove up to the Golan Heights.
A plaintive staccato from the green hills broke the silence.

They parked and headed towards the sound. A dozen or so men dressed in black *shirwals*, the traditional baggy black trousers of the Druze, with megaphones in their hands, shouted news across the border. Their words echoed in the vast surroundings.

Then the group of men on the Syrian side proceeded to do the same.

Farah blinked as she took in the scene of separated families on each side of a fence shouting their news across an armed border between enemy states.

A frisson ran through her body. Close enough to see, but not to touch. As sure as winter followed autumn, there was no hope of change.

Gerald took out his Kodak and clicked away. "You know, when you suggested we visit the Yelling Hill, I thought you were having me on, that it was a pun on the Wailing Wall."

They were in Majdal Shams, one of the five Druze villages in the Golan Heights that Israel had occupied after the 1967 war.

Farah thumbed through the guidebook. "According to this: *When Israel occupied the Golan Heights during the war of 1967, Druze families got separated. Some remained in Syria while others ended up in Israel.*' It seems this is a daily event."

Unable to peel her eyes away from the hill, Farah repeated what Gus had taught her long ago. "Nobody really knows anything about the Druze. They're kind of…a secret cult if that's the right word. They're considered heretics in Islam."

Gerald's phone rang. He puffed out a breath of annoyance and wandered off to answer the call.

Farah sat down on the grass next to Gerald's backpack. Another phone rang. She started and peered into the backpack.

The lights of the bulky cell phone lit up with each ring.

Farah stared at it in puzzlement.

Before she could entertain another thought, Gerald swooped up the phone, his lips clamped.

She stared at him. "How come you have *two* cell phones? People can barely afford one."

"I rented two at the airport, one for work, and the other for personal phone calls."

Farah tutted and yanked herself up.

On their way back to the car, they stopped at one of the tourist shops. Farah bought a small hand-woven carpet with intricate eye-catching knots, a typical Druze design, the vivid reds and greens contrasting against the white background.

Gerald tossed her the keys. "I need to find the loo. Meet you at the car."

She unlocked the vehicle and pulled out her suitcase from the back seat to see if she could fit the carpet in there.

Gerald's gift fell onto the ground with a smash.

With a cry of dismay, Farah bent down trying to gather up the pieces, but there were too many.

A heavy sigh escaped her lips as she crammed the fragments of pottery into a plastic bag she hid in her suitcase then slammed the door. She opened the boot to shove the carpet in there.

A cardboard box, right in the middle, spiked her curiosity. She peeked inside. Three bronze statuettes tarred by time, a couple of ancient-looking bowls, and some glassware lay there enveloped with bubble wrap. She banged the boot shut. What was Gerald doing with this stuff?

She stared ahead of her unblinking, her thoughts spinning for a moment, then laughed at her paranoia. Any archeologist dealt with ancient artifacts. Maybe he was transporting them to the Ministry of Antiquities.

Except that the Ministry of Antiquities was in Jerusalem, not Tel Aviv.

She rolled up the carpet and placed it next to her suitcase on the back seat.

Suddenly, a piercing pain shot through her side, forcing her to double over.

"Farah, what's wrong?"

Gerald was next to her, lines of concern creasing his face.

She pressed her hand against her right side and struggled to breathe. "I don't know. It's like…like a knife inside me, shredding me to pieces."

Groaning, she collapsed onto the ground in a heap. Bile rose to her throat.

"Easy now." Gently, he helped her into the car.

Farah stretched back in the seat and closed her eyes. Beads of sweat formed on her forehead, the intense pain making her dizzy.

"The closest hospital is half an hour away. I'll drive as fast as I can," he said, "let me know if you need me to stop."

She nodded and managed a weak smile. It was such a relief he was with her.

They finally reached the hospital.

"Wait here." Gerald pulled up in front of the entrance, yanking the parking brake. "I'll get a wheelchair." He patted her arm, murmured to her not to worry, then dashed off.

Unable to keep the contents of her stomach down, Farah stepped out of the car and threw up before foundering onto the ground.

"Hey, are you ok?"

She opened her eyes.

A pair of military boots stood before her.

Rallying her strength, Farah raised her head.

An Israeli soldier, probably not more than twenty-one, stooped in front of her. "Are you ok?" he repeated.

She nodded weakly and turned her eyes away. "Yeah."

He shrugged and strode off.

Gerald ran up with a wheelchair, helped her into it, and wheeled her to the entrance.

At the pristine hospital, the doctor pressed her stomach, tapped on her back, and checked her pulse. "From the kind of pain you describe, I'd venture to say it's your gall bladder. Except you seem far too young for that." His voice sounded puzzled. "I'm going to give you a shot for the pain, as well as some tablets. I suggest you do some blood tests. And I wouldn't go near greasy food for a while."

"Will I be ok by tomorrow?" Farah asked in a feeble voice.

"It would be a good idea to rest tomorrow."

Gerald leaned against the wall his arms folded. "We can drive to Acre now, and you can rest there."

Farah puckered her lips. What bad timing.

The needle pricked her as the doctor gave her the injection. "Ouch."

She stood up but collapsed back onto the chair, her legs too feeble to carry her.

Gerald stood by her side, and, in one swift movement, he lifted Farah off her feet, ignoring her loud protests. "Doctor's orders."

She attempted a smile.

He winked at her, their foreheads almost touching, then pretended to stagger at her weight.

She swallowed and clung to him, her fingers interlocking behind his neck as his strong arms carried her across the hallway and out onto the street. A fleeting thought shot through her mind. What it would be like to rest her head on his shoulder, against his clean-shaven cheeks that smelt of Pears soap.

Unlike the men in her family, Gerald didn't use cologne. Or was that because he was traveling?

She stopped herself.

Her heart had been empty since she had left Paris. How she longed for some romance in her life. This emotional vacuum could get dangerous.

They reached the car. With great care, he placed her on the seat.

Was he aware of the intimate thoughts she entertained about him? Did he share them?

After an hour and a half, the city of Acre came into view. The southern sea wall dipped into the blue water of the Mediterranean, fortress-like, an impressive defense line against sea or man.

Gerald parked in front of the hotel and went off to get her prescription.

Farah stared at him as he walked away. He *was* caring – but why? If he was attracted to her, why didn't he make a move? Maybe he just felt sorry for her?

A shadow crossed her face and she shivered, but not from the cold. Would she ever get out of this self-deprecating mood?

By the time they checked into the hotel, the sun was close to setting.

He carried her bag up to her room.

With a sigh of relief, she lay down on the bed. At least she could rest now.

"If you need anything, just give me a call. If I'm not in my room then on my cell phone. I'll come straight away. But try to sleep. I'll come back again later to check on you."

She nodded, swallowed her tablets, and dozed off.

The whole of the next day she stayed in bed, and by the following evening, all traces of the pain had vanished.

He knocked on the door and walked in. "Gosh, you look much better."

Farah grinned. "I feel much better." She drew the shawl around her shoulders tighter. "Thank you for looking after me so well."

"I've never seen someone go so white so fast as you did." He sat facing her and stretched out his legs. "Did you watch the news today? There was an explosion in Jerusalem this morning. Good thing we left."

Her hand flew to her mouth. "Jerusalem? East or West?"

"The infamous checkpoint on the way to Bethlehem." His tone was flat.

Farah took in a loud breath, her eyes wide. "Oh my God. I wonder if there were any Palestinian detainees there? Or if any of the same soldiers were on duty?"

She closed her eyes, the events of that night coming back to her in a rush, the prickling fear, the anger consuming her, the frustration at how helpless she was and…

In an abrupt movement, Farah turned to him. "Do you speak Hebrew?"

"What a bizarre question. Why?"

"I heard you that night at the checkpoint when you were talking to one of the soldiers."

He lifted a single eyebrow. "I learned a smattering of words from your guidebook."

She winced. It *had* been a stupid notion.

"How was the sightseeing?" she asked.

"The citadel is impressive. You'll have to come back when you're better. Unfortunately, I have an appointment tomorrow at twelve-thirty, otherwise, we could have done some of the sites, but there won't be time."

The next morning, they headed off to Tel Aviv. As they drove into the street, Farah followed the map and guided Gerald to Michele's posh neighborhood where the apartment building was located.

They stepped out of the car.

Her arms tensed as he handed her the suitcase.

"I'll give you a call in a couple of days so we can drive back together," he said, a soft look in his eyes.

She nodded slowly. With hesitant steps, she ventured into

the building glancing over her shoulder. Strange how she had grown accustomed to his presence.

***

Michele ushered Farah into the living room, drew the curtains, and sat down next to her.

"It's lovely to see you again, Farah. Great timing as well. One of my husband's colleagues is having a reception tonight, and I asked to bring you along."

"Sounds nice." Shame she couldn't ask Michele to invite Gerald as well.

Michele chatted about life in Tel Aviv and the stark contrast between living there and any other posting.

"Do you have any Arab Israeli neighbors here?" asked Farah, wondering about social dynamics.

Michele shook her head. "Oh no. You never see any in this neighborhood. Actually, very few in Tel Aviv in general. But you'll probably meet some tonight."

"Oh?"

"Yes, there'll be a good mix of people there – other embassy personnel, some UN officials. There might even be some Palestinians if they can get through the checkpoints," said Michele.

Chapter Sixty-three

Justin edged his way through the crowded apartment to the mini bar in the corner.

The doorbell rang again. Someone opened the door and Justin glimpsed the silhouettes of more guests arriving.

Conversations and laughter almost drowned the background music.

The bartender handed him a glass of orange juice. He loitered around observing rather than networking.

A waiter stretched out a tray filled with *kibbeh*. Justin reached out and helped himself to a deep-fried ball of finely chopped minced meat, stuffed with pine nuts. He glanced at his watch. He should make an effort to socialize, it was important for his job. He eyed the area, deciding who he could start a conversation with.

Well-dressed people filtered past him to the bar.

"I'll have a glass of white wine please," said an oddly familiar voice.

Justin froze then spun around, a flush of adrenaline tingling through his body. "Farah."

It was as if he had been shoved into a Kafkaesque scenario that he had never rehearsed. The noise around them stilled.

His heart squeezed in his chest.

"Justin…" Her face paled as if she had just seen a ghost.

During those seconds of silence, a valley of memories hovered between them.

It was only when someone turned up the music volume that the moment was shattered.

He put out a hesitant hand.

She recoiled. The glass in her hand quivered. Farah planted it on the table and rushed into the empty balcony, far from the blaring lights.

He was right on her heels.

"Farah. I have to talk to you." He was next to her now.

She had hardly changed, except for her eyes. They were harder now, not soft like they used to be.

His chin dipped down to his chest. He was to blame for that.

Before he knew it, her palm swung across his face in a resounding slap.

The vein in her forehead twitched. "You're ten years too late."

Justin covered his smarting cheek with his hand. He drew in a deep breath. "Please give me a chance to explain. I've been living in remorse for all these years. I tried to contact you. I even came to Paris…" He broke off.

Was she even listening to him?

Farah leaned over the balcony railing and stared into space before turning to face him again, her lips pinched tight.

He ran his fingers through his hair. "It's not what you might think."

She twisted the diamond ring on her left hand. The blue-mauve hues of the stone glittered.

When she finally raised her head to meet his eyes, hers were two glistening green pools.

Chapter Sixty-four

Tel Aviv – March 1995

Moshe cursed. It was almost 10.00 PM, and he was still stuck at the office *again*.

Someone rapped at the door. Saul, his deputy, walked in with a concerted look. "Moshe, the car you asked us to track, apparently, it's a rental. We checked the identity of the person who hired it, one Joel Lewis – turns out he's been dead for three years."

Moshe sat bolt upright, his eyes fixed on Saul. "Are you sure?"

"Yes, we ran the IDI database."

IDI was the most reliable state-of-the-art database worldwide.

Moshe tapped his pen on his desk and cleared his throat. "I want 24-hour surveillance on Avi Benjamin Cohen. I want all his phone calls tapped." Moshe ignored Saul's surprised look. "I want a background check on everyone, and I mean *everyone*, he talks to."

"What does your nephew have to do with this?"

Moshe slammed his hand on the desk "Just do it."

The phone rang.

THE DOUBLE-EDGED SWORD

Moshe waved Saul out. It was probably Carla in tears again. She would need comforting.

Instead, it was the Ministry of Defense.

"We just received information that The Avenging Sword has struck again," said the voice on the other end of the line, "this time from the strategic *Tel el Harra.*"

Moshe narrowed his eyes. *Tel el Harra* was an extinct volcano overlooking the Golan Heights in Syria.

Moshe placed his head in his hands and groaned in frustration at both his slippery, trouble-making nephew and this phantom group no one had managed to pin down. For a moment, he indulged in what he would like to do to each of them but quickly pulled himself together. He grabbed a file from the bookshelf. His phone rang again. "Yes," he answered wearily.

His niece's hysterical voice sounded down the line. "Uncle Moshe."

He sat up. "Tamar, stop screaming. What happened?"

"Ruth. She tried to commit suicide. The ambulance is here now. They're taking her to hospital."

Moshe's mouth turned dry. "I'm on my way." He slammed the phone down, seized his keys, and hurried out.

Saul rushed in. "Moshe, there's been another attack.," he panted, "Hebron."

Rasping, Moshe shoved him out of the way. "I've got to go. Emergency." His only focus was to get to his daughter.

Saul sprinted after him. "Moshe?"

Moshe gritted his teeth before he called out over his shoulder. "Get yourself to Hebron now. Take a team with you. I want a full report. Where, when, how." He paused and narrowed his eyes. "Take Avi in for questioning. Tell him I ordered it." Then he kicked the main door open and rushed to his car.

The Golan Heights and Hebron could all rot in hell.

Chapter Sixty-five

A wave of temporary relief coursed through Farah. Slapping Justin was the least he deserved.

How incredulous that after so long, he would pop up in Tel Aviv, of all places.

She braced herself. It wouldn't do to have a meltdown now. "Did you even care what I thought or felt when you walked away?" Her voice sounded like a high note out of tune.

"Farah, just give me a chance to tell you what happened. I know —"

"I don't think this is the right place to have this conversation." The tight knots in the back of her neck hurt her.

"Tomorrow? We could meet at the Helena Rubenstein Pavilion for lunch. Say 2.00 o'clock?" His voice was pleading.

Helena Rubenstein? Wasn't that a make-up brand?

"At the Tel Aviv Museum," he continued.

She desperately wanted to say no and walk away, her nose in the air. But she couldn't. Finally, she would find out why he had disappeared. "Fine. If you'll excuse me now."

Her eyes stung. She half-raised her hand and left without looking back.

Anxious to get away, she pleaded a headache to Michele and left, hailing a taxi as soon as she was on the street.

Her nose pressed against the windowpane, Farah clutched her throat and stared out into the moonless night. Were it not for a few stars scattered above, the blackness of the sky would have been morbid.

Had Justin left her for another woman? Impossible – she knew him well enough to be certain that this would be totally out of character.

The taxi stopped in front of Michele's building. She scrambled out and rushed upstairs, her rib cage about to explode from all the emotions, then rang Mariam.

Thanks to her Jerusalem ID and yellow car plates, Mariam could move around freely without the constraints faced by Palestinians in the West Bank or Gaza.

"Farah, what's wrong?"

"Listen, I know it's a *huge* thing to ask but would you be able to come to me now? I'm in Tel Aviv. I …" Farah broke and began to sob, shedding a decade's worth of tears.

"Give me your address and phone number. I'll be there shortly."

An hour later, Mariam was downstairs.

Her face tear-stained, Farah stepped into Mariam's car and they drove off. "Thanks for coming all the way, Mariam. I…I …" The words wouldn't come out.

"Don't worry about it. You're obviously distraught. Shall we go sit somewhere?

Farah shook her head and poked her tongue into her cheek.

Mariam drove to a beach, parked the car, and turned to face Farah. "What's wrong?"

Farah fumbled to find the right words. "I…I bumped into Justin after all these years. It was at a reception but I -I couldn't talk. It hurt too much. I left."

Mariam stared at her wide-eyed, her fingers tapping against the steering wheel. "Of course you're upset. But *why* did you leave? Didn't you want to hear his explanation?"

"At a party? And start crying? Come on." Farah pulled out a tissue and wiped her eyes. "Anyway, we're meeting tomorrow."

"Good. Would you like me to come over after you've met him?"

A tingling warmth ran down Farah's limbs. "Would you? I'm sure I'll be a total mess."

"Wa Lawwe." No problem.

Farah buried her face in her hands. "Oh God, Mariam. Just seeing him brought it all back." After a short moment, she climbed out of the car, her chest still tight.

A few people meandered on the promenade. Her shoulders stooped, Farah stumbled along, arms hanging by her side. Mariam caught up with her, a reassuring presence, and they walked side by side in silence.

A couple of teenagers skidded past on roller blades. Music blasted through from the kiosks dotting the beach while customers jostled one another to buy ice-creams.

The seashore stretched out in front of them, while black waves topped with frilly white edges, rose up then down again.

With a deep sigh, Farah flopped onto the sand, her energy drained.

Mariam squeezed her arm comfortingly.

"I feel so confused," said Farah in a tearful voice. "So much has happened in my life since he vanished. I never thought I'd be so affected."

Mariam murmured some soothing words. They sat for half an hour then headed back to the car.

As soon as she got home, Farah collapsed into bed.

Cracks of dawn were peeping through the darkness when she finally dozed off.

Her body clock woke her at 9.00.

She forced herself out of bed, revived herself with a hot shower, and dressed. At the sight of the dark circles under her eyes, she groaned. Thank goodness for concealer.

Desperate for coffee, Farah made for the kitchen.

Michele sat at the table eating breakfast. "Morning. Hope you managed to sleep off your headache." She offered Farah some orange juice. "Apparently, there were two attacks last night, one in the Golan Heights, and another in Hebron. The Avenging Sword claimed responsibility for the one in the Golan."

A drizzle of fear slithered through Farah's body. She gripped the edge of the table, her knuckles white.

***

The taxi stopped close to Rothschild Boulevard. Farah stepped out donned in jeans and flats, a brown suede jacket slung over her arm.
She was ten minutes late.

The pavilion itself, an extension of the Tel Aviv Museum, was nestled in a small but beautiful green park. Further beyond, stood a small bridge and upper walkways. Echoes of classical music cascaded through as if an orchestra was rehearsing.

Justin's head jerked back and forth as he craned his neck, his fair hair standing out amidst the crowd of dark heads bobbing up and down as people milled around.

It was a strange sensation, staring at someone who had one day been her entire world, and now almost a stranger. Or was he? The sight of him still stirred feelings within her. Yet how could she feel something for someone she no longer knew?

Butterflies fluttered in her tummy. She strolled towards him.

When he spotted her, Justin's eyes lit up.

She reached the table and held out her hand. "Sorry, I'm late. The news about the Golan Heights threw me off this morning. I was there only a few days ago."

Justin clasped her hand in his, both warm and clammy. "Golan Heights? What were you doing there?" He pulled out a chair for her.

Farah threw him a frosty stare before sitting down. Her heart pounded. "Tourism. What do you usually do in the Golan Heights?"

A waiter appeared and took their orders. She crossed her legs and asked, "what are *you* doing in Tel Aviv?"

"I live here. I'm working for the U.S. Embassy."

"Oh." Since when had he been with the Foreign Service? She frowned. "You're a diplomat?"

He shook his head. "I'm with the Public Information Services."

"How long have you been here?"

"I got transferred from Washington last September."

Her breath caught. So, they had been in Washington at the same time.

She lit a cigarette, trying to level her trembling hands.

"I didn't know you smoked."

"Well, now you do."

The tables next to them filled up with people on their lunch break.

Justin cleared his throat, his eyes darting around, an uncomfortable look on his face as if searching where to start.

Despite herself, a tad of satisfaction ran through her, though it was tinged with sadness.

"Farah, listen, I know I don't deserve you to talk to me after my behavior–"

"Your *despicable* behavior."

He swallowed, a pained look in his eyes. "I don't know where to start–"

"The beginning would be a good place."

Her stomach muscles gripped. If only she could hate him, or at least be indifferent.

Justin shut his eyes for a second and took a deep breath. "You're going to find this hard to believe but…I was given official orders to cut contact with you."

Farah stared at him. "What?" Had he gone mad?

"Before I asked you to marry me, I'd applied for a job with the NSA–"

"NSA?"

"National Security Agency. Something ten times bigger than the CIA." Justin combed his hand through his hair, a sheen of sweat forming on his forehead. "I never mentioned it to you because I hadn't heard from them in months and I was sure nothing would come out of it. Then, they contacted me and asked me for an interview."

"Without discussing it with me? In the midst of our *wedding* plans, you hid a job interview? With some secret service entity?"

He averted his eyes. "When I went for the interview, they questioned me about my time in Cairo. I told them about Danny –"

"Danny? Monique's ex?" This was getting more incredulous by the minute, like a play gone wrong.

He nodded. "They asked me if I knew any communists. Danny was the youngest member of the Communist Party in Yugoslavia. I had to be completely honest or risk losing that opportunity. Besides, they probably knew."

"OK, they asked you about Danny. Go on. What did that have to do with you vanishing?"

Justin stared into space before answering. A small frown played between his eyebrows. "They said I had to cut contact with all foreigners for a few weeks while they ran security checks." He tugged at his collar. "The weeks turned into months. They strung me along with promises that it would be 'any day now'. They made a condition that I change my phone number until they gave me the clearance. In the end, I didn't get the job. But it was too late for us by then…"

Farah went completely still and blinked slowly, a sense of paralysis overtaking her muscles. Even the wildest scenarios her mind had conjured up over the years, this one had never occurred to her. It was so far-fetched, were it not coming from Justin, she would never have believed it. But there was no doubt he was telling the truth; it wasn't in his nature to lie.

Everywhere, conversations continued uninterrupted. She glanced around without seeing anything. Life carried on for the rest of the world, even if hers had frozen in time.

She uncrossed her legs and leaned forward, inhaling a deep breath.

"*They* told you not to contact me and you *agreed*? I meant so little to you? You *sacrificed* me for the possibility of a job?"

"No. No. Farah, please." Justin dragged his hand through his hair, his Adam's Apple bobbing up and down. "You don't understand. I really had no other option –" The steely look of his interviewers as they had stated in no uncertain terms that he should have no contact with any foreigner overseas till they gave him the green light still sent shudders down his spine.

Her stomach in a knot, Farah raised her hand to shut him up, too scared of weakening.

Going back to Justin would be impossible, logically. But feelings had nothing to do with logic – never had.

Dallying around with him was a bad idea.

"Farah, we can't finish this over a cup of coffee."

Farah's chest ached as if her heart were about to split in half. She slumped back into her chair, her brain muddled, unable to think what next. A feeling of emptiness swept over her, draining her, as one kind of pain dripped out only to be replaced by another.

Justin's betrayal hurt like hell. He had placed his career over their life together, dropping her like an unwanted accessory.

Farah fumbled in her bag for a tissue, skirting his gaze. "I don't think there's anything left to finish, Justin."

She should leave but something inside her didn't want to. Despite the pain, hurt, anger, and resentment, the yearning for a life with Justin resurfaced.

Hope sprung eternal, just like Alexander Pope said.

The minutes ticked.

Farah feigned interest in the surroundings. A middle-aged couple cruised in, arguing loudly in English. A big group of tourists chatted in French as they waited to be seated. Different people, each with their own story – but definitely none like the one she was in the midst of living right now.

Justin fastened his eyes on her face, but she couldn't bear to look into them. She needed to be alone, to process her emotions before she made a decision that would impact her next steps.

Farah stood up abruptly. "I need to go."

He started. "Farah, please–"

She placed on hand on her hip. "Please what?"

"Can I see you again?"

"You dump all this on me and expect me to forgive you just like that?"

"There are still too many things left unsaid." A spasm of pain crossed his face. "Please."

"I...I don't know, Justin."

She began to walk away but couldn't resist one last glance.

His blue eyes, filled with remorse, smote her heart, and she was overcome with regret for what could have been.

***

Farah left the pavilion and headed for the beach. She walked around for a couple of hours in somewhat of a trance.

It was only when the pink-golden hues of the sun disappeared to be abruptly replaced by a dull greyness that she sat down close to the water.

Waves lapped against the sand, the soothing rhythm calming her soul. The lacy edge of foam splashed back into the sea just before hitting her shoes. A few seagulls squawked overhead as they glided above. As the minutes passed, the wind picked up and Farah slipped into her jacket. She swallowed a gulp of air, delighting in the fresh, briny scent of the Mediterranean.

Was it only yesterday she had driven here with Gerald, with no inkling of what awaited her?

She climbed some steps leading to the boardwalk, then rambled along while innumerable conflicting thoughts fenced one another in her mind as she replayed her meeting with Justin.

Would she be able to live here, tantalized by the bittersweetness of her first love only an hour away? This encounter with Justin had breached the dam, her emotions flooding through.

How was it possible to forget the happiness that had engulfed her when he had proposed in the picturesque gardens of Monticello? It had been the perfect ending for their enchanted love story. Two people embarking on a life together, young, happy, and in love. Full of dreams and hopes.

Dashed dreams that had ended in the NSA bin by the sound of it. Why would a man who claimed he loved her throw it all away, just like that?

Farah squeezed her eyes shut. She shuddered.

How on earth had Justin gotten involved with stuff like that?

No.

That wasn't the correct question.

How on earth had she *not* realized that an American studying Arabic with so much diligence wouldn't end up embroiled with such an agency? But even if she *had* figured it out, it would never have occurred to her that he would be asked to cut ties with foreigners.

"I didn't get the job," he'd said.

So, what was the Public Information Sector job? Probably some other spying business.

She stretched her legs and tilted her head back scanning the star-speckled sky as if it would reveal an answer.

On her way to find a taxi, she rang Mariam from a street phone.

"I'm sorry to bother you, Mariam, but if your offer's still standing, would you be able to pick me up this evening? I've decided to return to Jerusalem."

***

Farah picked up her suitcase and made her way to the living room, where Michele was waiting.

"I still don't get why you've changed your mind? I was so looking forward to having you here for a few days," said Michele, a perplexed look on her face.

"I'm sorry, but I need to return to Jerusalem and find out about the job."

"Why don't you phone them?"

"I prefer to go in person. Anyway, I'm sure we'll see each other again. If I stay, I'll only be an hour away." She hugged Michele. "Oh, my friend Gerald will probably call today or tomorrow. Could you tell him I've gone back to Jerusalem, please?"

When Farah walked out of the building, Mariam's car was idling by the curb. She shoved her bag in the backseat and jumped in.

"Thanks so much for picking me up."

Mariam smiled. "No bother." She picked up her cell phone. "I'll call home and ask them to prepare the guest room for you."

Farah put out her hand. "Oh no, please. I'll go back to the Notre Dame. I need to be alone." She took a deep breath. "Tomorrow I'll go to the center. Once I sign the contract, I'll start looking for a flat."

Justin was another life. A life she wasn't going to remain hostage to.

Did she really believe that or was she just trying to convince herself?

She sighed. An empty heart was a vulnerable heart.

***

Farah sat in Marco's office staring at him from the other side of his desk, her lips quivering. "But I don't understand. You said I could sign the contract in a week."

Her stomach hardened. Nothing made sense.

Marco looked away. "I'm sorry. Things have changed. We don't have the budget anymore to hire an Education Specialist."

A familiar ache crept up Farah's chest, the raw, throbbing pain of rejection. She had pinned her hopes on getting this job, wanting it more than anything. How could her world cave in around her from every side in just two days?

Was this a sign?

She sat there for a few minutes then rose to her feet, nodded goodbye, and walked out, a sour taste in her mouth as she headed back to the hotel.

Stretched out on the bed, Farah stared at the ceiling, disappointment eating at her.

The phone rang. She picked it up at the third ring.

"How did it go?" Were Mariam's first words.

"Bad. I'm returning to Amman tomorrow."

"*What?* I'm coming over now. Meet me on the terrace in fifteen."

Farah dragged herself downstairs, sat in the shade, and ordered a cappuccino. It wasn't long before Mariam joined her, concern written all over her face.

Her voice faltering, Farah repeated what Marco had told her.

Mariam scrunched her brow. "That's insane. How can they change their mind so fast?" She waved to the waiter to bring her the same as Farah. "Why go back to Amman? Stay with us and look for something else. There's so much need here."

A dull thud echoed in Farah's chest. "Thank you but no. This is probably the universe telling me that this isn't where I'm supposed to be." She shrugged. "I was happy in Amman before. I'm sure I'll find a job easily."

Mariam shook her head, her mouth twisted to the side. "That's such a shame. You could have made such a difference in the lives of those kids."

Farah looked down at her feet and stifled a yawn. "I never even got to see Abu Elias' brother. I thought I'd have plenty of time."

Chapter Sixty-six

Tammy spread a blanket over the bed in the guest room. "Sounds like you and Justin just weren't meant to be."

"I guess when I said goodbye, I thought I'd probably see him again."

"Do you *want* to see him again?"

"At times I don't want to have anything to do with him. Then sometimes I feel so lonely."

"Well, he was your first love. But honestly, Farah, would you be able to forgive him?"

Farah considered this. "If I'd stayed in Jerusalem, it would have been a tantalizing temptation." She swallowed the lump in her throat. "I guess I'll never know."

"Emotions are unchartered waters – you can never tell which way they will go. Unpredictable, really. But it's not like he went out of his way to find you. He treated you really poorly, Farah. How would you ever be able to trust him again?" Tammy tut-tutted. "Anyway, you got the answer to your question. You can move on."

Thinking of Justin wasn't going to get her anywhere. As weird and unsettling as it was to know that he was so close, Farah forcibly relegated him to the back of her mind. There were other more important things to think of now. Like getting a job.

The phone rang. Tammy went to answer. "Farah, it's for you."

Farah raced downstairs. It had to be Mariam, calling to ask if she had arrived. She picked up the phone. "Hello."

"Farah, it's Gerald. You left without even saying goodbye."

"Uuh…"

"I just arrived in Amman. Can we meet up?"

***

Farah took a cab to the Amra Hotel on the Fifth Circle, where Gerald was staying.

She offered him her cheek. "I didn't expect to see you here."

The hotel lobby swarmed with a group of babbling tourists waiting to check in.

"I was planning to come anyway. Because of the scrolls. So why not now?"

Farah nodded, unsure if she believed his reason but glad to see him nevertheless, though a bit guilty that he had slipped her mind.

Then, a thought occurred to her. "How did you get my number?"

"You gave it to me on our trip."

"I did?"

She had no recollection, but disoriented by all the events of the last couple of days, it didn't surprise her.

They hailed a cab and headed to the Amman Citadel, on one of the city's seven hills. The citadel boasted Roman, Byzantine, and Umayyad buildings, still visible on what was considered one of the oldest inhabited archeological sites worldwide.

Gerald paid and followed her to the archeological site. "You left so suddenly you threw me off balance. I had visions of touring more of the sights in Jerusalem with you. I guess you had an emergency?"

Farah flinched. "How long are you here?"

"I have a meeting tomorrow at the Ministry of Antiquities and should have a clearer idea by then. When are you going back to Jerusalem?"

"I'm not." A brief feeling of uneasiness flitted through her. Had he smuggled the artifacts into Jordan?

He leaned forward, a puzzled look on his face. "What about your job?"

"I didn't get it." Her voice went very quiet.

"I'm sorry to hear that." There was a moment's pause. "But maybe it's for the best. You never know when the Avenging Sword will strike again. Golan Heights was a close call for us." He adjusted his glasses. "What will you do now?"

She sighed. "Look for another job, I guess."

"Here?"

"I like Amman. I can make a life here."

She could visit Abu Elias, and help Fadi with his English.

They finished the sightseeing and went to Romero's, a cozy Italian restaurant on the First Circle. Another couple was standing at the door, their back to them, also waiting to be seated. The man threw a look over his shoulder.

"Layth," Farah beamed.

"Hey, Farah. You're still in Amman?"

The attractive brunette by his side smiled politely.

"Yes. And looking for a job, actually."

"Really? I might be able to help."

Farah inhaled a sharp breath. "Tell me more."

Layth grinned. "Now that Jordan has signed a peace treaty with Israel, I've started my own NGO to help Palestinian children. We're looking for someone in the Research Department." He pulled out a business card. "Listen, I'm traveling tomorrow for two weeks. Why don't you call me when I get back?"

"Thank you. I definitely will." Farah swallowed a shout of glee and put it in her wallet.

Layth winked at her, then guided his companion into the restaurant, his arm around her slender back.

Gerald scowled. "How do you know him?"

She shrugged. "Through someone."

A wave of sadness struck her heart. Gus's ghost hovered about, his laughter ringing in her ears.

Had she really referred to him as 'someone'?

"Are you going to get in touch with him?" asked Gerald.

"Of course. What a great coincidence bumping into him."

"Hmmm. He didn't give me a good vibe."

***

During the two weeks Gerald stayed in Amman, Farah saw him every day. It took her mind off the disappointment of not getting the job and eased the dull pain of Justin's betrayal.

On Gerald's last weekend, he rented a car and they headed to Machaerus, where Salome had danced for John the Baptist's head. It was a two-hour drive through winding roads.

Wild, dominating mountains stood amid deep silence against the desert backdrop. Raindrops drizzled from gloomy, grey clouds.

They parked and began their climb up the steep hill, Farah's hiking boots sinking into the muddy ground. Panting for breath, they made it to the summit. From their vantage point, despite the fog, the skyline of Jerusalem was visible, the sweeping panorama of the Holy Land.

A pang of regret flashed through Farah's heart. She could have been in Jerusalem now, helping Palestinian children. And Justin? Who knows what could have happened?

She shook off the troubled mood threatening to envelop her and focused instead on all the positives in her life.

As they began their descent, her foot hit a stone and she almost tripped. Her hand grazed against a rock. She let out a small cry.

Gerald caught her arm, saving her from tumbling down.

Light rain sprinkled down, and a gentle wind puffed against their back.

His fingers brushed against hers before they intertwined. He clasped her palm in his.

She peeked at him. His golden-brown eyes held a wistful look. Was he as satisfied as she was right now?

They took easy, unhurried steps down, a comfortable silence between them.

Farah thrust the past aside and embraced the moment. It was time to stop grieving for what could have been. Time to live in the here and now. *Carpe Diem.*

***

On the way back, they stopped to see Hanna.

Several glasses of wine later, Farah threw caution into the air. By the time they left, she was giggling at anything.

Gerald headed for his hotel. "I thought we could have some quiet time together," he said as he parked then went around to open her door.

She stumbled out of the car as waves of anticipation rolled through her stomach. Would he finally get romantic? He was a decent and stable man, with a successful career. What more could she ask for? She wasn't getting any younger and it was time to settle down. As for the artifacts, there had to be a logical explanation.

Up in the room, Farah downed a few more glasses of wine, ignoring the growls of her empty stomach.

Then, Gerald took her into his arms, his lips seeking hers. His hands roamed down her back. Sliding them under her shirt, he fumbled trying to open her bra.

Suddenly, out of the blue, Farah was overwhelmed with a sense of nausea. This didn't feel right. She burst into uncontrollable sobs, tears pouring down her face.

He cupped her chin in his hand and waited for her to calm down. "What's wrong?"

She shook her head, her lips clamped. Instead, she drew close to Gerald, yearning for his warmth.

He wrapped his arms around her. "You poor little thing. You're so fucked up."

She sobbed all the harder. Bile rose in her throat. She pushed him away, rushed into the bathroom and threw up. After rinsing her mouth, she collapsed onto the bed.

Gerald sat next to her stroking her hair until she fell asleep.

**

When she woke up it was already morning. Farah stared at Gerald with miserable eyes, her head aching from the hangover.

She scrubbed a hand over her face, conscious of a sense of dullness within her.

"You're packing?"

A pang of disappointment flitted through her. Would she ever have a stable relationship? The sense of loneliness was unbearable, like a knife cutting through her. And now she had ruined even this chance.

"Yes. I've ordered breakfast." Gerald paused and twisted his lips to the side before continuing. "It's funny, you know. I've taken more care of you in these few hours than I did of my wife in twelve years of marriage."

His confession did nothing to alter Farah's blue mood. She struggled to get out of bed. With slow, shaky steps, she crossed over to the bathroom.

A cold shower helped refresh her. Farah's nose wrinkled as she put on the same clothes.

Gerald came up to her and took hold of her hands. "Farah, I'm really sorry about last night. It wasn't planned. You're obviously not ready."

She rubbed her right eye, not sure what to say. "*I'm* sorry. I…"

Nothing had gone as planned. He was traveling tonight, leaving loose strings untied and the nagging echo of regret.

The next day Farah contacted Layth. He asked her to come in for an interview.

Within a week he offered her the job.

Chapter Sixty-seven

Three Months Later
Amman – June 1995

The meeting at work showed no sign of ending.
Farah diligently took down notes to type up the minutes once they finished. It had been three months now since she had started working with Layth, enjoying the challenge.

Her new job focused on devising practical ways to help Palestinian children living in Gaza or the West Bank who needed vital medical treatment only available in Israel.

Her work took her mind off her emotional landscape.

Layth raised his hands for emphasis. "So, if we can join our efforts with Peace Now, we might be able to accomplish something. After all, they've proven their ingenuity – they're the first Israeli activist group that managed, even if indirectly, to bring about the fall of Ariel Sharon as Defense Minister."

Skeptical murmurs filled the room.

Layth switched on the projector. **Neturei Karta – *Guardians of the City*** flashed on the screen.

He pointed to the words. "The Neturei Karta is an ultra-Orthodox Haredi Jewish group, founded in Jerusalem in 1938 when Palestine was still a British Mandate. They regard themselves as the 'pure Jews'."

"What does that mean? And what does that have to do with our work?" asked Selma, who was one of the most outspoken staff members in the office.

"They're blatant anti-Zionists," said Layth, "they refused to acknowledge the legitimacy of the State of Israel until the arrival of the expected Messiah because they believe it would be against God's will."

Farah raised a glass of water to her lips, her eyes fixed on the screen.

"Countless children suffering from debilitating illnesses end up scared and alone in Israeli hospitals, with no one to turn to, because the Israelis won't grant their parents exit permits from Palestinian territories." Layth adjusted the transparency sheet on the projector. "Different Organizations are identifying means to put pressure on the government and highlight that this is a matter of a child's life or death."

Selma folded her arms across her chest. "Do we know if this group would help us?"

"We need to explore that option. With the upcoming elections, if we can recruit even a small number of Israelis to our cause, that could perhaps provoke a ripple effect. Possibly even sway the current situation," said Layth.

With a gratified sigh, Farah leaned back in her chair.

Layth shot her a smile. "Kudos to Farah for discovering this group. I guess all those hours spent scouring in the library of the U.S. Embassy weren't in vain. You must be a microfilm expert by now."

She laughed, a warmth spreading through her body. The conversation they'd had the day Layth offered her the job rang clear in her mind.

"In the wake of the Peace Treaty between Jordan and Israel, it's important to open different channels of communication with like-minded groups. Kind of a natural progression – we need to look at what unites us rather than what divides us."

"Yes, I agree but –"

"No buts, Farah. Maslow's hierarchy of needs is the same for everyone regardless of religion or creed," he had said firmly.

Someone sneezed, interrupting her musings.

Layth handed out copies of a newspaper article. "Our next step is to establish contact and hope they'll cooperate with us."

Farah reached for a copy. The photo of a child not more than ten years old, a feeble smile on her stricken, gaunt face dominated the page. Her hair had either fallen out or had been shaved. Big, dark eyes full of sadness stared up at the camera, and pummeled Farah's heart.

Layth held up the picture. "Areej is a cancer patient. The Israelis allowed her to travel from Gaza to Nablus, but refused permits for either of her parents to accompany her. Her grandmother is her sole caretaker.

"We all know the restrictions the Palestinians face, despite Israel trumpeting that 'movement within the Palestinian territories is accessible to all.'" Layth grimaced. "The fact that a child has to go through the psychological strain of not having their parents with them during such an arduous ordeal is torture."

Selma raised her hand. "My neighbor's cousin who lives in Gaza was pregnant and needed specific medical attention not available there. She made it to the Eretz checkpoint, but the Israelis wouldn't let her through citing security reasons."

"What happened then?" asked Farah in a strained voice.

A shadow crossed Selma's face. "She went into labor at the checkpoint and delivered twins. They died immediately due to lack of required care."

There was a burst of curses and expletives from those present.

Layth raised his hands gesturing for quiet. "That's what we want to tackle. *Nobody* should have to suffer such indignity, nor be deprived of medical care, much less children."

Farah looked back again at the photo. Poor little angel, born in the midst of a political conflict through no fault of her own.

Selma tapped her pen on the desk. "What if we involve the United Nations? Wouldn't their backing give us a stronger stance?"

Farah snorted. All eyes turned towards her. She camouflaged it by turning it into a prolonged clearing of her throat.

"Did you want to say something, Farah?" asked Layth.

"Umm, well, I don't think it's a good idea to involve the UN. They've never been successful at compelling Israel to abide by any Security Council Resolution."

The meeting ended. Layth asked Farah to come to his office once she finalized the minutes.

Within half an hour, she at his door.

As she knocked and turned the handle, Layth's voice rumbled through. "Yes, of course, I will. Don't worry. *Inshallah ya Abu –*"

She stepped into his office.

A guarded look on his face, Layth waved her over and ended the phone call abruptly.

"Good you're here. I've designated you to initiate contact with the *Neturei Karta*. Since you have a French passport, it'll be easier for you to cross over to Jerusalem as my visa may take a while."

Return to Jerusalem?

Farah hesitated. "That's a daunting task."

"I wouldn't suggest it if I didn't believe you were competent."

Farah pressed her lips together and circled her thumb with her index finger over and over. A ripple of heat flashed through her body.

She drew in a sharp breath recalling the attack at the Golan Heights. It still unnerved her.

"What's wrong?"

"Last time I was there, the Avenging Sword–"

"Haven't you noticed that their targets are always military, never civilians?"

Farah's eyes drifted. Funny, Cyril had made the same observation a few years ago.

"Yeah." She still hesitated. The image of Areej's sad face flitted through her mind. That did it. She nodded. "Ok, I'll go."

"Great. I have to travel up north tomorrow to pick up some

documents. Come with me. I can brief you on aspects of your trip."

***

That evening, Farah lounged on the veranda, Gus's puzzle ring in her hand as she tried to soothe her frazzled nerves. Tomorrow she would find out more about what was expected of her.
Where up north exactly did Layth have to go? Um Quais, perhaps? The furthest northern tip in Jordan? Someone told her that he owned a house there, and visited frequently.

When the last circlet fell into place, Farah's mouth fell open. She had finally managed to put the puzzle ring back together.

A shooting star trajected over the dark skyline in blinking speed then vanished into the desert night beyond as if it had never existed.

Chapter Sixty-eight

One hand on her mouth, Farah stifled a scream, as she clutched the side of her car seat. The speeding Jeep swerved around the sharp corners of the mountainous road.

"Layth. Stop. I feel sick."

After driving for two hours, they reached the northern tip of the Jordanian border. In the distance, the Golan Heights soared up into the clouds.

Farah jolted from one side to the other, her nausea overwhelming her. "I need to get out. Now."

He slammed the brakes. The car skid before coming to a sudden halt.

Farah rushed out, bile rising to her throat. She lurched forward, gripping the closest boulder, and vomited.

Layth followed her to the edge of the road and reached out to steady her. "Feeling better?" He offered her some tissues.

Farah managed a nod and took a few deep breaths. Wiping her mouth with a tissue, she struggled back to the car.

Layth climbed in, switched on the motor, and shot off to the sound of screeching tires.

Below, across the border into Israel, the Sea of Galilee took on a sinister look as the afternoon sky swelled with dark clouds.

How ironic if she got killed in a car crash now.

The sky turned into a mess of thunder and streaking lightning, freak weather for this time of year.

Layth switched on the windscreen wipers, gripped the steering wheel, and glared at the pelting rain.

Farah shrunk into the seat, her hands tucked under her armpits. She chanced a furtive glance at Layth. A mere storm wasn't going to stop him or even slow him down.

How much further was it till they arrived at their destination?

The road wound up past blooming trees on either side, lush from early spring rain. Wildflowers speckled the grassy hillside with yellow and white.

They reached an isolated Moorish-style limestone villa set high up on the mountain.

By now the rain had eased to a drizzle, coating the air with a light, misty film. A few sun rays filtered through before dusk descended. Ahead, black iron gates stood open.

Layth drove in, past a garden dotted with rose bushes, the flowers in full bloom. He parked next to a shiny, black Mercedes.

Farah's legs shook as she got out of the car, the crisp whiff of 'after rain' piercing her lungs.

Layth's heavy boots crunched on the ground filling her with the urge to flee.

Within minutes, a starless black canopy overhead replaced the twilight.

"This way." He steered her towards a solid front door then tapped the brass knocker three times and waited. As if obeying some remote command, the door groaned open.

Her heart banged against her chest. Gerald's warning not to trust

Layth came back to haunt her.

With unsteady steps, Farah entered a large hallway, her eyes adjusting to the dim light. A double white marble stairway stood in the middle.

Layth's firm arm ushered her up the set of steps on the left. They climbed the stairs two at a time, their shoes clattering on the marble.

As soon as they reached the landing, Farah leaned against the banister, infused with an animal instinct of danger lurking, waiting to pounce. She shivered.

Layth hurried down a hallway to the left and she followed. He stopped in front of a room and opened the door.

The large room contained only a couple of wicker chairs, like those at any café in downtown Amman.

She stepped in.

Moonlight snuck in through a big window with half-drawn curtains, a faint light in a dark space.

The wooden floorboards creaked. Fear inched its way up her throat.

A shadow, indistinct in the hazy light, moved towards her, casting an eerie spell.

Time stood still.

From afar, a car's motor roared to life then faded. Farah cringed against the wall and clutched her throat.

She glanced around. Layth was gone.

***

Anxiety over his daughter tugging at him, Moshe picked up the phone on his desk and rang home. After a couple of rings, Carla answered.

"How is she, Carla?"

"She woke up half an hour ago and ate a little. Tamar is with her now."

"Do you think it was too soon to bring her home from hospital?"

"I'm not sure. Losing both Yossi and Jaleel in such a short time has devastated her. She'll need counseling…" Carla's voice broke.

Moshe's chest caved. He should be at home now, holding his wife and daughter in his arms. "I know. I'll leave work as early as I can."

He hung up with a sigh and glanced at the document on his desk. The tripartite meeting in Tel Aviv was due to start four days from now.

Unexpected details popped up daily. The phone rang non-stop whether from his own people, the Americans, or the Jordanians.

Moshe's mind drifted to the Hebron puzzle. Was his nephew involved? Curse the day Avi had become involved with settlers.

Exhaustion overcame him. He twisted a pen between his fingers. Perhaps Gideon was right. He should take his family and move to the U.S. Too many sad memories here. What was the point? The cycle of violence seemed destined to go on and on, with never-ending losses on both sides.

But how could he escape the hold this land had over him? The longings that turned into anguish. The deep love and raging anger where boundaries of right and wrong pushed and pulled against one another, leaving him and thousands like him, broken and sad.

This was where he had buried his son and his own dreams. Not only his – the dreams of every parent here whose child had been sacrificed on the altar of politics, Palestinian or Israeli – the pain of loss did not distinguish.

The door swung open. Saul, his deputy, charged in, taking Moshe by surprise. From the look on Saul's face, it was obviously bad news.

Moshe's heart plunged down to his stomach.

"I think you need to come to see what we found."

"Avi?"

Saul lowered himself on a chair and grunted. He pulled out a cigarette, drew a few breaths then stubbed it out. "When you asked me to keep Avi under the radar, I thought you'd lost your mind." He formed a steeple with his hands, his head gently rocking back and forth. "Avi the settler. Avi with his brood of children, one every year. Isn't that how you described him?"

Moshe's eyes narrowed, afraid of what would come next.

"Avi's selling weapons to the Palestinians."

Moshe gasped. The pen dropped from his hand. "WHAT?"

Saul nodded.

His breathing coming in rasps, Moshe clutched the edge of his desk. "This is totally warped. A surrealistic dimension."

"Money talks, I guess. Even to Zionists."

Moshe buried his face in his hands. "My poor, poor sister."

"Believe me, Avi is the lesser of your problems."

***

The shadowy figure drew near, close enough for Farah to touch. Her heart raced as the figure removed the *keffiyeh*.
She gasped.

Outside, an owl hooted. The cool breeze that rolled off the Yarmouk River on hot nights fluttered through.

The face etched for so long in her mind reappeared before her. Time hadn't dimmed his image, this specter risen from the land of shadows.

Overpowered by a feeling of light-headedness, Farah stood still, with no thought of pulling away. A familiar scent enveloped her, that intoxicating mix of cloves and citrus fruit. For a moment, everything else faded into nothingness.

The faint silvery glow struggled out through the clouds gave the scene a dreamlike quality like an impressionistic painting.

"There was a door to which I found no key
There was a veil through which I could not see:
Some little talk awhile of me and thee
There was – and then no more of thee and me."

Gus spoke the words thick with emotions and an edge of bitterness.

The quatrain from the Rubaiyat of Omar Khayyam was the link between the man she had once loved and the man who stood before her. The bonds forged between them in a past life had never melted.

Gus traced his fingers along her face, his eyes consuming her.

A tingling surged throughout her. Speechless, she stared at him, as her eyes welled with tears. How often had she longed for the sanctuary of his arms, to cling to his unshakable strength only to bow her head in defeat that he was gone.

But now, by an unexpected twist of fate, Gus stood before her once again bringing dead dreams to life.

Her chest hurt as if her heart was about to burst. Words failed her, her mind overwhelmed with this staggering encounter, both terrifying and awesome.

Screeching tires outside shattered the silence.

Gus plunged through the open window and swung down the pipes.

A convoy of military jeeps with flashing lights rumbled to a halt outside the remote villa. Members of the Royal Desert Forces spilled out, their red and white checkered keffiyehs flapping. Shouting, they charged into the woods in pursuit of the fugitive escaping through the olive grove.

Crack. A volley of shots lit up the darkness.

Farah's heart thumped. She slipped behind a curtain, her back drenched in a cold sweat, crouched, and hugged her knees.

The front door slammed open. Footsteps pounded through the empty hallway. The shouts grew louder.

"*Itala' la fawq.*" Upstairs.

She didn't move.

"*Yalla.*" Go.

Crack. Another gun shot.

Farah covered her ears. Someone yelled her name. She peeped through the gap in the curtain and gasped at the familiar profile before she fainted.

Chapter Sixty-nine

As soon as Ibrahim arrived, Moshe let him to the garden. They sat under the pergola.

The maid served their drinks and left.

Ibrahim picked up his glass. "It's been a while. How's life?"

Moshe didn't answer straight away, his mind still grappling with the info Intel he had received a couple of days earlier concerning Joshua. It hurt like hell.

He tilted his head to the side and fingered his parted lips. How could he tell Ibrahim that both of his nephews were part of the monstrous machinery of never-ending violence?

Ibrahim, relaxing in a big wicker chair, gulped some more beer.

Moshe wanted to freeze the scene into a mental photograph of calm and serenity – a fake, ephemeral calm about to shatter. He took a deep breath. "I'm thinking of leaving, Ibrahim."

Ibrahim placed his glass on the table, his eyes filled with disbelief. "Leaving?" he repeated, an audible shake in his voice.

Moshe nodded. He offered Ibrahim a cigarette, lit both, then drew in a long drag. He closed his eyes for a few seconds, an empty sensation filled his inside.

"I have nothing left to give, Ibrahim. I've failed. I'm powerless to change anything." He slumped backward.

"That's not true. In your own way, you've made contributions, no matter how small, to promote a more just society. Look at all the Palestinians you employed, how you improved the quality of their lives. How you fought in the Knesset. Even now, with Sechem, you're doing what no one else thought of doing."

"My heart is hard, towards Hamas for making Ruth a widow, and the Zionists for killing my son. The pain of losing him will never subside. And look at Ruth now."

Ibrahim nodded. "Yes, Yossi's death was a massive blow to all of us. We all loved him. What did the doctor say about Ruth?"

"He's seen cases like that before. Eventually, they overcome the trauma."

"See? There's hope."

Moshe looked at the ground. In this anguished land torn apart by endless rife, everyone's present was stained by past blood and irrevocable pain.

A war waged in that undefined area between Moshe's heart and conscience, but one he didn't want to fight.

A few small birds bent over the pool to sip some water.

Moshe's fingers traveled up and down his chin. "I read an interview with Mati Peled before he died a few months ago. I'm surprised it was published."

"*General* Mati Peled?" This was the man who had been a member of the Israeli General Staff during the six-day war of 1967.

"Yes. He maintained that Yitzak Rabin was stalling and dismissing any part of the agreement that would allow the emergence of a real Palestinian state. I agree with him. Rabin has no intention of ending Palestinian dependency on Israel. Oh, he'll allow them to collect their own garbage, print passports. But that's about it." Moshe snorted. "Israel will always be in control. Grieving parents, grieving spouses, grieving children."

"It has to change one day."

Moshe clenched his glass. "It turns out that Avi is selling weapons to the Palestinians."

Ibrahim let out a low whistle. "So, Avi is one of them."

"What do you mean?"

"Where did you think Palestinians got their weapons from, if not from settlers?" Ibrahim paused. "It must have been a shock to find out about Avi, though."

Ibrahim's pragmatic response made total sense. It was all so twisted and sick, the brainchild of convoluted minds.

"That's not the worst part, Ibrahim." Moshe paused, his guts tearing at him. He took a deep breath. "Joshua turned out to be a member of the *Kahane Chai*. Even the *Israeli* government considers them terrorists."

Ibrahim's eyebrows shot up. "He was your favorite."

Moshe clenched his right hand till his knuckles paled. "He called me a self-hating Jew for my stupid ideas of equality. He believes non-Jews should have their citizenship revoked and mixed marriages banned." He frowned. "Mixed marriages. Like Ruth and Jaleel."

Ibrahim nodded. "Any ideology that strips us of our humanity is evil."

The sound of laughter from the neighbor's garden grew louder.

"He almost accused me of being a collaborator – said we could have had the Avenging Sword by the balls instead of being unable to stop their attacks."

"What?"

Moshe dug his hand into his top pocket and pulled out a small, passport-sized picture of Farah.

Ibrahim peered at the photo and frowned. "That's Farah's photo."

"I found it stuck on a board in Joshua's place, among other things. All Joshua would say was 'every man has a price.'" Moshe thought for a minute. "Isn't she part Egyptian part French?"

"Yes." Ibrahim scratched his head. "How does Joshua know her?"

"Time will tell, I guess. As the Arabic saying goes, 'News that you have to pay for today, tomorrow you'll get for free'. I doubt I'll be around to find out, though."

"Moshe, you *can't* leave." Ibrahim edged his chair closer. "Listen, you need a break, but we *need* someone like you here. Can you imagine if people like you didn't exist? What the situation would be like?" He leaned forward and placed his hand on Moshe's knee. "I want to believe that one day, a new generation will understand that the violence can't continue and Israel will have to realize that the Palestinians aren't going anywhere. It's only people like you who can make this possible."

Moshe sighed. Perhaps Ibrahim was right.

Chapter Seventy

Farah opened her eyes to the sight of blue curtains. She pulled them open and frowned. Why was she on a hospital stretcher?

A figure in white floated by.

"Nurse?"

The young woman came towards her. "How are you feeling?"

"I'm fine. Who brought me here? And why?"

"You suffered severe shock and your blood pressure dropped dangerously low."

For a moment, Farah didn't say anything as the events of the last few hours came crashing back. She inhaled a deep breath, questions darting around in her mind like thunderbolts. She pinched the skin at her throat, unable to focus.

"I need to go home," she said.

The hospital released her and she made her way to the exit, jumped into a cab, and headed to Tammy's.

The house was in darkness. She crept upstairs, tiptoed into her room, closed the door, and heaved a sigh of relief, her heart thrumming.

Too tired to think any longer, she drifted to sleep.

The next morning, the maid walked in, carrying an exquisite bouquet of roses. "These came for you just now, Miss Farah, along with this letter." She placed them next to the bed, handed Farah the envelope, and walked out.

Farah bit her lip, a fluttery feeling in her stomach.

"Deep red: heartfelt regret and sorrow. Two dozen of them: love and gratitude, a perfect number; Twenty-four means I belong to you and you are constantly on my mind," she murmured to herself.

Gus and his obsession for roses. *He* had taught her their language, and the meanings different colors and numbers conveyed.

Her heart raced at the sight of his familiar slanted handwriting. She tore open the envelope with trembling hands.

Ma Chérie

Even a dead man can feel – though he has no right to do so. Yet how can I let go of the only ray of hope in my life – a life spattered with blood.

This was not the life I wanted. It was thrust onto me by virtue of my birth. My destiny was pre-ordained, sealed on a thousand suns and I am trapped in a conflict that preceded my existence by centuries.

I had no right to claim you – but such a love comes only once in a lifetime if you are lucky.

Your innocence and candor invaded the landscape of my parched being, igniting in me a passion I had never known before. That deep haunting love that burns like a blazing flame and feeds the heart and soul.

There is so much I want to say, but words are limited by our thoughts – and when our thoughts go beyond the firmament of our soul, words are useless.

In my country, among my people, we live by a law as ancient as time, an eye for an eye and a tooth for a tooth, wel bady azlam.[4]

In another world, I would have never let you go, would have protected you with my life – but my life does not belong to me.

I took you to the threshold of your dreams and hopes, only to crush them. Forgive me.

I have no right to ask you anything but my promise to you is that I will love you till the day I depart from this sorry world. Until then, your name is engraved on my heart.

Adieu,

Always your Gus

A tightness filled her chest as she devoured every word. She ached to be with him again, to be wrapped in his arms, to wake up next to him, enveloped in his scent.

Her cheeks stained with tears, Farah curled up hugging her knees as she whispered his name repeatedly like a mantra.

A gust of wind blistered through the window. The letter fluttered onto the ground.

Just then, Tammy popped her head through the door. "There's a man downstairs who wants to see you."

Farah snapped out of her thoughts. "Who?"

"I don't know. He wouldn't give his name and was very insistent. You'd better come down."

Hope swelled within her. She jumped into some clothes, flew downstairs, and crossed the hallway, her resolute steps echoing against the floor. When she reached the oak door, her hand on the handle, she hesitated. Something inside her told her that going through the door would be a rite of passage, one she wasn't sure she wanted to take. She swallowed. With a forceful twist, she pushed the door open and froze.

"Gerald?" He had only written once since he had left, despite her sending him at least five letters. "Why didn't you let me know you were

---

4   He who initiates is the guilty party.

coming?"

"I'm sorry, Farah. I ..." Gerald raised his shoulders, his palms spread outwards. "I just wanted to make sure you were OK after getting caught in the crossfire."

"H-how do you know?" She dropped into the sofa, her eyes narrowed.

He opened his briefcase, took out a document, and slid it over to her. "I shouldn't be showing you this."

"When did you get to Amman?" Farah glanced at the piece of paper. Gus's name caught her attention. She frowned her mind in a blur. "How do you know Ghassan Khodeib? And how do you know that I know him?"

"Just read it, Farah. It'll help you understand."

She swallowed and scanned the dossier detailing Gus's life. When she reached the part detailing his son's death, the pivotal incident in Gus's life, Farah stiffened.

Gus's wife and son were on their way to catch a flight to Paris when the vehicle was caught in the crossfire between Israeli troops and Palestinian militia. An Israeli bullet struck his son in the chest.

The Israelis continued to rain gunshots indiscriminately at passing cars and pedestrians, injuring and killing civilians.

When an ambulance finally arrived, the Israelis put a bullet through the driver's head. Gus's son died from internal hemorrhage in the arms of his bleeding mother, who had been in a coma since then.

That's why Layth wouldn't tell me anything about her.

What followed were stretches of time with scant information. There were suspicious indications that Gus left France and went to Ireland, where he got involved with the IRA before returning to Paris.

Farah was mentioned as a possible lead to his whereabouts.

Tremors rumbled through her. She pushed the document towards Gerald.

He stretched out a freckled hand.

Farah's eyes widened. It all came crashing back. That hand in the hazy light gripping the banister of her Paris apartment building.

"You broke into my flat in Paris, didn't you?"

Gerald squirmed in his seat, his ears turning red.

Farah clutched her arm. "Who are you, Gerald Naghton? Are you Mossad?"

"Mossad?" Gerald threw her a strange look as if confounded by her question. "No. Interpol. And before that Scotland Yard."

"You...you work for Interpol?" Farah closed her eyes for a second and repressed a derisive laugh. "I thought you're into the black market. Antiquities. I saw a stack of them in the car."

He nodded, biting his lower lip. "That was to willfully mislead you, I'm afraid."

"Why mislead me?" She controlled her voice.

"You've been under our radar since Paris. From the moment Ghassan Khodeib showed interest in you." Gerald paused. "We were investigating his possible involvement in illegal arms dealing when he 'died'." He took off his glasses, wiped them clean, and put them back on again. "His family has a finger in every pie. Weapons, transporting narcotics across the borders from the Beka'a valley. You name it, and there's probably a Khodeib involved. At times, they held the Lebanese economy hostage. And of course, with the ongoing war..."

Farah shrunk into the sofa. She recalled the cagey answers Gus used to give her whenever she asked about his business.

So, Interpol was interested in *her* as a lead to Gus?

"Our red lights started flashing when our Cypriot counterparts alerted us that a private plane carrying a passenger from the Middle East landed in Larnaca almost the same time as the news of the crash in Marka airport. Ghassan Khodeib arrived in Cyprus and presented a fake passport. At the time Cypriot authorities had no evidence that anything was out of order, and waved him through. He immediately boarded a boat for Lebanon. Not long after, the Avenging Sword appeared."

Farah's stomach lurched at the *déjà-vu* – Gus telling her when they first met how he would enter Lebanon despite being wanted - landing in

Cyprus and taking a boat to Tripoli.

She gasped as the rest of Gerald's words sunk in. Gus was involved with the Avenging Sword?

"B-but I was in Jordan for two years. How come Interpol didn't try to find him then?"

Gerald nodded. "Yes. At that point, Khodeib was busy setting up his operation. No time for sentimentality. Once everything was in place and he had time to think, it was a no-brainer that he'd try to find you again. *You* are his Achilles Heel, Farah. The one weakness the mastermind of the Avenging Sword has allowed himself."

She gave him an icy stare, her knees firmly together to stop them from shaking. "And are you here to arrest me then?"

"I'm not here in any official capacity. If my superiors find out that I communicated all this to you, I'll be in deep trouble. But I had to find out how you were doing. And get something off my chest. I was there with the Jordanian Desert Forces when they stormed in to capture Ghassan Khodeib. I took you to hospital."

Farah's mouth dropped.

One turned out to be a spy, the other a fugitive. And this one some international law official. What does that make me? A total idiot.

"Did you have anything to do with Nora Khoury canceling our meeting in Jerusalem?" A high-pitched laugh rolled from her. "Of course, you did. Otherwise, we wouldn't have spent any time together." Her hand flew to her cheek. "What about me not getting the job in Jerusalem?"

Gerald averted his eyes.

"I'll *never* forgive you for that." She glared at him, her heart pounding. "Did you get him?"

Farah held her breath.

He shook his head, a pinched expression on his face.

A sense of relief flooded through her. She stood up.

"I think it's best that you leave now, Mr. Naghton."

"Farah—"

"Hold on. That's not even your real name, is it? I caught a glimpse of one of your identity cards, remember? So, what's your real name then?"

"Ian. Ian O'Donoghue," he said as he rose.

"You're a good actor, Mr. O'Donoghue. You fooled me into believing you were interested in me."

***

As Gerald walked himself out through the front door, a sense of lightheadedness overtook Farah. Gus had escaped. Her thoughts jumbled with gratitude and a desire to sit still to let the relief sink in. She allowed herself to daydream for a few minutes before heading to the hallway.

"Tammy," Farah called. "I need to use your car if you don't mind."

Her sister leaned over the banisters with a look of concern. "Are you all right to drive?" She threw the keys down.

"Yes, don't worry," said Farah as she caught them, picked up her handbag, and headed to the car.

The drive to Shmeisani was quick, with hardly any traffic. Farah parked and checked the time. Layth should be coming out of the building any minute now.

She opened the door and stepped out.

The tall slim figure walked past, hands in pocket, towards his usual haunt for lunch.

"Layth."

He spun around, spotted her, and hurried towards her.

She leaned against the car.

"Farah, *hamdellah 'aal salameh* – thank God for your safety."

"It was you who sent the flowers and the letter."

He nodded.

"I need to talk to you. I'm sure you can guess why."

"Come, we'll go somewhere quiet."

Together they crossed the street and entered Cedars, a small Lebanese restaurant, then walked through into the courtyard. The man-made small waterfalls lapped against the artificial rock creating a gentle sound, pleasing to the ear.

They chose a shaded table in the far corner. The waiter delivered an array of Middle Eastern starters and a jug of freshly made lemon juice.

"I'm sorry about what happened, Farah. I had an inkling we were being followed but I thought I lost them. I would never have placed you in such danger. Nor Ghassan of course."

Farah swallowed, guilt eating her insides. It was because of *her* that 'they', whoever they were, had almost caught Gus. She pressed her lips together and looked at her plate.

"Farah, I swear to you. Ghassan would never have asked me to bring you if for one minute he thought there was any danger."

"I know, Layth. I'm not blaming you. I wanted to see you because…" Her voice faltered. *Why* had she wanted to see him? To tie up loose ends. But what did that mean? "Where is he, Layth?" She raised her eyes to meet his.

"He's safe, Farah. It would take more than something like that to stop him."

"That's not what I asked."

"You don't need to know."

She wrung her hands. "I need you to tell him something for me, please." Her voice trembled. Farah drew in a deep breath before continuing. "Tell him I'm torn inside but I have to go on my own journey now. I just want him to know that if I could, I would go to him straight away. Except I can't."

She couldn't repress a sob.

"I understand. Have you decided what you're going to do?"

Farah scrubbed away her tears, anxiety tugging at her heart. "I'm not sure."

Had she really just thrown away her chance of seeing Gus again?

"What about your job? You're doing great–"

Farah shook her head. "I need time to myself now." She paused. "What about you? What are you going to do?"

Layth shrugged. "What I've always done. Follow Ghassan. And

continue fighting for what I believe in."

"I want to ask you a favor."

"Sure."

"It's just that...well, actually I'm helping a Palestinian family here in Jordan. They're in Jerash Camp. I'm probably going to leave Amman and I wanted to ask you if you would make sure they don't need anything. I can give you some money now–"

"Of course, I'll help them. Just give me their details."

"Layth," Farah hesitated, not sure how he would take what she was about to say. "They're Christian–"

He silenced her with his hand, a deep frown between his eyebrows. "In Palestine, Farah, there are only Palestinians."

She nodded then turned her face away with a deep sigh, her chest weighed down by thoughts of Gus. It seemed like an eternity that she sat there in silence engrossed in her own world till she eventually stood up.

Her eyes glistening, she held out her hand to Layth.

He rose and clasped it.

She could say nothing past the lump in her throat.

"I'll give Ghassan your message. Be well, Farah."

Chapter Seventy-one

Tel Aviv – July 1995

Justin pushed both hands through his hair, his jaw clenched. He gazed out through the window onto the Mediterranean.

It was almost four months since his chance encounter with Farah, four months since he had been trying to get hold of her after she fled.

He learned from Michele Reynolds that she had gone to Jordan. But each time he rang, Tammy claimed that Farah was busy, or out or whatever excuse.

He didn't quit. The spark in her eyes had given him hope there was a chance, albeit slim, he could hold onto. Even if she wouldn't take his calls for now.

Justin glanced at the calendar hanging on the wall. Damn. Emily was arriving next week.

In all these months, Justin hadn't mentioned that he had bumped into Farah, not wanting to hurt Emily. But it wasn't right not to tell her. He stalked into the bathroom and reached for the bottle of Tylenol, popped a couple in his mouth then rubbed his forehead.

THE DOUBLE-EDGED SWORD

Sooner or later, Emily will find out. Look what happened when I wasn't upfront with Farah.

He headed for the door. Perhaps a stroll on the beach would clear his head.

Now that the sun almost set, the unbearable heat cooled down a bit.

Justin crossed the road and made for the seashore.

On the pier, a middle-aged woman played a dreamy tune on a digital piano. The music filled Justin with deep longings for a meaningful emotional connection, one that would banish the restlessness in his soul. A group of people crowded around to listen to her. Someone selling tapes approached him asking for ten shekels.

He bought one and continued walking. A few people in swimming suits lay around chatting and laughing, empty cans of beer littering the seashore.

He ventured a bit farther off to a less crowded area and dropped down onto the beach.

Rolling waves edged forward, only to die once they hit the sand. The sky transformed from a blazing orange horizon, with the sun one minute suspended in mid-air, to a blurry mauve grey within minutes.

Justin leaned back on his elbows watching the tiny stars beginning to appear, dreading the decision before him.

He sighed. His life was something like the movie *Casablanca* when Elsa bumped into Rick at his café.

Out of all the places in all the world, Farah, I bump into you in the one place I would never have imagined.

A soccer ball bounced so close it almost hit him, and two kids came running up. Justin threw it back to them and fixed his thoughts on next week. He traced his finger in the sand. How could he take another step with Emily when another woman was on his mind?

This was *his* moment of truth. He needed to summon the courage and be honest this time. It would be unfair for Emily to travel all this way when he wasn't ready to commit.

He wasn't willing to walk away again from Farah now that life had thrown together once more. The flame of love still burned.

He needed time. With Emily, time had run out.

It would be a hard conversation, and painful. But this was the only way to go.

***

Amman – July 1995

Farah lounged on the veranda, a light blanket thrown over her. As the skyline of villas disappeared fast with the setting sun, she contemplated the events that had taken place over the last five months. Fragmented scenes from the unfolding tapestry of her life.

The fact that somewhere on this planet Gus lived and breathed offered her some solace, though it was tinged with sadness.

What was this incredible hold he had over her, transcending time and place, making her unable to free herself from this bond? She had thought herself in love with Justin, a passionate love, and had been devastated when he walked away. Compared with her feelings for Gus, the difference was like a calm lake to a tempestuous sea.

Yet in the end, both men she had loved had let her down, each for his own reason. Ultimately, no matter what Gus said, his betrayal had been no different from Justin's.

Unresolved relationships, like threads sticking out of frayed material.

Abu Elias's words played in her mind: "Pain is a vehicle for growth. Without pain, there can't be change. No change means stagnation, wallowing in a murky muddy pond of self-pity."

How did the saying go? Life is like a wheel that turns, whenever there's a bad patch, you can be sure there will be a good patch after that.

Wasn't it time for her wheel to turn?

Tammy walked in and placed a bowl of strawberries on the table. "Justin was on the phone again desperate to speak to you."

Farah picked one up and nibbled at it. The mention of Justin filled her with longing for her lost innocence, and anger at what he had done.

"I think I've had enough emotional turbulence to last a lifetime."

"This too shall pass, as the Sufis say."

An army of starry hosts twinkled in the cloudless black heavens like little lanterns.

"What's it all about, Tams?"

It was incredible how different her and Tammy's lives had turned out.

"What?"

Farah lit a cigarette. Silvery plumes of smoke curled away into nothingness. "I mean, what's life about? Apart from pain, obviously."

The loud buzzing of cicadas drifted from the garden.

"What do you think it's about?" said Tammy.

Surprised that Tammy hadn't jumped at the opportunity to start preaching at her, Farah mulled the question over. "I'm not sure, really. I mean everything seems to be so random. And so much is determined by where we are born. If I'd been born in a refugee camp in Gaza, my life would have been completely different."

If Gus hadn't been born in Lebanon, his life would have followed a different path.

Tammy clasped her hands behind her head and closed her eyes.

Her sister's silence unnerved Farah slightly. It was almost spooky how she wasn't ramming her beliefs down Farah's throat.

The next morning after breakfast, Farah jumped into the pool to cool down. When she climbed out, Tammy was sitting on the grass reading the Bible.

Farah splashed some sunscreen on her arms and legs and dropped onto a towel. A light breeze ruffled through the trees. She sneaked a look at her sister. Tammy's face radiated peace.

The image of Abu Elias and his family gathered in prayer and giving thanks despite their living conditions still unsettled her, and still raised questions.

Then there was Cyril and his unshakable faith.

She shut her eyes and drew in a long breath. Was it possible that she might find the answers she was searching for?

***

That night, her back propped up against her pillows, Farah opened the Bible. Her eyes fell on the verse from St. John's Gospel: *And you will know the truth, and the truth shall set you free.*
She reread the verse five times, trying to understand. The words danced before her, their meaning out of reach.

Over the next few days, Farah kept returning to that same verse, scouring the different books in the Bible looking for similar words. The more she searched, the more frustrated she became.

One afternoon, when she was alone with Tammy in the living room, Farah asked her sister point blank. "What did Jesus mean when he said: The truth shall set you free? What's this 'truth' he's talking about? Set me free of what?"

"What do you think he meant?"

Farah drummed her fingers on the arm of the chair. "Could he set me free from this horrible pain I have inside me and the sense of brokenness and despair? The fear of the unknown?" She stopped, took a deep breath, then continued. "He talks about being free, so that means I'm a prisoner. But a prisoner of what?" Farah bit at her inner cheek while she considered the implication of what she had just said. "No one else said something like that. Ever."

"C.S. Lewis stated that there are only three options; Jesus was a liar, Jesus was mad, or, He was speaking the truth."

Farah narrowed her eyes. Now that was something that had never come to mind. Was she on the cusp of some life-changing discovery?

Epilogue

Farah glanced around her bedroom. This room had witnessed so many of her emotional upheavals in the last few months, from the reappearance of Justin to Gus returning from the dead, and the discovery of Gerald's duplicity.

Footsteps pattered in the corridor. Her niece, poked her head through the door.

"Mom says to hurry up or we'll miss our flight."

Farah nodded and picked up her handbag.

It was a weird sensation, leaving. She was heading into the unknown, returning to the one place she had tried to avoid at all costs. It was her own decision to return to Cairo, with no pressure from anyone.

She hummed to herself as she headed out the door.

This was going to be a special time. Not only were Tammy and her family traveling with her, but Cyril, along with Marc, Monique, and their daughter Sofia had already arrived in Egypt the day before.

One big family reunion.

How wonderful to be among people who loved her and gave her

strength.

All the while, the intriguing words from the Bible kept churning around in Farah's mind, '*The truth shall set you free*', filling her with a strange sense of hope.

It was time to find her own truth. Where better place to start than to go back to her roots, where her story had begun?

With a wide smile at her niece, Farah held out her hand, and together they went downstairs.

THE END

Acknowledgements

I am indebted to numerous individuals who played pivotal roles in the writing and completion of this novel. Firstly, Heba Abdel Latif who convinced me to revive a project shelved for more than two decades. Chahira Hallaba who persuaded me that this was a mission I needed to accomplish. Janie Aziz who provided invaluable input with her diligent reading and critiquing. Charmine El Guindy who was the first to glimpse the unfinished manuscript and who offered insightful comments. Anne Marie Evans, who came up with the expression "Mother of All Social Taboos." Angel Ortiz who patiently endured countless rough drafts. Their support, along with many others, made me determined to finish this work as best I could.

Above all, I am grateful for the opportunity I had to live in Palestine and for the amazing people I met there. In particular, I would like to mention the Abdel Shafi family, Dr. Haidar and Auntie Huda, who adopted me as one of their own; Bettina and Salah, whose home was always open to me; Gerry Shawa, who witnessed my tears as my marriage broke down; Manal Khalafawy, who was by my side as I navigated my way through tumultuous times; and the countless Palestinians I met who made me feel so welcome in their land.

To each and every one who contributed to this journey, thank you from the bottom of my heart.

Printed in Great Britain
by Amazon